Kate Charles, a past Chairman of the Crime Writers' Association and the Barbara Pym Society, is well known as a fictional chronicler of the Church of England and an expert in the field of clerical crime fiction. She is co-organizer of the annual St Hilda's Crime and Mystery Conference and a member of the prestigious Detection Club, as well as an occasional contributor to the *Church Times*. She has published twelve novels to date, including the popular Book of Psalms series, three standalone suspense novels and a series featuring curate Callie Anson.

Kate lives on the English side of the Welsh Marches with her husband and her Border terrier.

False Tongues

KATE CHARLES

Marylebone House

First published in Great Britain in 2015

Marylebone House
36 Causton Street
London SW1P 4ST
www.marylebonehousebooks.co.uk

British Library Cataloguing-in-Publication Data
A catalogue record for this book is available from the British Library

ISBN 978–1–910674–05–5
eBook ISBN 978–1–910674–06–2

Typeset by Graphicraft Limited, Hong Kong
Manufactured by Jellyfish
First printed in Great Britain by CPI
Subsequently digitally printed in Great Britain

eBook by Graphicraft Limited, Hong Kong

Produced on paper from sustainable forests

To quote Abraham Lincoln, 'All that I am, or hope to be, I owe to my angel mother'

In loving memory of Kathryn Lucile Fosher 1922–2013

Acknowledgements

As ever, I am indebted to a number of people for their encouragement and sharing of expertise. They include Suzanne Clackson, Deborah Crombie, the Revd Dr William Dolman, Ann Gray, Sharon Jones and Marcia Talley. I'm also grateful to Gladstone's Library for providing a wonderful writing space, and to my two agents, the late Dorothy Lumley and the amazing Nancy Yost.

Dramatis personae

In Cambridge

Callie Anson	Deacon
Tamsin Howells	Her friend, a deacon
Val Carver	Her friend, a deacon
Nicky Lamb	Her friend, a deacon
Adam Masters	Her ex-fiancé, a deacon
Scott Browning	Deacon
Jennifer Groves	Deacon
Margaret Phillips	Principal of Archbishop Temple House theological college
Hanna Young	Margaret's secretary
The Revd Dr Keith (Mad Phil) Moody	Lecturer in theology at Archbishop Temple House
John Kingsley	Retired priest

In London

The law

Sgt Mark (Marco) Lombardi	Family liaison officer, engaged to Callie Anson
DI Neville Stewart	Homicide detective
DS Sid Cowley	Neville's sergeant
DCS Idris Evans	Neville's boss
Dr Colin Tompkins	Pathologist
Danny Duffy	Computer expert
PC Dewi Jones	Uniformed officer
Sgt Salome (Sally) Pratt	Custody officer
Hereward Rice	Coroner
Walter Kendrick	Solicitor
Ray	Mortuary attendant

The press

Lilith Noone	Reporter for the *Daily Globe*
Rob Gardiner-Smith	Editor of the *Daily Globe*, Lilith's boss

Other Londoners

Peter Anson	Callie's brother
Serena di Stefano	Mark Lombardi's sister
Angelina and Chiara di Stefano	Serena's daughters
Brian Stanford	Vicar, Callie Anson's boss
Jane Stanford	Brian's wife
Dr Richard Frost	Anaesthetist
Miranda Frost	A & E surgeon
Sebastian Frost	Their teenage son
Hugo Summerville	Teenager
Tom Gresham	Teenager
Olly Blount	Teenager
Lexie Renton	Teenager
Georgie Renton	Lexie's younger sister
Becca	Teenager
Josh Bradley	Teenager
Paul Bradley	Josh's father
Iris Bolt	The Frosts' cleaning lady
Wendy Page	Parishioner of Brian Stanford
Philip Page	Wendy's husband, a churchwarden
Liz Gresham	Friend of Wendy Page
Giulia Bonner	Friend of Serena di Stefano
Emilia and Enrico Bonner	Giulia's children
Geoff Brownlow	Mark Lombardi's flatmate

Others

Charlie and Simon Stanford	Brian and Jane's twin sons, at Oxford
Ellie Dickinson	Simon Stanford's girlfriend

CHAPTER 1

Revisiting the past was a bad idea. Callie Anson knew that – especially given her own recent past – but there was something irresistible about the invitation she'd received.

It had arrived in the post not long after Christmas, among the late greetings cards and the glut of January sales catalogues, and had sat on her desk for about a week before she'd done anything about it. She'd opened the envelope, read the invitation, thought about it, then ... postponed a decision.

Deacons' Week at Archbishop Temple House, her old theological college in Cambridge. A time when those in their first year of ministry were bidden to return to the familiar precincts of the college to share problems and insights gained, to be reunited with friends and colleagues, with tutors and staff. A 'facilitator' would run the sessions, and these get-togethers had proved in the past to be beneficial experiences for those who took part. All deacons were strongly urged to attend, though of course attendance wasn't mandatory. It would take place in the spring, just after Easter.

Beneficial? Maybe ...

Callie might have postponed her decision even longer if Tamsin Howells, one of her best friends during her time at Archbishop Temple House, hadn't phoned her out of the blue.

'Well?' Tamsin demanded. 'Are you going?'

'I ... haven't decided,' admitted Callie. 'Are you?'

'Probably. Depends on who else goes, of course. I haven't returned my reply slip. I'm waiting to see.'

'But how will you know who's going?' That, in a nutshell, was the problem. Callie would love to see Tamsin again, and her other friends Val and Nicky. Some of the staff, and certainly her tutor. But not Adam. Definitely not Adam.

Tamsin chuckled. 'Facebook, of course. I've posted it as an event, and invited everyone from our year. I've asked them to RSVP. But the trouble is that hardly anyone has yet. Scott Browning said "yes" straightaway – he wouldn't miss it, of course. But none of our friends. Including *you*,' she added accusingly. 'I suppose no one wants to commit themselves until they know who else is going.'

1

'A bit of a catch-22,' said Callie. 'Actually, I don't really do Facebook.'

'You don't do Facebook?' Tamsin's tone of disbelief could not have been more profound if Callie had said that she didn't believe in God.

'I've never really got into it.' She knew that Tamsin lived and breathed Facebook, but Callie had too many things on her plate to spend the time necessary to get heavily involved in online social networking. Real life, she'd decided a while ago, was more interesting. Especially since Marco had become such a big part of her world.

'I can't imagine not doing Facebook. It's the first thing I look at in the morning, and the last thing at night.' Tamsin chuckled again, wryly. 'I suppose you're going to tell me I ought to get a life, right?'

It was exactly what Callie had been thinking, but decided it was better not to go there. 'It all depends on what you mean by a life, I suppose.'

'Well,' said Tamsin, 'Nicky still hasn't seen the light. If that's what you mean. But I continue to live in hope.'

Hope was a good thing, Callie acknowledged to herself. Especially for a clergyperson. One of the big three: faith, hope, charity. She wasn't convinced, though, that all the hope in the world would do Tamsin any good when it came to Nicky, and she was aware that her next words sounded lame. 'I guess you never know.'

'Well, Nicky says he's going to Deacons' Week, anyway. So I suppose that means I'll go. Unless he changes his mind or something.' Tamsin sighed. 'And *you*. Get on to Facebook, woman. It's about time you entered the modern world.'

Callie had a sermon to write, but the gauntlet had been thrown down, and she couldn't resist the challenge.

Facebook. It *was* time she entered the modern world, and proved that she could be as much of a dysfunctional time-waster as the next person, she said to herself as she logged on, delving deep in her memory for her password. She'd created an account months ago, at Tamsin's urging, but had never bothered to visit it since then.

Her home page was a poor thing, barely deserving the name. Instead of a photo there was a one-size-fits-all silhouette of a woman's head. Her profile consisted merely of her name and 'London'.

Yes, among all the other things that had piled up – requests to be her friend and reports on the daily activities of the few friends she'd already acquired in that short-lived burst of tepid enthusiasm – there was an invitation from Tamsin to attend Deacons' Week at Archbishop Temple House.

Callie clicked on Tamsin's name and was taken to her home page.

How, she wondered, did Tamsin find time to do her actual job? After all, there were only so many hours in a day, and Tamsin was a curate like Callie, with a parish to serve and a vicar to keep happy. Her vicar must be much less demanding than Brian Stanford, and her parishioners must be singularly without problems and needs. Clearly Tamsin had not exaggerated the scope of her activities on Facebook, which were truly prodigious. She had in excess of five hundred friends, with whom she evidently kept up a constant correspondence in the form of public 'wall' messages. There were probably private messages as well, and who knows what other methods of communicating with her vast network.

Callie couldn't help smiling at Tamsin's profile photo: it captured her so well. The word that summed up Tamsin was 'round'. Baby-blue eyes, round as saucers; bouncy blond curls; chubby cheeks; a body that was all curves. Tamsin wasn't exactly fat, but her short stature, combined with the generous size of her breasts – like over-inflated balloons – gave the impression of someone who would never win the Weight Watchers' Slimmer of the Year prize.

And yet to judge Tamsin by her appearance would be to vastly underestimate her. She was a woman of great intelligence and profound insights, as Callie had discovered very quickly at theological college. In their little circle of friends in their tutor group, Tamsin was undoubtedly the cleverest. People *did* underestimate Tamsin, all of the time, to their own cost.

Did Nicky underestimate Tamsin? On the whole, Callie didn't think so. She clicked through from Tamsin's home page to Nicky's.

Nicky Lamb looked utterly angelic in his profile photo, dressed in cassock, alb and his deacon's stole – butter wouldn't melt, Callie's mother would have said tartly. Again, appearances were deceiving. It wasn't that the Reverend Nicky Lamb, curate of St Ninian's Church, Brighton, was wicked. On the contrary, he was a good man with an integrity so deep that other people often found it daunting. But Callie knew that he had the most trenchant sense of humour she'd ever encountered. Much of it was self-deprecating, which took the edge off its sharpness. Yet he could cut the pompous down to size with just a few well-chosen words. And there had been plenty of pomposity resident at Archbishop Temple House, where Nicky Lamb had not always been the most popular of ordinands.

Except with Tamsin, of course. Tamsin adored Nicky unreservedly, and had done so from the beginning. Ignoring common sense and the

3

counsel of her friends, Tamsin lived for the day that Nicky would return her feelings. The trouble was, as Callie well understood, the train was never going to stop at that station. No, Nicky would be a far better match for her brother Peter. Callie had sometimes thought about introducing the two of them, during those frequent – if brief – periods when Peter was between boyfriends, except that it seemed vaguely disloyal to Tamsin. And probably a certain recipe for disaster, she acknowledged to herself.

Tamsin might not have a hope in hell, but that didn't stop her from taking a job in an adjoining diocese to Nicky's, so that she could travel to Brighton on her days off and spend time with him. They were good friends, Tamsin had explained to Callie. And if that's all it was ever going to amount to, it was better than nothing. Or so Tamsin reckoned.

Val was the one who thought Tamsin was crazy. 'Doesn't she realize?' she'd said so often to Callie. 'It's just not going to happen. And it's keeping her from meeting other people. Men, I mean. Straight men. Men who might conceivably marry her.'

Marriage was a subject which loomed large in Val Carver's mind. She'd been single when Callie and the others had met her, during that first week at college, and like the rest of them she seemed focused on her vocation to the priesthood. But it turned out that she had a secondary focus as well, and before the end of their first year she'd been sporting an impressive engagement ring. The lucky man was Jeremy Carver, the chaplain of the college; they had married last summer, during Val's final term.

Callie clicked on Val's name and was taken to her home page.

Val's expression looked smug, Callie decided. Not surprising, as she'd managed to achieve the two things she'd set out to capture: a clerical collar and a husband. Her relationship status was proudly proclaimed – 'Married to Jeremy'. And in the space for religion she'd put 'Deacon in the Church of England – to be priested next summer'.

She was an unlikely femme fatale, thought Callie as she studied the photo. Val was as angular as Tamsin was round, tall and flat-chested, with long, straight, mousy hair and square-framed spectacles. She looked like the quintessential schoolteacher – which is what she'd been, of course, before theological college and ordination. Val had been one of those women who'd always known she wanted to be a priest, but even though she'd come of age after that had become possible for her gender, she'd had the misfortune to be part of that generation which had been sent away by the ordination selectors and told to get some 'real world' experience before training for the ministry. She'd felt fairly bitter about it at the time, she'd confided to Callie, yet she'd served her time in the classroom with determination, if not distinction. And now, like the rest of them, she was almost there: a deacon, on the verge of being a priest.

Val might not be as prodigious a user of Facebook as Tamsin when it came to the quantity of friends, but she was more disciplined in the matter of organizing and posting her photos. Callie clicked on the list of Val's photo albums and discovered that there were a number of them, from 'wedding' to 'ordination' to 'parish activities'.

There was even an album devoted to snapshots from her theological college days, and Callie was surprised to find that she was tagged in quite a few of them. Val Carver, Tamsin Howells, Nicky Lamb, Callie Anson: they were there in various combinations, often without Val, who had been wielding the camera – devouring pizza at a favourite cheap eatery, lounging in the common room and even punting on the Cam.

Punting. Callie remembered that afternoon very well. A glorious day in April, during their first year. It had been so unexpectedly beautiful, after a long rainy spell, that they'd been drawn to the river, its banks lined with a profusion of blooms – daffodils, crocuses, hyacinths in their thousands.

'Let's hire a punt,' Nicky had suggested impulsively, and in spite of Val's reservations about his abilities, he had demonstrated quite a surprising facility for punting. The photos showed him handling the pole with a smug grin, while Tamsin gazed at him with wide-eyed admiration and Callie looked apprehensive.

What a lovely day it had been. Cambridge in the spring: there was nothing more glorious. Callie felt an uncharacteristic swelling of nostalgia in her throat – nostalgia for that day, that place, those people.

Deacons' Week was scheduled for April, after Easter.

She would go, Callie decided. If her boss Brian were amenable, she would go.

Brian hadn't been keen. Lukewarm, at best, Callie recalled several months later, as she packed her case.

Her request had caught him a bit by surprise, and Callie suspected that he wanted to run it by his wife Jane before committing himself irrevocably to any particular position.

'It's after Easter,' Callie had pointed out. 'And it's only five days.'

Brian tented his fingers together and regarded their tips. 'But we generally go away after Easter. Janey and I. To Wales. We can't really leave the parish unattended, can we?'

5

Last Easter she hadn't been there, Callie wanted to say to him. And all of the previous Easters. Evidently he'd left the parish unattended plenty of times before. Why was it different, now that he had a curate? 'It's only five days,' she repeated. 'I wouldn't be away on a Sunday.'

'And who would pay for it?' Brian asked, changing tack. 'There's no spare money in the parish budget to subsidize your little holidays.'

Callie made an effort to control her frustration. 'It wouldn't be a holiday. It's continuing ministerial education. CME. The diocese budgets money for that, I've been told. And if necessary I'd pay for it myself,' she added.

It had worked; Brian had eventually agreed that she could have the time off, as long as the parish didn't have to fund it.

But now that the time had come, Callie was having second thoughts.

Why had this ever seemed like a good idea? she asked herself as she contemplated the clothes she'd laid out on her bed.

Would people be wearing their dog collars and clericals? Or would it be more casual and informal, with the sort of clothes – jeans and sweats – that they'd worn as students? She would hate to be caught out either way, so she'd better be prepared for either eventuality. And maybe she'd need something smart in case they laid on a posh dinner.

Callie folded up an oversized college T-shirt – to sleep in – and tucked it into her case, then checked her sponge bag to make sure it contained everything she needed – the last time she'd used it was when she'd had to move into the vicarage for a few weeks. Thank goodness that particular experience was behind her. Her flat above the church hall, re-roofed after a storm had made it uninhabitable, felt like home to her, and it was so good to be back.

All the while that she was packing, a black and white cocker spaniel watched her every move from her position near the door with an expression that Callie interpreted as both accusatory and miserable. 'Oh, Bella,' she said, crouching down to stroke the dog's soft ears. 'Are you afraid I'm going to sneak out and leave you?'

Something else to feel guilty about, she told herself. Poor Bella. During Callie's weeks of enforced residence at the vicarage, she'd had to find a temporary home for Bella with her friend Frances Cherry in Notting Hill. Now, all too soon, Bella would be returning to Frances' for a few days. She'd be well looked after, if not thoroughly spoilt, but Callie felt bad about it all the same.

Her mobile phone rang in her bag and she scrambled to retrieve it, pressing the button to answer the call as she registered that it was her brother.

'Hi, Sis,' said Peter's breezy voice.

'Hi.' She took the phone away from her ear for a second to check the time display. 'I don't have too much time to talk right now,' she said. 'I have to finish packing, then take Bella over to Frances', and then catch a train.'

'Packing? Train?' Peter echoed.

She sighed. 'I told you. I'm away this week. Cambridge.'

'Oh, that's right. Meeting up with your chums.'

'Well, that's not really what it's about,' she protested.

'Whatever. Will what's-his-name be there?'

Adam. Peter had never liked him, and refusing to call him by name had always been his way of letting her know that. 'I sincerely hope not,' Callie said with feeling. She had monitored the replies to Tamsin's Facebook invitation, and Adam was down as a 'no'. 'And nice as it is to talk to you, I've really got to go.'

'Hang on a second,' Peter said. 'I can save you a bit of time. You won't have to take Bella to Frances'. I'll look after her this week.'

'What?'

'The thing is, Sis,' her brother went on in a remarkably cheerful voice, 'Jason and I have split up.'

'Oh, Peter, no!' It wasn't the first time, and with Jason's known pre-dilection for chorus boys, Callie had privately expected the break-up much sooner.

'Don't sound so upset,' he said. 'I'm not. Mutual consent this time. We just haven't been getting on, and it was time for me to move out.'

'So you're ...'

'Homeless again,' he chirped. 'And on my way to Bayswater, even as we speak. I'm in a taxi. I'll be there in ... oh, ten minutes at the most.'

Callie's heart sank, remembering the last time. She recalled it all too well: the wet towels on the floor, the dirty crockery in the sink ... 'But you *can't* stay here,' she protested. She'd only just moved back in and reclaimed her home. It wasn't fair!

'It won't be for long. Just a few days. I have my eye on a flat, so it's just a matter of some paperwork,' Peter said smoothly. 'And I'll be doing you a favour, Sis. Looking after Bella.'

'All right,' she capitulated, knowing she didn't sound very gracious about it. 'But you *have* to be out when I get back at the end of the week.'

'Done deal. See you in a few,' he said, hanging up.

Callie sighed, surveying her flat. Her lovely cosy flat, with everything just the way she liked it. That wouldn't last five minutes with Peter in residence.

But Bella would probably be happier in her own home, she told herself. Trying to inject some enthusiasm into her voice, she stroked Bella's ears and said, 'Uncle Peter's coming to take care of you. Won't that be nice?'

Her case was packed and she didn't have to take Bella to Frances'. That gave Callie a few spare minutes to check the invitation list one more time. She went to her desk and switched her computer on, navigating to her bookmarked Facebook home page.

The list was much the same as the last time she'd looked: in the 'yes' column were various names including Tamsin Howells, Val Carver and Nicky Lamb. But one name had been added at the bottom of the list. Adam Masters was now a 'yes'.

Callie caught her breath and uttered a single word which the average man in the street would not believe could ever pass the lips of a clergyperson.

Interlude: Facebook

DarthVader474 to RedDwarf287:

U make me sick u little wanker. U need to die. Y dont u just kill urself & save us the trouble?

CHAPTER 2

If there was anything that Detective Inspector Neville Stewart hated more than being woken out of a deep sleep by an emergency call, it was for the phone to go when he'd just managed to fall asleep after a bout of insomnia.

To be fair, it didn't happen that often. There weren't too many criminal incidents in the middle of the night that couldn't be dealt with by a more junior policeman – a detective constable or a detective sergeant, or even a beat officer. Traffic violations, drug busts, vandalism, drunken rowdyism: Neville need not be called from his bed for any of these.

But murder was something different.

And this murder was literally in his professional backyard: on the open common ground called Paddington Green, behind the police station.

A late dog walker had discovered the body – just the other side of the walk from the churchyard – and because of its proximity to the station it hadn't taken long for the police to reach the crime scene and cordon it off with plastic tape. As it was a Sunday night, though, and Easter to boot, few officers were on duty. When Neville arrived, feeling hard done by, the scenes of crime team was just beginning to assemble near the square bulk of the church and the photographer hadn't got there yet. Neither had Neville's sergeant, DS Sid Cowley, but at least the police doctor was there and had made the necessary examination to ascertain death.

It was to him that Neville naturally gravitated for a quick rundown of the state of play.

'He's dead, all right,' Dr Tompkins said with characteristic brusqueness. 'Stabbed. In the neck.'

Neville felt a chill like icy fingers on the back of his own neck. It was spring; the day had been warm, but that didn't mean it didn't cool off quite substantially at night. At least that was Neville's story, and he intended sticking with it. 'Do we know who he is?'

Colin Tompkins shook his head. 'Young lad. On his own. He might have some ID on him, but we've left him for you to have a look.'

Neville nodded approvingly; the less mucking about with the crime scene and the body, the better. 'Murder weapon?' he asked, falling in with Dr Tompkins' terse speech pattern.

'Knife. No sign of it yet.'

Another one, then. Neville closed his eyes and sighed. There had been so many of them lately: young men, little more than boys, killing each other with knives. What a waste. What a bloody, stupid waste.

Callie had very nearly changed her mind and stayed at home. Before the night was over, she wished she had.

Adam was a complication she had certainly not counted on. Spending the better part of a week in proximity to him – and in such emotive, evocative surroundings – was the last thing she needed at this point in her life. Just going back to the place they'd met was difficult enough to contemplate, let alone with him there.

It wasn't too late to change her mind, she'd told herself, breathing deeply to control her panic. After all, Adam had changed his, virtually at the last minute. The success of the week didn't depend on her being there. Tamsin would miss her, and Val and Nicky, but they'd get on fine without her.

Then Callie remembered Peter. He was on his way; he'd be here in a few minutes. To stay.

It was impossible. She was *not* going to share her flat with Peter again. Peter here on his own was bad enough; for her to be here with him just wasn't going to work.

She had to go to Cambridge. There was no alternative. No backing out now.

A bloody, stupid waste.

Neville looked down at the body in the feeble light of his hand-held torch, then crouched down for a closer look and swallowed hard. He wasn't squeamish; he'd seen enough violent deaths in his time that he knew he shouldn't be affected like this. But this was just a kid. Just a lad, with a tangle of dark curls and downy cheeks that had probably never seen a razor. He'd expected some street-hardened gang member, thick-set, covered with tattoos and scars from previous fights. This boy wasn't like that. He was tall and slender, clean, well-dressed. And so young.

He was someone's son.

Somewhere, perhaps not far away, his parents were wondering where he was. Wondering why he hadn't come home from an evening out with his mates.

10

The police photographer had arrived and was supervising the setting up of lights to illuminate the crime scene. 'Let's get on with it,' Neville muttered, mostly to himself, but the photographer heard him.

'Keep your hair on, mate. We're working as fast as we can.'

'Yeah, yeah.' Neville rocked back on his heels, then stood up.

The photographer threw a switch and suddenly the body on the ground was exposed in a glare of bright white light, lying in a pool of darkening blood.

'Jesus,' Neville said.

In addition to the stab wound in the neck, there was blood round the boy's mouth, difficult to see in the dark but now clearly visible. Neville turned to the doctor, who was still hovering nearby, and pointed down. 'What's that about, then?'

'His tongue,' said Dr Tompkins quietly. 'Looks like it's been split. With a knife.'

'Jesus,' he repeated with feeling. 'Jesus, Mary and Joseph.'

Travelling by public transport on a Sunday – let alone a holiday – was seldom a good idea, Callie recognized belatedly.

She'd spent longer talking to Peter than she'd planned, certain that the break-up with Jason was hitting him harder than he was willing to admit, then she'd made the mistake of taking the Tube to King's Cross rather than grabbing a taxi.

Services on the London Underground were greatly reduced at Easter, she discovered. In fact, the Circle Line wasn't running at all, due to engineering works, so she had to take the Bakerloo Line from Paddington to Baker Street. Once there, she lugged her case up twenty steps, round the corner, up the escalator and a few more steps to the Metropolitan Line platform only to see the tail lights of the departing train disappearing into the tunnel, and when she checked the electronic board for the next service, she was dismayed to see that there wasn't even one listed.

The platform was deserted; everyone else had made it on to the train. At least that meant she could sit down to wait for the next one, Callie told herself, dragging her suitcase to one of the plastic chairs bolted to the wall. She got out the envelope with her ticket and checked the time of the Cambridge train, synchronizing her watch with the electronic display board on the platform. If the Tube train came within the next ten minutes, she ought to make it.

The Tube train didn't come. A few more people rushed on to the platform, looking hopeful or desperate. An unshaven man with a can of cider in his hand wandered over and lowered himself into the chair next to Callie, giving her an appraising sideways look as he took a swig from his can.

She had debated about whether she should wear her dog collar for the journey, and had decided against it. Now she wasn't sure she'd made the right decision. Sometimes it seemed to her that a clerical collar was an open invitation to strangers to talk to her, but in a funny way it also felt like a sort of protection, especially for her as a woman.

Maybe she was being silly, she told herself. This man was almost certainly harmless. Nonetheless she was glad there were other people on the platform.

Eventually the train roared out of the tunnel, stopping with a squeal and a lurch, its doors sliding open.

DS Sid Cowley's comment on the dead boy was even more terse than Dr Tompkins': a single monosyllabic expletive said it all.

'Yeah,' Neville agreed, turning as his sergeant arrived at his side. Trust Sid to hit the nail on the head.

'He's – how old?' Cowley guessed. 'Fourteen? Fifteen?'

Neville clasped his hands behind his back. 'Something like that. And he's no street kid,' he added. 'Look at those clothes.'

The photographer was moving round the body, taking photos then stopping to scribble in his notebook. 'I'll be done in a few, Guv,' he said. 'Get him from all angles, then do a video just to be on the safe side. Then he's all yours.'

'What's a lad like that doing out here this time of night?' Cowley said. 'My mum would have killed me if I'd tried that.'

'We don't know how long he's been here,' Neville reminded him. 'Dog walker found him, as usual.'

Cowley turned round and surveyed the area. 'No houses anywhere near,' he observed. 'Not even a pub. Not likely anyone heard anything going on, unless they were up to no good themselves. We'll be bloody lucky to find any witnesses. 'Cept for them, of course,' he added, nodding in the direction of the church.

'Who?' Neville swivelled his head hopefully, then made out the dim outlines of several large tombs in the churchyard.

The sergeant laboured the joke. 'But I don't suppose you'll have an easy time getting anything out of them, Guv. Not even with your legendary detective skills.'

12

'Ha bloody ha,' Neville snapped. 'Thanks for that, Sid.' Thanks for stating the obvious.

Easy wasn't the word. This was not going to be an easy case in any sense; he could feel it in his bones.

King's Cross had once been a rather unappealing station at the best of times, Harry Potter notwithstanding. Now it had been tarted up beyond recognition. Callie had to stop, read the signs, and get her bearings. Harry and his chums would have been amazed at the crowd milling around Platform 9¾.

She had time to catch her train, Callie told herself, taking a deep breath. If she didn't dawdle and concentrated on finding the platform, she ought to make it before they closed the barriers.

Even with wheels, her case was cumbersome and heavy. Why had she packed so many clothes? A wheel caught as she rounded a tight corner; Callie paused and tugged it free.

The train was in sight. The barriers were still open.

And then she saw him: Adam, striding along on his long legs, a duffel bag slung over his shoulder, heading for the platform.

Callie stopped in her tracks; her suitcase banged into her leg. 'Oh, no,' she breathed, but not at the pain in her calf. He would see her – he was bound to see her. He would suggest sitting together and she wouldn't be able to say no. She would have to travel all the way to Cambridge with him, making awkward small talk. They'd share a taxi from the station to the college; they would arrive together.

No. She couldn't face it. Callie ducked behind a pillar and stayed very still. She didn't move as Adam reached the platform, as he boarded the train. As they closed the gates of the barrier behind him and a few other scurrying latecomers, as the train pulled out of King's Cross station.

'Oh, God,' she said in the direction of the vanishing last carriage. But Callie had no regrets about her decision. There would be another train, she told herself stoutly. She would still make it to Cambridge, sooner or later. On her own.

Callie pivoted her suitcase round and headed back into the concourse, towards the nearest cafe. A cup of tea – that's what she needed. She would sit down and have a nice cup of tea. That would help her to face the rest of the journey.

Neville winced as Sid Cowley, with a defiant half-look in his direction, pulled out a packet of cigarettes.

They'd moved to a bench in the churchyard to sit for a moment and discuss what they'd found in the boy's pockets while the SOCOs continued their search of the immediate area.

Let Sid have his fag, Neville decided wearily. He could bloody well do with one himself, but he'd given up that luxury a few years back. He was now an ex-smoker, with all the baggage that entailed.

'No ID, then,' Cowley said as he thumbed his lighter.

'Inconvenient, that.' Without any identification, there wasn't much they could do apart from waiting for someone to ring and report that their kid was missing.

The boy had been carrying a wallet but all it contained was a couple of ten-pound notes. There was a handful of loose change in his pockets as well, and a key on a bit of string. 'No phone,' Neville observed. 'Strange. Unless someone pinched it, which is possible. Kids that age, they never seem to go out without their phones.'

The tip of Cowley's cigarette glowed in the dark. 'My nephew,' he said. 'My sister's lad. Twelve years old he is, and it's like that phone is attached to his hand. Texting all the time. Used to be a right little chatter-box, but not any longer. Can't get a civil word out of him most of the time, he's so busy with that bloody phone. Not talking, just texting.'

What a world, reflected Neville. What a world it was for kids these days. Phones, computers . . . and knives. Sudden death in a churchyard in the middle of the night.

With an unpleasant jolt he remembered that in a few months his own child would be born into this world. Poor little bugger.

Neville shivered. Don't go there, he told himself. Not now.

More than two hours after Callie missed her train, she was finally on the next one bound for Cambridge. She'd managed to pass some of the intervening time in an unappetizing cafe with a cup of tea and a dried-out sandwich from the chiller cabinet. Then they'd started making moves to close the cafe for the night, so she'd gone in search of something to read. WHSmith had already shut its doors; eventually she'd found a few discarded sections of someone's Sunday newspaper and had made do with that while she waited for the platform to be announced and the gates to be opened.

Finally, though, she was on the train, her suitcase stowed in the luggage rack and a journey of about an hour ahead of her. The train wasn't too crowded; she'd found a seat without difficulty, facing forward and with a table.

She should ring Marco and let him know she was actually en route, Callie decided, and then she should ring Tamsin to tell her she'd been delayed. They'd arranged to have a pizza together at their favourite eatery; it wasn't fair to keep Tamsin waiting with no idea of her whereabouts.

Callie pulled her phone out of her red leather bag and pressed the button.

Nothing.

She'd forgotten to put it on to charge last night. And the charger, she now recalled, was at the very bottom of her suitcase.

Blast.

She tucked the dead phone back in her bag, then folded her hands on the table in front of her.

Her bare hands.

'Wear the ring, *cara mia*,' Marco had said. It was just about the last thing he'd said to her this afternoon.

The ring was on a silver chain round her neck, under her jumper. She fished it out, unthreaded it from the chain, slid it on the third finger of her left hand, then spread her fingers out to admire it.

A large sapphire, encircled by smaller diamonds, set on a gold band. Substantial, weighty, it had been worn by Marco's grandmother and her mother-in-law before her. Marco had put it on her finger for the first time about a fortnight ago, then they'd decided that perhaps she ought not to wear it until they'd officially announced their engagement. To her boss Brian, her congregation, her family and friends. And most importantly, to *la famiglia Lombardi*.

That was the biggie: Marco's Italian family. Callie had been nervous about telling them the news, and the two of them had agreed that the best occasion for the announcement would be Easter lunch, a festive meal when everyone would be round the table.

But it hadn't worked out that way.

Callie touched the sapphire, frowning at the memory.

It was, admittedly, not a good time for *la famiglia Lombardi* – too soon after the sudden death of Marco's brother-in-law Joe. Not only was the shock still raw, but his absence meant that the family dynamics were all askew. Joe should have been there at the table, teasing Chiara, joking with Angelina and praising Mamma's cooking. Instead, there was Callie in Joe's chair, feeling more of an outsider than she'd ever felt at one of their family gatherings.

This was her first Easter with them. The rest of them – Marco, his parents, his sister Serena and her two girls – had all been to Mass together at the Italian church, while she, of course, had been occupied with the Easter services at All Saints', so she'd arrived late. Late, self-conscious, and an Anglican curate, trying to fit in with an Italian family who were, for their part, struggling with a recent bereavement on a day which was supposed to be joyful. On reflection, the enterprise was doomed to failure.

They – most of them – had tried to make her feel welcome. Marco's mother had greeted her with double cheek kisses and '*Buona Pasqua!*' His father had done the same, taken her jacket and led her to the table.

The table was laden, as usual, and the food was fantastic – just as Callie had come to expect from the culinary genius who was Marco's mother. A special soup to start, then a mouthwateringly wonderful dish of stuffed artichokes.

'*Carciofi – sempre per la Pasqua,*' explained Grazia Lombardi. 'Always this day.'

Chiara, with the blunt candour of a thirteen-year-old, utterly without malice, asked Callie as the lamb was served, 'Why aren't you with your *own* family today? Your mum and your brother?'

That was a difficult one to answer. It would never have occurred to Laura Anson to have offered a meal to her children, on this or any other day, unless she had some sort of hidden agenda, but Callie couldn't very well say that. She settled for 'My mother isn't religious.'

That wasn't good enough for Chiara. 'Pasqua's not just about religion, about going to church. It's all about families being together.'

Marco's sister Serena lifted her head from contemplation of the lamb on her plate, shot Callie a sideways glance and said, 'Not quite, *cara. Natale con i tuoi, la Pasqua con chi vuoi.* That's the saying.'

Callie, whose grasp of Italian was fairly basic and didn't stretch to folk epigrams, looked at Marco for clarification. 'It means that you stay at home for Christmas, but can spend Easter with anyone you want,' he explained, adding, 'and we're all glad that you've chosen to spend Easter with us.' Under the table he reached for her hand and gave it a little squeeze.

'*Sì, certo,*' affirmed Mamma.

'*Certo,*' Pappa echoed.

'I think it's cool that Callie's here,' said Angelina.

Chiara nodded in agreement. 'Me, too.'

Callie raised her eyebrows at Marco, signalling that this might be a good time for their announcement, but he gave a tiny shake of his head. 'After lunch,' he murmured.

But at the end of lunch there was *la colomba*, the traditional Easter cake in the shape of a dove. And when Mamma brought it out of the kitchen, Chiara turned to her mother. 'Remember last year?' she said. 'Remember what Dad said about *la colomba*?'

Callie never found out what Joe had said about *la colomba*. Serena stood up, covered her face with her hands, and burst into tears – noisy, wracking sobs.

In the weeks following Joe's death, Callie had not seen Serena cry, not even once. It was not in Serena's nature to be outwardly emotional, but the fact that she could sit dry-eyed through her husband's funeral seemed extraordinary to Callie, who in the short course of her ministry had already dealt with a number of bereaved spouses, none of whom had displayed the degree of stoicism which Serena possessed.

Now, though, something had been triggered – some deep well of grief – and the floodgates were opened.

Serena wept copiously, surrounded by her family. Angelina, who seemed to have inherited her mother's stoic nature, put her arms round her, while Chiara – perhaps feeling guilty because she had said the wrong thing – began wailing as well. Mamma went in search of a box of tissues, while Pappa wiped his own eyes with his handkerchief. Marco hovered at the fringes, making soothing noises. Soon, though, they were all crying, even Marco – all but Callie. If she'd felt like an outsider before ...

And she was supposed to be the professional, the one who knew what to say in situations like this. Yet she was helpless – useless – in the face of so many tears, so much emotion.

There was no question of an engagement being announced. Not that day.

Feeling utterly inadequate, Callie tried to creep away unnoticed. She'd retrieved her jacket and just about made it to the front door when Marco caught up with her. 'I'm sorry, *cara mia*. So sorry,' he'd said, tears in his eyes. 'It's too soon. We'll have to wait to tell them.' That's when he'd told her to wear the ring.

As long as she only wore it around people who didn't know his family, presumably. And this week in Cambridge met that qualification.

Cambridge. She should be there soon, Callie reckoned, trying to remember the last station they'd announced. Meldreth, or was it Shepreth?

The train was slowing down. The train stopped.

But the doors didn't open, and there was no platform in sight. All Callie could see through the smeary window of the carriage was dark, featureless countryside. No lights – no streetlamps, no houses, no station.

People who had studiously been avoiding eye contact throughout the journey now looked at each other, raised their eyebrows, shrugged.

It was another ten minutes before a crackly announcement came over the tannoy. 'We apologize for the delay,' said the disembodied voice. 'There is an obstruction on the line. We will resume our journey as soon as possible. Once again, we are sorry for the delay, and any inconvenience it may cause.'

The man across the table from Callie frowned. 'They're not a bit sorry,' he muttered to no one in particular.

Callie sighed. Would she *ever* get to Cambridge?

'Hey, Guv, we've found something!'

Neville was still on the bench in the churchyard; he hadn't summoned up the energy to move, though he was feeling increasingly chilled. Cowley had finished his first fag – conscientiously tapping the ash and dropping the end in a styrofoam cup to avoid contaminating the crime scene – and had started on a second. They both jumped at the SOCO's shout.

She – it was a she – met them halfway, proffering an already-bagged item.

'A phone,' she said. 'An iPhone, in fact. The latest model, if I'm not mistaken. Smashed.'

Neville took the polythene bag from her with a sceptical frown. It was almost a matter of pride with him that he didn't see the need to follow the trends in technology. His old boxy computer worked OK, and so did his ancient mobile phone. This object didn't look anything like his phone: no keypad, no buttons at all. It was just a flat rectangular object with a screen which looked as if someone had taken a rock to it.

'Bugger,' said Cowley. 'Any idea how much one of them babies costs, Guv?'

Trust Sid to get to the heart of the matter. 'Not a clue. How much, then?'

'Five hundred, easy. Maybe six.'

'Bloody hell.' If it had belonged to the dead kid . . .

He moved closer to the spotlights and examined it more closely. 'Is that – was it – a glass screen?'

'A touchscreen,' confirmed Cowley.

'So that means fingerprints. Have you found the bits of glass?'

The SOCO held up her hand to display a drop of blood on the index finger of her rubber glove. 'Some of them. We're working on it now,

Guv. Fingertip search. We found the glass before we found the phone. Damn sharp, too. It went right through the glove.' Her voice was rueful.

Neville scowled at her. 'Well, for God's sake put on a new glove before you contaminate the scene with your own blood.'

'Yes, Guv.'

Another SOCO approached with a bag of glass shards. 'The glass seems to be confined to that area over there,' he reported, pointing. 'In the grass. It's a few metres away from where we found the phone.'

'Like someone smashed it, then threw the phone,' Cowley pointed out. 'Or dropped it.'

He hated having to defer to Sid Cowley, but in matters relating to technology Sid was streets ahead of him. Cowley knew his gadgets, even if he couldn't afford them for himself. An aspirational techie – that's what his sergeant was. 'OK,' Neville said. 'Tell me how this thing works. How do you turn it on?'

Cowley took the bagged phone from him. 'There's a button here at the bottom,' he explained, pointing at a small indentation in the surface. He pressed it; nothing happened. 'Broken,' he said.

'Which was presumably what the person who smashed it intended,' Neville said patiently. 'Does that mean we won't be able to get any information out of it?'

'Not necessarily.' Cowley turned it over. 'It must have a SIM card, like any other phone. If that's still in it, and hasn't been destroyed, then—'

'The computer blokes can sort it,' Neville concluded. At any rate, it wasn't going to happen tonight. They weren't going to drag Danny Duffy, the station's resident computer boffin, out of his bed tonight. It could wait till morning.

Neville was suddenly overcome with weariness – an overwhelming tiredness in every limb of his body, down to the bone. *Everything* could wait till morning, he decided, pushing down the niggling thought of worried parents somewhere, waiting for their son to come home.

He dragged himself back to the spot where the young man lay for one last look. 'You can take him away now,' he said to the people who were waiting on the periphery for him to give the order. 'I'm going home.'

About the time that Neville headed towards his bed, Callie finally reached her destination – hours later than she'd expected. The final part of the journey was no more straightforward than the rest of it had been; by the time she arrived at the station in Cambridge, most of the cabbies had given up for the night and she'd had to wait nearly twenty minutes for one to show up. Then, arriving at the college, she'd faced the problem of getting in. Obviously she no longer had a key, and in any case the front gate was locked and barred – at midnight, she seemed to remember.

Eventually she'd found the buzzer and roused an irate and grumbling porter from his bed. 'You should've rung to tell us you'd be late,' he said, glowering.

'I'm *so* sorry,' Callie grovelled. 'My phone is dead, and I never thought I'd be this late.'

She remembered him; he'd always been grouchy. Evidently he didn't remember *her* – she was just one of many who had passed through the institution over the years. One of the quiet, unexceptionable ones at that. He found his list and located her name, then made a great song and dance about getting the key off the appropriate hook and giving it to her.

'B23. Can you find it, or do you need a map?'

B23. 'I can find it,' she said.

She could find it in her sleep: her old room.

Callie dragged her case through the porters' lodge and out into the courtyard, the wheels rumbling noisily over the ancient, uneven pavement, echoing in the silence of the night. Fortunately it wasn't a long way to B staircase, which was in the front range of the college, the side of the rectangle closest to the road. But then she had to wrestle with the heavy oak door and get her suitcase up two flights of stairs. By the time she slid the key into the familiar lock of the room, Callie was ready to collapse with exhaustion.

Without any conscious thought on her part, her fingers found the light switch by the door.

Her room. The old stone fireplace, decorative but non-functional. The big oak desk with the wonky old chair and the bookshelves above. The comfy, tattered armchair. The basin in the corner. The battered chest of drawers, one knob missing; the imposing wardrobe which looked as if it had come out of some country house and would provide an entrance to Narnia. The incongruously modern bedside table, with its cheap laminate top. The bed.

The bed was the one thing that looked different. Callie had used her own flowered duvet cover, her own thick down duvet. Now it had a more institutional appearance, with a thin synthetic duvet encased in a dark-coloured, geometrically patterned cover. It didn't look very inviting, but at this point Callie didn't care.

20

She opened her case and found her sleep shirt. Then she quickly shed her clothes, tossing them on to the armchair, and pulled the shirt over her head.

She'd used the loo at the station, while waiting for the taxi, so she didn't have to make a trip down the corridor. Too weary even to clean her teeth or wash her face, Callie switched off the light, slid under the duvet, closed her eyes and fell asleep almost instantly.

A few minutes later – five? ten? – she was jolted back to consciousness by an insistent tapping. She prised her eyes open; the noise seemed to be coming from her door. 'What is it?' she called out, her heart pounding.

The door flew open; she'd forgotten to lock it.

A halo of blond curls was back-lit from the corridor for just a moment before Tamsin Howells slipped into the room and closed the door behind her. She put her hands on her hips. 'Callie Anson,' she said severely, 'where on earth have you *been*?'

CHAPTER 3

Waking in her bed on Monday morning, Margaret Phillips, the principal of Archbishop Temple House, reached for her husband Hal.

Hal wasn't there. As a matter of fact he had never shared this bed with her, but at least twice a week she dreamed about him, vividly, and woke expecting to find him with her. Margaret sometimes wondered when those dreams would stop. Probably never – or not until she stopped dreaming altogether, when they shut her up in a box . . .

The trouble was that she'd never stopped loving him – though she recognized all too well that sometimes love wasn't enough.

Sighing, Margaret turned over, looked at the clock and thought about getting up. It was Easter Monday, a holiday for most, yet that didn't mean it was a day off for her. Most of the students had gone home for the Easter holidays, but their places had been taken by the returning deacons. The daily services in the college chapel would be held as usual, and Margaret would want to be there, whether she was taking the services herself or not.

This was Margaret's second academic year as principal, which meant that it was also her second Deacons' Week. But this one was different, she'd already realized. Last year the returning deacons had been strangers to her, a legacy from the last principal. This year, though, they were *hers* – the fledgling priests-in-waiting whom she'd nurtured through their final year of theological training and turned loose on the Church of England in various stages of readiness. She felt responsible for them: protective, maternal. This first group would always be special to her, and she was looking forward to seeing them again.

Some of them – maybe most of them – would be at Morning Prayer in the chapel, whether driven by nostalgia, conscientiousness or curiosity.

Shaking her head sharply to rid herself of the remnants of the dream – until the next time – Margaret got out of bed and headed for the shower.

Coffee. Strong coffee: that's what she needed.

Miranda Frost had been up for most of the night working, in spite of the fact that it was Easter. She had, in fact, discovered over the years

22

that people were more rather than less likely to do themselves a mischief on a holiday. If the drink was flowing freely, the results often ended up in A & E – the victims of traffic accidents, fights or just plain carelessness.

Miranda yawned, stretched and climbed out of bed. She would let Richard sleep on. He had been working last night as well, but unlike his wife he had the bank holiday off today. Miranda was on call and had no illusions that she would be spending the day at home. Her eyes barely open, she groped her way down the stairs to the kitchen.

The Italian coffee machine was state-of-the-art, an object of great beauty, and had cost a bomb. Worth every penny, in Miranda's opinion, as it got more use than the rest of the kitchen appliances put together – with the possible exception of the microwave. She pushed a few buttons and within seconds the beans were being ground and the fabulous aroma filled the small kitchen.

The kitchen really needed re-fitting and extending, Miranda reflected – not for the first time – as she waited for her coffee to squirt into the cup. They'd just never got round to it. Couldn't face the aggro of obtaining planning permission, and then all of the disruption while the work was being done. And at the end of the day it still wouldn't be much more than a place to house the coffee machine and the microwave.

Funnily enough, of the three of them, Sebastian was the one most likely to be found messing about in the kitchen – though he would rather die, of course, than admit it to his mates. A few times Miranda had come home to find Sebastian watching cookery programmes on the telly. He had immediately switched over to MTV, as though an interest in food was too shameful to display even to his mother.

He'd been cooking something last night; it was evident from the pans piled in the sink. Unfortunately his covert interest in cookery did not extend to washing up. Miranda sighed as she snatched the coffee cup from under the nozzle of the machine, unable to wait a second more for that first scalding sip.

Sebastian didn't like coffee; he didn't even like the smell of it, and often complained that her prized machine ponged up the house. He was too young, Miranda thought: just wait until he got to university. That's where she'd first developed her addiction. All of those late nights, studying for exams, memorizing the bones of the hand or the components of the lymphatic system. And then the years as a junior doctor, on call, on endless night shifts . . .

Was it possible to be a doctor without caffeine? Miranda didn't think so.

Of course, there was a real possibility that Sebastian wouldn't go into medicine. She and Richard had always hoped that he would, following their footsteps into that noblest of professions. He did well in the necessary subjects at school – he seemed to have a facility for the sciences. But that didn't necessarily mean anything. Miranda knew that she was prejudiced where her son was concerned, but Sebastian was an all-rounder – good at sport, clever with computers, popular with his mates. He was capable of succeeding in just about any field he fancied. He might even want to be a . . . a professional footballer. Miranda shuddered at the thought.

She gulped down her first cup of coffee, and immediately made a second. That one she would savour. And she would make one to take upstairs for Richard, just in case he'd woken.

Balancing the two cups of coffee, Miranda went back upstairs. She paused for a moment outside Sebastian's firmly closed door, listening for any sounds to indicate that he was awake. It was the school holidays, of course, so there was no need for him to be up, but it wasn't all that early and he often could be heard at his computer in the mornings, playing games or music.

'Sebastian?' she said quietly; when there was no reply she juggled both cups into one hand and nudged the door open. 'Sebastian?' she repeated, blinking in the darkness.

He wasn't there, either in his bed or at his desk. And what's more, it was immediately apparent to Miranda Frost that her son's bed had not been slept in that night.

Tamsin hadn't stayed very long – just long enough to give Callie a hug, get an explanation for her delayed arrival, and promise to catch up with her after Morning Prayer – but Callie found that once she'd been woken up, it was impossible to get back to sleep. In spite of her exhaustion, she'd lain awake, her brain buzzing like a groggy bee, turning from one side to another in the narrow bed, listening to the various colleges' bells announcing the quarter-hours in their unsynchronized way.

If they'd given everyone their old room, she reasoned, that meant that Adam would be down the corridor. Sleeping like a baby, no doubt, in the bed which had once been covered by an old Indian throw.

But why, Callie asked herself wretchedly, was she obsessing about Adam? Why did it matter where he was, or what he was doing? Adam was ancient history. Marco was her present; Marco was her future.

What future, though, did she have with Marco, when he was unable to tell his family that he wanted to marry her? Would this engagement evaporate into thin air, the way the last one had? Adam was so deep in denial that he now seemed to regard their engagement as little more than a vague attachment, to be discarded without regret as soon as he'd met someone more appealing. It was true that he'd never given her a ring – hadn't been able to afford it, he'd said – but they had arranged curacies in neighbouring parishes, had even discussed the timing of their wedding. It was to have been this summer, in a few months' time, after they'd settled into their new jobs. Instead he had married the perfect Pippa just after Christmas.

And Callie was wearing Marco's ring. For whatever it was worth.

Finally, as the birds began their noisy dawn chorus outside her window – why did the birds in London not sing like that? – Callie fell into a deep sleep. The bell woke her at last: not her travel alarm, which she hadn't yet taken out of her case, but the loud bell which summoned the faithful to Morning Prayer.

No Morning Prayer for her, then. At least it meant she wouldn't have to wait for the loo or the shower, as presumably everyone else had already availed themselves of the facilities and were on their way to the chapel.

Not that long ago it hadn't seemed much of a hardship to Callie to share bathroom facilities with various other people. But now she was so used to having her own bathroom that she resented the necessary trip down the hall. Nevertheless she accomplished it briskly, aware that if she hurried she could still make it to breakfast.

Returning to her room, Callie threw her suitcase on the bed and rooted round for something appropriate to wear – something sober, conservative and clerical seemed the safest, until she discovered what everyone else was wearing. Then she delved for her phone charger, down at the bottom of the case, and plugged the dead phone in to re-charge.

Her room was still dark. Callie opened the curtains and, as she had done so many times in the past, paused involuntarily to admire the view. Yes, it was a perfect spring morning, limpid and blue, but that was just the proverbial icing on the cake.

Archbishop Temple House had been built round an elegant Victorian mansion, now the Principal's Lodge, on Cambridge's famous and pictur-esque Backs. The buildings – including chapel, refectory, lecture rooms, staff housing and student lodgings – formed a rectangle bordering the interior courtyard. The courtyard was beautiful, especially in spring, with a carpet of flowers lapping the trunks of mature cherry trees, and those whose rooms faced on to the courtyard counted themselves fortunate. The most envied of all, though, were the lucky few on the east side of the second floor of B staircase, whose windows provided a view across the Backs towards King's College and its magnificent chapel. The rooms on the ground floor and even the first floor weren't high enough; their inhabitants saw only the high brick wall surrounding the college. But from the top storey the view was breathtaking.

Callie could have stood there all day, watching the shifting light and shadows, observing the people coming and going – on foot or cycling madly – along the always-busy Backs. She'd spent not a few hours of her life doing just that, in years past. Now, though, there were more important things to do. Breakfast was waiting.

No matter how she may have felt about her son's absence, Miranda Frost stayed outwardly calm, because that was what she did. It was a persona honed through many years in her profession: people liked their surgeon to be cool, unruffled, in control. Miranda saw no reason why her private life should be any different; she'd observed enough histrionics in her patients to know that such behaviour was rarely helpful in any situation.

The first thing she did, after checking every room in the house and before waking Richard, was to ring Sebastian's mobile. He never went anywhere without his beloved iPhone, she knew. But there was no reassuring voice on the other end, not even a request to leave a message, just an automated message informing her that the phone was not in service.

That was odd.

She was by no means a paranoid, over-protective parent, but Miranda was an organized person who liked to have information at her fingertips, so at some point she had asked Sebastian to give her a list of his friends' mobile phone numbers. After taking a moment to regroup and locate the list in her Filofax, she rang Hugo, Sebastian's best mate.

''Lo?' Hugo sounded as if she'd woken him from a sound sleep – which was probably, Miranda realized, exactly what she'd done.

She took a deep breath and spoke calmly. 'Hugo, it's Miranda Frost. Is Sebastian by any chance with you?'

'Seb? No. Why would he be?'

Miranda answered with another question. 'You don't happen to know where he is, then?'

'No. Sorry, Mrs Frost.'

'When was the last time you saw him?'

Was there a fractional hesitation, or was Hugo just half asleep? 'Yesterday,' he mumbled.

'Yesterday afternoon?' she pursued.

'Yeah. I had this new game, see. *Blaster of the Universe*. He came round.'

Miranda could tell that she was on to a loser; she wasn't going to get any more information out of Hugo. 'Well, thanks, Hugo,' she said. 'If Sebastian turns up, or you happen to see him, could you please ask him to ring me?'

'Yeah, sure.' As a seeming afterthought he added, 'You might try Olly. Or Tom.'

Below Hugo's name on her list were Tom and Olly. She didn't really expect a positive result from either of them, and indeed they both averred that they hadn't seen Sebastian since Saturday night.

Miranda went back to the kitchen and checked round to see whether Sebastian had left a note anywhere – magneted to the fridge door, or on the worktop – which she might have missed in her semi-comatose pre-coffee state. The only evidence of Sebastian's presence in the kitchen was the jumble of dirty dishes in the sink.

It was, she decided, time to wake Richard. Perhaps Sebastian had mentioned something to him about plans to go out. He'd left for work later than she had yesterday; it was possible that he'd talked to Sebastian before leaving the house, or had even had a previous conversation with him on the subject.

She took one more look in Sebastian's room as she went by, regretting that she hadn't checked on him when she got home in the early hours of the morning. It was something she'd always done when he was younger, but now that he was a teenager it seemed an invasion of his much valued privacy. As she'd expected, his bed was still pristine; there was still no sign of him.

Richard was sleeping on his side, his knees drawn up towards his chest like Sebastian had always slept. In so many ways Sebastian was very like his father; the most instantly noticeable similarities were the long, lanky frame and the tightly curled hair. But Richard's curls were light brown, now liberally interspersed with grey, while Sebastian had inherited Miranda's much darker hair.

How Sebastian hated those springy curls – he claimed they made him look like a freak. Short of shaving his head, there was no way to get rid of them. Miranda, on the other hand, would have given anything for a bit of curl in her poker-straight locks. For years she had worn her

27

hair long — Richard preferred it that way — but now she kept it quite short, in a wash–and–wear cut that was more suitable for her demanding lifestyle as well as for her age. The only trouble was that every few weeks she needed to take the time to go to the salon and have it trimmed, or she would start looking rather like a shaggy dog. Sebastian liked to tease her about it. 'Time to go to the groomer, Mum,' he would say when she was overdue for a hair cut.

She woke Richard; she told him that Sebastian was missing, and explained what she'd done to try to find him. Richard knew no more than she did about their son's whereabouts.

'I think we should ring the police,' he said.

Breakfast was already in full swing, Callie saw, as she entered the dining hall. She grabbed a tray and headed for the serving station.

'Full English, love?' The man behind the counter, a youngish bloke with a cheeky grin, was the one who usually worked the breakfast shift. He gave her a wink, as he'd always done. Callie wasn't sure whether he reserved his winks for her or dished them out as indiscriminately as he served up eggs, bacon and sausages. She smiled and nodded.

'Hold the beans, right?' he remembered.

'Right.' She was impressed.

'And an extra toast.'

'Thanks.'

Callie collected her cutlery, poured herself a cup of tea from the pot at the end of the serving counter, then turned to the buzzing room to look for her friends.

Tamsin was the easiest to spot: her mop of yellow Shirley Temple ringlets always stood out in a crowd. She was sitting at a table on the far side of the dining hall, Nicky at her side, so Callie turned her steps in that direction.

But wait.

On Tamsin's other side, his head inclined towards her as he talked, was Adam.

Callie turned round, before any of them saw her, and went for the first empty seat she could find, her back to the treacherous Tamsin. Bending her face over her tray, she took a deep breath and tried to compose herself.

It was only natural and to be expected, she told herself firmly. Tamsin wasn't being disloyal to her by talking to Adam. By virtue of Callie's own relationship with Adam, he had been part of their little group up until the very end of their time at Archbishop Temple House. Until that ill-fated parish placement, when he'd met the wonderful Pippa. Still, Tamsin was *her* friend ...

She must get over it. Adam was here this week, and she couldn't avoid him for ever. She had to be a grown-up about it, and trust that he would do the same. After all, she'd endured the ordeal of dinner with Pippa, months back. And she had Marco now. Wonderful Marco, whom she loved deeply. Marco, with whom she was going to spend the rest of her life.

It was just that here, in this place ...

'Good morning,' said the woman across from her.

'Oh. Hi,' Callie replied, raising her head.

The woman wasn't someone she recognized – not one of her fellow deacons, then. She was perhaps a year or two older than Callie, she judged: early thirties, possibly. Neatly and unremarkably dressed – no dog collar – she had a rather flat, pale face with widely spaced eyes. Her mid-length hair was tinted a shade not found in nature, a sort of burgundy rinse over what was probably a nondescript brown.

'I'm Hanna,' she said, then amplified. 'Hanna Young. H-A-N-N-A. No H at the end.'

'I'm Callie Anson. I'm here for Deacons' Week.'

Hanna Young nodded. 'Right. I recognize your name.'

'How ... ?'

'I'm the principal's secretary,' she explained. 'Her *personal* secretary. PA, really, to be honest. And I've had quite a lot to do with organizing Deacons' Week.'

Callie remembered that the principal's old secretary had been planning to retire at the end of last year. This was her replacement, then. 'It must have been a fair amount of work,' she said.

'Oh, yes. You have no idea. The admin nightmares ... People unable to commit, changing their minds ...' Hanna tutted in displeasure.

Blushing guiltily and averting her face, Callie made an attempt at a sympathetic noise. It may have taken her a while to make up her mind and commit, but at least she hadn't pulled out at the last minute, as she'd been tempted to do.

'Would you believe that I had one person who didn't decide until yesterday to come? Easter Sunday! Did he think the housekeeping staff would be working yesterday to get his room ready? How inconsiderate can you be?'

Adam. Clueless as ever. Callie tried not to smile. She bent over her tray and applied herself to eating her breakfast.

Hanna lowered her voice, glancing towards the top table. 'The principal – I worry about her, to be honest. Don't you think she's looking tired?'

'Well ... I suppose.' The principal didn't look appreciably different to Callie, but it was easier to agree.

'I don't think she's ever got over what happened with her husband, to be honest,' Hanna went on in a loud whisper. 'But then you wouldn't, would you?'

Callie shrugged; it was all she could do, since she had no idea what the other woman was talking about. She knew that Margaret Phillips had been married, and that she had been one of the first female archdeacons in the Church of England before coming to Archbishop Temple House as principal. Beyond that she had no knowledge of the principal's private life.

Hanna was looking at her, seemingly waiting for a more satisfying response. 'What *did* happen with her husband?' Callie asked obediently, spearing some egg and bacon on her fork.

It was Hanna's turn to shrug. 'I couldn't possibly say.' She compressed her lips, then added, 'I'm in a position of trust, you realize. To be honest, the principal hates it when people talk about her.'

We're over-reacting, Miranda Frost told herself as she made another coffee for Richard; the first one had gone cold while she was ringing round Sebastian's friends. When Sebastian comes home he's going to be furious.

'I'm not a child', 'Don't baby me, Mum'. Her son's angry words sounded in Miranda's head.

But Richard had insisted on ringing the police. Now he was showering, getting dressed. Waiting for them to arrive.

Surely it wouldn't be long. The police station was nearby, and a missing teenager ought to have some sort of priority over traffic accidents and other routine business. Miranda wasn't sure why she was gripped by such a sense of urgency; she tried to calm herself down with deep breaths.

Still, it seemed an eternity as they drank coffee and Richard re-inspected the entire house, top to bottom. 'No. He's not here,' he reported a moment before the doorbell chimed.

The policeman on the doorstep was in uniform: a shortish but powerfully built young man with spiky dark hair who identified himself as PC Jones. He checked the piece of paper in his hand. 'And you're

30

Dr Frost?' he asked, looking between Miranda and Richard. 'Both of you, they said?'

'I'm Dr Frost,' said Richard. 'My wife is a doctor as well, but she's a surgeon, so technically she's Mrs Frost.'

PC Jones shook his head in confusion. 'Whatever.'

Miranda invited him into the front room and offered him coffee, which he refused, getting out his notebook as he took a seat on the sofa. 'If you can just give me the details, Mrs Frost. Or Dr Frost.'

'I told them on the phone,' Richard cut in impatiently. 'Our son is missing. Sebastian. He's not in the house, he's not answering his phone, and his friends don't know where he is.'

'He didn't sleep in his bed last night,' added Miranda.

The policeman turned his head and looked at her, frowning, then scratched his head with his pencil. 'How can you be sure of that, Mrs Frost?'

To her it was obvious, not deserving of time-wasting explanations. 'Because his bed is made. It hasn't been slept in.'

'How do you know for sure that he didn't sleep in it and then make it?'

Miranda took a deep breath. 'Sebastian never makes his bed. Never. Nothing I can say to him ever makes any difference. He just won't do it. So every afternoon the cleaner makes his bed. While he's at school.'

'*Every* afternoon?' pursued PC Jones. 'Yesterday was Sunday, Mrs Frost. Easter Sunday, in actual fact. Was your cleaner here yesterday?'

'Yes, she was. Briefly. As a special favour to me.' He was looking at her strangely; Miranda felt compelled to explain. 'My husband and I both work long and irregular hours. In A and E. Mrs Bolt has been with us for many years. She's more than just a cleaner.'

PC Jones made a note. 'Mrs Bolt, you say. Have you been in touch with her regarding your son's whereabouts?'

Why on earth hadn't she thought of ringing Iris? Miranda turned to Richard, almost gasping with relief. 'That's it. She'll know where he is. Can you ring her now?'

'Yes, of course.' Richard reached for his mobile.

But Iris Bolt didn't know where Sebastian was; she hadn't seen him since yesterday afternoon.

Having invested so much in that brief hope, Miranda now felt the panic rising again, more insistent than ever. Someone should be doing something; someone should be out there looking for him.

'The hospitals,' PC Jones went on methodically, as if consulting a mental checklist for missing persons. 'Have you been in touch with them? With A and E?'

'We work there,' Richard reminded him with more than a touch of ironic impatience. 'We were there last night. Both of us, until late.'

'There are other hospitals in London,' pointed out the policeman.

Oh, God. What was he suggesting? Miranda didn't even want to think about it.

PC Jones moved on. 'So could you tell me about the last time you saw your son? When was it? And where?'

'Yesterday afternoon,' Miranda said promptly. 'Early afternoon, just before I went to work. He was in here, in this room, watching the telly.' She indicated the enormous plasma screen mounted on the wall. 'A film. Sebastian has a telly in his room, of course, but sometimes he likes to come in here and watch the large screen, especially if it's a film.'

'I think it was a James Bond film,' Richard added. 'I left a bit after Miranda, and it was nearly over at that point.'

'So you left him on his own? Did he indicate his plans for the rest of the day?'

'Sebastian is fifteen,' Miranda said, hoping she didn't sound defensive. 'He's quite capable of being left on his own.' She ran her finger over the knobbly fabric on the arm of the chair. 'And no, he didn't say anything about his plans. His friend Hugo told me that Sebastian went to his house later in the afternoon to play a video game. And,' she remembered, 'he must have come home and cooked something for himself later on, after Mrs Bolt was here. He left some dishes in the sink.'

PC Jones' pen moved across the page of his notebook, scratching, scratching. So slowly; Miranda wanted to scream at him, but she clamped her lips together and stared down at her lap. She knew that if she caught Richard's eye, one of them would probably say something they'd regret.

'Now,' said the policeman, looking up from his notebook after what seemed like hours. 'Could you please show me your son's room?'

Jane Stanford prepared breakfast for her husband while he was saying Morning Prayer in church. On his own, no doubt; what parishioner in their right mind would turn out on Easter Monday, after an intensive run of services? Maundy Thursday, Good Friday, the Easter Vigil and Easter Day: even Jane, who took her role as vicar's wife seriously, had had enough of church for a few days.

Making Brian's breakfast was something she did every day, unquestioningly and dutifully, but today she was feeling cranky and out of sorts. She just couldn't get out of her mind something that she'd overheard on Saturday afternoon, during the annual ritual of doing the Easter flowers.

Wendy Page, wife of one of the churchwardens and leading light of the flower rota in her own right, had been working on arranging the pedestal in the Lady Chapel, chattering away to someone whose murmured acknowledgements didn't immediately identify her to Jane. Obviously Wendy didn't realize how far her voice was carrying in the reverberant acoustic of the church, and Jane – doing the altar flowers in the chancel, on the other side of the screen – didn't bother to alert her.

'I ran into Mildred Channing at the greengrocer's the other day,' Wendy said. 'Moaning as usual. She said that the vicar hadn't brought her home communion for a while – he's been sending the curate instead.'

Jane couldn't quite make out what her companion said in reply. Wendy went on, 'Mildred says she doesn't object to women clergy, per se. But she thinks it's terribly dangerous, letting these young women loose in the Church like that. Working hand-in-hand with susceptible middle-aged men. "I know they're priests," she said, "but they're men for all that. Even Father Brian. I wouldn't be surprised if he had a soft spot for that young woman," she said. "Or even more than that. No fool like an old fool."' Wendy chuckled knowingly. 'I'm not saying it's true, mind, but it does make you think.'

It had certainly made Jane think. Not that she believed it. Not for a minute. Brian ... and Callie? No way. It was ridiculous – of course it was.

But if that's what people were saying ...

'No smoke without fire,' had been the quiet but audible reply.

Did anyone seriously imagine that Brian was casting longing looks at Callie in the stalls at Morning Prayer, or surreptitiously groping her behind the font?

Jane's first impulse was to storm into the chapel and confront them. Don't be ridiculous, she wanted to say to Wendy Page.

But if she did, she told herself, they would probably only take it for confirmation. Protesting too much ...

'I don't suppose Jane knows what Mildred is telling people,' Wendy continued, lowering her voice. 'They do say the wife is always the last to know.'

'She's probably in denial,' agreed her companion.

In denial, indeed. Jane gritted her teeth as she plopped the cereal box on the table with unnecessary force.

It was no wonder she was out of sorts.

And then there was the fraught issue of this week's holiday – or non-holiday, as it had turned out.

Brian had always taken the week after Easter as holiday, ever since he'd been in parish ministry. Most clergy did: after the rigours of Lent, and the heavy-duty Holy Week and Easter services, they were entitled to a bit of R & R. Usually the Stanfords went to Wales, where they had the free use of a cottage which was owned by an old school friend of Brian's. It was a good place for the boys, with lots of outdoor activities on offer, and Jane always looked forward to their annual week there as a family.

But this year it hadn't happened, and wasn't going to happen.

To be fair, the boys hadn't helped, with their alternative plans. Simon had spent Easter with his girlfriend Ellie's family, and was going with them to the South of France this week. And Charlie, after a few days at home, had returned to Oxford to do some work in the Bodleian. He had an essay due right after the hols, he said, and the only way he was going to finish it was to go back up to Oxford.

Things just weren't the same now that the twins were at university, Jane acknowledged unhappily. But she and Brian still could have gone to Wales. This year, with Brian's inheritance from his Australian uncle, they wouldn't even have been limited to Wales. They might have had a romantic week in Venice, taken a cruise, flown to the Caribbean, or gone on safari. Just the two of them: a holiday to remember.

Brian had said no, though, and the reason was Callie.

Callie – that woman again. Glancing at the clock to judge the timing of Brian's return, Jane filled the kettle and switched it on. Callie Anson needed to go to Cambridge for something to do with her old theological college, and Brian felt he had to be a martyr, to make a point, and to stay at home this week so that the parish wouldn't be left unattended.

It was ridiculous. As ridiculous as the suggestion that there was any-thing between Brian and his curate, Jane told herself. Last year this time he had scarcely known of the existence of Callie Anson. He didn't have a curate then, and it hadn't occurred to him to be worried about leaving the parish unattended, at Easter or any other time. He'd always taken his Saturdays off, his weeks after Christmas and Easter, his summer holidays. He was entitled to time off, like anyone else. Why, this year, did he feel that he had to make a point?

34

Callie.

Jane filled the milk jug and slammed it down on the table, splashing more than a few drops of milk on the cloth.

She'd made such an effort to tolerate her husband's curate, and she actually felt she'd been making progress lately. In spite of everything, she'd begun warming to her; there had even been a few times when she'd thought they might eventually be friends.

Now, though . . .

Mopping up the milk, Jane knocked over Brian's juice glass. The juice soaked the tablecloth and the glass rolled off the edge, shattering on the floor.

'Oh, great.' Jane felt the tears welling up. What was the matter with her?

She crouched down and started gathering up the jagged bits of glass. Maybe, she thought suddenly, it was PMS. Wasn't she about due for her period? With all of the frenetic busyness of the last few days – Holy Week, getting the church ready for Easter, all of the services, Charlie coming and going – she hadn't really had time to think about it.

The calendar was on the side of the fridge, with all of the relevant days circled and notated. After disposing of the largest pieces of glass and sweeping up the tiny shards, Jane looked at the April calendar page.

She heard Brian letting himself in through the front door, calling out a greeting to her, as the realization struck.

She was overdue.

Was it possible?

Could she be pregnant?

CHAPTER 4

After a short night, Neville Stewart's morning had begun very early, and very badly.

Of course the first problem was Triona. This was a bank holiday; naturally she wasn't working, and he was meant to have the day off as well. He had arranged for them to go to the house they were in the process of buying, and measure up the rooms so that they could start buying furniture.

This wasn't the first time he'd let Triona down, and they both knew it wouldn't be the last. He had expected that she would shout at him with something along those lines. But on this occasion Triona didn't shout, and somehow he found her resigned disappointment – the slope of her shoulders, the averted face – even more upsetting than an out-and-out row would have been. Instead of defending himself, he'd heard himself apologizing – almost grovelling. Neville didn't like to grovel.

Not a good start to the day.

And then, before anything else, he'd had to go to the mortuary, to witness the post-mortem examination of the nameless boy. Neville wasn't squeamish, but he couldn't help finding it distressing. Dr Tompkins was so matter-of-fact, so taciturn, that Neville wanted to shout at him. This is someone's son, he wanted to say. Don't you feel *anything*, man?

When the procedure was over, Colin Tompkins went to the basin to wash his hands, turning his head to address Neville in the longest speech he'd ever heard him make. 'Some of these boys really carve each other up, but this one was quite efficient. Death was caused by a single stab wound to the neck. Severed the jugular. It would have been fairly quick,' he added as he reached for a towel. 'Maybe that will be a consolation to the parents.'

Some consolation. 'Do you have children?' Neville heard himself asking.

'Four, as a matter of fact. Two boys, two girls.'

'Then how do you ...?'

The doctor smiled faintly. 'I can't let myself think about it. This is my job. I do it. And when I go home I forget about it.'

Neville wondered, as he headed for the police station for an inevitable meeting with his boss, how it was possible to achieve that level of detachment. If only he could manage to do the same – to remain uninvolved with the dead, to view them only as pieces of meat on the table, unconnected with the living and breathing human beings they had once been. Would it make his job easier, or would it mean that he would be unable to continue doing it? He knew that he was a good detective – was it because he felt so deeply for the dead?

One thing he was sure about: it would certainly make his personal life easier if, like Dr Tompkins, he could leave his work behind when he went home at the end of the day.

'You're *engaged*?!' Tamsin squealed at a volume that would have woken the dead – had there been any dead nearby. She grabbed Callie's hand and scrutinized the ring. 'Oh. My. God. But who? You've been holding out on me, girl! Tell me everything!'

Callie smiled at her friend, bemused. She was glad that they'd retreated to her room – with its thick, soundproof walls – for their after-breakfast chat, rather than a more public place. 'Where do you want me to begin?'

'At the beginning! Since you haven't bothered to tell me anything at all about this mystery man. I mean, as far as I knew, you were still pining after that love rat Adam. And you haven't put anything on your Facebook page about it.'

'I know. I know. Guilty as charged.' Callie put her hands in the air in mock surrender.

'Well? Who is he?'

'His name is Mark. Mark Lombardi. I call him Marco.' Saying his name conjured him up in Callie's mind, vividly, and she couldn't help smiling.

'And?' demanded Tamsin.

'He's a policeman. A family liaison officer, in fact – he deals with families of murder victims and that sort of thing. And he's Italian,' she added.

'Oooh. The dark and handsome type, I suppose.' Tamsin rolled her eyes. 'Do you have a photo?'

There must be some on her phone, Callie realized. Probably not very good, yet better than nothing. 'Hang on a second,' she said.

The phone, plugged into the wall, hadn't fully recharged yet, but there was sufficient juice in it to access the photos. She clicked through them till she found one that seemed to represent him with reasonable accuracy. She handed it to Tamsin. 'Here.'

'Umm.' Tamsin squinted at the photo. 'Gorgeous. How did you meet him, and how long has it been going on?'

'I met him on an aeroplane, actually. Coming back from Venice, right after my ordination.' Relaxing on the bed, Callie recounted the story: how she'd chatted with the attractive man sitting next to her, and the way things had developed since then. She left out the part about his demanding Italian family, his sister's insidious attempts to undermine their relationship, and a few other messy details that she didn't consider relevant or necessary.

Tamsin sighed happily. 'He sounds perfect. Lucky old you. But why didn't you tell me about him before?'

Why hadn't she? 'I suppose I didn't want to jinx it,' Callie admitted. 'I didn't want to assume too much. Not until he actually went down on his knees and asked me to marry him. I mean, after what happened with Adam . . .'

'That toerag,' snorted Tamsin, then had the grace to look slightly guilty. 'Sorry about breakfast. I was sitting there chatting with Nicky, and Adam came along and sat on my other side. Just like nothing had happened. Like we were still good friends. I didn't even want to speak to him, after what he did to you. But I didn't feel I should cause a scene by getting up and leaving. I hope you didn't think . . .'

Callie sat up, waving her hand dismissively. 'No, of course not. I wish he hadn't come, but since he's here we just have to deal with it. All of us.'

'How *do* you feel about Adam?' blurted Tamsin.

It was a subject she tried not to dwell on – and had been fairly success-ful, until yesterday afternoon. 'Angry, still,' Callie admitted, probing her feelings like a tongue relentlessly seeking out a sore tooth, trying to be honest. 'I'm not in love with him any longer, if that's what you mean. I don't fancy him. I don't even like him, much. But when he's here, where everything happened between us, I can't just ignore him and pretend it didn't happen.'

Tamsin chewed on her lip, looking as if she was sorry she'd asked the question. She got up from the chair where she'd been sitting and crossed to the window, studying the view silently.

That gave Callie the chance to observe the top Tamsin was wearing – something that had been difficult to do when Tamsin was seated. It was a sort of T-shirt, periwinkle blue in colour, made of a stretchy jersey fabric, but tailored to Tamsin's ample figure and topped with a dog collar. She was about to mention it when Tamsin shook her head, sending her curls into bouncy mode, and changed the subject.

'Let's not talk about him any more – he's not worth it. I want to hear more about your wonderful Marco. Is it true what they say about Latin lovers? Is he fantastic in bed?' She gave Callie a lascivious grin, then smacked her lips.

Oh, no – the question she'd hoped Tamsin wouldn't ask. Callie flopped back on to the bed, pulling the pillow over her face, aware that she was blushing. 'Actually,' she said, 'I don't know. Yet. We haven't—'

Tamsin shrieked. 'You haven't? Why not? Don't tell me you've developed scruples, now that you're ordained?'

'It's not that, exactly.' Why was she telling Tamsin this? It was something private between herself and Marco, none of Tamsin's business, but Callie couldn't stop herself now that it had gone this far. 'It's not me, it's Marco. He's Italian. He's Roman Catholic. He has this thing about priests being holy. He says he just can't, until we're married.'

'My God. But he's a red-blooded man, isn't he?' Tamsin yanked the pillow from Callie's hands and stared down at her.

'I didn't say it was easy. And I've tried.' Callie pressed her palms to her burning cheeks. How humiliating – to have to admit, even to one of her best friends, that her fiancé didn't want to sleep with her. That wasn't strictly true, though, she reminded herself: he *did* want to sleep with her, and had clearly demonstrated how much on a number of occasions, but she hadn't yet managed to overcome all of those cultural barriers that were standing in their way.

'You haven't tried hard enough, obviously.' Tamsin grinned, irrepressible. 'I know what we'll do. We'll sneak away from the college sometime this week and go into town. That sexy lingerie shop in Rose Crescent, near the market ... We'll find something there that will do the trick.'

She'd had enough of this conversation; it was Callie's turn to change the subject. 'Speaking of clothes,' she said firmly, 'tell me about your ... um ... clerical shirt. I've never seen anything like it.'

Tamsin struck a pose, arms outstretched and chest thrust forward. 'Good, isn't it? One of my parishioners is in the fashion business, and she designed it for me. I have them in all sorts of colours. Every colour in the rainbow, for every day of the week.'

'But ... why?'

'I can't wear a normal clerical shirt.' Tamsin looked down at her chest and gave her blond curls a rueful shake. 'My boobs are too big.

The buttons won't stay done up over them, and nothing looks more unprofessional than a curate with her boobs hanging out. I have a difficult enough time being taken seriously without that.'

Callie laughed. 'Well, whatever works for you, I suppose.'

Neville's meeting with Detective Superintendent Evans had taken exactly the path he had expected. Evans' main concerns, apart from the obvious ones of solving the crime and finding the perpetrators, were to identify the victim and to manage the press. 'It's mainly why I've put you on the case,' Evans said. 'The press are going to go mad over this. Another teenager stabbed to death. Sort it, Stewart.'

Fortunately that meeting had been short, if not sweet. He knew what was expected of him; it was time to get on with it. DS Cowley was waiting for him, and together they went to see Danny Duffy, the station's resident techie. Danny was disgustingly young – as one would have to be to do that job – and seemed revoltingly chipper this morning, when Neville was feeling old and weary.

'There was no ID on the body,' Neville explained to Danny as Cowley handed over the evidence bag with the damaged iPhone. 'And nothing very helpful turned up at the PM. No tattoos, no birthmarks. No dental work, either. Kids these days – they take better care of their teeth,' he added ruefully.

'In other words, you're counting on me.' Danny smiled, holding the bag up.

'You've got it in one. We're counting on you.'

'It's all right for me to take this out?'

'They've already tested it for prints,' confirmed Cowley, who had been to the forensics lab while Neville was at the post-mortem. 'Not a lot to go on, apparently. Some smeary prints – nothing conclusive. And we don't even know that it belonged to the dead kid,' he added. 'It wasn't on the body. They found it a few metres away.'

Danny tipped the phone out on to the table in front of him and bent over it, frowning. 'Someone wanted to make sure this phone was never used again,' he observed. He fiddled with the switch at the top, pressed the 'on' button, and shook his head.

'But there must be something inside that you can get out,' Neville suggested, remembering what Cowley had said in the wee hours of the morning. 'A SIM card?'

'These phones have internal memory chips – quite substantial ones – as well as removable SIM cards.' Danny opened a drawer, poked round in it for a moment, and took out some implements, including a pair of tweezers. 'Let's see what we can do.'

Cowley was practically salivating, Neville observed. 'That is one slick bit of kit, that phone,' the sergeant enthused. 'That would set you back ... what? Five, maybe six hundred quid? More?'

Danny probed the top of the phone with the tweezers. 'It's a dead cert I couldn't afford one. Not even on a contract.'

'Me, neither. But if I won the lottery ...' Cowley leaned forward, obstructing Neville's view.

Time to get rid of Cowley. 'Sid, there's something you could do for me,' Neville said.

'Can't it wait?'

Neville ignored the plaintive question. 'I haven't had a chance to talk to the desk sergeant this morning,' he went on. 'Could you pop down to see him, and make sure he knows we have an unidentified body? If he gets any missing persons reports involving teenage boys, he needs to ring me straightaway.'

Cowley went, reluctantly but obediently, with a longing backwards glance, as Neville turned back to the table and watched the delicate operation.

After what seemed a very long time, Danny gave a grunt of satisfaction and held something up with the tweezers: a tiny rectangle of bent plastic. 'Ordinarily,' he said, 'I could put this card into something else – another phone, a card reader – and retrieve the information off it quite easily. But you can see how badly mangled this is. Whoever broke this phone, they were pretty thorough.'

'So you can't do anything with it.' Neville frowned: another dead end.

'I didn't say that. The information may still be there. Or on the chips inside the phone. But I'm going to need specialized equipment, and it will take time.'

Time. That was something they didn't have much of, Neville was well aware. The press ... as soon as they got a whiff of this, they'd be on it like vultures on roadkill.

Bracing the phone on the table, Danny inserted a thin blade along the side and twisted it. 'They don't design these things to be opened up,' he said. 'But where there's a will—' The phone came apart, revealing a mysterious interior stuffed with tiny black squares and silvery bits, none of which Neville could begin to put a name or function to. Danny grinned. 'We'll see what we can do with this.'

Neville asked the big question. 'How long?'

41

'Oh, give me a day. Or two. It might take up to a week, depending.'

Trying to hide his disappointment, Neville turned away from the table, just as his phone rang.

Sid, the caller ID told him. 'Yes?' he rasped into the phone.

'I was too late,' Cowley said. 'There's been a missing person report this morning. A fifteen-year-old boy. They've sent Dewi Jones.'

Neville's expletive caused Danny Duffy to drop his blade on the table with a clatter.

'Steady on,' said Danny, looking shocked.

Pregnant?

Jane managed to get through breakfast, maintaining an outward semblance of normality for Brian's benefit.

'No one at Morning Prayer,' he said conversationally as Jane poured his tea. 'Not a soul. Just me and God.'

She bit back a tart comment on the fact that everyone else – everyone with sense – was away. As they could have been. *Should* have been.

None of that mattered if she was pregnant. Nothing else mattered.

It was all she'd wanted and longed for, tried so hard to achieve.

More than eighteen years since the twins were born. Eighteen years since she'd held a tiny, warm, fragrant new life in her arms. Through all those years she'd longed for a daughter – a little girl she could dress in frilly clothes, with whom she could join in dolls' tea parties and share delicious girly secrets.

And for eighteen years it had been utterly out of the question. On a vicar's stipend, bringing up the twins had been a constant struggle. Jane hadn't worked outside of the home – she strongly believed that the role of a vicar's wife was a calling in itself, and it was part of her job to make sure that the meagre resources stretched as far as she could make them stretch. Bills, school uniforms, the untold costs associated with growing boys: most of the time just feeding the four of them was a major financial achievement.

But then – miracle of miracles – a bequest had come out of the blue, an inheritance from an uncle. Not enough money to allow Brian to give up his job and live in the lap of luxury; enough, though, to make a difference to their lives.

And what could make more of a difference than to fulfil the dream of making their family complete, with a new baby?

Brian had been sceptical at first, even incredulous: they were both over forty, after all. Eventually he'd been won over by his wife's passionate arguments, and in spite of their GP's discouraging advice, they'd embarked on a regimen in which their love life was regulated by the calendar and Jane's obsessive temperature-taking.

The irony was, of course, that over Easter she hadn't had the time to worry about it. And now ...

'I was thinking,' Brian said, buttering his toast, 'that since things are quiet this week, maybe we could go out for lunch today? Just the two of us?'

Jane stared at him. Obviously he was feeling guilty, and this was his way of being conciliatory, trying to make it up to her for not taking a week of holiday. But this was a first. He'd never, as long as they'd been married, suggested going out for lunch.

She wasn't ready to let him off the hook. Not yet, anyway. 'I'll see,' she said. 'I have an errand to run this morning.'

Brian gave her a puzzled frown. 'What sort of errand?'

'To the shops,' she said vaguely.

'Are the shops even open? On the bank holiday?'

'Yes, they'll be open.'

At least Jane hoped so; she knew she couldn't bear to wait another twenty-four hours.

She did manage to wait until breakfast was over and she'd done the washing-up and tidied the kitchen. By then the shops would be opening, she reckoned. Grabbing a jacket and her shopping bag, she headed along Sussex Gardens towards the nearest branch of Boots, on the Edgware Road.

Why hadn't she bought a testing kit already? Jane asked herself as she turned the corner into the busy road. She should have had one in a drawer at home, ready for this moment. It had been superstition that had prevented her: that perverse, niggling fear of tempting the fates, jinxing her luck, by assuming too much. She'd never acknowledged it as such, and she knew that as a Christian it was unworthy of her to succumb to such nonsense, but it had been at the back of her mind nonetheless.

Well, now was the time.

The testing kits were towards the back of the shop. There were various ones on offer, a confusing array. Jane, deciding that they would all do the same job, chose one more or less at random and started to make her way back towards the tills at the front.

'Jane!' Coming up the aisle towards her, smiling, was Wendy Page.

Instinctively, without even thinking about it, Jane shoved the test kit behind a bottle of shampoo on the shelves and picked up the first thing her hand fell on: a home hair-colouring kit, as luck would have it. 'Oh, hello, Wendy,' she said, striving for a normal tone of voice.

'Out shopping today?'

Jane, put out at the interruption, was torn between one sarcastic reply ('What does it look like?') and another ('Actually, I'm on holiday in Wales. You just *think* you see me.') Instead she did the proper vicar's wife thing and returned Wendy's smile. 'Just a few bits and bobs.'

Wendy made a little face. 'I had no intention of coming out to the shops today,' she revealed. 'But would you believe it? Philip has run out of mouthwash. And nothing would do but I had to get him some.' She shook her head and rolled her eyes, adding 'Men!' in an exasperated voice.

'I know what you mean,' Jane improvised. 'Brian's run out of . . . para-cetamol.' She looked at the box in her hand and put it down hastily.

'I'm not surprised he has a headache, with all he's had to do over Easter.'

Jane nodded. 'Yes, well, it's all part of a vicar's job.' She knew she probably didn't sound very sympathetic. Brian didn't really have a head-ache, after all, and if he did it was no more than he deserved.

Wendy took a step back and gave her a long, searching look. 'We all have our crosses to bear,' she pronounced, her words heavy with meaning.

Sid Cowley, to give him credit, had organized things swiftly. He'd got a car and was already waiting for Neville in the car park at the back of the station, smoking a cigarette.

'Bloody Dewi Jones,' Neville growled, slamming the car door as he got into the passenger seat. 'PC Dewi Bloody Jones. Give me strength.'

'What do you have against Dewi Jones?' Cowley pinched out his fag and started the engine.

He knew that Sid was just winding him up, but Neville couldn't help himself. 'Welsh twat,' he said acidly. 'Wanker. Thinks he looks like bloody Robbie Williams.' Neville conjured up a mental picture of him: spiky gelled hair, tattoos. Muscle-bound body. 'All brawn, no brains. Thick as you-know-what. The only reason he hasn't been kicked off the force on to his fit little backside is that he's Welsh. Evans has a soft spot for him.'

'Oh, you're just jealous, then.'

Neville decided not to rise any further to the bait and changed the subject abruptly. 'Where are we going, then?'

'Not far.' Cowley eased the car out into traffic. 'St Michael's Street. Do you know it?'

'Doesn't sound familiar.'

'The other side of Praed Street. Round the corner from the Tesco Metro. There's a decent pub in St Michael's Street,' Cowley added.

'That would explain your familiarity with it.' Neville waited for the comeback, involving the words 'pot' and 'kettle', but Sid seemed to have settled down to concentrate on his driving and was no longer engaged in point-scoring.

He needed to settle down as well, Neville realized. For some reason this case really had him on edge. Maybe it had something to do with the fact that he was about to be face-to-face with the parents of a missing boy, and that he was almost certainly going to have to tell them something that no parent ever wants to hear. There were a lot of things he hated about his job – the unpredictable and unsocial hours, the soul-destroying paperwork, getting chewed up by the press, being answerable to Evans, having to work with idiots like Dewi Jones – but this was the very worst part of it, the thing he hated the most.

Cowley turned the car off busy Praed Street, then turned again into a quiet residential road. 'You'd never believe there was a street like this so close to everything, would you?' he remarked.

It was a very attractive short street of immaculate terraced houses, brown brick with red brick accents and painted white trim, set back from the pavement and protected by original spiky black iron railings. As Cowley said, it seemed a world away from the multicultural food joints of Praed Street, from the hospital and the railway station. St Michael's Street was genteel, old-fashioned, beautifully maintained. And quiet.

The north side of the street was marked out for parking, and contained a solid line of cars. 'Residents' parking,' Cowley pointed out, crawling along slowly, looking for an empty space. 'Bank holiday today. No one's gone to work.'

Another police car had been parked illegally, outside of the designated spaces. Dewi Jones, Neville thought sourly. 'Pull up behind him,' he directed.

It had to be done; no point putting it off by cruising round looking for a legal parking space. God only knew what sort of damage was being inflicted by Dewi Jones in the meantime.

Cowley parked the car, consulted his bit of paper, and checked the house numbers. 'This one,' he said, pointing to the middle house in a three-house terrace. It had a shiny black door, flanked by bay trees in pots.

'Right.' Neville squared his shoulders. 'Let's get this over with. What are they called, then?'

'Frost. Doctor and Mrs Frost.'

'A doctor. That makes sense, this close to the hospital. And a posh house like this.' Neville opened the gate, marched the two steps to the door, and rang the bell.

The woman who opened the door was probably in her early forties, Neville judged. Short black hair, with large eyes magnified even more behind round spectacles. Thin – scrawny, even. Very pale, though whether habitually or as a result of the current circumstances was impossible to determine. Her eyes widened at the sight of them.

'Mrs Frost?'

She nodded, swallowing visibly.

'I'm Detective Inspector Stewart, Ma'am, and this is Detective Sergeant Cowley. We'd like to have a word with you and your husband. May we come in?'

'There's a policeman here already,' she said, opening the door wider. 'PC Jones.'

Dewi Jones appeared behind her in the entrance hall, notebook in hand. Neville glared at him with contempt. 'You can bugger off now.'

'But—' PC Jones waved his notebook. 'I need to talk to you.'

'Later.'

Dewi Jones went, sputtering. Mrs Frost showed them into the front room, furnished with an expensive-looking three-piece suite and dominated by an enormous plasma screen. Neville glanced at Cowley, who was, as he'd expected, staring at the screen with naked lust.

A tall man with curly greying hair stood up and introduced himself as Richard Frost, shaking hands with grave courtesy. Mrs Frost offered them coffee; Neville declined, though he would have loved one. Coffee could wait.

He took the plunge, before she could invite them to sit. 'About your son, Mrs Frost. Dr Frost. He's missing?'

'Sebastian. Yes.' She nodded, her eyes widening still further as they met his.

'Do you by any chance have a recent picture of your son that you could show me?'

'Yes,' said Mrs Frost. 'Yes, I do.'

Callie had time, before the first session was due to start, to ring Marco. Taking the precaution of locking her door to avoid interruption, she unplugged her phone from the charger and settled into the chair. It embraced her like an old friend, far more comfortable than any chair she now possessed; she gave its faded arm a fond pat.

Marco answered on the second ring. '*Cara mia!*' he said, his voice anxious. 'Are you all right?'

'Yes, I'm fine.'

'I've been trying to reach you, ever since yesterday afternoon. Your phone's been switched off. I've left a few messages . . .'

She hadn't listened to them yet, but could imagine their content. 'Yes, I'm sorry. My phone ran out of juice. I've only just got it charged up again.'

'Your trip was OK?'

'Actually,' she confessed with a sigh, 'it was the trip from hell.'

Interlude: a phone call

WENDY: Hi, Liz. I'm just back from the shops.

LIZ: Were they crowded?

WENDY: Surprisingly so. You'd think people would have better things to do on Easter Monday than go to the shops, but there you are. Anyway, you'll never guess who I saw in Boots.

LIZ: The Duchess of Cornwall?

WENDY: Oh, very funny.

LIZ: Surprise me, then.

WENDY: Jane Stanford.

LIZ: I thought the Stanfords always went away after Easter.

WENDY: Not this year, evidently. Anyway, guess what she was buying?

LIZ: Let me think. Porn? Not in Boots, I suppose. (*Laughing*)

WENDY: Oh, you *are* witty today. (*Dramatic pause*) No, she was buying hair dye!

LIZ: Well, what's so amazing about that? I colour my hair. So do you, come to that.

WENDY: Yes, but Jane *doesn't*. Or at least she didn't, before now. Think about all that grey she has at the front.

LIZ: I suppose she decided it was time to get rid of it.

WENDY: Yes, but here's the thing. She was looking at *red* dye. The name on the box was 'Miss Scarlett'. Can you imagine Jane Stanford with red hair?

LIZ: Not easily, I admit. But I suppose we'll be seeing it quite soon.

WENDY: She tried to hide it, even. She told me she was there to buy paracetamol for Father Brian. But I saw the box in her hand, plain as day. 'Miss Scarlett.' I think it must mean that Mildred Channing was right, you know.

LIZ: About the vicar and the curate, you mean?

WENDY: Absolutely. And it means that Jane knows about it. Don't you see? Jane realizes that Father Brian fancies his curate, so she decides to dye her hair – red! – to make herself more attractive to him. To rekindle the spark, so to speak.

LIZ: I'm not sure it's going to do that much good, to be honest.

WENDY: Jane Stanford with red hair – the mind boggles. But it just shows how desperate she must be, don't you think?

LIZ: Well, like I said before, there's no smoke without fire. Poor old Jane.

CHAPTER 5

Mark Lombardi was, unusually for him, at the desk in the police station which was his official 'office'. It was no more than a cubicle in a large room full of such cubicles, the desk top furnished with a computer, a phone, and some trays for his files. He generally spent as little time there as he could decently manage, much preferring to be out actually doing his job. But he, like his friend Neville, had found that paperwork was becoming an increasingly important part of that job. It was a paradox, verging on travesty: for the police to be seen to be fulfilling their function, they had to be ever more transparent, which meant documenting everything they did. Writing things down in notebooks, transferring their notes to official forms, transcribing everything on to the central computer. Those who were conscientious about it could spend most of their time at their desks and very little time actually working.

Neville, Mark knew, was the opposite of that. He avoided paperwork like the plague, resorting to it only when there was absolutely nothing else to do – or when the pressure increased on him from above to produce something in writing about a specific case. He was always behind, always snowed under.

While Mark hated the paperwork nearly as much as Neville did, he tried to tread a middle path and to exercise some discipline so that it would neither take over his life nor burden him with guilt over 'leaving undone those things which he ought to have done'. So he usually forced himself to go to his desk on Monday mornings, as a matter of routine, to put his head down and get things in shape for the week to come.

Today was a holiday; he wasn't on duty and needn't have come in at all.

Other years, Easter Monday had meant a family outing of some sort. This year no one had even suggested it – thank God for that. And Callie was away.

Furthermore, his flatmate was at home, lounging round their none-too-spacious flat and catching up with the Sunday papers. Theirs was a business arrangement, not a relationship; they tended to keep out of each other's way as much as possible. So Mark had decided that it might as well be business as usual. He'd get a head start on the week, he told himself smugly.

He might as well not have bothered; he was finding it impossible to concentrate.

He couldn't stop thinking about the fiasco that had taken place at the family table yesterday. It should have been such a joyous occasion; instead it was a disaster of enormous proportions. And he'd been helpless to do anything about it. Mortified, Mark re-played the scene over and over in his head, looking for a point at which he might have brought about a less horrendous outcome.

He'd let Callie down: he knew that, and yet he couldn't see how he could have done anything differently.

To make matters even worse, he and Callie had parted so abruptly that he hadn't had a chance to make amends to her.

And now she'd gone away for a few days, and he hadn't been able to reach her. She'd not rung him, and his repeated efforts to ring her had resulted only in increasing frustration on his part. Her phone was off; Mark was getting sick of the non-human voice telling him to leave a message.

Had she switched her phone off on purpose? Was she that angry with him, and not ready to talk about it?

Had he really, truly blown it with her this time?

Mark hadn't been all that happy about her plans to go away this week, feeling insecure at the thought of her stepping back into a past that hadn't included him, surrounded by people he didn't know and memories he didn't share.

He hadn't told her that, of course. He'd encouraged her to go, to revisit a place that had been important to her. Especially since she'd said, with a casualness that didn't fool him, that Adam wouldn't be there. That was the one thing that made it bearable, from Mark's point of view: no Adam.

Mark had never met Adam, even though her former fiancé lived in the next parish to Callie in London. He didn't want to meet him. Adam was married now, but that made no difference. Adam's very existence touched Mark's insecurities at the deepest level: a man who had loved Callie, who had been intimate with her, who shared memories with her that Mark would never know about. Adam had hurt her deeply, yet before that she had loved him, and the thought of that was more than Mark could bear.

His own romantic history was much simpler: it scarcely existed. Before Callie, he'd gone out with a few girls, but there'd never been anything serious. His family had seen to that. Mamma's insistence that he marry a nice Italian girl had affected him powerfully, always there at the back of his mind when he met an interesting woman at work or socially. The Italian girls who had been paraded before him on a regular basis had failed to click with him – possibly because they were as brainwashed and screwed up as he was when it came to relationships.

And then he'd met Callie. Intelligent, attractive, empathetic, caring. Committed to her vocation. Vulnerable, as well, in a way that touched his heart at a deep level. They'd met entirely by chance, unless you believed in a Higher Power who arranged these things somehow, and Mark wasn't sure that he didn't. From the first he'd been attracted to her in a way that he'd never before experienced, strongly enough to overcome the insistent voice of Mamma in his head, telling him that she wasn't suitable. It wasn't just that she wasn't Italian; that would have been bad enough, but it was far worse than that. She was outside their faith, to the extent of being an ordained minister in the Church of England. Not just English, but Anglican.

Yet she was the woman for him. His certainty had grown as he'd got to know her better. Of all the women he'd ever met, she was the one. He loved her. It was as simple – and as complicated – as that. Twist of fate, cosmic joke – whatever. When he realized that he couldn't imagine a future without her, Mark knew he would have to leave his comfort zone and fight for their future together.

It hadn't been easy, but he'd done it. Was he to get this far, only to fall at the last hurdle? Sabotaged, once again and fatally, by *la famiglia*?

Mark stared, unseeing, at a document on his desk. It may as well have been written in Swahili.

And then his mobile rang, with the special ringtone assigned to Callie. He lunged for it. Be cool, he told himself. Concerned, not accusing.

He managed pretty well with the preliminaries, though in his over-whelming relief he knew he was running on a bit more than he should have about how many messages he'd left for her. And then he asked her, belatedly, about her trip.

'It was the trip from hell,' she said.

All sorts of horrible images flashed into his mind, along with a panicky guilt that he'd been worrying about himself and their relationship rather than taking seriously the possibility that something dreadful had befallen her. 'Oh, no! What happened?'

There was a sigh on the other end of the phone. 'Tube trains not running. Missed train. Obstruction on the line. And my phone dead as a dodo. Some day I'll tell you all about it, in excruciating detail. At the moment I don't even want to think about it.'

'You're OK, though?' he demanded anxiously.

'Oh, yes. I'm fine. Apart from lack of sleep, anyway. And missing you, of course,' Callie added, a smile in her voice.

Mark smiled in return. 'Likewise, *cara mia*.'

There was a tiny pause on the other end of the phone. 'And Adam's here,' Callie said. 'He changed his mind at the last minute, apparently. I've managed to avoid him so far.'

His heart plummeted. Adam – there! It was bad enough, missing her, without having to deal with the torment of knowing that she was spending the week with Adam instead of with him.

The phone on his desk emitted its harsh double ringtone. Mark jumped and stared at it: this phone never rang, or at least if it did he was seldom here to answer it. As far as he was concerned it was little more than desk furniture, there to balance the computer on the other side.

'Just a second, *cara mia*,' he said into his mobile. 'My other phone is ringing.' He checked the caller display before picking it up. Neville Stewart.

'You're a hard man to track down,' Neville said without preliminary. 'Your mobile's engaged, and your flatmate says you're not at home.'

Mark sighed, knowing this was no social call. 'Well, you've found me now.'

Easter Monday was not, generally, a very active day in the world of journalism. Most of Lilith Noone's colleagues were, she supposed, at home with their families, making themselves ill by over-indulging in chocolate Easter eggs. Tomorrow they would stagger back to work, jaded and bloated.

Lilith, however, had no family. And she didn't particularly care for chocolate.

Besides, she had some ground to make up at the *Daily Globe*. A recent high-profile assignment had left her with a bit of egg on her face, and she knew that her boss, Rob Gardiner-Smith, was keeping an eye on her performance. She needed to prove to him that she was up there with the big boys, capable of producing the goods.

He'd called her into his office and had actually questioned her vocation as a journalist. That hurt: Lilith had never wanted to do anything else. Growing up as the daughter of the proprietor of a weekly provincial paper, she'd set her sights on the national journalistic scene from an early age. She'd worked hard, starting at the bottom, putting in her time, earning the respect of her colleagues and putting fear into the hearts of not a few people.

Now here she was keeping a low profile, writing features and other rubbish just to stay out of Rob Gardiner-Smith's sights for a while. It wasn't good.

And Lilith had something to prove to herself, as well. She'd been offered a job – a very good job – with *HotStuff*, the top celebrity gossip magazine, and had turned it down. It wasn't that she had scruples about gossip-mongering, and wasn't above engaging in it herself in pursuit of a larger goal, but she wanted to feel that what she did had some value in the greater scheme of things. She was a real journalist, she'd told herself, as she turned her face against *HotStuff*. Now she needed to do something to demonstrate that she'd made the right decision – to herself and to her boss. She was tired of hiding from him; it was time to beard the lion in his den.

So on that morning when other employees of the *Globe* were having a lie-in, Lilith got up at the usual time, dressed in clothes which said 'professional journalist', and did a careful job on her make-up.

She had to get past Rob Gardiner-Smith's secretary, who consulted with him by phone before waving Lilith into his office, so he was expecting her, looking rather bemused as he sat behind his desk.

'Lilith,' he said with an ironic smile. 'I haven't seen you for a while.'

'No.' She forced herself to look him in the eye. 'But I was wondering whether you had anything for me. I'm keen to get my teeth into something ... challenging.'

'Are you, indeed?'

'Yes.' Lilith held his gaze, unflinching.

'Well, well, well.' He put his elbows on the desk and tented his fingers, regarding them thoughtfully for a moment. 'Perhaps there is something, then.'

'Yes?'

He seemed to hesitate for just a second, then nodded decisively and met her eyes again. 'I've had a tip-off from a reliable source. Never mind who.' His smile was without mirth. 'Another teenage stabbing. An unidentified fatality, I understand. In the Paddington area. No one else should have it yet. Just check it out for me, see what you can find. And the quicker the better, obviously,' he added.

'Obviously.' Lilith was already on her way to the door. You won't be sorry, she wanted to say, but decided she had better produce the goods first.

Neville hadn't needed to look at the photo – not really. Once he'd seen Dr Frost's curly hair and tall frame, he'd been in no doubt that they were at the right house. But there were procedures to be followed.

The next order of business – now that he'd seen the photo and satisfied himself that Sebastian Frost was the boy in the mortuary, now that he'd broken the news to the parents, now that he'd tracked down Mark Lombardi to step in as family liaison officer – was to arrange for a formal identification of the body. One of the parents would have to do it.

Neville asked himself which of the two was stronger. They were both doctors, he'd discovered, which meant that they'd seen their share of blood, mangled flesh, probably even dead bodies. They wouldn't be squeamish and faint, have the vapours and need to be carried out like some people he'd dealt with in the past. He observed the two of them and decided that he would put his money on Mrs Frost. She was in shock, yes – deathly pale and quiet – but there was a steeliness at her core that was palpable even in these circumstances. Her husband was less sure of himself, more at a loss.

He would leave it up to them – let them decide between them which one of them to put through the ordeal. Not quite yet, though. He needed to wait for Mark Lombardi to arrive, and in the meantime there were questions he needed to ask the Frosts. It would be difficult, undoubtedly, but he did have an investigation to conduct.

And it was time for that coffee, to fortify him. 'Would you like Sergeant Cowley to make some coffee, or some tea?' he suggested.

Mrs Frost shook her head and headed for the door. 'No, I'll do it.'

Her husband offered them a wan smile. 'No one touches Miranda's precious coffee machine,' he said. 'Not even me. It's one of those monsters like you see in restaurants. I won't say it cost as much as the house, but it certainly cost several times more than the plasma television. And it makes the best coffee you've ever tasted.'

Out of the corner of his eye, Neville registered Cowley's incredulous expression.

The coffee arrived more quickly than he would have expected, and lived up to its hype. Strong, smooth, delicious – Neville savoured it for its own sake, and as a brief but welcome respite from the difficult work of the morning.

'Now,' he said, putting the empty cup on the nearest table with not a little regret, 'as the senior investigating officer, I do have some questions

I'll need to ask you. About your son's friends, and his . . . lifestyle. That sort of thing.'

Richard Frost gave a weary nod, but his wife, beside him on the sofa, sat up straight and glared at Neville. 'You're going to ask me if Sebastian did drugs, aren't you? The answer is no. Definitely not.'

Neville opened his mouth to defend himself, but she went on. 'I read the papers, when I have time. I work in a hospital, for God's sake. I know that the kids who get stabbed are into drugs and gangs. Sebastian isn't . . . wasn't . . . like that. He was a good boy. Bright, academically gifted, good at sport.'

'Sometimes parents are the last to know what their kids are up to,' Cowley said, stepping into the line of fire. 'My sister had a boyfriend once. He died of a drug overdose, and his parents were the most surprised people on the planet. They had no idea – they would have sworn blind that he never touched drugs.'

It was, Neville thought, like watching a car crash in slow motion. Miranda Frost went even paler, rose to her feet, and advanced on Cowley, who was leaning against the door jamb. He stood up straighter, his face registering alarm, as she reached him. 'Sorry,' he said hastily, 'I didn't mean . . .'

'You did.' Miranda Frost poked her finger into his chest. 'How dare you? You didn't know him. Don't you *ever* try to tell me that I didn't know my own son.'

'Sorry,' Cowley repeated, raising his hands in mock surrender.

'Now get out of here,' she ordered, in the manner of one who was used to having her orders obeyed. 'I don't want you in my house.'

Cowley looked beseechingly towards Neville, who nodded. What else could he do? 'Why don't you step outside and have a fag, Sid?' he suggested. 'I'm sure you're ready for one.'

'Thanks, Guv,' Cowley mumbled, making himself scarce.

Neville sighed. He was used to Sid and his little ways – the endless anecdotes about his sister and other members of his family, his tendency to speak without thinking – but could see how other people might not find these things very endearing.

'I'm sorry about DS Cowley,' he said by way of apology, adding, 'he means well. And he's quite young.'

'That's no excuse.' Miranda Frost, not in the least mollified, returned to the sofa. 'Now, Inspector. I'm sure you'll want to speak to Sebastian's friends. I can provide you with a list of them. So what else would you like to ask us about our son?'

As Jane arrived home, her purchase – finally achieved – tucked safely and secretly into her handbag, the phone was ringing.

'Can you get that, Janey?' Brian called from his study, evidently having heard her key in the lock.

She sighed, went through to the kitchen, and reached for the phone.

'Hi, Mum,' said Charlie.

'Oh, hello.' Jane smiled in spite of herself. She dropped her handbag and her shopping bag on the table and pulled out a chair.

It used to be that Simon was the one who rang her, just for a chat. But now that he had a girlfriend – a serious one, who seemed to consume his every waking moment – those chatty calls were few and far between. Now it was far more likely to be Charlie who made those calls. On her part, Jane was always reluctant to ring her sons, in case they were in lectures or tutorials, or busy with important coursework.

'I'm bored,' Charlie said. 'Up to my eyes with this blasted essay. And there's no one else around. So I thought I'd ring you for a bit of a gossip.'

Well, Jane thought philosophically, it was better to be a last resort, a relief from boredom, than the alternative of no call at all. And she always enjoyed Charlie's gossip: unlike the more earnest Simon, he had a tendency to be amusingly ironic. He was observant, as well – a useful characteristic for the priesthood. That was Charlie's chosen career, though of course it would be up to the Church whether to accept him or not. From a young age he'd stated his intention to follow his father into the Church, and was reading theology at Oxford with the aim of going straight on to theological college.

'I don't have any gossip,' Jane admitted. Charlie wouldn't be interested in the churchwarden running out of mouthwash, the only thing she could recall from her recent encounter. She emptied her shopping bag on to the table and lined up the items she'd bought as cover: a box of paracetamol tablets, a packet of sausages, a cucumber. Just in case Brian asked about her urgent errands.

'Well, I do.' Her son paused, then went on. 'I was in the Bodders on Saturday afternoon. After a few hours I had to go out and get some air. I stopped at a little caf to grab a cup of tea, and who do you think I saw?'

The Archbishop of Canterbury? Lady Gaga? 'Surprise me,' Jane said obediently.

Charlie launched into a long and highly coloured account of the sighting of one of his lecturers, 'that dry old stick' as he described him, having tea with a pretty undergraduate. 'Honestly, Mum,' he said. 'You should have seen the way he was looking at her. It was exactly like something out of a Barbara Pym novel. *Crampton Hodnet*, to be precise.'

'Oh, really?' Jane wasn't a huge fan of Barbara Pym's novels – she always found them uncomfortably close to her own life – but for some reason Charlie adored them.

'I mean, who would have thought it of old Mathieson? He looked positively besotted!'

Ordinarily Jane would have relished this titbit, and the fact that her son had shared it with her. Today, though, with the memory of Saturday's overheard conversation – Brian, Callie – still fresh in her mind, it struck her as vaguely unpleasant, if not indecent. 'You might be reading more into it than you should,' she heard herself saying, more sharply than she'd intended. 'I'm sure it was perfectly innocent.'

'You didn't see the expression on his face.' Charlie laughed. 'Practically drooling. You know what they say, Mum – no fool like an old fool.'

That *was* close to the bone. 'Well,' Jane said, 'that may be, but I really ought to ring off now, and get a start on your father's lunch.'

When she'd hung up, though, she only opened the fridge to put the sausages and cucumber away, before heading to the lavatory.

In just a few minutes she had her result.

She was pregnant. Staring at the unmistakable lines on the test stick, Jane didn't know whether to laugh or cry.

The one thing she wasn't going to do – not yet, anyway – was tell anyone. Not even Brian.

After her conversation with Marco, Callie spent a few minutes leaning on the windowsill of her room, enjoying the amazing view. King's College Chapel, in all its Late Gothic splendour. And spring: it was about time, she told herself, after the long, cold winter. Green grass, greening trees, yellow drifts of daffodils and concentrated clumps of crocuses, yellow and purple and white. Cambridge was a magical place in the spring, and there was no better vantage point to enjoy it than this window.

A bell chimed somewhere, from one of the colleges. Callie looked at her watch and saw she'd been standing there for far longer than she'd realized. She was going to be late for the first session.

No time to do her make-up properly. She took a quick look at herself in the mirror, ran her brush through her hair, put on some lip gloss, and decided that would have to suffice.

Callie clattered down two flights of stairs and headed through the courtyard towards the lecture hall. There was only one other person in the courtyard, seemingly headed in the same direction; as she overtook her, she recognized her friend Val.

'Callie!' Val stopped and they hugged each other.

'We're late,' Callie said, glancing at her watch.

Val put up a hand. 'Don't worry. I have inside information. The facilitator hasn't arrived yet – his train has been delayed.'

That sounded familiar. 'Oh, we're all right, then.'

'We have a few minutes.' Val gestured towards the bench under the cherry tree. It was a favourite spot of Callie's; when the weather was fine she used to sit there often, reading heavy tomes for her essays.

They sat down and Callie took a good look at her friend. Val seemed much the same, with her long, mousy hair and her glasses, yet there was something different about her: that indefinable extra glow that came from happiness, from living the life she wanted to live. 'I didn't see you at breakfast,' Callie said.

'We usually have breakfast at home.' Val pointed across the courtyard at the block of modern flats and terraced houses, the accommodation provided for faculty, staff and married students. 'Jeremy doesn't much like having to make conversation first thing in the morning,' she added with unmistakable wifely smugness.

'How is Jeremy?' Callie asked dutifully.

Val smiled. 'Oh, he's great.'

'And marriage is . . . everything you thought it would be?'

'And more. It's wonderful.' Val held out her hand so that her solitaire diamond sparkled in the sun, contemplating her rings intently. Then she turned to Callie with a somewhat shamefaced expression. 'Listen, Callie. I'm really sorry that I haven't been better about keeping in touch.'

'It's my fault,' Callie said automatically.

'No.' Val shook her head. 'It was me. I felt so bad for you, about . . . Adam. And all that. It just seemed so unfair. I had everything I wanted, and you had . . . nothing. It made me feel guilty, and I didn't want to keep reminding you about it, and rubbing your nose in my good fortune.'

Callie was astonished; it had never occurred to her that she was such an object of pity that her friends were deliberately avoiding her. 'It's not like that,' she said, searching for the right way to say it. 'I'm . . . fine.

Really. My job is ... an interesting challenge. I love parish ministry. And I'm over Adam. Truly. Good riddance to him.' It sounded to her own ears almost as if she was protesting too much.

Val, though, seemed to buy it. 'Oh, I'm so glad!' She gave her a hug. 'Wait a minute. What's that on your finger?'

It was Callie's turn to hold out her hand. 'I told you I was over Adam.'

'Oh my God!' Val squealed in an unclerical way. 'Tell me! Tell me everything!'

The first thing Lilith Noone did, after taking leave of Rob Gardiner-Smith and before she departed the *Globe*'s offices, was to check the Metropolitan Police's website. She did it without a great deal of optimism, and indeed the Met press office had nothing at all to say about the stabbing death of an unidentified teenager; the most recent press release online had to do with the theft of a large quantity of Easter eggs from a corner shop in Bethnal Green. Lilith snorted in disgust and shut the computer down.

Just as well, really, she told herself as she headed for the Tube. If it were on the website, then every journalist in town would have access to the information and there would be no chance of getting in there first. She would have to employ a bit of ingenuity and lateral thinking.

The Paddington area, Rob had said. That was where she would go. Straight to Paddington, then up the road to the police station. Maybe she would strike it lucky there.

But she had reckoned without the heavy security on the door; the armed guard was adamant that she couldn't go in, even when she flashed her press pass, and she had to resort to her mobile phone to speak to the desk sergeant. 'I understand that there's been a stabbing,' she said, without giving her name. 'An unidentified boy?'

There was a palpable hesitation on the other end, measured in several heartbeats. 'I'm afraid you've been misinformed,' came at last.

'Identified, then?' Lilith persisted.

'No.'

'Could you put me on to someone else? The chief superintendent, perhaps?'

The desk sergeant cleared his throat, loudly. 'The press office is what you want, Miss. I can give you their number, if you like.'

'No, thank you.'

More lateral thinking. A fatality in this area would almost certainly be taken to the mortuary at the hospital, back down the road. Maybe someone at the mortuary would be more forthcoming than the police. And if she couldn't find the pathologist, or a communicative mortuary assistant, she could always ring the coroner's office. Coroner Hereward Rice had a soft spot for her, or at least she knew how to play him to get information. It had worked in the past, and she was sure she'd lost none of her powers where he was concerned.

Lilith found the mortuary, tucked behind the hospital buildings which faced on to Praed Street. Unfortunately for her, the first person she encountered there was less than helpful: a sour-faced woman who glared at her and claimed ignorance. 'I'm just covering for Ray,' she said begrudgingly. 'He's on break.'

'I'll wait,' said Lilith, and sat on a metal folding chair, trying to breathe through her mouth. The place smelled of bleach, antiseptics and other fluids she didn't want to think about.

Ray, who arrived within a quarter of an hour, proved to be a middle-aged man of Caribbean descent with steel-grey hair and deep, liquid brown eyes which turned down at the corners, sad pools brimming with all the sorrow he'd seen in this place over the years. But his smile was cheerful. 'Can I help you?' he said.

'I hope so.' Lilith returned his smile, feeling that perhaps her luck had changed.

'So do I. We don't often get pretty ladies like you in here. Not live ones, anyhow.'

Lilith tried not to think about that. 'You've had a young boy brought in recently?' she said, half statement and half question. 'A teenager. A stabbing, I understand. Unidentified.'

Ray shook his head; Lilith's heart sank. Then he explained. 'Yes and no,' he said. 'He's here, all right. A young kid. Stabbed, for sure. But I've had a call, just a few minutes ago, from the police. The parents are on the way. They'll be here pretty soon to identify him.'

Lilith couldn't suppress an uncharacteristic, face-splitting grin.

CHAPTER 6

The chocolates had started appearing on Margaret Phillips' desk at Christmas; the first was a chocolate reindeer, sitting in the middle of her desk on a Monday morning. She had assumed it was a thoughtful gesture from her new secretary, Hanna Young, to whom she had mentioned her fondness for chocolate. But Hanna had – reluctantly, Margaret perceived – claimed herself unable to take credit for it.

Every Monday after that, there had been another chocolate. Most of them were small offerings, a single rich bite which Margaret recognized as having come from the posh confectionery shop in All Saints Passage. On the Monday nearest to Valentine's Day, though, there had been a chocolate heart. And today, of course, there was an Easter egg, fist-sized, wrapped in colourful foil. She rolled it round her desk bemusedly, considering the mystery.

No note, ever. She'd never seen anyone sneaking into her office, yet it was always there waiting for her on a Monday morning.

Margaret's office was on the ground floor of the Principal's Lodge, immediately adjacent to the chapel, so anyone in college, potentially, could be passing its unlocked door on a Monday morning. It was a wide open field; she might never know who was responsible. That wasn't going to stop her from enjoying the chocolates, whatever their source.

Tempting as it was, she would save the egg till after lunch, Margaret decided. She would hate to appear for the opening session of Deacons' Week with a smear of chocolate round her mouth. And the opening session, temporarily delayed by the late arrival of the facilitator, could begin at any moment.

Her secretary – or PA, as Hanna preferred to style herself – came into Margaret's office, waving a cordless phone. 'He's nearly here,' she announced. 'He says he's just caught a taxi at the station, so he'll be here in about ten minutes.'

'Oh, good.' She would go across in a few minutes, then, and meet him at the porters' lodge.

Hanna crossed to the window and looked out into the courtyard. 'Just a few stragglers,' she observed. 'Mad Phil is in a rush – I don't suppose he knows there's been a delay.'

61

Margaret perceived a note of disapproval in her secretary's voice. 'I don't think that punctuality has ever been a priority for Dr Moody,' Margaret said, smiling indulgently; as far as she was concerned, his slipshod timekeeping was far outweighed by his other unquestionable gifts. Keith Moody was, by a long way, the most popular tutor at the college, loved by his students. There was always a waiting list for his tutor group: that, in Margaret's experience, was unprecedented, and a good indication of his positive qualities.

Not that she knew him very well on a personal level. In her year and a half as principal of Archbishop Temple House, Margaret had got to know some members of staff better than others. Keith Moody seemed to her to be a very private man, so things she knew about him were largely matters of observation and hearsay. She knew that he was a middle-aged bachelor with a receding hairline and spectacles, that he had been on the staff for several years, that he favoured professorial tweed jackets and bow ties. She knew about his punctuality issues and his popularity, that in addition to being considered highly intelligent and theologically astute, he had a reputation for being both kind and fair-minded. And there was one other thing she knew.

'To be honest, I've always wondered,' Hanna said. 'Why does everyone call him "Mad Phil"? Isn't his name Keith?'

'The Reverend Dr Keith Moody,' Margaret confirmed. 'It's a bit of a long story, and it goes back a few years. Before my time, obviously, but the way it was explained to me by a helpful student, it started with a typo. On the college's prospectus, I believe. There was a list of the tutors, with their qualifications behind their names, and the typesetter left out a comma. So instead of "MA, D Phil", it said "MAD Phil".' She found a bit of scrap paper on her desk and wrote it out, showing it to her secretary. 'Like this.'

Hanna nodded. 'Right.'

'And then there was the Harry Potter thing. I haven't read the books myself,' Margaret confessed, 'but I believe there's a character in them who's called "Mad-Eye Moody"?'

'I haven't read them, either, to be honest,' admitted Hanna.

'So apparently one of the ordinands at that time, who was a big Harry Potter fan, thought the typo was funny and decided to call her tutor "Mad Phil Moody". And it stuck.' Margaret shook her head; it seemed a poor joke to her. But it was now firmly entrenched in college usage, and Keith Moody didn't seem to mind, so there was no point trying to put a stop to it – even if she had the power to do so.

She herself always referred to him as 'Dr Moody', feeling he was owed that much respect.

Margaret tucked the chocolate egg into her cassock pocket, looking forward to the delayed gratification of eating it. 'I suppose I'd better think about going across to meet our facilitator,' she said.

'Would you like me to come with you?' Hanna suggested. 'Or I could go and fetch him, and bring him back here.'

'That's not necessary. And I'll need to take him straight on to the lecture hall. We're already half an hour late.'

And what a joy it was to get outside on such a glorious day, Margaret reflected, as she walked along the courtyard towards the porters' lodge. The temperature was perfect – even her cassock felt a bit too warm – and the combined scents of the trees and flowers made a heady perfume.

A taxi was just pulling up at the gates; a man was getting out. A distinguished-looking man, with a thin, kind face and a sheaf of silky silver hair. He smiled at her and took her outstretched hand.

'Margaret Phillips,' she said. 'You must be Canon Kingsley. Welcome to Archbishop Temple House.'

'Please, call me John.' He followed her through the porters' lodge and into the courtyard, carrying his rather battered case. 'I'm so, so sorry about the delay,' he apologized. 'I spent Easter in London with my daughter, and it didn't even occur to me that the trains might not be running properly on the bank holiday. Apparently there was some sort of problem on the line last night, and everything was backed up.' The canon stopped, forcing Margaret do to the same. 'Oh, what a wonderful spot!' he exclaimed. 'It's like a little oasis, isn't it?'

'We like it,' said Margaret, with proprietorial pride.

Dead. Not missing. Not injured. Not skiving off with his friends somewhere. Dead.

Sebastian was dead.

Miranda's brain refused to process the information. On some level she understood what they were telling her, but it had no relation to reality.

She had seen death, many times. It was part of her job. She worked hard to save lives; she wasn't always successful. The people whom she worked on in A & E, though, were often on the brink of death when she encountered them. For them it was a small step, her efforts to save them fruitless.

But Sebastian? Sebastian was life. The very essence of life.

Life, from the moment she felt that first small kick. She'd been a bit ambivalent about the pregnancy before that – how would it affect her career? – yet as soon as she'd felt that kick, there had been no doubt that it was the best thing that had ever happened to her. And then holding newborn Sebastian in her arms, seconds after his birth. A wriggling baby, gulping hungrily for air. Toes clenching, fists waving. Even his hair – those black curls, in astonishing profusion already – had seemed alive.

As a toddler, as a boy, he crackled with energy. Some children were lethargic; Sebastian was the opposite of that. Even when he was sleeping there was something about him that seemed ready to spring into action at a moment's notice. And when he entered his teens, a time when so many children morphed into slug-like beings, conserving their energy for physical growth, he had retained his vitality. It was his natural state, without benefit of caffeine.

Now they were trying to tell her that he was dead. Stilled, inert. For ever.

Impossible.

The Irish police inspector and his objectionable Cockney sergeant had gone. They'd been replaced by someone else, a nice young Italian who had said complimentary things about her coffee machine. Miranda trusted his air of competence to the extent that she'd given him instruction in using the machine – the first person ever to be allowed to touch it. He'd mastered it quickly, producing very good coffee on his first attempt. He would be with them for a while, he said; they called it family liaison.

But it was time for him to take one of them to the mortuary, he told them. The police needed a formal identification; it was a necessary step in their investigation.

'I'll go,' Richard offered.

Miranda shook her head, adamant. 'We'll both go.'

If she didn't see it for herself – Sebastian, dead – she would never really believe it. In her head, maybe, but not in her heart.

As she and Val slipped into seats at the back of the lecture hall, Callie did a quick visual check: Adam was safely seated in the second row, on the other side. She realized, with a shock of painful honesty, that there might have been some subconscious force at work in making her the last to arrive. It meant that she was in control; she could sit wherever she wanted without the danger that Adam would come in after she did and sit next to her.

Not that she couldn't handle sitting next to Adam, but − Callie justified to herself − she had been in enough of these situations to know that they were likely to be broken up into smaller groups, or even pairs, to carry out various exercises. It wasn't something she even wanted to think about doing with Adam.

She and Val weren't quite the last, she observed with a smile as her former tutor pushed the door open and took a seat nearby. Not surprising, really. Mad Phil had been late to every tutorial she'd ever had with him, and would have been late for their weekly tutor group breakfasts as well if they hadn't been held in his house. As it was, she and Val had had to organize the cornflakes, put the kettle on and make sure there was enough milk.

He looked round, seeming surprised that proceedings were not yet under way. Val leaned in his direction and whispered, 'We're waiting for the facilitator. He's been delayed.'

Mad Phil nodded, smiling at the two of them. 'I'm not surprised. He was never any better at being on time than I was.'

Callie processed that statement. 'You know him, then?'

'Oh, yes.' Their former tutor scooted along a few seats, stopping just behind them, and leaned forward to whisper to them. 'He was my training incumbent, years ago. I was the one who suggested asking him to do this week.'

'So who is he?' Val asked, adding, 'Jeremy doesn't know him.'

'John Kingsley. Retired priest. Spent most of his career in Malbury diocese. For years he had a parish near Ludlow − that's where I was his curate. Then he was a canon at Malbury Cathedral. Now he's retired, and lives in Ludlow. I haven't seen him for a few years, but we keep in touch.' Mad Phil smiled, a fond expression on his face. 'He's one of the best. One of those old-fashioned kinds of priest that the Church used to be full of, but are few and far between these days. A wise old bird. Absolutely genuine. Terrifyingly so, sometimes.'

Callie wasn't sure what that meant. How could someone be terrifyingly genuine? She was about to ask for clarification when the door swung open and the principal came in, escorting a man with silver hair and an apologetic smile.

'This is Canon Kingsley,' Margaret Phillips addressed them. 'He's going to be leading us this week, and I'm sure we'll all be learning a great deal from him.'

The next half hour − a discussion of the relationship between curate and training incumbent − went by quickly, until that inevitable moment when they were asked to find a partner for one-on-one role playing. Callie, who hated that sort of thing, turned reluctantly towards Val, only to find that Val had already been claimed by someone else. She looked round, panicking, to see a man bearing down on her with intent.

'Callie! I haven't seen you yet,' Nicky Lamb said accusingly. 'Come and be my partner, darling.'

'Nicky!' She smiled at him, relieved. Nicky was so beautiful that people just naturally smiled at him, Callie had observed, but that didn't stop her from doing it as well.

He kissed her on both cheeks. 'You're looking uncommonly well, darling.'

'And you. But you always do.'

'Flatterer.' Nicky took her hand and led her to the back corner of the room. 'Let's get away from all of these ghastly people. With any luck they won't notice that we're not role playing.'

'We're not?'

He shuddered. 'Not in a million years. We're catching up, one-on-one. Apparently we have twenty minutes to do it.'

'Oh, good.' What a relief, thought Callie. 'I thought you and Tamsin would be partners,' she added. It was the perpetual elephant in the room: everyone knew that Tamsin was in love with Nicky, but no one ever said so directly.

Nicky shook his head. 'No way. Tamsin actually *likes* this sort of thing. Role playing – it appeals to her inner drama queen.'

'And not to yours?'

'I don't have an inner drama queen, darling,' he smirked. 'My drama queen is right out there, for all the world to see.'

That was the honest truth. 'How does that go over in your parish?' Callie asked him.

'Oh, they're fine with it. Mostly. They learned right away that what you see is what you get, with me. And it *is* Brighton,' he added archly.

'Well, yes.' Hairdressers, interior designers. The gay capital of Britain.

'Actually, London must be much the same. Isn't it?'

Callie thought about that for a moment. 'Maybe some places in London. The traditionally spiky churches in the East End. Not in my parish, though.'

'You disappoint me. I pictured you right in the middle of the gin-and-lace crowd, darling.' He gave her a wicked grin and pantomimed knocking back a large drink.

'There's very little of either gin or lace at All Saints',' she laughed. Not with Jane firmly in charge.

'What's your incumbent like, then?' Nicky swivelled his head round and surveyed the earnest role playing which was already under way in the room. 'That's what we're supposed to be role playing, isn't it? A conversation with our incumbent?'

'Oh, Brian. He's all right.'

Nicky raised an eyebrow. 'Surely that's *Father* Brian?'

She smiled. 'Well, he does encourage the congregation to call him Father. But I certainly don't. He's just Brian to me.'

'My dear!' Nicky looked scandalized. 'I can't imagine what would happen if I were to call Father Stephen *Steve*. Or even Stephen. Maybe that's the root of your problems with him.'

'Who said I had problems with Brian?'

'Everyone has problems with their incumbent,' he stated knowingly. 'If it's not one sort of problem, then it's something else. That's what being a curate is all about.'

'Brian's all right,' Callie repeated. 'He's a bit lazy, I must admit – if he can push something off on to me, he's happy to do it. I think he's been coasting for quite a few years.' As she said it, she knew it was true: she'd never thought about it in those terms before, but it was true. Maybe there was some point in role playing after all ... 'Actually,' she added, 'I think I'd get on with him just fine if it weren't for his wife. Jane. She hates me, for some reason. And resents me.'

'Oh, a *wife*!' Nicky gave an exaggerated shudder. 'He's a *family* man! No wonder you're having problems with him. It was the beginning of the end of the Church of England, when they allowed married clergy.'

'But there's always been married clergy!' she protested.

'And the Church of England is in terminal decline.' He nodded smugly. 'It's taken a few hundred years, but ... Elizabeth the First had the right idea. She refused to acknowledge clergy wives.'

Nicky was just being provocative, she told herself. He didn't really believe what he was saying. It was part of the way he operated: to stir things up a bit, to get people to think about their positions.

'Something I've always wondered about.' Callie deliberately removed the focus from herself. 'If you're so very High Church, why did you decide to come to Archbishop Temple House? It's so middle-of-the-road. Why didn't you go to St Stephen's House, or Cuddesdon, or even Westcott House? Or Mirfield?'

He laughed. 'I've asked myself that question a million times. But it was my bishop, darling. I wanted to go to Staggers, but he insisted. Said it would be good for me, for my formation, to see how the other half lives.'

'How grim for you,' she smiled.

'At least he settled for middle-of-the-road. Broad Church, he called it. Liberal. He could have sent me among the Evangelicals, to Ridley Hall or Wycliffe Hall.'

'I don't think you would have survived.'

'The Bible thumpers would have torn me apart,' he said quietly, serious for once.

Callie had seen enough of the extreme Evangelical faction in London to know what he was talking about. Evangelicals like Adam's incumbent, with their fear and loathing of homosexuality and their utter certainty that they were right. About everything.

Adam had become rather like that himself, she had observed in the limited contact she'd had with him in London. He'd taken up the Evangelical banner with every semblance of sincerity.

Involuntarily Callie looked over towards him, to where he was earnestly role playing with Tamsin. Poor Tamsin, who would, of a certainty, rather be with Nicky.

Surely Adam hadn't always been like that? A hard-line Evangelical? When they were here at Archbishop Temple he had seemed like the rest of them − liberal-thinking, inclusive, willing to listen to other people's points of view. His parents had been missionaries, yes, but he had never seemed to possess that missionary zeal to convert everyone to his way of thinking or his brand of churchmanship. What had happened to him?

Nicky must have followed the direction of her eyes. 'He's changed,' he said, as if reading her thoughts. 'Adam. He's much more ... judgemental ... than he used to be. About me, and what he calls my "lifestyle". Not that he knows anything about that,' he added bitterly. 'We had a chat last night, in the bar. He came over really heavy. I must admit that it got to me.' He leaned forward and took Callie's hands, squeezing them hard. 'You're not still hung up on him, are you? Tell me that you're not.'

'No,' said Callie. 'No, I'm not.'

In his years as a family liaison officer, Mark had done this more times than he cared to think about: taken people to the mortuary to identify the body of a relative. Wives identifying husbands, husbands identifying wives; sisters and brothers, children and parents. All horrible, but this was the most difficult of all. There was something particularly repugnant – something unnatural, in the true sense of the word – about parents outliving their children. It wasn't supposed to be this way. And this was the Frosts' only child: their only link to the future of the planet, their only hope of genetic immortality.

So the last thing he needed, as he carried out this sensitive and difficult facet of his job, was to encounter the ghoulish press, in the person of Lilith Noone, at the mortuary.

She waited until the deed had been done – until a white-faced but composed Miranda Frost had entered the viewing room with her husband and said, 'Yes, that's Sebastian' – and they were on their way out.

At least Lilith didn't have a photographer with her. A small blessing, but a blessing nonetheless. Miranda Frost's face was not something that belonged on the front page – or any other page – of the *Daily Globe*. Mark, recognizing Lilith in an instant, glared at her and put his hand up to ward her off.

It all happened so quickly after that.

Lilith Noone ignored him and went straight for the bereaved mother. 'Could I have a word?' she asked in a soft voice, warm with sympathy.

Miranda Frost stopped and turned towards her, blinking, as though the voice had come out of the blue. 'Yes?'

'Your son, was it?'

Mrs Frost nodded automatically.

'I'm so sorry. You must be devastated.'

Richard Frost, at his wife's side, seemed to snap out of his own private hell as he became aware of the intruder. 'Who are you?' he demanded.

'I think it's time for us to go,' Mark tried to interpose.

But somehow Lilith Noone had established a connection with Miranda Frost. They stared at each other for a moment, as if no one else were in the room. 'Sebastian was my only son,' Miranda said.

'How terrible for you. Do you have any idea who could have done this to him?'

Miranda shook her head. 'Why would anyone want to kill Sebastian?'

'He didn't have any enemies, then? He wasn't involved in drugs, in—'

Now, Mark realized, Lilith Noone had gone too far. Miranda took a step backwards, her eyes widened, and the colour suddenly returned to her cheeks. 'No,' she said sharply. 'No. Who *are* you?'

Lilith carried on. 'Could I ask your name?'

'You can ask all you like,' Mark asserted, regaining control of the situation. 'No one is going to tell you anything.' He put an arm around Miranda Frost's back and propelled her towards the door.

Sebastian Frost: it was official. Mark had rung to tell Neville that the identification had been made, so now the investigation could proceed properly, with a named victim.

Tracing Sebastian Frost's last movements – his final hours – was the priority, and for that, Neville decided, the logical place to start was with his friends.

Miranda Frost had efficiently written out a list of the three boys she knew to be her son's closest friends, including their addresses and phone numbers. Neville studied it: Hugo Summerville, Olly Blount, Tom Gresham. Eventually he would need to talk to all three of them himself, and most likely quite a few others as well, but for now he reckoned it was important to get to all of them as quickly as possible. 'I'll start with this Hugo Summerville,' he said to Sid Cowley when they'd got back to the station. 'You can deal with one of the others. Tom Gresham.' He gave him the address.

'Right, Guv.'

'And I don't need to tell you, do I, not to antagonize him by suggesting straightaway that he and his friends are druggies?'

'They probably are,' Cowley stated.

'See if you can be a bit subtle about it.' Neville sighed. 'Ring me when you've finished, and we'll decide where to go from there.'

Hugo Summerville lived not too far from the Frosts, Neville discovered. His house was in one of the exclusive squares of Georgian terraces between Praed Street and Sussex Gardens.

It was an impressive house. Whatever Hugo Summerville's parents did, they were not short of a bob or two, Neville realized as he mounted the steps to the front door. He hoped the parents weren't going to be difficult when it came to him interviewing their son.

He needn't have worried; the door was opened by a boy who was almost certainly Hugo himself. 'Are your parents at home?' Neville asked.

'No, they're not. Can I help you?' said the boy; his voice was polite and his accent all that one would expect, given the neighbourhood. He looked, in fact, like a typical, quintessential public schoolboy, tall and slim, with floppy fair hair and the sort of bland good looks that would doubtless set young female hearts aflutter.

'Are you Hugo Summerville?'

'That's right.'

Neville produced his warrant card. 'I'm Detective Inspector Stewart, Mr Summerville. I'd like to talk to you, if you don't mind.'

Hugo frowned. 'It's about Seb, isn't it? His mum rang looking for him.'

'Yes, it's in regard to Sebastian Frost,' he confirmed.

'I told her I didn't know where he was.' Hugo hadn't moved from the door. 'He's not here, I swear it.'

'Could I come in? I need to ask you a few questions.'

'I told his mum. He came round in the afternoon to play a video game. I don't know where he went after that.' But Hugo had stepped aside, allowing Neville into the entrance hall.

'You're here by yourself?'

'My dad is playing tennis,' Hugo explained. 'And Mum is shopping. She won't be back for hours.' He hesitated for a moment, then led Neville up a flight of stairs and into a handsome formal drawing room which overlooked the leafy square.

Neville, wanting to establish who was in charge, took a seat in a wing-backed chair and gestured for Hugo to do the same. He may as well get it over with, he decided, rather than beating about the bush. 'I'm afraid I have some bad news for you,' he said, watching the boy's face closely for his reaction.

Hugo leaned forward and swallowed hard, his Adam's apple bobbing in his throat. 'Yes?'

'Your friend Sebastian is dead, I'm afraid.'

The boy blinked. 'Dead?'

'He's been killed. Murdered.'

The brutal words fell between them. Hugo sat still, not moving a muscle, and Neville did the same, waiting. The silence stretched out interminably. Then Hugo exhaled, a long and painful breath. 'Oh, no.'

'You're sure you didn't see him last night?'

The boy swallowed again. 'No.'

'And you had no knowledge of his movements, or his plans? Whether he was planning to meet someone, for instance?'

'No.' His eyes flickered away from Neville.

It occurred to Neville that for an articulate boy, Hugo seemed suspiciously at a loss for words. Neville might have expected questions from him at this point. Where? How had it happened? How had he been found? And above all, why would anyone want to kill Sebastian?

Maybe Cowley was right. Maybe it had to do with drugs. Dealing? Perhaps, if they were in it together, Hugo knew exactly who had killed

71

his best friend, and why. A drug deal gone wrong? Something as prosaic, as tawdry, as that?

It could happen, even in the best families.

Hugo turned his face towards the expanse of windows. 'I thought ...' he said slowly, then stopped and began again. 'That is, I rather thought that Seb was seeing Lexie last night. Since his parents were working.'

Lexie? It was the first time he'd heard that name. Miranda Frost hadn't mentioned any Lexie when she listed Sebastian's friends. 'Who is Lexie?' he asked sharply.

Hugo's head swivelled back again in Neville's direction, and at last he resumed eye contact. 'Lexie Renton. Seb's girlfriend.' He shrugged. 'We call her Sexy Lexie. His parents ... well, they thought he was too young to have a regular girlfriend. They thought he should be concentrating on his GCSEs.'

Quite right, too, was Neville's immediate thought. A boy of fifteen ...

It was amazing how one's perspective changed with the years. He didn't even want to think what he'd been up to at fifteen. Or would have done, if he'd had the opportunity and had thought he could get away with it. Neville resolutely put that out of his mind.

'A regular girlfriend, you say? They were ... serious?'

Hugo gave another shrug. 'He was shagging her, if that's what you mean. Whenever he could. When his parents were both at work.'

'And he told you about this?'

The boy nodded.

Of course he did. They were best friends, and they were boys. Bragging about their sexual exploits, real or imagined, to each other – that's what boys did.

This, Neville realized, changed everything. Drugs suddenly seemed much less likely than ... what? A lovers' row? A crime of passion? Two boys fighting over the same girl?

He was only fifteen, for God's sake, Neville reminded himself. Fifteen.

But he was dead, and that fact was unmistakable. Someone had killed him. For whatever reason, someone had stabbed him to death.

'I think,' he said, 'that you need to tell me how to get in touch with this Lexie Renton.'

Lilith stared helplessly at the departing parents. Where had she gone wrong? She'd so very nearly been there. She had connected with the mother – she knew that she had; the connection had been real. And then she'd lost it. Blown it. And that officious family liaison officer ...

They were gone, taking their names – and probably Lilith's future career – with them.

She turned to Ray, the helpful mortuary attendant. He was her only hope.

'Is there any way you can check the paperwork and give me those people's names?' she asked, with her most beguiling smile.

Ray shook his head, and her heart sank. That was it, then. She was stumped. Screwed, to put it bluntly.

'I don't need to check the paperwork,' he said. 'That's Miz Frost. And Dr Frost, her husband.'

'Frost? You know them?'

He nodded. 'They work here. At the hospital.'

'Both of them?' This was too good to be true.

'That's right,' Ray confirmed. 'In A and E. Miz Frost is a surgeon, and Dr Frost – I think he's an anaesthetist.'

Their first names would be a matter of public record, easy to find on the hospital's website, even if Ray's knowledge didn't stretch to that. And their son was called Sebastian. Sebastian Frost. She had a name.

She had a story.

'Thanks, Ray.' Once again she produced her most brilliant smile; this time it came naturally. 'Thank you so much.'

Interlude: a mobile phone call

HUGO: Hey.

TOM: Hey.

HUGO: Seb. He's—

TOM: Yeah. I know. I've had a cop here.

HUGO: Me, too.

TOM: It totally sucks.

HUGO: Poor Seb.

TOM: You didn't tell them, did you? About—

HUGO: Of course not, dickhead. Do you think I'm mental or something?

TOM: I just—

HUGO: *You* didn't tell them, did you?

TOM: No. But he's dead, Hugo. Don't you think—

HUGO: My point exactly. He's dead. Nothing we say is going to bring him back. We've got to think of ourselves now.

TOM: Yeah, I guess you're right.

HUGO: You know that I am. You know what would happen if it all came out.

TOM: Yeah, my parents would kill me, for a start.

HUGO: And that would just be the beginning. We would be so totally screwed. So just keep your mouth shut.

TOM: Yeah, OK.

HUGO: I'm going to ring Olly now. See you.

TOM: Yeah, see you.

CHAPTER 7

They may have had a late start, Margaret reflected, but the first session had been a great success. She was particularly pleased with the facilitating style of Canon Kingsley, who had achieved more in a morning than some people could have done in a whole week. It had been a gamble to invite someone with whom she'd had no personal experience. She'd followed her instincts, though, and trusted Keith Moody's recommendation. It had clearly paid off.

After the communal − and satisfyingly convivial − lunch in the dining hall, before the next session was due to begin, she sought out Dr Moody to thank him. She caught up with him in the courtyard, where he was sitting on a bench, evidently enjoying the sunshine.

'No one is going to want to be indoors this afternoon.' He turned towards her as she approached. 'I suspect we may lose a few people to the temptations of the river and the other attractions of Cambridge.'

'Mmm.' She sat down beside him and lifted her face to the sun. 'Maybe we should just acknowledge defeat and give them the afternoon off.'

'We could always have an informal session in the bar this evening instead,' he suggested.

Margaret thought about it for a moment. 'If John Kingsley doesn't mind, I think it's worth considering.'

'I'm sure he wouldn't mind. He had a difficult journey, I understand, and he's not as young as he used to be.'

'And the deacons would be delighted.'

He smiled. 'As I said, I suspect more than a few of them would skive off anyway. And I could probably tell you which ones.'

'I don't doubt it.' Margaret closed her eyes; the sun was making her feel sleepy already. Napping in the afternoon was not − had never been − her style, but after her night of interrupted sleep the thought was very tempting. Reminding herself of why she had come looking for Keith Moody in the first place, she forced herself to open her eyes and look at him. 'Actually, Dr Moody, I wanted to thank you for suggesting Canon Kingsley. He was brilliant this morning.'

'Please,' he said. 'Call me Keith. Or Mad Phil, if you'd prefer,' he added with a grin.

Margaret laughed. 'All right, then. Keith.'

'And I'm delighted that it's working out with John Kingsley. I knew he'd be good.'

'He's a lovely man,' she said with complete sincerity. 'I'm looking forward to getting to know him this week.'

Keith Moody took his spectacles off and polished them with his handkerchief. 'Could I suggest something?' he said. 'If you're truly considering cancelling the session, I'd really like it if you and John would come and have tea with me this afternoon. In my garden. It would give you a chance to get to know *both* of us a bit better.'

'What a good idea.' She had, Margaret recalled, only just been thinking about how little she knew Keith Moody, and this would be an excellent opportunity to remedy that situation. Reluctantly she stood up. 'I suppose it's time for me to go and deliver the good news. We're all having an afternoon off.'

When he'd finished with Hugo Summerville, Neville tried to ring Cowley to compare notes and plan their next interviews. Annoyingly, Cowley's phone went directly to voicemail, so he left a message to tell him to pay a call on Olly Blount.

He would tackle Lexie Renton himself. Sexy Lexie. He certainly couldn't trust Cowley with someone with a nickname like that. Not so long ago he would barely have trusted himself, but he was a respectable married man now . . .

First, though, food. Neville realized, as he got in the car, that he was ravenous. He hadn't eaten all day. It had been an early start, and he had learnt a long time ago that it was never a good idea to eat before a post-mortem. After that things had happened non-stop; food had been the last thing on his mind. Now his stomach rumbled, reminding him that it had been grossly neglected.

Once upon a time, these circumstances would have called for a quick pub lunch. A sarnie, a pint, a fag. But things had changed. He'd been off the fags for a few years, and pubs were now non-smoking anyway. The pint wouldn't be a good idea just before an interview. And most of the pubs in this part of London had gone so upmarket – gastropubs, they called themselves – that a quick lunch was out of the question.

The Paddington area was notoriously bad for parking, but another thing that Neville had discovered years ago was that there were definite advantages to driving a police car. He pulled up on a double yellow in front of a grimy-looking kebab shop, went in, stood at the counter, and ordered a large doner kebab with extra chilli sauce. He'd patronized this place before, more than once. It might not boast the most elegant decor, but the food was very much to his taste, and they provided a counter in front of the window where he could perch on a high stool and keep an eye on the car while he wolfed down the greasy concoction. And there were plenty of cheap paper napkins to wipe his hands afterwards. Doner kebabs were something best kept out of police cars, Neville felt. Their pungent smell lingered on like stale fag smoke, and that was assuming you didn't dribble chilli sauce on the upholstery as a lasting reminder of a culinary indiscretion.

Suitably revived, he chucked his detritus in the bin by the door, lifted a hand in a gesture of farewell to the proprietor, and retrieved his car.

Hugo had been vague about where Neville might find Lexie Renton. 'She lives in a flat. Somewhere round here,' was the best he'd been able to provide.

Fortunately Renton wasn't a very common name. A quick phone call to an obliging colleague with access to a telephone directory yielded a promising result: an S. M. Renton at an address just off the Edgware Road.

The block of flats may have been close geographically to the genteel Georgian squares of Bayswater, but architecturally it might as well have been on a different planet. Evidently a bomb had been dropped on the spot – a German aiming for Paddington Station, no doubt, maybe after a glass or two of schnapps – and at some point after the war it had been deemed a good idea to fill in the space.

They shouldn't have bothered, Neville decided, as he regarded the ugly, angular building, already ageing badly. His own flat was nothing to write home about, but this one was even worse.

S. M. Renton's flat was on the second floor, and there was no lift. There also wasn't an exterior bell to check whether anyone was at home, so Neville puffed his way up two flights of stairs, hoping that after all this he was in the right place.

The door was opened by a young girl who looked about ten, though Neville was no reliable judge of children's ages. 'Does a Lexie Renton live here?' he asked.

The girl nodded. 'Lexie!' she yelled over her shoulder. 'It's for you. A man.'

After lunch, which she'd eaten with Tamsin, Nicky and Val, Callie excused herself to make a quick phone call to Marco. Their previous conversation had been cut frustratingly short, so she wanted to make sure that all was well in London. She sat on her favourite bench under the cherry tree in the courtyard and rang his mobile.

'*Cara mia,*' he said. Her heart gave a thump at the sound of his voice. 'I'm afraid I can't really talk. I'm on a new assignment.'

'On a bank holiday? I thought you weren't working today.'

'I wasn't supposed to be. But . . . things happen. A boy's been killed.'

She caught her breath. 'Oh, no. And you're with his family.'

'That's right.' Marco gave a sigh. 'Maybe this sounds silly, *cara mia,* but could you pray for them? Nothing will bring their son back, but . . .'

'It doesn't sound silly at all. And of course I will. Tell me their names.'

'They're called Miranda and Richard Frost, and their son was Sebastian.'

'I'll pray for them,' she promised. 'And so will other people. My friends.'

'I wish you were here,' Marco said quietly.

'So do I.'

And she did, Callie realized. Even here, in one of her favourite spots on earth, she would rather have been with Marco.

'I'd better go. I'll try to ring you tonight, *cara mia. Ti amo,*' he added.

Callie smiled; her grasp of Italian was minimal, but that was one phrase she understood. 'Love you, too.'

She put the phone in her pocket and sat for a moment, closing her eyes and lifting her face to the sun, saying a silent prayer for the Frost family.

'There you are,' called Tamsin. 'We've been looking for you!'

Callie opened her eyes. Tamsin and Nicky were coming up the path towards her. 'Have you heard?' Tamsin said, grinning. 'We're free this afternoon! The weather is so nice that they've given us the afternoon off.'

'So we were wondering what to do,' Nicky added. 'I think we should hire a punt.'

'And I think we should go shopping,' Tamsin stated.

Nicky pulled a face. 'So we need you to cast the deciding vote. What's it to be?'

A punt on the river – that would be bliss. Just like old times. 'Punt,' Callie said without hesitation.

'That's settled, then.' Nicky turned to Tamsin with a smug smile. 'See, I told you that she'd make the right decision. She's a sensible woman.'

'A traitor to womankind,' pronounced Tamsin, but she was smiling fondly at Nicky as she said it.

'Did I hear the word "punt"?'

They all turned as Adam Masters sauntered up from behind them.

'Sounds like a great idea,' he said. 'You don't mind if I join you, do you? It will be just like old times.'

'Lexie Renton?'

Neville couldn't help staring: she was a reasonably pretty girl with shiny pale hair, but it was her body that was spectacular. She did nothing to conceal it, either; she was wearing a short black tank top with spaghetti straps, showing off hot pink bra straps on her shoulders and a bellybutton stud on her bare midriff, above the briefest of miniskirts. She was no more than fifteen, Neville reminded himself.

'I'm Lexie,' the girl confirmed, returning his stare challengingly. 'And who are *you*?'

'Detective Inspector Stewart.' He produced his warrant card.

Usually a mere flash of the card was all that was required, but Lexie Renton was evidently of a more suspicious turn of mind than most; she took the card from him and examined it, then handed it back with a nod. 'OK,' she said, then turned to the younger girl, who was watching with interest. 'Piss off,' she ordered.

The girl complied, with a glare.

'How can I help you?' Lexie asked, leaning against the door.

Neville decided he should play it safe, just in case. 'Are your parents at home?'

'Mum's working today,' she said. 'And Dad doesn't live with us.'

'Is there a place where we could talk for a few minutes, Miss Renton? In private?'

'Miss Renton.' She snorted. 'Call me Lexie.' Without waiting for a reply, she turned and walked down a corridor. Neville followed, his eyes fixed on the butterfly tattoo in the small of her back.

Fifteen. Good God.

When he was fifteen, his chief delight had been in a girl called Norah Kelly. He hadn't thought about her for years, but he thought about her now. A tumble of red curls, and eyes as blue as the sky. Behind the bike shed, she had unbuttoned her white cotton blouse and allowed him to look. Two perfect pink rosebuds. God. Neville's mouth went dry, remembering.

Even now, he found white blouses highly erotic. That was probably why he'd been so attracted to Triona, the first time he met her, in her prim solicitor's suit and a crisp white shirt.

Norah Kelly. Those knowing blue eyes, promising so much. God, how she could kiss. And her mam would have killed her if she'd known the things that girl could do with her hands . . .

It hadn't gone much farther than that, of course. Not in that time and place. They were too frightened of the consequences. A baby would have been catastrophic, would have brought disgrace on both families and condemnation from the Church, in the terrifyingly authoritarian person of Father Flynn. Even Neville, inflamed with adolescent lust as he'd been, had known it wasn't worth the risk.

Where was Norah Kelly now? Probably married to some dim farmer, mother of half a dozen brats, her red hair faded to greying ginger. Pushing forty, just like he was. She might even have grandchildren.

Neville swallowed hard as Lexie pushed open a door and led him into her bedroom.

It was a small room, furnished with a single bed and a desk. The walls, painted a pale purple, were decorated with posters and pictures of boy bands and other pop stars, mostly unrecognized by Neville. A few books were piled on the desk, next to a shiny laptop computer of a type which would have sent Sid Cowley into raptures of techno-lust.

Lexie Renton sat on the bed and looked at him, her head to one side, as he turned the desk chair round to face her and took a seat. This was going to be tricky, he realized, pulling out his notebook. Probably in more ways than one. He couldn't read her expression; she was bound to be apprehensive, if she wasn't expecting this visit and didn't know what it was about, yet there was no sign of that in her demeanour.

'Sebastian Frost,' Neville began. 'I understand he's your boyfriend?'

She smiled, more to herself than at him. 'Is that what Seb told you?'

The girl was wrong-footing him already. 'It's what I've been led to believe,' he said carefully.

Lexie nodded. 'OK, then. We'll go with that. He's my boyfriend.'

'You met him . . . where?'

'We're at the same school,' she said, adding, 'it's a posh school. My dad pays the fees. Guilt, for dumping Mum and leaving us.'

That figured, Neville thought. From what he'd seen of their poky flat, the Rentons wouldn't be moving in the same circles as the Frosts or the Summervilles. 'And you and Sebastian . . . have been intimate?' he said with uncharacteristic delicacy.

'Like you said, he's my boyfriend.' She shrugged. 'It's not a big deal.'

Once again, unwillingly, Neville's mind was dragged back to his fifteen-year-old self. It had been a big deal for him, and for Norah Kelly.

Or it would have been a big deal, if it had happened. A *very* big deal. Things had certainly changed. At least kids today had easy access to contraception, so they wouldn't have to worry about nasty surprises, and he trusted that Lexie was smart enough to insist on safe sex.

Lexie's eyes widened; she clapped a hand over her mouth. 'Oops,' she said from behind her hand. 'Is that what this is about? Statutory rape, or something like that? Because I'm fifteen? In that case, I take it all back. Seb's never shagged me. I never said he did.'

'Nothing like that,' he assured her quickly. 'My interest is in ... another matter.' He would have to tell her sooner or later, but he wanted to get as much from her as he could before it became necessary.

'That's OK, then.' She removed her hand and visibly relaxed.

Neville made a couple of sketchy notes, to buy himself a bit of time before framing his next question. 'Did ... does ... Sebastian come here? For your ... um ... intimate times? Or did ... do ... you meet at his house?'

'His parents work at night a lot. So that's pretty convenient.' She flicked her long fringe out of her eyes. 'My mum works evening shifts, too, sometimes – at Tesco – but *she's* always around.' Lexie jerked her head in the direction of the lounge, presumably a reference to the younger girl who had answered the door.

'Your sister?'

'Yeah.' She made a disgusted noise in the back of her throat. 'Georgie. She's a pain in the bum.'

So they'd had their romantic trysts at the Frosts', then. Neville made a note, wondering whether Lexie's mother knew that she left her little sister home alone to go and shag her boyfriend. 'Did you see Sebastian last night?' he asked, recalling Hugo's assertion that a meeting had been planned.

She didn't hesitate. 'Last night? No.'

'Were you supposed to meet him?'

'No.' She shook her head.

'When was the last time you saw Sebastian, then?'

Lexie narrowed her eyes at him. 'Why are you asking these questions?' she demanded. 'What's happened? Is Seb OK?'

There was no getting round it now. Neville cleared his throat. 'I'm really sorry to have to tell you this, Miss Renton, but Sebastian Frost ... is dead.'

He was in no doubt that the look of astonishment and shock on her face was totally genuine.

The free afternoon gave Margaret Phillips a chance to work at her desk and catch up on some admin. But she found that her mind kept drifting to other things. Normally a very focused person, she could only blame it on spring fever. Outside the open window of her office the birds were chirping away and the gentlest of breezes stirred the cherry blossom, wafting its faint yet intoxicating scent towards her. She longed for . . . what? Something different. Something other than this panelled and book-lined room, attractive as it was.

Margaret leaned back in her chair and buzzed her secretary's desk. A moment later Hanna Young appeared in the doorway. 'Yes?'

'What are you doing at the moment, Hanna?'

'Photocopying the handouts for tomorrow's sessions.' Hanna waved a handful of papers as evidence.

'I was thinking about calling it a day,' confessed Margaret. 'As the weather's so nice. I just can't concentrate, if you want to know the truth.'

Hanna's brows drew together for a split second in what Margaret feared was disapproval. 'So you can leave as well, if you like,' she added hastily. 'Go home early. Put your feet up.'

'I have to finish this photocopying, to be honest. Canon Kingsley's only just given it to me.'

Now Margaret felt guilty. 'Well, I can help you, I suppose,' she offered.

'Photocopying is a one-person job,' Hanna stated. 'I'll just carry on. And I'll lock up when I've finished.'

'All right, then. I'll see you tomorrow morning.' Feeling now like a naughty schoolgirl skiving off from her lessons, Margaret left her desk and went upstairs to her sitting room. The house had been built in the Gothic style, and this room featured a large stone-mullioned and leaded oriel window, also overlooking the courtyard. She crossed to the window and pushed open as many of the leaded panes as were openable, breathing in the aromas of spring. A few people lingered in the courtyard, but most had scattered to enjoy their afternoon of freedom elsewhere.

Aimless still, Margaret wandered to the table near the window which held a collection of framed photographs. All of them contained the same person: her son Alexander. From his earliest baby pictures to his school photos to the most current, a formal studio portrait with his partner, Alexander was the focus, the photos charting his progress from adorable child to extremely good-looking young man, as handsome as his father. She picked up the studio portrait and smiled at her son's serious expression. His partner, Luke, appeared somewhat more cheerful.

There were no grandchildren, of course. And there wouldn't be, unless Alexander and Luke were moved to adopt at some point. They'd shown no inclination to do so, and they'd been together for several years now. They'd entered into a civil partnership; they were a stable couple. Margaret knew she must be grateful for that, at least, though there were brief moments when she longed for a grandchild. For a new generation, a new beginning.

Automatically her eyes sought for her favourite photo of Alexander: the one with Hal, the two of them – the teenaged Alexander and his father – looking like peas in a pod. It wasn't there, of course. There were no photos of Hal.

Margaret suddenly felt overheated, even with the windows open. She was wearing her black cassock, as she customarily did at the college as a mark of her position. Now she went to her bedroom and took it off, hanging it up carefully, contemplating her wardrobe as she stood there in her slip.

She was going to a garden party, she reminded herself. It had been several years since she'd been to one, even one as small and informal as this one. What should she wear?

A floaty summer frock would be ideal, and would suit her un-characteristically frivolous mood, but there were none such in her very clerical wardrobe.

Then Margaret remembered the jacket. It was hanging at the far end of the wardrobe, unworn for years, somehow having escaped relegation to the local Oxfam shop.

It wasn't a frivolous jacket, but it was quite unclerical. The abstract print was in shades of soft dove grey and blue, and had been selected to complement Margaret's colouring: her blue eyes and her wiry salt-and-pepper hair. It would do nicely, she decided, over a black skirt and pale blue clerical shirt. She pulled it out of the wardrobe and laid it across the bed.

The archdeaconry clergy garden party: it all came back to her now. The hot day, the crowds of clergy with axes to grind, their dowdy wives in their best summer frocks. And Hal, dazzling in his cream linen suit, pouring Pimm's and acting the perfect host.

Perhaps she wouldn't wear the jacket today, after all.

The fact that it was a bank holiday meant that Neville didn't have Detective Superintendent Evans breathing down his neck, and as far as he was concerned that was a blessing. Evans had been in his office first thing in the morning to give Neville his orders, but after that he had decamped home for an Easter egg hunt with his children and grandchildren, leaving Neville to get on with things.

Now, though, it was time to check in with Evans and discuss the next steps in the investigation. Evans, obviously hoping that it would be a cut-and-dried case, had ordered him to 'sort it', and he hadn't even begun to do so.

Well, Neville told himself defensively, he had *begun*. This morning they hadn't known who the dead boy was; now he had a name. Sebastian Frost had left behind parents and friends, so that was a beginning.

But still. It wasn't exactly going to fill Evans with joy.

Summoning up all of his courage, Neville rang Superintendent Evans' mobile number. His boss, he discovered, was still at home with his family, and not about to return to the police station. 'Come here and brief me,' Evans said. It wasn't a suggestion; it was a command.

'To your house, Sir?'

'That's right.'

He made little effort to hide his disbelief. 'You want me to drive—'

Evans cut him off. 'It's Bromley, Stewart, not the bloody moon. Ten miles from London Bridge. Not much traffic today. Won't take long. Bring Cowley, if you like.'

At least that would give him a chance to talk things over with Sid, Neville reflected, as he tracked his sergeant down.

Cowley's phone was back on, and he was at the station. Neville drove there to collect him.

'Bromley?' said Cowley, getting into the car. 'Bloody Bromley? You have to be kidding me.'

'If only.' Neville made an attempt at mimicking Evans' sing-song Welsh accent. 'Ten miles from London Bridge, boyo. Won't take long.'

'That's all right then.' Cowley snorted. 'In the middle of an investigation, we have to drive to bloody Bromley, because the boss can't be bothered to leave his family.'

Some family it was, too: two families, really. Neville and everyone else at the station had watched with considerable interest a few years ago as Detective Superintendent Evans had wooed and won the hand of the fair Denise, a secretary with awesome physical assets. To do so he'd had to ditch an inconvenient middle-aged wife, one who had long since provided him with the offspring who had made them grandparents. With Denise he had embarked upon creating a new family, and they now had three children under five.

Not bad going, Neville reflected, for a bloke as monumentally ugly as Evans, with his whacking great jaw and his eyebrows like furry black caterpillars. You could only hope that the kids took after their respective mothers.

'Look at it this way,' Neville said. 'We have ten miles, give or take, to talk about what we've found out so far, and to decide what to tell him.'

'Well, I've found out bugger all,' Cowley confessed, fumbling for his packet of fags.

Neville knew it would be a waste of his breath to tell Cowley to put his fags away. It was against regulations to smoke in police cars, but Cowley was very skilled at doing it in a way that left no traces. So he sighed, loudly enough to make the point that he wasn't happy about it, then addressed himself to Sid's confession. 'You talked to his mates, didn't you? To Tom and Olly?'

'Snotty little rich kids,' Cowley pronounced with a sneer. 'Butter wouldn't melt. The idea of them being part of a gang – well, it's just laughable.'

'Yes?' Neville encouraged him to elaborate.

'They go to a posh school. They have all the latest kit: computers, laptops, iPads, games consoles, smartphones, iPods, video cameras. Parents with bottomless pockets. It's not a world I know anything about, Guv.' He took a deep drag on his cigarette and blew the smoke out of the window. 'Gangs are for kids like the ones I grew up with. Kids with time on their hands, nothing else to do. Bored kids. Not kids with Xboxes and Wiis and iPhones.'

Neville took his point. 'And if another kid stabbed him, it wasn't to nick his stuff, either. His phone was smashed, not nicked.'

'That's exactly what I'm saying.' Cowley shook his head. 'What a waste. My nephew – he'd practically kill to get his hands on that phone. Hell, Guv – I practically would myself, to be honest.' He grinned. 'But these kids don't need to. If they want something, they just ask Mum and Dad.'

'What about drugs, then?'

'Possible,' admitted Cowley. 'When you've got that much money, you could certainly afford drugs if you wanted them.'

Again, though, Neville reflected, it just didn't fit the picture they'd started to build up. It was usually bored kids who got their kicks from drugs, as well as from gang membership. 'The Frosts were adamant that their son had nothing to do with drugs,' he said. 'They're doctors, so they would know what to look for. I suppose I'm inclined to believe them.'

'Well, what's left, then?' Cowley tapped ash into the little portable ashtray he carried in his pocket.

'Sex,' said Neville, allowing himself a quick sideways glance to see the effect on Cowley.

The sergeant's reaction was gratifying; he raised his eyebrows and grinned. 'Oh?'

'I talked to his girlfriend. Sexy Lexie, I understand she's known as.'

'Tell me more, Guv.'

'I'd say she earned the nickname, fair and square.' He shook his head, remembering. 'She was quite blasé about the whole thing, really, but it's clear that our boy Sebastian was having it off with her regularly while his parents were at work. Fifteen, the both of them,' he added meditatively.

'Good on them.' Sid's grin widened. 'But how does that add up to a motive for murder? You're not saying that she's the one who stabbed him, are you?'

'No. But say one of his mates fancied her. Or shagged her, and he found out.'

'A crime of passion, you're saying?'

Put like that, it didn't sound very likely, even to Neville's own ears. They were fifteen years old, for God's sake. Love – or lust, more accurately – might be intense at fifteen, but it was understood to be fleeting. Would he have pulled a knife on one of his mates if he'd found out that they'd managed to get into Norah Kelly's knickers? Not likely. Even making allowances for a different time and a different place . . .

Still, at this point it was the best angle they had.

Gangs? Unlikely. Drugs? Probably not. Sex? Well, just maybe . . .

Now Cowley's grin split his face from side to side. 'Guv, can I ask a favour?'

'Ask away.'

'Next time you go to talk to Sexy Lexie, can I go along?'

Once again Neville put on his Evans voice, though he couldn't help smiling. 'Not on your life, boyo. Not on your bloody life.'

If only he would just shut up.

Callie closed her eyes and tried to tune out the sound of his voice, to concentrate on other sounds instead: the birds in the trees on the riverbank, the rhythmic splash of the pole hitting the water, the shouts and laughter from other punts.

She didn't remember that Adam had talked this much when they were together. If he had done, how had she borne it?

Maybe he was just nervous, she told herself. After all, if it was awkward for her, it must be awkward for him as well. Yet he seemed supremely confident as he rattled on. He talked in glowing terms of his incumbent, recounted amusing anecdotes of parish life, and of course there were endless stories about the exemplary Pippa, the wonderful girl for whom he'd abandoned Callie. Pippa, his wife.

Nicky was punting, standing on the flat ledge at the rear of the boat, concentrating on his steering and ignoring the chatter of the others. Tamsin, for her part, tried valiantly to interject comments and to turn it into something other than a monologue.

Callie had given up. Lost the will to live, almost. She leaned back against the cushions in the punt and wished herself somewhere – anywhere – else.

'Where are we going?' Tamsin asked brightly, in Nicky's direction, during a brief instant when Adam stopped to draw breath.

'Grantchester, of course,' said Nicky. 'The Orchard. I feel very Rupert Brooke-ish today. Tea under the apple trees – with honey, of course – will be just the thing.'

'It will be crowded,' Adam stated. 'Everyone and his granny will be there today. We might not be able to get in.'

Please God, thought Callie. In any other circumstances, sitting under the trees at the Orchard, consuming a cream tea, was her idea of heaven. If Adam didn't shut up, though, it would be more like a vision of hell.

Interlude: a close encounter observed

By the time she left the office, having photocopied every bit of paper required for the next day, Hanna Young was feeling both self-righteous and fed up. She had done her duty while others – many others – had shirked theirs; the moral high ground was hers, but at the cost of having missed out on enjoying the delicious afternoon. The galling thing was that no one else even noticed, or probably cared.

She locked the door to the office and headed for the car park, tucked behind the terrace of houses and flats which provided accommodation for tutors and married students.

Someone was coming out of the back door of one of the houses, moving through its garden towards the car park. Hanna stopped, watching and listening.

Mad Phil Moody – it was his house – and with him a young girl. Not one of their students, but a girl Hanna hadn't seen before. Too young to be an ordinand, almost too young to be an undergraduate. Long honey-coloured hair, long bare legs, much flesh on view.

Hanna held her breath.

Mad Phil's arm was round her waist. They stopped for a moment; he leaned down and whispered something in her ear. She laughed, smiled up at him, twined her arms round his neck. He bent his head down; a kiss was exchanged, loud enough for Hanna to hear the smack, though his head obscured her view.

A tight, lingering hug, then the girl slipped away through the back gate into the car park, turning to wave as she unchained a bicycle from the railings, climbed on it and cycled away with her long bare legs.

Hanna stood for a long moment as Mad Phil looked fondly after the girl, then turned and went back into his house.

Disgusting. An old man – fifty, if he was a day. And a girl like that.

It didn't require much imagination for Hanna to determine what Mad Phil Moody had been up to on his free afternoon.

She wrinkled her nose in distaste and resumed her progress towards her car.

CHAPTER 8

'It's good, as far as it goes. I want more.'

More?

Lilith read the brief email for the tenth time, fuming. She'd knocked herself out, tracking down the dead boy and getting an ID. She'd written a story, padding out the little she knew with skill: incorporating platitudes, speculation and flashes of brilliance. And no one else had the story – she was sure of that. Nothing had appeared on the Met website yet; the fact that it was a holiday was working in her favour.

Yet it wasn't good enough for Rob Gardiner-Smith. He wanted more.

What else could she give him?

An interview, that was what. Quotes. But trying to get through the police family liaison officer to the family was a non-starter. He would be guarding them jealously against press intrusion, whether she rang on the phone or turned up at their door. That was part of his job.

And her job was to do what her editor wanted.

Lilith read the email again. She narrowed her eyes; she tapped her well-groomed fingernails on the desk.

And then it came to her. Lilith knew what she had to do, where she had to go. She shut down the computer, grabbed her bag and headed for the door.

It had been an act of madness, Margaret acknowledged to herself, as she stood in front of the mirror. Not like her at all. But she didn't regret it in the least.

Not even stopping to think about it, she'd grabbed the jacket from the wardrobe, stuffed it into a carrier bag, gone downstairs and retrieved her long-unused bicycle, then cycled across the river, through the narrow streets going into the town, along by the Round Church to the Oxfam shop. There she'd handed over the jacket. And there she had spied the loveliest of summer frocks: floaty, flowery, the very essence of a garden party. Her size.

She hadn't even tried it on. Margaret, who pondered over additions to her wardrobe, sometimes for weeks, before committing herself to a purchase. She'd bought it without a second thought and cycled back to the college.

After a quick, reviving shower – cycling into town had been warm work – she had slipped into the dress. It was a perfect fit.

She looked at herself in the mirror, scarcely recognizing the person she saw. Her cheeks were flushed a becoming pink – from the unaccustomed exertions of cycling, she told herself – and her eyes sparkled at the joy of breaking out of her routine and doing something so utterly un-Margaret-like. A touch of lipstick was all she needed to make the transformation complete.

Margaret hoped that her secretary had gone home by now, that she wouldn't run into her looking like this. Somehow she suspected that Hanna would not approve.

But she didn't really care. She was going to a garden party.

Neville allowed Cowley to drive back into London, and for the first part of the journey he was silent, lost in his own thoughts.

Strangely enough, he wasn't thinking about the things Evans had had to say about the Frost case, but about parenthood. Fatherhood, to be precise.

Evans, whatever else you might say about him, was a good father, Neville realized with a sense of revelation. The way he got down on his knees to play with the toddlers, the look on his face when he held the baby . . .

Evans, of all people. It was beyond belief.

Of course he'd had plenty of practice, Neville reminded himself cynically. Years and years of it, with two families. Still, he seemed like a natural. And the children obviously adored him, from the grown-up ones all the way down to the baby.

Who would ever have thought it?

He wondered whether it had always been so easy for Evans – back in the beginning, with the first baby and wife number one. He must have been quite young when the first one came along. Much younger than Neville was now.

And yet Neville felt so totally unprepared for fatherhood. He was, he acknowledged to himself in his most honest moments, terrified by the prospect. The baby hadn't been planned; he hadn't even known about it until several months into the pregnancy. He still didn't feel he'd had enough time to get his head round it.

A little person in his life. Always there, dependent on him for everything.

What if he didn't know what to do? What if he didn't hold it properly, and dropped it? Those things were supposed to be instinctive, but were they really? He wasn't even sure that Triona would know what to do with a baby; he'd never seen much evidence of maternal instinct in her.

How would they cope? There were so many ways in which he could fail. So many traps for the unwary. So many ways in which he could screw up a kid's life so that he would be blamed for ever.

Like my da: the thought popped unbidden into Neville's mind and he pushed it away. He hadn't consciously thought about his father in years and wasn't about to start now.

He just wasn't ready for this baby. He hadn't had time to get used to being a husband, let alone a dad.

But it was too late for that. It was going to happen. By the end of the summer . . .

'What do you reckon, Guv?'

Cowley's words cut across his thoughts; Neville turned to him. 'Hmm?'

'I left you alone 'cause I could see you were thinking about what Evans said. So what do you reckon?'

What *had* Evans said? 'Remind me.'

Cowley flashed him an incredulous look. 'About us assuming that another kid killed him,' he said with exaggerated patience.

Yes, they *had* made that assumption, as Evans pointed out. Because of the MO, primarily. Teenagers stabbing each other was an epidemic in London, and had been for several years.

Evans had warned them not to assume anything. Wise advice, when it came to detective work.

'I see what he's saying,' Cowley went on. 'But if some villain had done it, he would've nicked the phone, not smashed it.'

Neville nodded. As he'd said to Evans, it just didn't have the feel of an opportunistic crime. It was more deliberate than that, his instincts told him. At this point he couldn't see why anyone would have wanted Sebastian Frost dead, but someone had done, and it was up to them to find out who. 'If we can figure out *why* someone wanted to kill him,' he thought aloud, 'maybe that will tell us who did it.'

'But it's going to take time, Guv,' Cowley stated. 'If we have to talk to all his mates, everyone at his school . . .'

As Evans had pointed out to them, in no uncertain terms, they'd been lucky that this had happened on a bank holiday. No press breathing down their necks, for a start. That wouldn't last long, Neville was well aware. Tomorrow they'd have to hold a news conference. And then all hell would break loose, for sure.

In the meantime, though ...

'Where are we going now, Guv?' Cowley asked as they crossed the river, looking to him for instructions.

Neville sighed, then made a sudden decision. 'I don't know about you, Sid,' he said. 'But I'm going home.'

The first day of working with a family after a bereavement was often the hardest, Mark reflected, before reality really kicked in, and practicalities demanded to be dealt with. At this point it was still surreal; people were in shock. They needed time to let the horrible truth sink in. His job on that first day was a matter of being unobtrusive, giving them space yet being attentive to their needs.

All too soon the press would be on their doorstep. There would inevitably be more police questioning, involvement with the coroner, funeral arrangements to be made, condolences pouring in. Friends and family to comfort and be comforted.

But not today.

This was a day for the Frosts to begin to come to terms with the fact that their son would not be coming home.

After their return from the mortuary, Mark had done little apart from making coffee. In his experience, some people dealt with the early stages of grief by talking ceaselessly, as if their words would somehow bring their loved one back to them. Others went the opposite way and retreated into their own heads, hoarding their memories internally. The Frosts – both of them – were of the latter type. They scarcely spoke to each other, let alone to him; their early tears had given way to a sort of quiet stoicism.

In some way the blabbers were easier to cope with, he reflected. Their grief might be uncomfortable to observe, but at least you knew where you were with them. The Frosts' stilted politeness was painful, heavy with the weight of what wasn't being said.

So when Mark's phone rang he looked at it eagerly, hoping for the respite of a chat with Callie. He'd had to give her short shrift earlier; now that things had quietened down – literally – he was ready to excuse himself and take her call in another room.

But it wasn't Callie, he realized as he looked at the caller display. She wouldn't be ringing him, after he'd put her off and said he would ring her tonight.

It was his niece Chiara.

Chiara had only recently obtained a mobile. Her mother had always said she was too young to have one, in spite of the fact that all of her friends did, but Serena had finally given in, buying it for her almost as a sort of consolation prize after her father died. 'It might help her to deal with it if she can talk to her friends,' Serena had explained her change of heart to Mark.

'Uncle Marco?' Chiara whispered.

'*Ciao, nipotina.*'

'Can you talk? Or are you working?'

He took his phone through to the kitchen. 'Yes, it's fine. What's up?'

'I just . . . wanted to talk,' she said. 'I was thinking about last year. Easter Monday. Remember?'

Mark did. They'd gone to the London Eye, all of them. *La famiglia.* In that now-unimaginable time before Callie had entered his life. 'The London Eye,' he said.

'It was so much fun.' Chiara sighed.

'You didn't think it was going to be,' he recalled.

'I didn't want to go. I was scared,' she admitted. 'It looked so high from the ground.'

There had been tears, Mark remembered. His brave little niece had revealed a previously unknown fear of heights. 'But you did go.'

'Dad talked me into it. He said I wouldn't even think about how high it was, once I was up there. Because it moves so slowly, and because there's so much to see.' There was a long pause. 'And he was right. I didn't think about it at all. And it was . . . magic.' Chiara gulped, loudly. 'Oh, Uncle Marco. I miss my dad.'

'Of course you do.'

'I just can't believe I'll never see him again.' She was crying now: he could tell from her voice.

Mark hadn't always seen eye to eye with Joe di Stefano, especially in recent months when Joe had broken Serena's heart by having an affair. But even at the lowest point of Joe's relationship with Serena, Mark had never doubted the bond between Joe and his daughters.

'And it upsets Mum when I talk about him,' she continued before Mark could say anything. 'It makes her sad.'

For just an instant Mark felt a twinge of resentment. Was he never to be allowed to escape from people in the throes of bereavement? It was his job; now it seemed it was going to be a permanent feature of his family life as well. He closed his eyes.

'It's all right, *nipotina*,' he assured her. 'If you don't want to upset your mother, you can talk to me. Any time.'

She proceeded to take him at his word. While she was talking – and crying – Mark kept half an ear attuned to the rest of the house in case he was needed elsewhere. After a few minutes he thought he heard someone in the corridor and went out to investigate.

The front door was closing; the latch clicked into place.

No one had come in. That meant that someone had just gone out.

Well, they weren't his prisoners, he reminded himself. The Frosts were free to come and go as they liked.

'You look wonderful.' Keith Moody's eyes travelled up and down Margaret, frank with admiration. 'You should take off your cassock more often, Principal.'

It had been a long time since Margaret had been conscious of being looked at like that by a man – as a woman rather than as a priest, an asexual creature in a dog collar. The sensation was unexpected, if not unpleasant, and she felt herself blushing. That was something she hadn't done in years. 'Thank you,' she said, smiling. 'It's not every day I'm invited to tea in the garden.'

'We'll have to do something about that, then. Come on through to the garden. John isn't here yet.' Keith led her through the French doors in his main reception room and into the small but immaculately maintained garden, where a table and chairs had been set up to take full advantage of the late afternoon sunlight.

Margaret observed with admiration the neat, well-weeded beds of spring flowers and the pruned rose bushes, still a long way from blooming. 'I didn't know you were such a keen gardener.'

'I find it relaxing,' he said. 'It clears my head. When I'm worrying about some little theological niggle – something that has come up in tutor group, usually – nothing is as therapeutic as an hour in the garden, pulling weeds.'

'Well, you know that saying. "You're nearer—"'

'"Nearer God's heart in a garden than anywhere else on earth",' he finished for her with a smile. 'I can't tell you how often I ran into that one when I was in parish ministry. Usually embroidered on a cushion in the home of someone who never set foot in church.'

Margaret laughed. 'It makes a good excuse, doesn't it?'

'One of the better ones. There isn't as much folk wisdom justification for spending Sunday morning washing the car instead of going to church. But somehow it's OK if you're in the garden.'

The doorbell rang; her host went to answer it while Margaret sat down on one of the rather faded garden chairs. She should have put on some sunblock cream, she realized. With her fair skin she would soon be sorry she hadn't done. But it had been so long since they'd had a day like this that she wasn't even sure she could find her bottle of sunblock without a major search operation.

There was a cat curled up on another of the chairs, she realized. A plump tabby, sound asleep in the sun.

Without thinking, Margaret leaned over and stroked the cat. It began purring: a deep, satisfied rumble. After a moment it opened one very green eye, stared at her, and jumped down from its chair. It stretched, forwards and back, yawned hugely, then jumped up on her lap and curled up once again into a ball.

Keith Moody and John Kingsley came through the French doors. 'Sorry I can't get up,' Margaret said, indicating her burden.

'Oh!' Keith raised his eyebrows. 'You should feel very honoured, Principal. Evie is quite particular about laps, and has paid you a great compliment. But feel free to push her off if she's bothering you.'

'Not at all. She's lovely.' Margaret rubbed behind the cat's ears and was rewarded with another burst of purrs. 'She's called Evie, then?'

'Evie, short for Evensong.' He gestured John Kingsley into the chair recently vacated by the cat. 'Because that's when she adopted me. One afternoon I came home from Evensong and found her here. Inside the house, curled up on the sofa, as if she owned the place. I'd left a window cracked open and that was all the encouragement she needed. She's been here ever since. Ruling the roost, I don't have to tell you.'

'My daughter has a cat,' Canon Kingsley contributed. 'She keeps telling me that I should get one, to keep me company. I think she worries about me, living on my own. But I'm used to it.'

Maybe *she* should get a cat, Margaret told herself. It would certainly make her house feel less empty. She didn't think she would *ever* become accustomed to living on her own.

'And I'm afraid I would neglect it. Forget to feed it, or something. I'm a bit like that,' John Kingsley admitted. 'Sometimes I don't even remember to feed myself.'

'There's no danger of neglecting Evie.' Keith Moody laughed. 'She's very good at letting me know when she's hungry. And speaking of food . . .'

He disappeared for a few minutes, then came back with a tray of plates, tea things and cutlery.

'Can I help you?' Margaret offered guiltily.

'Not at all. Everything is organized. And you're a guest,' he added. 'With a cat on your lap.'

'So I am.'

On his next trip he brought out a cake on a platter, iced extravagantly with chocolate. 'Chocolate cake,' he announced.

It looked wonderful. And homemade – not just any old shop-bought cake. 'Oh! I love chocolate,' confessed Margaret. 'It's my absolute favourite.'

'Yes, I know.'

There was something in his voice . . . something that made her turn her attention from the cake and look at him more closely. The tiniest suspicion wriggled into her mind.

Keith Moody met her eyes, holding her surprised gaze without looking away. He raised both eyebrows for a second . . . and then he winked.

It was there, on Paddington Green, as Lilith had guessed it would be. The shrine.

The crime scene tape was still in place, cordoning off an area of the green. But the shrine had appeared against the railings on the perimeter. Bunches of flowers, most wrapped in cellophane. Cards, notes.

And they were there, as well. Sebastian Frost's friends, sitting round on the grass, talking quietly among themselves in small groups or withdrawn into their own thoughts and memories. A dozen or so young teenagers, mostly boys and a few girls, dressed in what Lilith recognized as the latest teen fashions.

She approached cautiously, afraid of scaring them off. But those who could be bothered to turn their heads or open their eyes looked at her incuriously; the others ignored her.

Lilith wished she'd thought to bring some flowers herself. The fact that she hadn't brought any to add to the shrine didn't stop her from crouching down beside the floral tributes and reading the messages.

'Seb – I won't forget you.'

'Good mate. You'll be missed.'

'I can't believe your gone, Seb. This sucks.' Lilith grimaced and mentally corrected the grammar.

They went on in that vein, more or less grammatical but scarcely articulate, let alone poetic.

Lilith left the messages and studied the gathered teenagers for a likely target. She chose one who was sitting on his own, leaning against the trunk of a tree with his eyes closed. Easing herself down beside him, she wished she'd been wearing something more appropriate for sitting on the ground than her tight skirt. It wasn't often that Lilith got caught out wearing the wrong clothes – she prided herself on dressing for the occasion – but she hadn't anticipated this venue when she'd chosen her wardrobe for the day. Her outfit was suitable for confronting her editor, not for this; she made the best of it by tucking her legs to the side, knees demurely together.

'Hi, I'm Lilith,' she said to the boy, her voice as quiet as she could make it and still be heard. 'Are you one of Seb's friends?'

He opened his eyes, narrowing them in her direction. They were a bit red, with some evidence of tears. 'We were mates, yeah.'

'And you are . . . ?'

'Olly.'

'Nice to meet you, Olly.' She didn't offer her hand, but he nodded in acknowledgement. 'Do you mind talking about Seb?'

'Suppose not.'

He was not the most prepossessing of boys, being a bit spotty and rather short, though his dark hair had been styled into fashionable spikes. Lilith hoped he would make up for in articulateness what he lacked in looks.

'How did you hear about Seb's death?' Lilith asked, putting on an expression of sympathy and concern. She wished she could employ a tape recorder, or at the very least a notebook, but sensed it would scare him off. She would just have to rely on her excellent memory.

Olly looked at her as if she'd just asked the stupidest question possible, rolling his eyes. 'Duh. One of my mates texted me. Stuff like that gets round pretty fast. It was on Facebook like hours ago.'

Facebook! She hadn't even thought of checking there. 'There's a memorial page, then?'

'Yeah, of course.' He rolled his eyes again.

Lilith tried to come up with a question which would demonstrate that she wasn't as thick and out-of-touch as he seemed to think she was. She settled for the simplest of all: an open invitation. 'Tell me about Seb.'

The boy sighed as he considered the matter; he pulled up a blade of grass and shredded it, then began tentatively. 'Seb is . . . was . . . special.

You know? Seb did things that other kids only thought about. Or didn't even think about, till Seb did them. Then everyone else did them too.'

A leader. That's what this boy was trying to say, in his tortuous way. Sebastian Frost had possessed leadership qualities. 'Can you give me an example?' she urged.

Olly picked at a spot on his chin and took his time to answer. 'I can't really think of anything,' he said at last, then corrected himself. 'Well, there was this sort of game that Seb invented. This was a long time ago, like. We all had names of *Star Wars* characters. You know?' He shredded another blade of grass and added apologetically, 'It all sounds kind of stupid now. Sorry.'

Lilith was beginning to wonder whether she might have better luck with one of Sebastian's other friends when her attention was drawn to a new figure on the scene. The man walked slowly towards the makeshift shrine, his head bent as if he hadn't the strength to hold it up. A tall, lanky man with curly brown hair, flecked with grey. He stopped in front of the shrine and squeezed his eyes shut, pressing his lips together.

Lilith recognized him immediately, from the mortuary. Dr Frost. Sebastian's father.

It had been a good day for her: a dollop or two of luck, added to solid journalistic instincts and hard work. This, though, was the icing on the cake. She'd hit paydirt.

With the weather so delightful, Callie found her room oppressive and the courtyard enticing. She needed to make a couple of phone calls and decided to take a chance on doing it from her favourite bench, hoping she could remain undiscovered and undisturbed while she did so.

Peter was the first, mainly to check up on Bella. 'She's fine,' he said blithely. 'We had a long walk this afternoon.'

For a change he didn't seem inclined to engage in idle chit-chat, which suited Callie just fine. She promised to ring tomorrow and ended the call.

If Peter had started probing – or worse, teasing her – about Adam, she didn't think she could have borne it. Likewise, she really wasn't ready to talk to Marco just yet, after what had happened. She'd had to tell Marco that Adam was there, but that was as much as she wanted to say to him on that subject. By unspoken mutual consent, she and Marco didn't talk about Adam; they both preferred it that way. Perhaps one day, when they were married and thoroughly secure in their relationship, they would be able to discuss her former fiancé, but not yet.

Her friend Frances was the person she really wanted to talk to. Frances would understand why Callie was upset; Callie wouldn't have to make excuses or try to explain.

Frances, though, wasn't answering her phone; Callie's call went straight to voicemail. She hung up without leaving a message. How could she condense into thirty seconds – a few sentences – the horror of the afternoon she had just endured?

Yet she desperately needed to talk about it, to try to make some sense of the way she was feeling. Maybe she could find Tamsin and have a private chat.

'Hello,' said a voice close by, and Callie recognized Canon Kingsley as he approached along the path.

'Oh, hello.' She wasn't at all sure what prompted her next words. 'Do you have a minute, Canon? To talk?'

'Yes, of course.' He sat down beside her on the bench. 'I don't think we've been properly introduced.'

'I'm Callie Anson. One of the deacons,' she added unnecessarily.

He didn't press her, and he didn't try to fill the initial silence with small talk. He just sat and waited while Callie tried to think how to begin. Maybe it was a mistake, she told herself. Why should she think it was a good idea to burden a total stranger with this? But there was just something about this man, something that made her certain she could trust him.

'When I was studying here, the last few years, I was involved with someone,' she started tentatively.

Then it all came out, in a flood of words. Adam, the growing relationship, the commitment, the physical intimacy which had seemed so natural and right at the time. The plans they'd made for the future, and the way it had ended. Adam's obtuseness as he'd told her that he'd met someone wonderful, and hoped she and Pippa would be good friends. The pain she'd suffered in the months after that. Then Marco, and the difference he had made in her life. The healing, the hope, the love.

And now this week. Today. This afternoon. Adam again, bringing with him the reminder of things she'd tried so hard to forget.

Canon Kingsley was the perfect listener: attentive, encouraging her with his body language as she told the story, never interrupting her. Not judging.

'I don't know why I'm letting it get to me so much,' she finished. 'It's over. In the past. I've moved on, just like he has. Why am I allowing this to upset me?'

He seemed to weigh his reply carefully, treating her question as more than a rhetorical one. 'You don't love him any longer,' he said, a statement rather than a question.

'No. Absolutely not.' Callie wasn't just saying it; she knew it was true. 'In fact, being with him this afternoon made me wonder what I'd ever seen in him.'

'But he clearly stirs up very strong emotions in you. Not love – something else, then.'

'Yeees . . .'

'Anger,' said John Kingsley. 'Adam makes you very angry, doesn't he?'

Callie didn't consider herself an angry person. But Canon Kingsley was right. He was absolutely right. It hit her like a blow to the solar plexus. 'Yes,' she admitted. 'Yes, he does.'

'Then the next thing you need to ask yourself—'

'Callie!' Tamsin's voice cut across his words from several feet away. 'I've just been up to your room, looking for you. I figured I'd find you here. We're going to be late for dinner!'

'I'm sorry,' Callie said quickly to Canon Kingsley, before Tamsin reached them. 'I have to go. But thank you so much for listening.' Her regret, and her gratitude, were real.

He smiled. 'We can continue this conversation another day, if you like.'

'If you really mean it . . .'

'Oh, I do,' he said.

Lilith had thought for a moment that he wouldn't talk to her – Richard Frost. That he would blow her off, tell her to go away and leave him alone.

But it hadn't been like that. Not at all.

It was almost as if he'd come looking for her, hoping she would be there. He was aching to talk, desperate for it.

'It's always about the mother,' he said to her. 'Everyone focuses on her. Like she's the only one who's grieving. Yes, it's hell for Miranda. Of course it is. But what about *me*? He was my son too. I've lost him as well. Why do I have to be strong for Miranda, when I've lost my son?'

They had connected. It had been palpable, that connection – almost sexual in its intensity. Richard Frost had talked, and she had listened. He had bared his soul to her, shared his pain and his frustration. He'd told her the things he couldn't tell his wife. Miranda, who was hurting so much that she didn't want to know about his pain. Things he couldn't tell the family liaison officer, who after all was just a policeman being paid to do a job. But he had told *her*, Lilith Noone.

And he had talked about his son. About Sebastian, that gifted boy with so much to offer, his whole life in front of him. But now there was no future for Sebastian; his life was behind him. All of that promise, cut short. Sebastian Frost might have discovered the cure for cancer one day; he might have scored the winning goal at the World Cup in a dozen or so years; he might have been prime minister. Now they would never know what he could have achieved. It was a vast tragedy, a loss for the world, a story without an ending.

In a sense it was a story that he had handed to her, like a gift wrapped in shiny paper and tied with a bow.

She owed it to Richard Frost – and to Sebastian – to get it right.

Front-page stuff? Almost certainly. At the end of the day it would be up to the subeditors to write the headline. But as Lilith sat down at her computer to compose the story, she knew what she wanted the headline to say: A Father's Anguish.

John Kingsley had excused himself from the tea party earlier, pleading tiredness, saying he needed a few minutes to put his feet up in his room before the evening meal. 'I'm not as young as I used to be,' he'd said.

Margaret thought she should probably go as well, and began to make a move to shift the cat from her lap. But Keith Moody intervened. 'You don't have to go yet,' he said quickly.

So she didn't. She remained, and accepted a refill of tea. She even had a second sliver of chocolate cake. The conversation flowed, covering all sorts of topics from theology to Cambridge to favourite music. Talking to Keith Moody was effortless; Margaret wondered why she'd never really done it before. It wasn't until the sun dropped behind the trees that she realized she was chilled, and feared that she may have outstayed her welcome.

'I must put in an appearance at dinner,' she said. 'And there's that session in the bar tonight. That was *your* idea, remember?'

'I'll be there,' he assured her. 'And I'll even buy you a drink.'

'I should buy *you* a drink. You've given me such a splendid tea.' Margaret finally managed to remove the cat and stand up.

'I hope you'll come back another time.'

'Of course. And you must come and have a meal with me sometime,' she heard herself saying.

'I would be delighted.' He gave her a courtly, old-fashioned bow.

'Thanks so much for this. Really. It's been lovely.'

Keith Moody smiled. 'My pleasure, Principal.'

'Please,' she said. 'Please, Keith. Call me Margaret.'

CHAPTER 9

Neville turned over in bed and snuggled against Triona, fitting himself round her sleeping body. His hand moved lazily over the smooth satin of her nightdress, tentatively exploring, just in case . . .

'Mmmm.' She opened one eye, then reached out a hand and grabbed the bedside clock. 'Oh, Lord. Is that really the time?' she groaned, struggling up on to her elbow.

'There's no rush.'

'Oh, but there is!' She turned towards Neville, gave him a chaste peck on his bristly cheek, then pulled away from his questing hand and got out of bed, more nimbly than he would have thought possible with the size of her bump. 'I have a meeting with a client first thing this morning. I did tell you last night.'

Last night he'd had other things on his mind. He probably hadn't even been listening, he admitted to himself – if not to her.

'And I have to get clear across town,' she reminded him.

Her flat was in the City, very close to her office. But they were at his Shepherd's Bush flat instead. She'd spent the day there yesterday, while he was working, giving the place a thorough spring clean, the likes of which it hadn't seen since he'd moved in over fifteen years ago. He'd heard that pregnancy sometimes did that to a woman: brought on a cleaning frenzy, part of the nesting instinct. His flat, and the people who were going to buy it in the near future, were the beneficiaries of that primitive drive.

Last night they'd slept on freshly laundered sheets, under an aired duvet, in a room that had been scrubbed within an inch of its life. Neville scarcely recognized the place. Its familiar fug was gone; maybe now Triona wouldn't have as many objections to staying there, at least until they were able to move into their new house. And please God that would be soon. Before the baby. Then maybe they'd start to feel like a real family, instead of a couple of people making do.

Not that Neville had many grounds for complaint at the moment. The pregnancy hormones, in addition to producing the laudable cleaning frenzy and an even more laudable boost in her libido, seemed to be making Triona more mellow in temperament, less likely to take exception to his failings as a husband. And then there were the fantastic breasts, always delectable but now grown to unprecedented lusciousness. If only, he thought with a guilty sort of regret, she could stay pregnant like this for ever, so he could reap the benefits without having to worry about the inevitable conclusion: the arrival of that life-changing baby.

For a full thirty seconds Neville managed to forget what he had ahead of him over the next few hours, and then it hit him. He had no illusions that Sebastian Frost's killer would have turned himself in during the night. Evans would be back at his desk, poised to jump on Neville at the earliest opportunity. And if the press hadn't got hold of the story yet, they would be having a field day very soon. He was going to have to come up with something good to feed to them at the news conference.

Neville groaned aloud and threw off the duvet.

Callie made it to Morning Prayer on Tuesday, arriving even before the summoning bell. Tamsin wasn't quite so prompt, slipping into the pew next to Callie in the middle of the General Confession. Distracted, Callie glanced at her and stumbled over 'miserable offenders'; Tamsin shrugged with a significant roll of her eyes in Callie's direction. 'I'll tell you later,' she whispered as soon as absolution had been pronounced.

'Later' turned out to be after breakfast, before the morning session began. Callie went back to her room to clean her teeth and collect a notebook; Tamsin followed and closed the door behind her.

Callie's curiosity was piqued. 'What's this all about?'

'Gossip,' said Tamsin. 'Juicy gossip.'

She knew she shouldn't encourage her, but Callie couldn't help it. 'Tell me,' she demanded.

'Have you met that new secretary woman?'

'Oh, the principal's PA, isn't she?' Callie recalled. 'Hanna, with no H at the end.'

'That's the one,' Tamsin confirmed. 'She spelled it for me. Anyway, she waylaid me outside the chapel. I was running late anyway. There wasn't anyone else about, so I suppose that's why she told me.'

'Told you what?'

'I'm getting to that.' Tamsin plopped down on the bed. 'She said she was so upset that she just had to tell someone.'

'Upset?'

Tamsin shook her head. 'She didn't seem that upset to me. But that's what she said.'

If this was all meant to increase the impact of the gossip, it wasn't working: Callie was beginning to get bored. She crossed to her basin, twisted the cold tap and reached for her toothbrush.

'It's about Mad Phil,' Tamsin revealed.

Callie applied a squeeze of toothpaste to the brush and started on her back teeth. Mad Phil Moody seemed to her the least gossip-worthy of people, from what she had seen of him as her personal tutor and in tutor group. He appeared to have no private life as such, living alone as a bachelor in his little college-provided house. The main interest of his life was theology. What on earth could he have done to provoke upsetting gossip? Forgotten to put his bin out on the proper night, perhaps? Nicked an extra sausage at breakfast?

'She said he has a girlfriend.'

'A girlfriend?' Callie spoke through a mouth full of toothpaste, turning to face her friend with an incredulous look.

'A *young* girlfriend. An undergraduate, most likely.'

Callie turned back to the basin, spat and rinsed her mouth before dignifying that with a reply. 'That's absolutely ridiculous.'

'She saw him. Them. That's what she said.' Tamsin shook her head, causing her curls to bounce. 'I'm just telling you what she said.'

'She *saw* them,' Callie repeated scornfully.

'Kissing,' Tamsin added with ill-disguised relish. 'In his back garden. Hugging and kissing.'

Callie stared at her.

'That's what she said. That's what she saw. I'm not making it up.'

'No,' said Callie. 'No way. Mad Phil? I don't believe it. Not for a minute.'

The way that grief – bereavement – affected different people in diverse ways was something that had always interested Miranda Frost. Professionally, she had often observed it and had concluded that there was no way to predict how people would react. Yes, there were stages of grief which were fairly predictable, but they manifested themselves in ways that were not. And it wasn't just individuals: it was families – couples – with their own dynamics which combined in various ways to make things either easier or more difficult. In Miranda's experience, grief could either bring a couple together, or it could drive them apart; rarely was there a middle ground, with a relationship which remained untouched.

So often, she had observed, guilt and blame were involved, muddled together and liable to turn from one to the other in an instant. It was

105

a toxic formula. 'If only you hadn't given her the car keys ...', 'If you hadn't said that ...', 'If you'd just noticed ...'.

It wasn't, though, something she'd been thinking about consciously in the last twenty-four hours. Her own feelings were muddled, chaotic, anything but rational or analytical.

She'd taken a sedative. That was something she always prescribed for people who had suffered unexpected bereavement, and she'd decided it would be foolish to ignore her own advice.

Richard, however, had refused to have one. He was a grown-up; she couldn't force him to do it.

And he was no longer in bed beside her, Miranda realized as she woke up, groggily, to the sound of a distant telephone ringing. It stopped, abruptly, but it was too late: she was awake.

She groaned and struggled up into a sitting position as everything came back to her. The sedative had given her a full night's sleep, had suppressed her dreams, and that was a blessing, but it couldn't take away the living nightmare that her life had now become. Sebastian was dead. Fact.

Dead this morning, dead tomorrow. And every day from now on. Miranda didn't know why she should even bother to get out of bed.

There was a mug of coffee on the bedside table. Miranda reached for it automatically.

Cold. As cold as her dead son, on the slab in the mortuary.

But where had it come from? Presumably that nice policeman, the Italian one, had made it for her. That seemed to be his main function, along with answering the phone.

She put the cold coffee back on the bedside table and, telling herself that she had to get up whether she wanted to or not, reached for her dressing gown.

Brian Stanford had gone out to visit a few of his devout but housebound parishioners and take them their Easter communion, so Jane had a bit of time to herself. She started a load of washing – Brian's alb and some other whites – then did the breakfast washing-up, and finally sat down for a few minutes with a cup of coffee, alone for the first time since she'd discovered her condition.

This time next year she would be washing nappies. It was an old-fashioned thing to do, she knew – these days everyone used disposable ones. Easier, yes, but even if she could afford them, Jane knew she wouldn't be going down that road. Easier wasn't always better; she'd learnt that

106

at her mother's knee, and a good thing too. Life as a vicar's wife had its compensations and she wouldn't have chosen any other life for herself, but ease wasn't one of the qualities associated with that particular path.

How was she going to tell Brian? He was going to be shocked, she knew: even though they'd been trying for a baby, she didn't think that Brian really believed it would happen. Had *she* even really believed it? Jane wasn't sure, in retrospect. It *had* happened, though, and it was too late to second-guess now. Nappies, sleepless nights, noise, mess. Their lives were certainly never going to be the same again. Not for another eighteen years or so, anyway. And by then Brian would be nearing retirement age, facing other momentous changes.

The phone rang, startling Jane out of her reverie. It was probably just a parishioner, wanting to bend her ear about the flower rota or talk to Brian about some personal problem. She answered it. 'Hello?'

'Mum?'

It was Simon, the twin to whom Jane had always felt closer. She knew that parents weren't supposed to have favourites, and she didn't – not really – but Simon was the one she understood better. He was more sensitive and intense, more like her than his breezy and sometimes cynical brother.

She hadn't seen Simon for weeks. At the start of the Easter vac he'd gone to stay with his girlfriend's parents in Northamptonshire, and was due to travel with them to the South of France. He'd rung on Easter Day, of course, but his own parents would be lucky if he found the time to come to London before the start of Trinity term.

'Simon!' she said. 'Aren't you supposed to be on the way to France?'

'Later today,' he confirmed. 'We're flying from Luton this afternoon.'

Jane didn't approve, though she knew she didn't have any say in the matter. It wasn't just that she felt Simon's place was at home, with his own family. She resented the fact that Ellie's parents, the Dickinsons, were wealthy enough to subsidize her son's holiday travels, and that they assumed it was all right just because they had the means to fund it. Simon and Ellie, sharing a room, a bed, in some villa in the South of France ... They wouldn't have to bother observing the proprieties as they did when they were under Jane's roof, in the separate rooms she insisted upon. It wasn't right.

'Well, I hope you have a nice time,' she said as neutrally as she could manage.

107

'Actually, Mum, there's something I need to talk to you about. Before we go.'

Jane's heart leapt. Simon had always confided in her, in the old days. The days before Ellie. Had he seen the error of his ways? Had he realized that Ellie wasn't the right one for him after all?

'Yes?' She tried not to sound too eager.

'Is Dad there?'

'No, he's not. He's doing home communions.'

'Good,' said Simon, and Jane smiled to herself. Simon *did* want to talk to her about something important. Something Brian might not like.

'The thing is, Mum...' Simon paused, long enough for several scenarios to unfold in his mother's brain. 'The thing is... we're having a baby,' he blurted out.

Jane's brain wasn't working fast enough. 'A baby...?' she echoed.

'We didn't plan it, of course,' he added quickly, defensively. 'Sometimes things just happen.'

'Yeeees...'

'I know the timing isn't good,' he went on. 'Ellie will barely finish Michaelmas term. She'll probably have to take a term or two out after the baby's born.'

Jane reminded herself to breathe. She couldn't believe what she was hearing. 'Ellie's having a baby,' she stated, trying to persuade herself that she wasn't dreaming.

'That's what I said. We'll get married, of course,' Simon added. 'As soon as possible.'

'But... Simon! You can't get married. You're too young. And your studies. Oxford...'

He gave a wry laugh. 'I'm old enough to have a baby, Mum. It's going to happen. So the rest is a non-issue.'

'Oh, Simon.'

'Don't worry, Mum. We'll make it work. One way or another. Ellie's parents can help us financially, even if you and Dad can't. We'll find digs in Oxford after next term. As I said, Ellie may have to take a couple of terms out, but I'll carry on. It will be fine – you'll see.' His voice was hearty, as if he were attempting to convince himself.

Jane seized on something he'd said. 'Ellie's parents... they know about this?'

'Yes, of course. She told them straightaway, as soon as she was sure. Right after she told *me*.' Simon added, 'Ellie's very close to her mum. And they've both been really supportive. Just like I know you'll be,

Mum.' He gave a little laugh. 'Once you get used to the idea of being a granny.'

'Oh.' Jane's eyes widened: she was going to be a granny. A *granny*.

'I know it's a bit of a shock, Mum. Out of the blue like this. But you'll cope. And,' he added smoothly, 'I'll leave it up to you to tell Dad. When you think he can handle it. You'll know when the time is right to tell him.'

Simon went on for another minute or so in that vein, breezily conveyed Ellie's love – which Jane knew to be insincere – then rang off.

Jane stood with the dead receiver in her hand for what seemed like hours, staring at the phone on the wall. She felt numb.

Just a few minutes ago she'd been thinking about how she was going to tell Brian that he was going to be a father. Now she had something else to break to him. Now she would have to tell him that he was going to be a granddad as well.

'Lilith Noone!' said the furious voice on the other end of Mark's mobile phone. 'Why in God's name didn't you tell me she was on to it? You must have known.'

Mark had never heard Neville in a lather like this, at least not directed at him. 'I'm sorry,' he said straightaway. 'She was hanging round the mortuary when I took them there. I should have mentioned it to you.'

'Damn right you should have.'

'I'm sorry,' Mark repeated contritely.

Neville sighed down the phone; his next remarks were in a more reasonable tone. 'Not that it would have made any difference. That pestilential woman – she just seems to have a sixth sense. For making my life a misery.'

'I haven't seen the story,' Mark admitted.

'Neither had I. But Evans had. You can imagine.'

Mark could: Evans didn't like being bested by the press in any form, and Lilith Noone was the worst of the lot. He was glad he hadn't been in Neville's shoes at that particular interview.

He was on his way to Westminster Coroner Court, for a meeting with the coroner, to discuss on behalf of the parents what the plans were for the inquest into the death of Sebastian Frost. As it was a beautiful morning, he'd decided to go on foot, admitting to himself that he was in no great rush to resume his duties at the Frosts' house.

'Anyway,' Neville went on, 'there's to be a news conference this afternoon. A bit of damage control at this point, as well as seeing if anything useful to the investigation comes out of it.'

'You don't have anyone in the frame at the moment? One of his friends, maybe?' Mark suggested.

'Nothing. No one. No witnesses, and no one claims to be able to think of any reason why Sebastian Frost was stabbed.'

Mark wove between two people who were walking abreast on the pavement; they both glared at him. 'But someone did stab him.'

'Thanks for pointing out the bloody obvious,' Neville snapped.

'Sorry,' Mark repeated.

Once again Neville sighed. 'I'm sorry, mate. I shouldn't be taking it out on you. I just don't know where we're going with this thing. With the school holidays, tracking down every one of his classmates and talking to them is impossible. Half of them are probably abroad, for God's sake. It's a bloody nightmare. At this point, the news conference is just about our only hope of coming up with something.'

'Will you want the Frosts to be there?'

'Yes. It might help.'

The grieving family was now a set piece in most news conferences of this sort, Mark knew. An impassioned plea for information from a bereaved parent or spouse, tugging at the heartstrings, occasionally elicited some crucial clue from a member of the public. In this case he wasn't sure it would work: if Sebastian's parents remained self-controlled and subdued, as they'd been yesterday, their presence wouldn't have the desired impact.

'All right. I'll make sure they're there,' he said.

'I'll be sending a team to the house this morning,' Neville added. 'To do a thorough search of the boy's room. Bring in his computer for Danny to have a look at, and that sort of thing. Diaries, papers, anything that might have a bearing.'

'Right. If you could hold off for a bit, it will give me time to get back and prepare the Frosts for the invasion.' Mark explained his current errand of liaising with the coroner.

'I'll give you an hour,' Neville stated. 'I can't afford any more delay than that.'

'Thanks.'

'And if you could ring me if there's *anything* I need to know—'

'Yes,' Mark promised guiltily. He had almost reached the coroner's court building, where he was due for the meeting in Hereward Rice's office. But there was one thing he needed to do first. He popped into the newsagent's across from the court and bought a copy of the *Daily Globe*, its front page emblazoned with the headline 'A Father's Agony'.

Miranda came down the stairs, heading for the kitchen, when she heard the rustle of a newspaper in the front room. She put her head round the door; Richard was on the sofa, reading his *Guardian*.

'Nothing in there about ... Sebastian?' she asked.

He didn't look up. 'No.'

'Is the policeman here?' She knew his name was Mark; he'd invited them to address him that way, but Miranda didn't yet feel comfortable using his Christian name. It gave him a status that she didn't feel he had earned.

'No,' Richard repeated. This time he glanced up at her. 'Mark told me last night that he was meeting with the coroner this morning. And he's unplugged the phone,' he added. 'He warned me that the press would probably be on to us first thing this morning.'

She held up the mug of cold coffee. 'He didn't make the coffee, then?'

'I made it,' her husband admitted.

Miranda's eyes widened. 'You used my coffee machine?'

He nodded. 'I thought you'd want some coffee when you woke up.'

Anger flared in her, pure and hot. 'But I've told you not to touch that machine! It's delicate! You could break it if you pushed the wrong button!'

'It's not that complicated. I'm a grown-up.'

For some reason that made her even angrier; she had an almost irresistible urge to dump the cold coffee on him, curbed only by the realization of what it would do to the furniture and the carpet.

'Don't you ever touch it again!' she snapped, turning her back on him and stalking to the kitchen.

How dare he? She set the machine in motion, fuming at her husband's audacity. His insensitivity.

Using her coffee machine. Then sitting there reading the paper, like it was an ordinary day. What sort of a monster was he?

Her first cup of coffee, quickly gulped down, helped to restore her and put things into some sort of perspective. Maybe he *was* just trying to be helpful and considerate, Miranda told herself begrudgingly.

She made herself another cup and carried it up two flights of stairs to the top floor, where on either side of the landing, under the eaves, was tucked a small room serving as an office. Hers was on the right, and Richard's on the left. They each had their own books, their own computer.

Miranda was awake now, and wanted to see whether anything about Sebastian's death had been picked up yet online. She switched on her computer, waited for it to boot, then googled 'Sebastian Frost'.

A moment later she stared at the screen, unable to believe what she was reading. 'A Father's Agony.'

Richard had told a reporter, for all the world to read, that his wife was too wrapped up in her own grief to realize that he had lost his son as well, that he was hurting as much as she was.

Unbelievable.

Outrageous.

She went to the top of the stairs and shouted down. 'Richard! Come here – now!'

Margaret made an effort to get to her desk early on Tuesday morning, before the first session was due to begin, determined to show her secretary that she was working hard. She wasn't sure why Hanna Young brought out these feelings of guilt and inadequacy in her. Hanna didn't usually say anything, but she had a way of looking at Margaret that made her feel she was being judged, and often found wanting.

The look she gave Margaret this morning, though, was slightly different: her brows drawn together, as though something was worrying her. 'All right, Hanna?' Margaret said cheerfully. She couldn't help it. Last night she'd slept better than she had in weeks, unhaunted by troubling dreams. Today was another beautiful day, and she was planning to enjoy it.

'Yeees . . .' Hanna paused by Margaret's desk, seemingly on the brink of asking or telling her something.

Margaret decided that whatever it was, she didn't want to hear it. 'I'll be away from the office for most of the day, of course,' she said briskly. 'It's important for me to be there for the sessions, even just as an observer. So is there any post I need to look at before I have to go?'

'Nothing urgent,' Hanna said. She indicated a neat pile of opened post in the centre of Margaret's desk. 'There's a card from your son. I've put that on top.'

Margaret smiled as she opened it. An Easter card – very thoughtful of Alexander, even if he hadn't managed to post it soon enough to get here in time. It was signed 'with best love from Alexander and Luke'. She propped it up on her desk where she could see it.

'Well, then,' she said, getting up, 'I suppose I'll—'

'Actually, there *is* something,' Hanna interrupted her. 'Something I think I should tell you, to be honest.'

She was going to hear this whether she wanted to or not, Margaret realized, resigned. 'Yes?' She turned her face towards her secretary, assuming an expression of interest.

'It's about—' Hanna stopped and looked in the direction of the door, which was swinging open.

Keith Moody came in, sharing a tentative smile between the two women. 'Hope I'm not interrupting anything,' he said apologetically.

'No,' said Hanna. She turned and retreated to her own office, shutting the connecting door after her.

Keith raised his eyebrows at Margaret. 'Was it something I said?'

'I don't think so.' Margaret couldn't help feeling relieved at the interruption, and grateful to Keith for providing it, however inadvertently.

'Anyway, I didn't mean to intrude. If it isn't convenient, just tell me to go away.'

She smiled. 'Actually, I was just leaving. For the lecture hall. If you're heading that way, we can walk over together.'

'Perfect.'

He fell into step beside her. 'I wanted to ask you something. You like music, don't you?'

'Of course.'

'When I found out that John Kingsley was going to be here this week, I ordered a couple of tickets for tonight's concert at King's College Chapel. Ensemble Sine Nomine – that fantastic early music group. It sold out almost immediately, so I was lucky to get the tickets.'

'He should enjoy that,' she said.

Keith gave her a rueful smile. 'The thing is, when I told him about it at breakfast, thinking he'd be really pleased, he said that he doesn't go out much in the evenings these days. Too old, he said, and he needs to save his strength.'

'Oh!' Margaret felt guilty; were they demanding too much of an old man? Canon Kingsley didn't seem that frail, and his mental acuity wasn't lacking in the least, but he *was* getting on in years.

'So I was wondering,' Keith went on, 'whether you would be free to go with me this evening? So the ticket doesn't go to waste? It should be an excellent concert,' he added.

'I'd love to,' she said promptly. 'You don't need to convince me. I'd love to go.'

Interlude: from the Metropolitan Police website, Tuesday morning

Investigations are under way in the stabbing death of a teenage boy.

Police were called at 00.13 hrs on Monday morning re: a body found on Paddington Green. The victim was pronounced dead at the scene and was later identified as Sebastian Frost, age 15, of Paddington. A post-mortem gave cause of death as a stab wound to the throat.

DI Neville Stewart heads the investigation, based at Paddington Green. He is appealing for any information which could lead to the apprehension of the perpetrator. A news conference will be held at 14.00 hrs on Tuesday.

CHAPTER 10

Coroner Hereward Rice was a busy man – as he constantly reminded anyone who would listen – so Mark had to wait a few minutes outside the inner sanctum of his office before his turn came to speak to him. That gave him a chance to read the lead story in the *Daily Globe*, then put the paper in the bin.

It was bad. Really bad. No wonder Evans was having a coronary. The only good thing about it, Mark reflected, was that Miranda Frost was unlikely to see it. She didn't strike him as a *Globe* reader, and in any case they were shut up in their house, not wandering down to the local newsagent's. Unless some well-meaning person called her attention to it, she might never know.

Nonetheless he wasn't exactly looking forward to getting back to the Frosts' house. They probably weren't going to be best pleased about the invasion of Neville's team, and he wasn't sure how they would feel about appearing at the news conference.

The meeting with the coroner was straightforward and to the point: an inquest would be opened on Wednesday afternoon, and unless the police made a huge breakthrough within the next twenty-four hours or so, it would be adjourned to a future date. The parents' attendance was not necessary, though they could come if they wished.

He made his way to Paddington by Tube, and walked quickly to St Michael's Street, where he was relieved to see that there were neither press photographers in waiting nor evidence of police presence.

Richard Frost let him in with a thin smile and a semi-apologetic shrug.

Over the last few months, within his own family, Mark had become sensitive to atmosphere within a house. And this morning the Frosts' house possessed an atmosphere you could cut with a knife.

'Miranda's not very happy with me, I'm afraid,' Richard told him.

That was an understatement. Miranda was not speaking to Richard, which, from Mark's point of view, was perhaps a good thing. She had evidently given him the full blast of her fury before Mark's arrival, and was now ignoring him.

'My husband couldn't talk to me about it, but he saw fit to tell some stranger – some scumbag of a tabloid journalist – that I wasn't sufficiently

115

sensitive to his feelings of bereavement,' she told Mark, with a sideways glare in Richard's direction.

'But . . . how did you find out?' he blurted out, realizing as he said it that he was betraying his own knowledge.

'Internet,' she said succinctly, then turned her back on him – on both of them – and stalked towards the kitchen, presumably to refill her coffee mug.

Of course. He should have thought of that, Mark berated himself. Of course she would have been on Google to see what was going on.

It was a funny thing about humans, he reflected: sometimes you bonded with them, and sometimes you didn't. You never could tell which way it was going to go.

In the course of his job, working with people who had suffered a loss very close to them, Mark possessed a natural sympathy, generally accompanied by empathy. Even in cases where the family members were themselves suspects, possibly guilty of murder, he could find himself liking them, rooting for them to be innocent.

When it came to the Frosts, though, Mark was struggling. Of course he had sympathy for them – they had lost their only child, and in brutal, horrible circumstances – but the empathy wasn't there. Richard seemed to him to be ineffectual and self-pitying, while Miranda was brittle and controlling. And he had the feeling that they didn't like him much either, resenting his presence in their life. It made it so much more difficult to carry out his job. He didn't ask for gratitude – that was a bit much to expect – but a semblance of co-operation would be useful.

'I don't want to go to the news conference,' Miranda stated when he put it to her. 'I don't want to be a grieving parent for the benefit of the gutter press. My husband has already done a good enough job of that.'

'We never know what may turn up from a news conference,' Mark attempted. 'You *do* want us to catch Sebastian's killer, don't you?'

That elicited a withering look.

'I think we should go,' Richard put in, touching her arm. 'I'm going to do it, even if you don't. I think we need to help the police as much as we can.'

Miranda jerked away from him. 'Oh, all right then. But only for Sebastian's sake.'

The doorbell rang. Mark went to answer it.

Sid Cowley was lounging against the railings, smoking a cigarette, with two other officers behind him. 'The guv sent us,' he said, dropping his fag and grinding it out with his heel. 'To get the computer and have a butcher's at the lad's things.' He stepped through the door, into the entrance hall.

The poisonous look Miranda had given Mark was nothing compared to the one she now directed at the unfortunate Cowley. 'Out!' she commanded, adding to Mark, 'I will *not* have that man in my house. It's outrageous. Get him out of here – *now.*'

Callie had found the morning session interesting, if a bit intense. There had been role playing, and this time she hadn't managed to get out of it: she'd had to impersonate a difficult parishioner in conversation with Tamsin.

After lunch she escaped to her room for a bit of downtime. Much as she enjoyed being with her friends, it *was* wearing, she admitted to herself, and she felt she needed to be on her own for a few minutes.

She collapsed into the comfy chair and got out her phone to ring Peter. First she tried her home number; when there was no reply she rang her brother's mobile. He answered after a couple of rings. 'Where are you?' she asked him.

'In the park. Walking Bella. See, Sis – I told you I'd take good care of her.'

Callie was impressed; she hadn't expected him to be that conscientious. 'How is she?'

'Not missing you in the least,' he said callously. 'We're having a grand time.'

'I hope you aren't spoiling her. With treats and things.'

Peter chuckled. 'Just the odd sausage. Did you know she loves sausages?'

'Oh, Peter! You mustn't give her sausages.' She'd *known* it was a bad idea to leave Bella with Peter. Now she wouldn't be able to eat a meal without Bella begging at her feet.

'But she loves them. They make her happy. Why shouldn't we have things that make us happy?'

It was, Callie told herself, a reasonable philosophical question. Theological, even. If it had been anyone but Peter asking it . . . He was just trying to wind her up. Time to change the subject, she decided.

'Is everything else all right? Any messages, or urgent post?'

'You had a visitor,' Peter said. 'Yesterday afternoon.'

She hadn't been expecting anyone. Frances knew she was away, as did anyone else who was likely to drop by. 'Well, who was it?'

'The new vicar of St John's, Lancaster Gate. Said he was just calling by to introduce himself.'

'Oh!' Callie knew that her neighbouring church had a new vicar; Brian had been invited to the induction a week or two ago and had told her about it. 'Michael something, isn't he?'

'That's right. Father Michael.' Peter sighed loudly and expressively down the phone. 'Sis, he's gorgeous!'

'Gorgeous?'

'No mere clergyman has the right to be that fanciable. It's against the laws of nature.'

Callie hoped, fervently, that he was just winding her up again. That was the last thing she needed – to have her brother pursuing a colleague in the next parish. 'Oh, Peter, don't,' she said.

'I'm just telling you the truth. A dish in a dog collar. And he has a dog, as well,' he added. 'A black Lab. I was rather hoping we might meet by chance, walking in the park.'

So that explained the conscientious dog-walking: Bella was being used in pursuit of a romantic dream. She should have known it would be something like that.

'Leave him alone,' she said sternly. 'I mean it.'

'Got to go now, Sis,' Peter said, as if she hadn't spoken. 'I think I see a black Lab in the distance.'

Disconnected. Callie stared at the symbol on the phone screen, shaking her head. What was she going to do with him?

While pondering that question, she leaned back in her chair and looked at the stone fireplace. It was original to the room, and once would have been the sole source of heat for its occupant. Some years ago the building had acquired central heating in the form of rather old-fashioned radiators, and the fireplace chimneys had been blocked up, removing their functionality but retaining them as a decorative feature. When this room had belonged to Callie, she had put a basket of flower-bedecked fairy lights in the fireplace to provide a bit of atmosphere; the current resident was more practical, using it as a storage space for theology books. A guy? Probably, she thought idly, examining the room for clues to its inhabitant's gender.

There weren't any other clues in evidence. The curtains and bedspread were generic, provided by the college, and no personal belongings – other than the books – were visible. Callie knew that between terms the students were expected to remove their possessions from their rooms so that the college could utilize the accommodation for conferences, retreatants, and tourists on a tight budget. Somehow the books had been left behind, tucked into the fireplace.

Something tugged at Callie's memory. A hiding place . . .

A little shelf, up in the chimney. She remembered it now: she'd discovered it at some point during her first year, and had used it to secrete things she didn't want Tamsin to see. Had the current resident found it as well?

Curious, if guiltily so, Callie got up from the chair and knelt on the hearth, sticking her hand under the hood of the fireplace and up the chimney. Her fingers encountered stone, then the hard edge of the shelf, and finally something that felt like a bundle of paper. Feeling really guilty now, she grasped the paper and pulled it out into the light of day.

News conferences: Neville hated them. He'd hated them back when they were called 'press' conferences, and attended largely by print journalists. Now they were far worse, with the inevitable presence of television cameras, not to mention bloggers and people posting live updates via Twitter – or so he'd been told.

This news conference, he was sure, would attract more than a normal amount of attention. Teen stabbings were flavour of the month anyway, and this one was out of the ordinary. Not a street kid, not a gang fight, but a middle-class boy with professional parents.

And no obvious suspects. No one in the frame.

The press would be salivating, out for blood. The police's blood – *his* blood.

Neville hadn't had time to prepare his statement properly, to his liking. He'd been working away on it at his desk when he'd been called back to the Frosts' house. Emergency: bloody Miranda Frost wouldn't allow Sid Cowley through the door. Sid and his big mouth, buggering things up. So Neville had had to drop everything and do the job himself.

Now it was almost show time, and Neville was in the gents, trying to make himself look respectable. If he'd thought about the news conference when he got dressed that morning, he'd have been more careful about his wardrobe. He'd have put on a telly-worthy suit, rather than his old beat-up tweed jacket. As it was, he'd even had to borrow a tie off a fashion-conscious DC. He draped it round his neck and squinted into the mirror above the basin, attempting to make a good job of tying it in the horrid glare of the fluorescent lights. He adjusted the knot, ran his hand over his chin – should have shaved with a bit more care – and over his head, smoothing his hair into some semblance of shape.

He'd run out of time. Now he just had to get on with it.

Callie stared at the bundle in her hand, her brain refusing to believe what she was seeing. It was a thick wad of papers and photos, tied round with a silver ribbon.

Hers.

She went hot, then cold, then hot again.

After a minute she realized how uncomfortable she was, kneeling on the hearth, and found her way back to the chair, where she rested the bundle in her lap and plucked at the ribbon with trembling fingers.

The bow came undone; Callie closed her eyes, then opened them again.

Still there, loose now on her lap. Photos, notes, cards.

Without volition she picked up the top photo. It showed a smiling Callie, a smiling Adam. His arm tightly round her shoulders as she stretched her left hand towards the camera. On her finger was the only ring he'd ever given her, fashioned out of a gold metallic sweet wrapper in a moment of romantic high spirits. All he could afford . . .

Beneath that were various scribbled notes in Adam's nearly illegible handwriting, passed to her during theology lectures. Ragged-edged, torn out of his notebook. Undated, but through them it was possible to trace the progression of their relationship. The early ones were mostly just funny; they grew increasingly romantic, and the later ones were declarations of love, festooned with doodled hearts and flowers.

More photos of them together.

And greetings cards, with printed sentiments of love. Signed with hugs and kisses.

She'd kept them all, treasured them. Tied them up with a silver ribbon.

And hidden them in the safest place she could find.

Why were they still there?

Callie tried to think. Why hadn't she removed them, destroyed them?

Adam's bombshell – that he had fallen in love with someone else during his parish placement – had occurred right at the end of their time at Archbishop Temple House, as they all prepared to move out and relocate in their new parishes. She'd been in shock, obviously. She hadn't seen it coming, and it had knocked her sideways, into a state of denial for weeks. In the midst of that she'd packed up and set off to start afresh in Bayswater.

The last thing on her mind had been retrieving the tangible reminders of the love she and Adam had shared. She couldn't wait to get out of that room, out of the college, out of Cambridge. Away from everything that held memories of Adam.

She had, in her numb-minded distress, simply forgotten that the bundle was there.

What if the new inhabitant of the room had discovered it? Again Callie went cold, then hot.

How embarrassing. How humiliating. If he had . . .

But he probably hadn't, she told herself firmly. If it was a 'he' . . . He probably didn't see the fireplace as anything other than a convenient receptacle for his overflow of books, not as a hiding place for precious personal memorabilia.

Oh, God.

Callie took a deep breath. If only she could kindle a fire in the fireplace right now, and reduce these things to a pile of ashes, she would do it.

Lilith positioned herself in the front row at the news conference. She felt she'd earned that position, as the only journalist who had covered the story to date. That, she was aware, was about to change. There was bound to be a great deal of interest in it – for a few days at least, or until the police caught the killer. She looked round the room: it was pretty well full, with print journalists filling the chairs at the front, bloggers and tweeters in the middle, and video cameras at the back.

Not just a couple of down-and-outs whose no-hoper son had been knifed by some other loser. The Frosts were an attractive professional couple, the sort who didn't have this kind of thing happen to them. That's what made them interesting. That's what made the whole thing interesting. There was nothing cut and dried about this case.

As the principals filed on to the stage, she looked down at her note-book, avoiding eye contact with any of her known police adversaries, or with Dr Richard Frost. He probably wasn't feeling too anxious to establish contact with her, either. She observed, from under lowered lids, that his wife put some distance between them as they took their seats, moving her chair a good six inches farther from him.

If the Frosts *had* been a couple of down-and-outs, Lilith doubted that the proceedings would have merited the presence of Detective Superintendent Evans, but DS Evans was indeed there, in all his grotesque ugliness. His prognathous jaw was thrust out even further than usual, she fancied, as he welcomed the audience, thanked them for coming, and introduced Detective Inspector Neville Stewart, the senior investigating officer.

Stewart, she was interested to see, was looking a bit seedy this afternoon. Was this case getting to him, or was it something else? He hadn't exactly dressed up for the occasion, and the lines round his eyes were more pronounced than she remembered.

'As Detective Superintendent Evans has indicated,' he began in that maddeningly sexy Irish voice, 'we've invited you here today to talk about the murder of Sebastian Frost.' He pulled a ragged bit of paper out of the pocket of his tweed jacket and read from it. 'Sebastian Frost, aged fifteen, of St Michael's Street, Paddington, was stabbed to death on Paddington Green late on Sunday night, or in the early hours of Monday morning. A post-mortem examination has been carried out, and the cause of death was established as a knife wound to the throat, severing the jugular. We appeal to anyone who was in the area at the time of the incident who may have seen or heard anything suspicious, or has any information about this incident, to contact us in confidence.' He gave the phone number, then added, 'Anonymous information would also be welcome at Crimestoppers, on 0800 555 111. We do need your help to find the person or persons who carried out this horrific murder.'

He seemed to have run out of words on his paper; at that point he stuffed it back in his pocket, looked up and said, 'We'll be happy to take your questions in a moment or two. Now, though, I'm going to ask Sebastian Frost's parents to say a few words.'

Richard Frost leaned towards the microphone on the table, between him and his wife.

She had loved Adam. He had loved her; she had loved him. There was no doubt about that. The bundle of memories, tied up with a silver ribbon, brought it all back with a force that was almost physical.

Over the past months that was something Callie had tried to forget, to downplay in her own mind. As Marco had become more important to her, her previous relationship with Adam had been reduced to a passing thing, a romance of a lesser magnitude.

But she *had* loved him, truly. However little worthy of her love he had proved to be, she had loved him. He'd been in her thoughts constantly; he'd brought her happiness in that present, and in that present – now past – her future was tied up with his.

Except that it hadn't been. He'd gone his own way, left her behind. He'd made his own future, one in which she had no part.

And her own future now included – revolved round – Marco.

Or did it?

Was she just falling into the same trap, all over again? Out of the frying pan, and all that?

Marco wasn't anything like Adam. But would he hurt her as well, maybe in a different way yet with equally painful results?

In a year's time, would she be looking back on her relationship with Marco, and wonder how she'd ever let herself get involved with him?

Callie's hands were shaking; she clasped them together in her lap.

She loved Marco, she told herself; she believed that they could make a future together.

But she had believed that – just as fervently, just as honestly – about Adam as well. A year ago she'd been in love with him, wrapped up in plans for their shared future. Now she couldn't bear the sight of him.

Marco and his family, *la famiglia Lombardi* . . .

Would he always, in a crisis, put them first? Would he ever be strong enough to stand up against them?

Adam, whatever else you might say about him, was strong. He knew what he wanted, and he went after it. There was a certainty about him that had once attracted her – a quality that she, who lived her life in a much more tentative way, knew that she lacked.

That certainty was now manifesting itself in a rather unattractive brand of religious fundamentalism, and she liked him the less for that. But Adam's strength of mind and purpose had much to be said for it. If Marco had just a bit more of that sort of strength . . .

He wouldn't be Marco, she told herself firmly. She loved Marco, just the way he was. Gentle, empathetic Marco.

And he loved her, and wanted her to be his wife.

Callie twisted the ring on her finger. The ring which had belonged to his grandmother, a symbol which bound her into the Lombardi family. But would she ever truly be a part of it? Would they be able to accept her – English, Anglican, a priest? – into that tightly knit Italian unit?

And was that what she really wanted for herself? To be sucked into that matriarchal world, where Mamma reigned supreme, with Serena not far behind, and Marco falling in with whatever they decreed, all for the sake of a quiet life?

She swallowed hard, gulping back a sob, and twisted the ring off.

Adam had been a mistake – she could see that now, very clearly, though it hadn't been at all clear at the time.

Maybe Marco was a mistake as well. Maybe he had come along too soon, when she was needy and vulnerable, and it had all happened too fast.

And maybe, Callie told herself, she needed to give it a lot more thought before she committed herself to another big mistake.

When Mark's brother-in-law Joe had been murdered, not that many weeks ago, there hadn't been a news conference. It had been altogether a more private death, at least as far as public interest was concerned during the investigation. That had been one of the few mercies, Mark reflected, as he sat beside Miranda Frost on the platform. Serena and the rest of the family had been spared this ordeal.

It was part of his job to be there, to provide support for the family. Sometimes, when the family were too distraught to speak – or too inarticulate – he might be called upon to read out a prepared statement on their behalf. In this instance, though, the Frosts were more than capable of speaking for themselves, even if it was reluctant in Miranda's case.

They knew what the police expected of them, and why it was important for them to be seen by the press. Richard, who spoke first, was pitch-perfect. His voice wobbled; his eyes filled with tears; he ran a distraught hand through his springy brown curls.

'Our son Sebastian was a fine young man,' he said. 'He had so much to live for. He was a gifted student, a gifted athlete. He was popular with his friends. He loved life. He could have accomplished so much if he had lived. His . . . death . . . is a tragedy not just for us, but for everyone.' He stopped for a moment, drawing a deep breath before continuing, as the television cameras zoomed in for a close-up. 'Please, please. If you know anything that will help to catch the monster that did this to our son, ring the police. It won't bring him back, but we need to know. For ourselves, and for everyone else who loved him. And so that justice may be done.' The tears spilled over and rolled down his face; he got out a handkerchief and wiped them away, then leaned back from the microphone and closed his eyes, his part done.

124

It would make good television, Mark judged. An effective performance.

Lilith Noone, he saw, was sitting on the front row, smiling. Pleased with herself, obviously. For an instant he caught her eye, then she looked away deliberately.

Now it was Miranda's turn. Mark could feel the anger rolling off her in waves as she pulled the microphone towards her. She yanked it out of its stand and rose to her feet. 'I had a son,' she said with quiet force. 'Just one. My only child. Now he's dead. The person who murdered him has not only killed the best son in the world. They've also destroyed our family.' She narrowed her eyes and turned her head slowly, sweeping the room, staring down every person in it, ending with the television cameras. 'I hope they're happy,' she concluded. 'And I hope they rot in hell.'

Mark sensed the collective indrawn breath as she sat down, her face set, refusing to shed tears on demand. Yet she'd done what had been asked of her, and had done it superlatively well. He found himself liking her a bit more for it.

Interlude: an anonymous phone message, left on Tuesday night

Umm ... is this the number to ring about Seb Frost? I guess it is.

The thing is, you've got it wrong. Seb Frost wasn't a saint. Nothing like it. His parents might think the sun shone out of his bum, but they were wrong. He was a nasty piece of work. An arrogant bastard, and worse. Whoever killed him, I reckon he deserved it.

If you don't believe me, ask his mates. Ask that Hugo. Ask him about the bullying. Not that he's any better, mind you. He'll lie through his teeth to protect them all – Seb and all his crowd. But ask him.

I'm telling you the truth. The real truth.

CHAPTER 11

Margaret was smiling when she woke up. No nightmares of Hal; only pleasant dreams.

She was smiling as she showered, as she dressed. Not even the thought of Hanna, waiting for her in her office with a disapproving expression, was enough to wipe the smile off her face as she went to Morning Prayer.

Involuntarily her eyes searched the chapel for Keith, then she reminded herself that he wouldn't be there, nor would he be at breakfast in the dining hall: this morning he would be hosting his old tutor group, and they would have their own act of worship, their own breakfast. All of the tutor groups were having reunions this morning, so the congregation for Morning Prayer was minimal.

She tried to keep her mind on the liturgy, but it was difficult. The words were familiar, ingrained, and tripped off her tongue without any intervention from her brain. 'O Lord, open thou our lips . . .', 'Our Father, which art in heaven . . .'

It had been a wonderful evening. The weather had continued to be unseasonably balmy, so the walk across the Backs to King's College Chapel was a sensory delight. The earthy smell of the spring flowers, the touch of the breeze on her warm skin, the laughter of the punters on the river, the glint of the water, sparkling in the slanting rays of the setting sun as she and Keith crossed the bridge.

And the concert was superb – a feast for the ears, balm for the heart. In the amazing acoustic of the soaring Perpendicular chapel, a few perfectly tuned voices filled the space completely, ravishingly. Margaret didn't want it to end, ever.

Of course it did end. Keith seemed to sense – and share – her mood of elation at the beauty of the music, so he didn't descend to meaningless chit-chat as they walked back through the water meadows and across the bridge.

In the dark, in the silence of their wordless communion, it was even more magical. They paused on the bridge, leaning on the side rails, watching the water – black now – as it flowed beneath them. His arm, in its rough tweed sleeve, brushed against hers, and she shivered slightly.

For the first time, she was aware of him as a man, and the sensation was both disturbing and pleasurable. The faint spicy scent of his aftershave, the feel of his sleeve . . . And then he reached for her hand, lacing his fingers with hers. It was natural, unforced, unthreatening, and shocking only in the warm rush of physical pleasure it elicited in Margaret. How long had it been since a man had had this effect on her?

Keith Moody was not a prepossessing man in any sense. He was middle-aged, losing his hair. He'd probably never been very handsome, even in his prime. Yet when he held her hand like that, she didn't want him to stop.

Margaret had been married to a handsome man. She'd been there, done that. Hal was the kind of man who was a joy to look at. Achingly, heart-stoppingly handsome, more handsome than any man had a right to be. The kind of man whom other men's wives fell in love with . . .

A disturbing man in many ways. And that comeliness had turned her life — and the lives of several other people — upside down.

Keith was nothing like that. He was comfortable, like a well-fitting shoe.

But still, Margaret's pulses were beating faster at the touch of his fingers on hers. And she didn't want him to stop . . .

'The grace of our Lord Jesus Christ . . .'

Morning Prayer was over. Margaret had daydreamed her way through it, on autopilot.

Feeling a bit guilty, but still smiling, she decided to skip breakfast and go straight to her office. Maybe she could get there before her secretary arrived, and have a few uninterrupted minutes with her post and her emails.

The office door was unlocked; the post was unopened on her desk, delivered first thing by the porter.

And on her desk, as well, was a box of chocolates. Not just one chocolate, but a whole box. A *large* box. Expensive chocolates, from the poshest shop in town. Tied up with an extravagant bow.

It wasn't even Monday.

Margaret's smile spread across her face, from ear to ear.

Neville scrunched the computer printout into a ball and lobbed it into his bin. 'Rubbish,' he said.

'You can't do that, Guv!' Cowley sounded outraged as he retrieved it. He uncrumpled it and smoothed it out on Neville's desk. 'What if they're telling the truth? And even if they're not, you can't just bin it.'

Neville sighed; Sid was right. Even if it was rubbish, it would have to be saved and put into a file. That was the way of bureaucracy: file it and forget it, but be sure you've covered your backside.

'I think we need to look into this,' Cowley went on. 'Check it out. It could be true.'

'It's anonymous,' Neville pointed out with exaggerated patience. 'We can't follow up on it.'

Cowley's finger stabbed the transcript. 'It says to ask his friends, to ask Hugo. We can do that, Guv.'

Neville had things to do that morning; apart from anything else, he needed to draft his statement for the inquest. He had no wish to speak to the posh Hugo Summerville again, and besides, the caller's claim was patently unfounded. He shook his head. 'I'm sorry, Sid. I just don't buy it.'

'Why not?' Cowley demanded.

'Sebastian Frost was a good kid. A *normal* kid, for God's sake. His parents knew him better than anyone, and if he'd been into something unsavoury like bullying—'

'But he got himself killed, didn't he? There has to be a reason for that. If it wasn't drugs, or gangs—'

Neville cut across Cowley's interruption. 'You're saying you believe that Sebastian Frost was a bully? And that someone killed him because of it?'

The sergeant crossed his arms across his chest. 'I'm saying it's possible, Guv. You know what schoolkids are like. If someone's different in any way – a little bit of bullying happens. Someone starts it, other people join in. Sometimes it gets out of hand.'

Suddenly, vividly, Neville was transported back in time over thirty years. A schoolyard in another land, another time. Connor O'Brian, Fergal Flaherty, Donal Ryan: he could see them as clear as day, remember the looks of scorn on their faces, the mocking voices. 'What kind of a name is Neville Stewart? You call yourself Irish, boy, with a name like that?' He'd wanted to curl up and die. He'd wanted to change his name. He'd wanted to strike out with his fists . . .

He shook his head abruptly to clear the image. 'What about *you*, Sid? You seem to be an expert on the subject. Were you ever bullied at school?'

Cowley shifted from one foot to the other and looked away. 'Well, no, Guv. Not me.'

Not me. Neville realized, in a flash, what that meant: Sid Cowley had been a bully. Not a victim, but a perpetrator. No wonder he was an expert on the subject.

He found that it wasn't difficult to believe, or imagine. Sid Cowley, taller than the other kids. Chippy. A bit of a smart-aleck, a know-it-all. Mouthy, then as now. If he couldn't intimidate the other kids with his fists – and he'd have been perfectly capable of it – he could always do it with his mouth.

Was it possible? Could Sebastian Frost have used his height and his educated, middle-class superiority to bully kids who were less blessed by nature or circumstances?

Well, he told himself, nothing else of value, no credible leads, had been forthcoming from the news conference and the appeal for information. No witnesses, no one stepping forward to say they'd seen Sebastian that night. Much as he disliked the thought, he needed to take this seriously, to follow it up. Maybe something would come of it. Neville sighed.

'All right, Sid,' he conceded. 'We'll do it. We'll talk to his friends about this. Let's do it and get it over with.'

'It's just like old times,' Tamsin said happily as she and Callie crossed the courtyard. 'Getting up early on Wednesday morning for tutor group.'

Callie rather enjoyed *not* having to get up early on Wednesdays since she'd left Archbishop Temple House, but she nodded her agreement.

'Except that I had to get up *really* early to do Facebook,' Tamsin added. 'I've been so busy the last couple of days that I feel like I'm falling behind.'

'How are you doing it? Did you bring a laptop?'

Tamsin shook her head, sending her ringlets bouncing. 'Phone. I had to get an iPhone so I could keep up with Facebook when I'm not near my computer.'

Callie laughed incredulously. 'Has anyone ever told you that you're seriously addicted to Facebook?'

'I don't deny it.' Tamsin grinned. 'The only trouble with the phone is that the keyboard is so small. What I really want is an iPad. Or maybe an iPad mini. I'm saving up for one,' she added.

They'd reached the row of staff housing, tucked at the back of the courtyard. It *would* be good to meet with their tutor group again, Callie told herself. Not least because Adam wasn't part of the group. At the time, she'd regretted that he'd been in a different group, but now it was a source of great relief. A couple of hours with no danger of running into Adam was something she was looking forward to unreservedly.

129

Mad Phil greeted them at the door with the sort of friendly hug that was permissible now that he was no longer their tutor. 'Come in,' he said. 'You know the drill. Worship first, breakfast after.'

They weren't the first to arrive; Nicky was already in the lounge, Mad Phil's cat on his lap, having appropriated the most comfortable chair. He scooped the cat on to the floor, rose and gave them hugs.

'I see you've snagged the best chair,' Callie observed.

He bowed with mock gallantry, swooping his arm in an exaggerated gesture. 'Just saving it for you, my dear lady,' he said. 'I'm going to sit on the sofa with Tamsin.'

Tamsin beamed with pleasure as he led her to the sofa and settled himself beside her, draping a casual arm round her shoulders.

Poor Tamsin, thought Callie. No wonder she was in love with Nicky: he certainly didn't do anything to discourage her, whatever his protestations to the contrary. She didn't stand a chance when he turned on the charm like that.

Mad Phil took the least comfortable chair, as was his custom. 'I'll be leading the worship, as soon as everyone gets here,' he said. 'I decided it wasn't fair to ask anyone else to do it.' He yawned suddenly. 'Oh, excuse me.'

'You look tired, Dr Moody,' Tamsin said.

Nicky removed his arm from around Tamsin, leaned forward and squinted at their ex-tutor. 'Yes, you do,' he pronounced. 'Did you have a hot date last night?'

While Callie gasped at Nicky's temerity, Mad Phil merely smiled. 'I suppose you might say that,' he said, just as the doorbell rang. 'Excuse me,' he repeated, rising and heading for the door.

'Saved by the bell,' Nicky whispered. 'Oh, that sly dog. Who would have thought it of Mad Phil?'

Tamsin's eyes were even rounder than usual. 'Oh, Callie! Maybe it *was* true! What that Hanna said about him!' She put her hand over her mouth.

'What?' Nicky turned to her accusingly. 'Have you been holding back some juicy gossip from me, woman? Tell me everything!'

'I don't know what you're talking about.' Hugo gave them a blank stare.

Once again Neville was in the handsome upstairs drawing room, in the wing-backed chair across from Hugo Summerville. This time Cowley was with him, and Neville could tell that his sergeant was not impressed – either by the surroundings or by Hugo himself. Neville was trying to keep an open mind about Hugo; though the boy had never been anything but polite to him, he had the nagging feeling that something about him didn't ring quite true. But at least he had the advantage of familiarity. Cowley seemed to be thrown off by it all – by Hugo's posh accent and general air of superiority.

'You're saying that you know nothing about Sebastian Frost and bullying,' Cowley demanded.

Hugo shrugged. 'Seb was my best mate. Don't you think I would have known about it if someone was bullying him?'

'Bullying *him*?' Cowley gave a contemptuous snort. 'Don't make me laugh, Sunshine. If anyone was doing the bullying, it was your mate Sebastian.'

'That's ludicrous.'

'Is it?' Cowley leaned forward and eyeballed him.

If he'd been hoping to intimidate Hugo, it wasn't working. Hugo gave a little smile and shrugged again. 'Don't you think I would have known?' he repeated. 'And why would Seb want to bully anyone?'

Neville, in spite of himself, had to admire the performance. If performance it was ... Hugo was clearly in charge of the situation, answering questions with questions, winding Sid up to breaking point. 'I think we're wasting our time here, Sergeant,' he interjected.

A complete and utter waste of time, just as he'd feared. Nothing but an anonymous phone call to go on, no evidence to back it up, and an adversary who was giving nothing away. A smooth customer, cleverer than the two of them put together. They could stay here all day, ask Hugo Summerville every question in the book, and they wouldn't get one inch closer to discovering the truth about this.

Meanwhile Sebastian Frost's killer was out there. And everyone – Evans, the press – wanted to know why they hadn't caught him yet. Then there was the little matter of the inquest ...

Five minutes later they were back at the car. 'Tosser,' Cowley pronounced. 'Smooth toffee-nosed bastard.'

Neville sighed. 'I suppose we'll have to give this up as a bad job.' He refrained from adding that he'd predicted that from the start.

'Not yet, Guv.' Cowley slid into the driver's seat. 'One more, at least. Let's try his mate Tom before we give it up. I talked to him before, remember? He's not as much of a clever clogs as bloody Hugo. If we can catch him on the hop—'

'All right,' Neville conceded. One more, before he had to start preparing his statement for the inquest.

131

'You shouldn't have told Nicky,' Callie reproved Tamsin. 'You know what a terrible gossip he is.' The worship session had ended; they'd moved on to breakfast, and the two of them had volunteered to make the toast.

Tamsin widened her eyes. 'I know,' she admitted. 'But I can't say no to Nicky. He would have wormed it out of me, sooner or later, so I thought I might as well just get it over with and tell him.'

'Tell Nicky what?' Val came into the kitchen to assist. She had been the last to arrive at the gathering, even though she lived almost next door, so she'd missed the gossip session.

Callie shot Tamsin a warning look. 'Don't.'

'Nicky will tell her, if I don't,' Tamsin reasoned.

'Then let Nicky tell her. Let it be on his conscience.'

'Tell me what?' Val put her hands on her hips and looked back and forth at the two of them. 'What's going on?'

'Nothing,' Callie stated firmly.

'Just some gossip,' Tamsin added. 'It's probably not true, like Callie says.'

Callie shook her head. 'It's not true. Let's just drop the subject, OK?' She had a horrible feeling that it wouldn't end here, nonetheless. Val would ask Nicky, or he would seek her out to impart the juicy gossip and his own spin on it.

'OK,' Val agreed amiably. She snatched the first slices of toast out of the toaster and piled them on a plate while Tamsin slotted in more bread. 'Sorry I was late,' she went on, smiling smugly. 'Jeremy wouldn't let me get out of bed this morning. If you know what I mean.'

Callie experienced a twinge of envy, and immediately felt guilty about it.

Tamsin made a face. 'Oh, rub it in, why don't you? Flaunting your marital bliss in front of us sad spinsters—'

'You may be a sad spinster, Tam, but Callie has her Italian stallion waiting for her in London. She only has to be away from him for a few days.'

'Oh, but they're not sleeping together,' Tamsin blurted out. 'He wants to wait till they're married.'

Callie felt her face burning; it must, she thought, be the colour of the fuchsia-pink clerical T-shirt that Tamsin was wearing that day. She wished that Mad Phil's kitchen floor would open and swallow her up.

'You're joking!' Val turned to her, eyebrows lifted.

'He's Roman Catholic,' Callie muttered, looking down at that floor. 'He's Italian.'

Tamsin snorted. 'So is Silvio Berlusconi!'

'And so was Casanova,' added Val.

'Rudolph Valentino. And—'

Callie cut her off. 'All right, all right. I get the picture.' There was just something wrong with *her*, then.

But Tamsin was not to be stopped. 'I told Callie she needs some sexy underwear,' she addressed Val. 'You know that shop—'

'Oh, the one in Rose Crescent! It's fantastic. Jeremy—'

'Let's take her there and get her sorted. We could go this afternoon, right after lunch.'

'That's settled, then.'

Settled. Sorted. If only it were that simple, Callie said to herself.

But there was one good thing that had come out of the dissection of her intimate problem, she realized. It had diverted her friends from the gossip about Mad Phil. If her own finer feelings had to be trampled on, so be it. It was worth it.

'Tom's mum,' Cowley warned as he and Neville arrived at the door of another well-appointed Georgian town house off Sussex Gardens. 'She's a bit protective.'

'Maybe we'll be lucky and she won't be here,' Neville said optimistically.

His optimism had no grounding in reality, and he soon realized that Cowley's warning had been an understatement. The woman who answered the door seemed reluctant to open it more than a crack.

'Mrs Gresham?' Neville said. 'I'm Detective Inspector Stewart. I believe you've met Detective Sergeant Cowley before. We need to have a word with your son Tom.'

She shook her head. 'You've talked to him once. I don't see why you need to harass him again.'

Neville made a supreme effort at patience. 'Mrs Gresham, this is an ongoing investigation. I'm sure you can appreciate that. As we receive information, sometimes we need to ask different questions.'

The door opened a tiny bit wider, then finally wide enough to admit them. 'He's taken his friend's death very hard,' she said. 'Please don't do anything to make it worse.' She called up the stairs. 'Tom, could you come down for a moment?' While they were waiting for him to emerge, she told them, 'He's revising for exams, you know. They start after the school holidays. Very important, too. We insist that Tom spend at least a few hours every day on his revision, even during the holidays.'

133

Cowley snorted under his breath; Neville could just imagine what he was thinking.

A young man loped down the stairs, long-legged and slender, towering over Neville and Cowley as he reached the bottom of the stairs. They grew them tall in W2, Neville reflected, reminding himself that this boy, like Hugo and Sebastian, was only fifteen.

Or maybe not quite. As Mrs Gresham ushered them into the lounge, Neville noticed that the mantelpiece displayed several greetings cards with the number 16 in large figures.

'It's your birthday, is it?' he asked in a falsely jolly voice, hoping to break the ice.

The boy glared at him. 'Last week. What of it? Who are you, and what do you want?'

'I'm Detective Inspector Stewart, with just a few questions for you. We won't keep you from your revision for very long.'

Tom glanced towards Cowley. 'I told you everything I know, the last time. Which is nothing, basically. I didn't see Seb at all that day.'

Out of the corner of his eye Neville could sense Tom's mother, hovering. They needed her out of the way, for starters. 'Mrs Gresham, I wonder if you'd be good enough to make us some coffee?' he suggested.

'All right,' she agreed with obvious reluctance.

'Two sugars for me,' Cowley requested, catching Neville's eye.

No more time to waste, so straight to the point. 'Tom,' Neville said, 'we were wondering whether you could tell us anything about ... bullying. In respect of Sebastian Frost.'

Tom's head was turned, watching as the door closed behind his mother. That was unfortunate, Neville realized: when he turned it back to face them, he'd had a critical few seconds to arrange his expression to reflect polite disbelief. 'Seb? Bullying? I don't know what you could mean, Inspector.'

The police were not the only ones who had received an anonymous phone call about Sebastian Frost. When Lilith arrived at her desk at the *Daily Globe* on Wednesday morning, she discovered a message on her answerphone. 'I thought you might like to know. Seb Frost was a nasty piece of work. He was a bully. Ask his mates about it if you don't believe me.'

Unlike Neville, she didn't hesitate. This, she knew in her bones, was a breakthrough. Whether the police had the same information or not, she was going to run with this, as far as it would take her. Though she was planning to attend the inquest, this was far more important. The inquest would be a formality; this was a huge advance.

She looked through her notebook in the vain hope that she'd obtained any contact details for Sebastian's friend Olly. No, just the first name. And in the end she hadn't even needed to use that – or his lame stories of Sebastian's leadership qualities – in her story, once she'd latched on to Richard Frost.

Never mind. She would soon track him down. She'd look for him at the shrine if necessary, but there was probably a better way.

Lilith switched on her computer and went to Facebook. She logged in, then searched for the name 'Sebastian Frost'. Within a few seconds she was viewing the memorial page.

The tributes to Sebastian were as inarticulate – and in many cases, incomprehensible – as the notes left at the shrine on Paddington Green, but that didn't matter. What did matter was the list of friends who had 'joined' the page to show their support.

One of them was Olly. Olly Blount. She clicked through to his page. A quick glance at his profile photo confirmed the identification: spiky hair and spots.

And not only was his email address there for all the world to see – his mobile phone number was, as well.

Without hesitation, Lilith pulled out her phone and rang the number.

After a couple of rings, Olly answered. 'Hullo?' He would probably be looking at the caller ID, trying to work out who it was.

'Is this Olly Blount?'

'Yeah, that's right. Who's this?' he asked suspiciously.

'My name is Lilith,' she said. 'We met at Paddington Green, a couple of days ago. We talked about Sebastian.'

'Yeah, I remember.'

This, Lilith decided, was something that ought to be done in person. It would be all too easy for him to hang up the phone – or to deny it, to lie – if she asked him a question that cast his mate in a bad light. She needed to see his face when she put it to him.

'Could we meet up, do you think?' she suggested.

'Why?'

She would tell him at least some of the truth. 'I'm a journalist,' she said. 'I'm writing a … tribute piece about Sebastian. And I liked some of the things you said about him. I'd like to do a proper interview with you, so you can be credited in the article.'

'You mean you'll put my name in the paper?'

'If you want me to.'

There was a pause on the other end of the phone. 'What about Hugo? Are you talking to him?'

Who was Hugo? She'd be able to find out on Facebook if she needed to, Lilith was sure. She tried to guess what answer Olly wanted to his question. 'No. Just to you.'

'Well . . .'

Had she made the wrong guess? 'I'll meet you at the McDonald's, Paddington Station,' Lilith put in swiftly, hoping that would be a sufficient lure. 'By Platform 1. I'll buy you a Big Mac.'

'Yeah,' said Olly. 'Yeah, all right. With fries and a Coke,' he added. 'Deal?'

'Deal!'

When breakfast had finished, Callie volunteered to stay behind and do the washing-up.

'That's not necessary,' their host said. 'I can deal with it later. You don't want to be late for the morning session, do you?'

Callie wasn't at all bothered about that. 'I don't mind, really,' she insisted, gathering up the cereal bowls from the coffee table. 'You've told us often enough that the role of a deacon is to serve other people.'

Mad Phil grinned at her. 'Well remembered. And quite true. I can't argue with that, so get on with it.'

'I'll help,' Tamsin said promptly.

Callie stifled a sigh. She'd been rather looking forward to being on her own for a few minutes; much as she loved her friends, she was finding Tamsin particularly trying at the moment.

But Tamsin was on her best behaviour as the two of them worked through the stack of dirty crockery and cutlery. She didn't bring up Callie's sex life again, or the speculation about Mad Phil's romantic exploits. Her gossip was confined to their fellow ordinands. 'I didn't think it was possible,' she said, 'but Scott Browning is more pompous than ever. I'm sure he thinks he's going to be a bishop.'

'He probably *will* be.' Callie rinsed a plate and slotted it in the drying rack.

Tamsin snatched it out and dried it vigorously with a tea towel. 'Probably. But he's going to have to get out of that dump of a parish first. And as quickly as possible. From what he's said in the sessions, his incumbent is an idiot.'

'I'd take what Scott Browning says with a pinch of salt,' Callie cautioned. 'I feel a bit sorry for his incumbent, actually. It must be difficult to have a curate who knows everything.'

'And doesn't mind telling you so,' Tamsin added. 'And anyone else who will listen.'

Callie tried to turn the conversation in a more positive direction. 'I like Jennifer's new hair style,' she said. 'It suits her.'

'I think she might have a new man in her life.' Tamsin added another plate to the pile on the kitchen table. 'One of her parishioners, maybe? She's not saying, but the signs are there. New hair style, smart wardrobe, and I think she's lost a bit of weight, as well. Classic signs.'

Back to men and sex, then, Callie realized resignedly. Wasn't there anything else to talk about? She tried again. 'Val hasn't said too much about her job,' she said. 'I don't know whether the churchmanship of that parish is really to her taste. But I suppose she was really lucky to find a curacy in Cambridge, with all of the ordinands and wannabes floating round the place.'

It was one of the issues faced by married women clergy, she reflected, especially ones married to other clergy: their employment options were limited, dictated by geographic necessity. In London it wasn't as much of a problem, with the sheer number of churches, as well as schools, universities, hospitals, prisons and other institutions requiring chaplains. Other parts of the country were not as blessed.

Tamsin sighed. 'I think churchmanship is the last thing on Val's mind at the moment. She's being priested in a few months, and that's the important thing for her. Plus she has the wonderful Jeremy to make her happy, and keep her warm at night.' She sighed again, rolling her eyes. 'Not that I'm jealous or anything.'

'Oh, come on, Tamsin.' Callie's voice sounded falsely jolly, even to her own ears. 'There must be some nice, eligible young men in your congregation—'

'Not blooming likely. Even if I thought it was a good idea to get involved with a parishioner, which I don't,' Tamsin stated firmly, 'there just aren't any of those sort of men in my parish. It's a family congregation. All of the nice men have wives and babies. And you know that men don't take me seriously, anyway,' she added, gesturing expressively at her generous breasts. 'They never have. They look at my boobs, at my blond hair, and they think "airhead". "Ditzy blonde." It's so unfair.'

137

It *was* unfair. Callie had realized a long time ago that Tamsin was an extremely intelligent woman, probably the brightest in their little group of friends. She deserved to be taken seriously.

And she deserved a man who would see past the surface and value her for the incredible person she was. But that probably wasn't going to happen, reflected Callie. Not as long as Tamsin was hung up on Nicky. Even though she'd never admit it, even to Callie, Tamsin's heart had a 'reserved' sign on it. And that meant she sent out the wrong signals to men – subconscious messages that she was unavailable. Tamsin wanted a man, but not just any man. She wanted Nicky.

'We're nearly finished,' Tamsin said, and pointed at the stacks of clean crockery on the table. 'I suppose we ought to put them away before we go. But I need to pop to the loo.'

'You go ahead. I'll finish up here.' Callie washed the last few teaspoons, put them in the drainer, emptied the sink and wiped it down, then opened cupboard doors till she found the proper places for the plates and cereal bowls.

'Oh. My. God.'

Tamsin wasn't shouting, but now that the running water in the sink was off, her voice echoed loud and clear down the stairs and in the kitchen.

'What is it?' Callie, alarmed, raced up the stairs to the bathroom door. 'Tamsin, are you all right?'

The door flew open. Tamsin stared at her, eyes wide and mouth in an O.

Had she hurt herself somehow? Was she bleeding? 'Are you all right?' Callie repeated.

Tamsin took a step back and pointed at an open drawer, then finally regained the power of speech. 'Look,' she said. 'I finished off the loo roll, so I was looking for a spare. I opened this drawer.'

Callie leaned over and peered into the drawer. It held an electric hair straightener with a long cord, a jumble of make-up, and at the bottom a packet of Tampax.

'Oh, God, Callie,' Tamsin breathed. 'She was right. That Hanna woman was right about Mad Phil. He's having it off with an undergraduate!'

Lilith peered through the glass which surrounded the McDonald's outlet on the far side of Paddington Station. It wasn't lunchtime yet, but that didn't prevent most of the people within from chowing down on burgers, she observed with some distaste.

Olly, she saw, had arrived and was sitting by himself at one of the plastic tables, intent on his phone. She watched him for a moment: he was apparently playing some fast-paced game, punching the little screen vigorously with his finger, oblivious to his surroundings.

She went in, joined the queue, and ordered a Big Mac meal for Olly and a coffee for herself. Then she carried the red plastic tray to the table and stood beside Olly, waiting for him to finish his game and notice her.

'Oh, hi,' he grunted eventually, putting the phone down.

Lilith slid the tray on to the table and sat down across from him. Olly reached for the sandwich carton with one hand and fed a fistful of fries into his mouth with the other.

She sipped at her coffee, which was surprisingly good – though ridiculously emblazoned with a message warning her that the coffee might be hot – and watched him eat. He applied himself to the task with the single-minded concentration of a starving man or a teenage boy, not looking at her. One would think, she reflected, that he hadn't eaten for weeks.

The food consumed, he guzzled down about half of the large Coke, then belched and put the cup down on the table in front of him. He grabbed a straw from the tray and stuck it into the Coke, taking one more sip from it before finally raising his eyes to Lilith.

'Thanks,' he mumbled.

'My pleasure.' Lilith leaned back in the moulded plastic chair and smiled across the table at him.

'You wanted me to talk about Seb?' Olly frowned, as if dimly grasping the fact that he was now under obligation to her. 'Like I told you before, he was a good bloke. A good mate.'

Now, she decided, was the time to strike. 'I believe what you're telling me, Olly. But someone's told me something a bit disturbing about your friend Seb. Someone has said that he was a bully.'

Olly's eyes widened; for the first time he made real eye contact with her, before he quickly looked down at the table. 'Who told you that?'

'I'm sure you know I have to keep my sources ... secret,' she said carefully. 'And anything you tell me, Olly, will be just between the two of us. If that's the way you want it.'

He swallowed hard, his Adam's apple bobbing up and down. 'It wasn't like that,' he said, so quietly that Lilith had to lean forward to catch his words. 'Not really. It was just a bit of fun.' Olly reached his hand out and fingered his phone.

CHAPTER 12

The morning session had been particularly good, in Margaret's estimation. She continued to be very impressed with John Kingsley as a facilitator: he seemed possessed of extraordinary sensitivity and empathy, enabling him to draw out issues from the participants that otherwise would have remained buried and unaddressed.

After the fact, Margaret felt a bit guilty that she hadn't offered Canon Kingsley accommodation at the Principal's Lodge, rather than assigning him to one of the college's guest rooms. Apart from anything else, she had cheated herself of the opportunity to get to know that exceptional man better. By the end of lunch she had resolved to do something about it. If it was too late to move him – and to suggest that would perhaps point up her initial failure – she could at least invite him for a meal. A meal she would cook herself.

It had been quite a long time since Margaret had cooked a proper meal. Since her arrival at the college, it had been much easier for her to take her meals in the dining hall than to assume the responsibility of cooking for one person. The standard of the college food was more than acceptable, and it seemed a good thing to let herself be seen at mealtimes, providing opportunities for informal interactions with staff and students. If she needed privacy, or didn't feel up to communal dining, the kitchen staff were always happy to send a tray to her office or her living quarters.

Once upon a time, in what seemed to her a previous life, she had quite enjoyed cooking, and had been pretty adept at it; Alexander had never complained, nor had Hal. Now, though, she was so out of practice that the prospect was more than a bit daunting. Not allowing herself to think about that, she took her lunch tray to the clean-up station and slotted it into the rack, then went to where John Kingsley was lunching, with former students on either side of him and Keith Moody across the table.

She forced herself not to make eye contact with Keith straightaway, addressing herself to Canon Kingsley. 'Canon, I was wondering whether you might be free to have supper with me tonight at the Principal's Lodge,' she said, smiling. 'It would give us a chance for a good chat.'

He returned her smile. 'That's very kind,' he said. 'I'd be delighted, if it's not too much trouble for you.'

'I'm a bit rusty at cooking,' Margaret admitted, 'but I'm going to have a go. Is there anything you don't eat?'

The canon gave a dry laugh. 'I'm a clergyman. I'll eat anything.'

She felt a tug on her sleeve, and looked down at Keith Moody, smiling involuntarily at his cheeky grin. 'Please, Ma'am,' he said. 'Am I invited too? I'm very well behaved, and I'll eat anything as well.'

'Yes, Dr Moody,' Margaret said formally, conscious of the openly eavesdropping deacons. She attempted to rearrange her expression to something more befitting her position, but was afraid she was less than successful; the smile refused to be suppressed. 'You're invited. I'll see you both at seven.'

The interview with Tom Gresham had been as big a waste of time as Neville had feared. As big a waste of time as talking to Hugo Summerville. Tom had professed himself baffled about any suggestion of bullying, and no line of questioning had produced anything but a flat denial, a blank stare.

Now Neville was working against the clock, sitting at his computer and trying to draft his statement for the inquest. And Sid Cowley wasn't making it easy, as he paced round Neville's desk and interrupted his train of thought.

'What about the girlfriend?' Cowley suggested. 'That Lexie. We ought to talk to her, for definite. She'd know what her boyfriend was up to. When he wasn't shagging her, that is.'

'And you think she'd tell us? Come on, Sid. None of these kids are giving up a thing. They're all in on it together, and none of them is going to crack.'

'I could try, Guv. Let me have a go at her.'

That was all he needed, Neville told himself. He was more determined than ever that Cowley would never come face to face with Sexy Lexie. He sighed. 'No way. Just forget it, Sid.'

'But—'

'We'll think about it after the inquest,' he stated firmly, and glanced at his watch. The time was slipping away; he was going to be every bit as unprepared as he'd been for the news conference.

He needed Sid out of his hair, and now. 'Could you go and get me a cup of coffee?' he asked in desperation. 'A proper cup of coffee, I mean. Not out of the machine. Not from the canteen. I really fancy a Starbucks.'

Cowley stared at him in amazement. 'Starbucks? But that's on the Edgware Road! It'll take me ten minutes to get there, at least.'

'Then you'd better get a move on, hadn't you?'

'What sort of coffee do you want, then?' Cowley shook his head, as though the guv had lost his last remaining marbles.

Neville hadn't the faintest idea. Triona would have known; she was the one who was always going on about Starbucks. He was more of a greasy spoon man himself. 'Oh, I don't know. Surprise me. As long as it's good and strong . . .'

'Right you are, Guv.' With a final bemused shrug, Cowley departed.

Head down. Neville reviewed what he'd written already, added a few words, and sighed. He knew that this account needed to be accurate rather than literary, but it just didn't seem to be working. Something was missing . . .

Like maybe a clue as to what this investigation was really about, and where it was headed.

Neville pushed that thought away from him and took refuge in procedural jargon. 'The police were called to the scene at 12.13 a.m. and I myself arrived at approximately 12.50. The victim was a young male who appeared to be approximately fifteen or sixteen years of age. He was later identified as Sebastian Frost, aged fifteen. The pathologist confirmed death at the scene and surmised that the cause of death was a knife wound to the throat.' He had already decided not to mention the other knife wound, the one to the tongue – it hadn't yet been made public, either in the press release or at the news conference. They hadn't even told the parents about it. It was one of those little details that probably only the killer would know, so there was good reason to withhold it in the hopes that it would prove useful in future. That, and the smashed iPhone . . .

It seemed like only a few minutes had passed, but Sid was back already. 'Sorry, Guv,' he said, plopping a white and green paper cup on the desk. 'It took for ever. The queue was out to the pavement! I got you a French Roast with a shot of steamed milk,' he added. 'They said that was the strongest.'

'Thanks, Sid.' Neville sighed again and returned his attention to the screen. It wasn't going to get any better, and they were already cutting it close for time. He pushed 'print' with one hand and reached for the coffee with the other.

It had cooled off sufficiently for a cautious sip. To his surprise, it tasted pretty good; maybe Triona was on to something with all her

142

Starbucks nonsense, he admitted to himself. He could have done without the steamed milk, but the coffee itself was flavourful and strong. 'Thanks, Sid,' he repeated.

The page churned out of the printer; he grabbed for it with his free hand. 'Time to hit the road,' he announced. It wasn't strictly necessary to take Cowley along, but it was one way of keeping him from getting into mischief – and he could drive, so Neville could focus his attention on other things.

They were halfway down the corridor, heading for the car park, when a voice hailed from behind. 'DI Stewart! Just the man I was looking for.'

Neville turned: it was Danny Duffy, the boy wonder from the techie department, waving a sheaf of papers.

'We're in a bit of a hurry,' Neville said, looking pointedly at his watch. 'Inquest.'

'For the Frost boy? That's what I wanted to talk to you about. I've been into his computer. He had it pretty well protected – passwords and firewalls and all that. Didn't make it easy for me, I have to tell you. But I found some things that might interest you.' Once again he waved the papers, with a self-satisfied grin.

'It will have to wait.' Neville turned and added over his shoulder, 'We'll be back in a couple of hours. I'll come and find you then.'

Brian had gone out to do some hospital visits, so Jane, feeling a bit adrift, decided it was time to pay a visit to the church and check on the flowers. By mid-week, things were usually looking rather sad, and some intervention was advisable to keep the flowers going for a few more days: topping up the water, judicious removal of wilted blooms, moving things round a bit to cover the gaps.

She wasn't the only one who'd thought about the flowers, Jane discovered as she went into the chancel. Wendy Page was standing, back to her, plucking a drooping lily out of one of the pedestals.

'Hello,' she said, and Wendy turned.

'Oh, hello, Jane.'

'I see you're tidying the flowers,' she said unnecessarily.

'They need it.'

'How far have you got?' Jane looked round the chancel.

'I've done the ones on the altar. You can do the other pedestal, if you like.'

Jane went obediently to the other side of the chancel and contemplated the bedraggled arrangement, trying to decide where to start.

'Actually, Jane, I'm glad I've seen you,' Wendy said. 'There's something I'm a bit worried about, and I thought you . . .' her voice trailed off.

It happened all of the time: people used Jane as a conduit to their vicar. They knew she was discreet and trustworthy, that she had his ear. So if they felt awkward about approaching Brian directly, they often had a word with her, knowing that it would be passed on in the right way, at the proper time. Jane considered it part of her job. Part of the privilege of being a vicar's wife.

'What is it?' She smiled encouragingly.

'It's Liz,' Wendy said. 'Liz Gresham.'

Wendy's great friend. 'Does Liz have some sort of problem?'

'It's her son. Tom – you might not know him.' Wendy shrugged. 'He doesn't come here very often, admittedly. Only at Christmas, and then only under duress. But he *was* christened here at All Saints'.'

Jane tried to picture Tom Gresham and failed. 'How old is he?'

'He's just had his sixteenth birthday, I think. Much younger than my two. He was a late baby,' Wendy added, smiling. 'A bit of a surprise for Liz, to be frank. And her husband.'

Late baby. Jane's hand went involuntarily to her belly; she hoped that Wendy was too distracted to have noticed. 'Oh?' she said neutrally, re-focusing her mind. Tom was a few years younger than the twins, then; she probably wouldn't have had any reason to have registered him, especially if he never came near the church. 'Is Tom in some sort of trouble?'

'I'm not sure,' admitted Wendy, yanking on another wilted bloom. 'But Liz is in a real state. The police have been round to talk to Tom. Twice. About that boy who was stabbed.'

Jane hadn't really been following the story – she had other things on her mind – but was aware that the murder had featured prominently on the evening news, and that it had happened locally. On Paddington Green. Not in the parish, but not far away.

'Do the police think that Tom was involved?'

'He was a friend of the dead boy. Liz knows that much, but Tom won't tell her anything else. For all she knows, he might be a suspect.'

'How dreadful for Liz. Does she have any reason to think—'

'Oh, no.' Wendy shook her head. 'He's a good boy, even if he doesn't come to church. Very polite, never been in any real trouble. Liz thinks the world of him.'

Which still didn't mean he wasn't involved, Jane said to herself. She'd seen enough as a vicar's wife – if not as a parent – to realize that mothers didn't always have the most realistic view of their children's capacity for getting into mischief.

'Do you think it would help if Brian ... had a word with Liz?' she suggested delicately.

'Oh, yes!' Wendy turned to face her with a grateful smile. 'I'm sure Liz would appreciate it. I've tried talking to her, telling her there's nothing to worry about, but she doesn't take any notice. She'd listen to Father Brian, though.'

'Leave it with me,' said Jane.

'Still ...' Wendy frowned.

'What is it?'

'I just can't help thinking. Liz thinks the sun shines out of Tom's ... you know. But Liz is the one who always says it. "No smoke without fire." Makes you wonder, I have to say.'

'I can go on your behalf,' Mark offered. 'You don't have to go.'

Miranda Frost narrowed her eyes at him. 'Don't be ridiculous,' she said icily. 'Do you think I might have something more important to do today than attend my son's inquest?'

He tried to explain. 'I just thought I might spare you something unpleasant.'

'Something more unpleasant than having my son murdered, do you mean?' She turned her back on him and stalked away, saying over her shoulder as she reached the bottom of the stairs, 'I'll be down in five minutes. Ready to go. Whether my husband chooses to go or not.'

Richard Frost gave Mark an apologetic smile, lifting his shoulders in a shrug. 'Are you married?' he asked as soon as Miranda was safely out of earshot.

'Not yet. I'm engaged.' He smiled involuntarily at the thought of Callie.

'Well, good luck, mate. You might find that you need it.'

Callie is nothing like your wife, Mark wanted to say. But he realized how rude that might sound.

Inevitably his mind slipped into Callie-mode; he wondered what she was doing at that moment, and tried to imagine her in Cambridge. He'd talked to her the night before on her mobile, but it had been less than satisfactory. She'd been in the college bar with her friends, and – not surprisingly – she'd sounded distracted, not really engaged with him or their conversation. Had Adam been there, then, dazzling her with witty chit-chat and reminding her about what she'd once had? Mark pushed the thought away from him.

'She hasn't always been like this,' Richard continued, as if he'd heard Mark's unspoken comment on his wife. 'I don't think she knows how to cope with a situation that she can't control. Miranda's a take-charge sort of person.'

'Yes, I'd noticed.' Mark tried to keep his voice neutral, un-ironic.

'In her job she has to be. If someone's brought into A and E with a traumatic injury, or a catastrophic illness that requires surgical intervention, she's right in there. Making decisions, taking action.' Richard shook his head. 'You should see her. She's bloody brilliant.'

'Was that how the two of you met?'

'It was, as a matter of fact.' Richard smiled, and in that smile Mark could see the depth of his love and admiration for his wife. 'I'm an anaesthetist. Our eyes met in theatre, over the inert body of a traffic accident victim. Very romantic.'

'Love at first sight?' It had been that way with Callie; they'd met on an aeroplane, by some sweet twist of fate – or divine intervention – seated next to each other, and by the time they'd reached their destination Mark was besotted.

'Something like that.' Richard's mouth twisted in a self-deprecating way. 'For me, anyway. I never did understand what she saw in me. But it's lasted for almost twenty years. In spite of . . .' His voice trailed off; he looked away. 'Oh, God,' he said in a totally different voice, so quietly that Mark strained to hear him. 'I don't want to do this. But I have to. Or Miranda will despise me even more than she does already.'

'It won't be so bad.' Mark tried to sound cheerful, encouraging, but he suspected it wasn't very convincing. 'It's just a formality today. I've been to more of these things than you've had hot dinners, and—'

'But it's not your son.' Richard's voice cut through his weasel words, and as he turned his head Mark could see that his eyes were welling up with tears.

'No. It's not.'

'I'm ready,' Miranda announced, appearing at the door. 'Let's do this.'

'No,' said Callie. 'No, I don't want to.'

'Come on. It will be fun.' Tamsin was practically bouncing up and down.

'We mustn't miss the afternoon session.'

146

'You know how you hate role playing,' Val chipped in. 'You haven't been called on to do it in front of everyone yet. I think it's about time for your luck to run out on that score. Your turn is coming.'

'Well . . .' Callie really didn't want to skive off, and she certainly didn't want to go shopping for skimpy underwear. Not now, not ever. 'We can't go dressed like this,' she said lamely. 'Not in our clericals. Can you imagine?'

'That's a point,' Val admitted, taking charge. 'We'll have to change our clothes, then. Tam, you take Callie to her room and help her choose something to wear. Something inconspicuous – jeans, maybe. Then you can do the same.' The look she directed at Tamsin said 'Don't let her escape.' She went on, 'I'll go home and get into some mufti. We'll meet at the porters' lodge in – what – quarter of an hour?'

'Make it twenty minutes,' Tamsin said, grabbing Callie's arm.

'But I don't want to,' Callie protested, knowing she was on to a loser. Tamsin, at this point, was like a force of nature, not to be resisted.

They went up B staircase, Tamsin following close on Callie's heels – as if, Callie thought, she was afraid she would turn and make a run for it. Maybe she would, given a chance . . .

Once in Callie's room, Tamsin went straight for the wardrobe. 'Boring,' she pronounced as she pulled out one thing after another. 'Too clerical. You might as well wear your dog collar, or tattoo 'clergy' on your forehead. Don't you have anything the least bit sexy?'

'No. This is a theological college, not a lap-dancing club. In case you hadn't noticed.'

'Oh, Callie, lighten up!' Tamsin ordered. Eventually she settled on a pair of jeans and Callie's favourite stripy jumper. 'Not very exciting, but at least it won't make you look like a nun,' she declared.

As Callie pulled off her dog collar and started unbuttoning her blouse, Tamsin fished her phone out of her handbag. 'I'll ring Nicky,' she said. 'I'm sure he'll want to go with us.'

'Absolutely not!' Callie stared at her in horror. 'You must be mad!'

'But he'll be hurt if we leave him out.'

'He'll never know, if you don't tell him.'

Tamsin pouted. 'He'll know if we're all not there at the session this afternoon – you, me and Val. He'll figure it out.'

'No,' Callie said in her firmest voice – the voice she used when Bella did something naughty.

Then it was Tamsin's turn to stare. 'Oh, Callie, you can't!'

'Can't what?'

147

'Wear that bra. To go shopping for underwear.'

Callie looked down at her bra. It was perfectly serviceable – Marks & Spencer's, identical to all of the ones she owned. 'What's the matter with it? It's clean. It doesn't have any holes in it.'

'But people will see it. And it's so ... booooring. What did you do, go into Marks and say "Give me your most boring, least sexy bra"?'

'I don't have anything else,' Callie said with exaggerated patience. 'And anyway, I thought that was the whole point of this exercise. To get something more ... alluring.'

Tamsin snorted. 'Trust me. That won't be difficult.'

Lilith Noone was the first person Neville noticed in the coroner's court. She was sitting front and centre in the press area, and she was smiling. Her smile, he fancied, was directed at him – a self-satisfied smirk that made him distinctly uneasy.

Did she know something? *Could* she possibly be on to something? He knew from experience that one underestimated Lilith Noone at their own peril. She was cunning; she was sneaky. Nothing was too low or underhanded for her. She wasn't, in his opinion, as clever as she thought she was, but that didn't stop her from being dangerous. It might even make her more so.

Neville made a mental note that, whatever happened today, he would have a look at the *Globe* tomorrow morning, before he had any contact with Evans. Just so he wouldn't be caught out, in case she pulled some sort of a fast one.

Lilith Noone turned her head to the side and he followed her line of sight: Mark Lombardi had just come in and was settling Miranda and Richard Frost in the seats reserved for the family of the deceased. So he hadn't been able to talk them out of coming; Neville wasn't surprised. He couldn't really imagine Miranda Frost opting out of the procedure, distressing as it might prove to be. And if Miranda wanted to come, Richard would be there too, whether he wanted to or not.

A moment later, Hereward Rice swept into the room in all of his self-important majesty, smoothing back his wavy salt-and-pepper hair as everyone stood. He bowed formally, then asked the assembled crowd to sit and waited a moment for them to settle.

'I open formally the inquest touching the death of Sebastian Frost,' he said.

An audible sigh was heard in the courtroom. Neville glanced at the Frosts, from which direction the sound had come. Not from Miranda, he judged; she was pale but composed, or at least under control – her lips pressed together in a tight line and her hands clasped in her lap. Richard, though, was bowed over with his head in his hands, and looked as though he were about to be sick. Mark murmured something in his direction; he shook his head.

Neville glanced towards Lilith Noone, who was scribbling something in her notebook. Smirking, damn her.

Hereward Rice ignored all of the drama and ploughed on. 'I shall call upon Detective Inspector Neville Stewart, senior investigating officer, to make a statement.'

Show time, then. Neville rose and went to the witness stand, where he was sworn in.

Next to the Savile Row tailoring of Hereward Rice's immaculate suit, and his suave, in-control manner, Neville felt shabby as well as under-prepared. But he was resolved to hold his own and not allow himself to be intimidated.

'Mr Stewart,' said Hereward Rice, 'you are the senior investigating officer in charge of the investigation into the death of Sebastian Frost?'

'That is correct.'

'And the police are treating this death as a homicide?'

'Yes, Sir.'

The coroner nodded. 'I would like you to tell the court about the state of play of your investigation, including the identification of the deceased, which is the chief concern of the court at this time.'

Once upon a time, Neville knew, the pathologist would have been called to give testimony as to the identity of the deceased. But pathologists were busy men with limited time for that sort of thing, and the inquest at this point was a mere formality. Dr Tompkins would doubtless be required to give expert testimony when the inquest was re-opened in a few months' time; for now, Neville's sworn word would have to do. He pulled the computer printout from his jacket pocket and unfolded the single sheet of paper.

He was determined not to look at the Frosts, nor at the press area, so he focused his eyes on his paper and read it out, formally and mechanic- ally, trying not to think about what the words meant. It sounded impos- sibly stilted and formulaic to his own ears.

'Thank you, DI Stewart,' said Hereward Rice, when he had finished. 'Now I have a few questions for you.'

'Yes, Sir.'

'Has anyone been arrested or charged in connection with this homicide?'

Neville knew it was a formal, legal question which had to be asked, but he couldn't help feeling affronted at the implications of failure on his part which it contained.

'No, Sir.' His eyes were drawn in spite of himself to Miranda Frost, who stared at him stonily.

'And you said that no witnesses to this fatal assault have come forward.'

'No, Sir. But we continue to appeal for witnesses, or any information that is pertinent to our investigations,' he added.

'And your investigations are ongoing.'

'Yes, of course.'

'Then I will adjourn this inquest, pending further investigation, until . . .' Hereward Rice paused and consulted a calendar. 'The fifteenth of July. Is it reasonable to expect that someone will have been arrested and charged by then, DI Stewart?'

Bastard. 'I would hope so, Sir,' Neville said stiffly.

'Good.' The coroner switched his attention from Neville to the seats reserved for the family. 'And, in line with Department of Justice guidelines, I would like to inform the family that the body will be released to them within a maximum of four weeks.'

Now Neville couldn't bear to look at the Frosts; instead he turned his eyes to the press area.

Lilith Noone was still smiling.

Callie hoped, as she returned to college, that she wouldn't run into anyone to whom she'd have to explain her absence. She was on her own; Tamsin had, in spite of Callie's protests, texted Nicky, who had joined them on their shopping expedition, and the two of them had gone to Auntie's Tea Shop afterwards, while Val had decided to stop at Sainsbury's for some groceries. Callie, though, was sufficiently overcome by guilt that she wanted to be back in time for Evening Prayer.

She moved quickly through the porters' lodge, holding her shopping bag behind her, then kept close to the building as she skirted the courtyard towards B staircase. Dodging round a pillar, she nearly collided head-on with someone coming, equally furtively, the other way. They both jumped, hands clutched to their hearts, and stared at each other.

'Oh! You nearly scared the life out of me!' Callie gasped.

'You almost gave me a heart attack!' It was Jennifer Groves, one of Callie's former classmates – she of the gossip-worthy new hair cut. It nearly rendered her unrecognizable: once mousy brown and long, it had been cut in a stylish wedge and skilfully highlighted with warm gold.

'I was just ... well, I didn't want anyone to see me,' admitted Callie, still trying to conceal her shopping bag. It was a posh one, stiff and shiny, with braided handles and the logo of the shop in gold on the side.

'Me, too.' Jennifer gave a sheepish laugh and produced the book she'd been holding behind her. 'Library book,' she confessed. 'From the college library. I found it in my stuff at home recently, and thought I'd try to sneak it back when no one was around.'

'I was trying to get back in time for Evening Prayer.' Callie's breathing was returning to normal.

'Skiving, were you?'

'I suppose you could say that.'

Jennifer nodded. 'I didn't think I'd seen you at the afternoon session. You, and Val and Tamsin and Nicky.'

Oh, dear. It had been a bit naïve, Callie realized, to think that their absence, en masse, would have gone unnoticed. 'Retail therapy,' she admitted.

'Lucky you. I'm not saying the afternoon session wasn't interesting. But I'm beginning to suffer from deacon overload. Not to mention a numb bum.'

They both laughed. 'I hear you,' Callie said with feeling. 'On both counts.'

'Where are your co-skivers, then? Didn't they come back with you?'

'Val went to the supermarket, and Tamsin and Nicky opted for tea at Auntie's.'

Jennifer gave her a shrewd look. 'She's still after him, then? Tamsin's an intelligent woman. Doesn't she realize that it's never going to happen? I mean, come on.'

The words echoed Callie's own feelings, but she felt compelled to defend her friend. 'She can't help the way she feels,' she said. 'Sometimes it's like that. No matter what your brain tells you, your heart has a mind of its own. And intelligence has nothing to do with it.'

Jennifer lowered her voice and glanced over her shoulder. 'Like Mad Phil, you mean? Mad Phil and his young girlfriend? I always thought Mad Phil was more or less asexual. I mean, who would ever have thought he would succumb to the lures of the flesh? It just goes to show you.'

Not that again. 'That's just a bit of malicious gossip,' she said curtly.

'Nicky seemed to think it was true.'

'Nicky doesn't know everything.' And he can be a gossipy old queen, she said to herself. 'I'd better get on,' she added, and made her escape, sensing that Jennifer was staring at her retreating back.

Callie didn't want to think about it, much less discuss it. Even if it *were* true – and there was increasing evidence to support it, she had to admit to herself – there was nothing constructive to be achieved in repeating and embroidering the gossip. And what business was it of anyone, what Mad Phil did in his spare time, or with whom?

She charged up B staircase and hurried along the corridor towards her room. A few metres short of her door she came face to face with someone going the other way, and it was just about the last person she wanted to meet: John Kingsley.

He was, she knew, staying in the room at the far end of the corridor – the college's best guest room, with the same coveted view that Callie's room boasted, and the added benefit of en suite facilities.

There was no way to avoid him now. 'Good afternoon,' she said, hoping to carry on without having to make any explanations, but he stopped.

'Oh, Callie. Well met, my dear. I was hoping to see you.'

Was he going to tell her off for missing the session? She hoped not, though he would be completely justified if he did.

The canon smiled at her. 'I've been thinking about you quite a bit since we chatted the other day, and there's something I wanted to tell you.'

'Yes?'

'We can talk more about this, maybe tomorrow if we have a few minutes. But I just wanted to say that you've been holding on to your anger for long enough. I think it's time for you to forgive Adam.'

She was completely taken aback. 'Forgive him?'

'Forgiveness is a gift from God,' he said. 'And now, if you'll excuse me, my dear, I must get on to Evening Prayer.'

CHAPTER 13

Neville couldn't stop thinking about Lilith Noone and her self-satisfied smirk.

'Do you think she knows something?' he said, almost to himself, as Cowley negotiated traffic on the way back to the station.

'Who? Lexie? I think we need to talk to her, Guv.'

That proved he'd been right in bringing Sid with him, keeping him out of temptation's way. 'No. Lilith Noone. That wretched woman. Didn't you see that grin on her face?'

'I didn't notice.'

Well, worrying about it wouldn't help, he told himself. Short of ringing her up and asking her, there was nothing to do but wait for tomorrow morning's *Globe*.

Now he needed to concentrate on his own next steps.

Danny Duffy, obviously. Whatever Danny had found on the computer, it could provide him with new leads, fresh directions for the investigation.

But before he saw Danny, before they got back to the station, there was something else he really needed to do. Unpleasant though it was certain to be ...

'We need to call at the Frosts',' he said to Cowley decisively.

'What for?'

Neville sighed. 'I have to ask them about the bullying. They're not going to like it, and I'm sure they'll deny it, but if I want to dot the i's and cross the t's in this case—'

'I'm not going into that house,' Cowley frowned.

'I'm not asking you to.' Neville shook his head. 'You can stay in the car. She'd just chuck you back out, anyway. Unless she's softened up a bit. But I doubt that.'

He hoped the Frosts were back from the coroner's court; he hoped they would be able to find a place to park in St Michael's Street.

The latter was a lost cause on a Wednesday afternoon. So it was just as well that Cowley was staying with the car – he could stop on a double yellow and wait for Neville to finish.

'No problem,' said Cowley, rolling down the window and pulling out a packet of fags as Neville got out of the car. 'Take your time, Guv. I'll be here.'

Neville was dismayed to see a straggle of journalists on the pavement in front of the house. He recognized a couple of them from the news conference, and was determined not to make eye contact. 'Hey, Stewart! Anything new?' one of them called out as he marched by.

'No comment,' he stated.

'They've just got back from the inquest,' another one volunteered. 'And *they* didn't have any comment, either.'

Mark would make sure of that. For a moment Neville felt sorry for the Frosts, having to run the gauntlet of journalists on their doorstep to get into their house.

Not surprisingly, no one came to the door when he rang the bell. Neville fished his phone out of his pocket and rang Mark's number. 'I'm outside,' he said. 'Can you let me in?'

'No problem.'

Mark was there in a matter of seconds. 'I didn't know you were coming,' he said, opening the door just enough for Neville to slip through, then closing it quickly behind him. 'We've just got back, actually.'

'Sorry, it was a spur-of-the-minute thing.'

'I was just organizing some hot drinks,' Mark went on. 'Would you like tea? Or coffee?'

'If the coffee's coming out of that fancy machine, I'll have some of that.'

Mark ushered him into the front room, where the Frosts were evidently waiting for their drinks. The room was dark: the curtains had been drawn, presumably because of the journalists outside, but no one had bothered to put the lights on. Feeling at a disadvantage, Neville pressed the wall switch.

In the sudden glare from the overhead bulb, Miranda Frost scowled at him. 'Is that necessary, Inspector?'

'I think so.' He sat down across from her with an apologetic smile. 'You may be used to finding your way round your house in the dark, but I'm not up to it.'

She seemed to unbend a little. 'All right, then.' After a moment she went on, 'Listen, Inspector. I want to thank you for ... well, for what you said at the inquest. It was very ... professional.'

'I was just doing my job, Mrs Frost.' Neville was astonished, both at her words and at the concession they represented on the part of this stiff-necked woman. He hadn't done anything out of the ordinary; he'd only stated the facts as he knew them, and pretty woodenly at that, in his own opinion. Had she been expecting him to say something disparaging about her son?

Now, more than ever, he regretted what he was going to have to say to her now.

Neville waited until Mark had returned with the coffee and withdrawn discreetly. He might have asked Mark to stay, but decided to brief him later; the Frosts might be less guarded if he was on his own.

'Dr Frost. Mrs Frost,' he addressed them impartially. 'I've come to speak to you about a rather delicate matter, and I apologize in advance if it offends you. I hope you'll understand why I have to ask.'

He could almost see the guard going up, the barriers being erected. 'Yes?' Miranda said, narrowing her eyes at him. Richard put his head down, showing Neville nothing but his brown curls.

'We've had an anonymous phone call to our hotline. It suggested, in fairly ... strong ... terms, that Sebastian was involved in bullying.'

'Bullying!' Miranda stared at him in astonishment. 'You *are* joking, aren't you?'

'It's not a joking matter, Mrs Frost.'

'But it's ridiculous! Laughable.'

'We've spoken to some of his friends,' Neville admitted. 'To Hugo and Tom. They more or less said the same thing. Do you mind telling me why you think it's so ridiculous?'

He wouldn't have been surprised if she'd shown him the door there and then, accompanied by a stream of furious invective. But she considered the question thoughtfully for a moment, twisting her coffee cup between her hands, and answered with obvious care.

'Bullying is for losers,' she said at last. 'And Sebastian wasn't a loser.'

Losers? Instinctively, he would have thought just the opposite. In his experience, bullies were big and strong. Sure of themselves. Connor O'Brian, Fergal Flaherty, Donal Ryan. And Sid Cowley, he reminded himself. 'What do you mean?'

'They're inadequate people, damaged in some way, who are compensating for something. Something they lack. The only way they can feel good about themselves is to tear down other people and make them feel bad.' She gave him a bitter, knowing smile. 'I'm a doctor, Inspector. I've studied psychology, and I've seen things you can't imagine. I know what I'm talking about. Trust me. From what you know about Sebastian, can you honestly say that he fits the profile of a screwed-up loser?'

* * *

Forgive Adam?

Forgive him?

Callie couldn't get the words out of her head. She went into her room and dropped the posh shopping bag on the bed; it tipped over, spilling a creamy froth of lace and silk over the institutional geometric duvet cover. She ignored it, plopping down in the comfy chair, all thoughts of going to Evening Prayer vanishing.

Forgive Adam.

Had John Kingsley talked to him – to Adam – then? Had Adam indicated that he was deeply sorry for what he'd done to her?

Forgiveness. A gift from God.

And a big step, indicating a new phase in their relationship – if you could call what remained between them a relationship. Coming to terms with what had happened. Moving on.

Repentance, forgiveness.

Was he sorry enough to deserve her forgiveness?

Adam had been the one with the power in the relationship, when he had so abruptly terminated it.

Now, Callie realized, she was the one with the upper hand: the power to forgive him for what he had done and the hurt he had inflicted.

If he really *was* sorry . . .

Without conscious thought, Callie got up from the chair and went to the window, leaning on the sill. Cambridge in its spring glory virtually flaunted itself: the greening grass, the profusion of bloom and blossom. Cherry-blossom pink and daffodil yellow, all providing nature's set dressing for the magnificent architecture of King's College Chapel, beyond the cut of the river.

She had known such happiness in this room . . .

As previous springs had come and gone, shading into the lush growth of summer, she had rejoiced in the growing sense of her vocation to the priesthood, and her growing love for Adam. Twined together somehow, coming to fruition. All of a whole, the future before her. Before *them*. A shared future.

A future that was not to be, for a love that had proved as fleeting as spring sunshine, as transitory as the fragile cherry blossom.

She'd had a lucky escape – of course she had, and she knew that now. But that wasn't really the point. The point was that she had suffered, and terribly, when he had rejected her so cack-handedly. His blithe dismissal of all she had thought they meant to each other had

156

made her question seriously her worth as a woman, as a potential priest, and even as a human being.

Adam Masters had a lot to answer for.

Could she forgive him?

She opened the window a crack and breathed in deeply.

There was a knock on her door; Callie started guiltily. Was Tamsin back already, then?

She went to the door and pulled it open.

Adam was lounging against the wall in the corridor, hands in his pockets. 'Can I come in?' he said. 'I think we need to talk.'

'She has a point, Sid,' Neville said as they drove the short distance back to the station. He'd never been comfortable with the bullying scenario, he reminded himself. He'd immediately dismissed it as rubbish. Everything that Miranda Frost had said about the psychology of bullying had re-inforced that belief, had given solid backing to his instinctive rejection of the anonymous caller's claims.

'Then what do we have left, Guv? Where does that leave us?'

Cowley was frowning. He'd liked the bullying angle, Neville realized. It was something he could relate to.

'It leaves us with bugger all,' he admitted. 'Square one.' Then he remembered Danny Duffy, with his sheaf of papers, and felt a surge of optimism, not unlike a caffeine-induced jolt of adrenalin.

They found Danny in his lab, surrounded by all of his techy bits and bobs. He had some piece of computer kit on his work table and was bending over it with a tool, performing an operation as delicately as a surgeon might do. An A & E surgeon like Miranda Frost, even.

'Oh, hi,' he greeted them, straightening up. 'I wondered whether you'd got lost.'

'Not lost. Just delayed,' Neville said.

'I'm glad you caught me. Another half an hour and I'll be out of here. But I think you'll be interested in what I've found.' Danny was wearing latex gloves; he stripped them off, dropped them on the work table and went to his piled-up desk in the corner. He picked up a paper-clipped pile of printouts. 'That kid, Sebastian? Awesome stuff.'

'Awesome?' Neville echoed.

'The most egregious case of cyber-bullying I've ever seen.'

'Egregious?' Cowley frowned. 'What the hell does that mean?'

At the same time, Neville said, 'Cyber-bullying? What the bloody hell is that?'

157

Danny Duffy grinned. 'Cyber-bullying. You know. On a computer.'

As far as Neville was concerned, bullying required face-to-face contact. Words might be involved – hurtful, hurtful words, in spite of the 'sticks and stones' rhyme – but so, often, were fists. And other parts of the anatomy. A swift knee to the groin, a sneaky foot stuck out to trip you. It wasn't possible to beat someone up on a computer. Was it?

'Explain,' he demanded.

'It's all the thing now. Works pretty much like old-fashioned bullying, except that it's much easier to do. People gang up online.'

'My nephew knows about this,' Cowley confirmed. 'He was telling me that someone in his class got bullied by email.'

'But how can that hurt someone?' Surely, Neville reasoned, if someone sent you a nasty email, you'd just delete it? And the next time you had one from that person, you wouldn't even open it.

'Oh, it can be pretty effective. I'll show you.' Danny flipped through his sheets of paper. 'Our Sebastian, now, he was pretty clever. Covered his tracks – he knew his way round a computer, all right. He didn't send emails. He did it all on Facebook.'

'On Facebook? Is that one of those social network things they keep going on about?'

Cowley gave a great, condescending sigh. 'Surely you know about Facebook. Even you, Guv. It's where you go to catch up with everyone who was ever important in your life,' he explained pityingly. 'And to meet new people, as well.'

Why should he know? Why would he be interested? The last thing he wanted to do was to hook up with Connor O'Brian or any of his thuggish mates to share reminiscences about the old days. The past was the past, over and done with, and that was the way it was meant to be, thank you very much.

'By meeting new people, I suppose you mean women,' he sneered. 'Fine for you, Sid. But I'm a married man now, remember?'

Danny intervened. 'OK. I'll show you what I mean.' He waved the papers round to get their attention. 'He didn't use his own regular Facebook account for this. He opened a new account, using the name Darth Vader.'

'How original,' said Cowley.

Neville was listening now, re-focusing, his skin starting to prickle. This could be important, he realized. 'And you have proof of this?'

'Absolutely.' Danny put the papers on his work table, removed the paper clip, and thumbed through them till he found the sheet he was looking for. 'Here's the account information. Then he – as Darth Vader – started a page on Facebook, called "Red Dwarf Must Die".'

'Red Dwarf?'

'It was a show on the telly,' Cowley told him in the same patronizing tone of voice. 'Back when I was a kid.'

'And it was the name he used for another boy, it would seem,' Danny explained. 'The target for the cyber-bulling.' He shook his head. 'Man, he did not like this kid.'

Neville snatched the paper and scrutinized it. It was a printout of a series of messages: scurrilous, scatological, crude. And cruel – deliberately, excruciatingly cruel. Written in the almost indecipherable shorthand of texting, they painted a very ugly picture indeed.

'Bloody hell,' he said with feeling.

'You'll see that not all of the messages are from Darth Vader,' Danny pointed out. 'Lots of other people joined in.'

'Let's see.' Cowley craned his neck over Neville's shoulder. 'Luke Skywalker. Chewbacca. Han Solo. Padmé. Princess Leia. Do I detect a theme here?'

This, Neville was beginning to realize, changed everything. Sebastian Frost had not been what he appeared, had not been the sunny darling his mother portrayed. There was something dark and deeply unpleasant in all of this. Something that made Neville want to drop the paper and wash his hands. With strong carbolic soap.

Cowley was beginning to catch up with the content of the messages. 'This is nasty stuff, Guv,' he said, stating the obvious. 'If I was this Red Dwarf kid, and read all this, I think I would have killed myself.'

Or someone else.

'I just have one question at this point,' Neville said slowly.

'Ask away,' Danny invited with a smug grin. 'I'll do my best to give you an answer.'

If Danny could do that, Neville would be a happy man. He swivelled his head and looked Danny in the eye. 'Who is Red Dwarf?'

For a long moment Callie just stared at Adam. 'We need to talk?' she echoed at last.

'Can I come in?' he repeated.

She stood back silently and he entered her room, seeming to fill it with his presence.

Callie looked involuntarily at the bed, suddenly conscious of the tangle of lace and silk spilling out of the shopping bag. Turning her back on Adam, she swept her purchases back into the bag, then moved it to the floor beside the bed.

Her legs, she realized, were no longer capable of holding her up. She sat down in the chair.

That might have been a mistake, she decided as soon as she'd done it. Her sponge bag and dressing gown were on the desk chair, leaving nowhere but the bed for Adam to sit.

The bed. Oh, God. He must be as conscious as she was of that narrow bed, and all it represented. How many nights they'd spent there, snuggled together like spoons ...

But Adam didn't sit down; he began pacing the length of the room – with his long legs, it didn't take more than a few strides for him to cover it in each direction. It made her nervous, but it was better than having him on the bed.

How strange it was for him to be here, Callie thought with one part of her brain. It had been strange enough for her to re-inhabit this room, but adding him to the oh-so-familiar setting, when he no longer had a part in her life, was bizarre.

John Kingsley, wise man that he was, had been right. It was now time for repentance and forgiveness. Time to move on. And what better place than this room, where they had shared so much?

Judging by his pacing, Adam was obviously nervous about asking her to forgive him. She could have made it easier for him, but decided that the words needed to come from him first.

'I wanted to talk to you,' Adam finally said.

Callie prepared her face with an encouraging smile. 'Yes?'

'The thing is, Callie ...' He turned and paced the other way. 'The thing is ... I've missed you. I'd like to start ... you know. Seeing you again.'

Those certainly weren't the words she'd expected. 'Seeing me again? But ... but you're *married*.'

By which she meant: you made your choice. And it wasn't me.

Adam stopped, frowned and waved his hand as though banishing a pesky insect. 'I'm not talking about sleeping together, if that's what you thought I meant.'

She stared at him. 'What *do* you mean, Adam?'

He ignored her question and carried on. 'Because, apart from the fact that it would be wrong, and sinful in the eyes of God, that's one area in which I have been truly blessed in my marriage. Pippa is a wonderful lover. Our sex life is brilliant. God has been very good to us.'

160

Way too much information, Callie said to herself in shocked disbelief. She wanted to cover her ears, but found her muscles incapable of movement.

Adam didn't seem to notice. He turned and traversed the room again. 'What I miss about you, Callie, is your . . . I don't know. I suppose your brain. We used to have such interesting discussions about all sorts of things. We were on the same wavelength. Remember how we used to talk half the night, about theology and our vocations?'

She remembered, but her vocal cords were as paralysed as the rest of her.

'I just don't have that with Pippa,' he said, with a baffled shrug. 'In every other way she's a wonderful helpmeet, and of course she's the wife God chose for me. But lately I've been missing those talks we used to have, you and I.'

In other words, Pippa was thick. The realization gave Callie a little thrill of guilty pleasure, and somehow unfroze her stunned brain – that brain that Adam so unexpectedly valued.

He turned towards her with a gesture of appeal, and a smile that once would have melted her heart. 'How about it?' he said. 'Shall we be friends again, then?'

He had not come to apologize, Callie said to herself. He had not come in repentance, to ask for her forgiveness. To turn over a new leaf, to move on.

He wasn't sorry for what he'd done to her. He didn't even seem to realize that he should be.

It was all about him, and his needs. All about Adam.

'How dare you?' she said quietly.

Now it was Adam's turn to stare. 'I beg your pardon?'

Callie stood up, and found that her legs were capable of holding her after all. She moved towards the door. 'It's time for you to leave, Adam,' she stated as she yanked the handle and opened the door. 'Go. Now.'

'Who is Red Dwarf?' Danny echoed. 'Ah. Unfortunately, that's not such an easy question to answer.'

'Why not?' Neville demanded.

'Like I said, this Sebastian – Darth Vader – was really good at covering his tracks. Everything was done through Facebook. And I reckon quite a few of the messages were posted from his phone,' he added. 'He might have sent texts, as well, if he thought they couldn't be traced.'

'His phone! Then we can get his phone records, can't we?'

Danny sighed and shook his head. 'Think about it.'

'His phone was smashed,' Cowley reminded him. 'We don't even know what his number was.'

'I can try to get the information off the SIM card,' Danny offered. 'As I said the other day, it will take some time, the condition it's in, but if it's important . . .'

'The first thing we need is his phone number,' Neville stated. 'Then we can get the ball rolling with his service provider. It's a murder investigation. They'll give us his records, no questions asked.'

Danny slapped his palm against his forehead. 'Duh. If all you need is his phone number, why can't you just ask?'

'Ask who?' Cowley demanded. 'He's dead, in case you forgot.'

'His mates. His girlfriend. His mum.'

Of course. 'Get on to it, Sid,' Neville said. 'Not his girlfriend,' he added hastily.

'And not his mum,' Cowley reminded him, scowling.

'Hugo, then. Ring him. Get the number. Don't ask him any other questions – nothing more about the bullying,' Neville said, thinking aloud. Hugo, he knew instinctively in his gut, was Luke Skywalker – that floppy blond hair made it a dead cert – but getting him to admit it was going to require some careful strategy. 'We don't want to go there just yet. Not till I've had a chance to absorb all of this.' He waved his hand at the printouts. 'And when you have the number, you can contact his service provider.'

'I'll stay on for a while and make a start on resurrecting the SIM card,' Danny volunteered.

'Good man.' Neville scooped up the pile of printouts. 'And I'll get on with these.' He stopped before he got to the door. 'Thanks, Danny,' he said belatedly. 'I really appreciate this. You've done great work.'

John Kingsley was the first of Margaret's guests to arrive. She met him at the door and took him upstairs to the drawing room, then went to the kitchen to get him a drink.

She returned, a glass of wine in each hand, to find him at the table by the oriel window, studying the framed photos of Alexander.

'Thank you so much,' John Kingsley said, accepting a glass and indicating the photos with his other hand. 'This is your son?'

'That's right,' she confirmed. 'Alexander. He lives in London. He's an architect.' Margaret smiled, as she always did when she thought about her son. 'You have a . . . a daughter, isn't it, in London? You were visiting her before you came here?'

He nodded. 'Yes. Lucy. Her husband is a vicar, and pretty tied to his parish, so if I want to see them, I have to be the one who does the travelling. Especially at the major festivals like Easter,' he added. 'You know how it is.'

Margaret did know. 'I've been a parish priest.'

'I have three sons as well,' John Kingsley volunteered. 'So I do a fair bit of travelling about these days, now that I've retired. It's good to be able to keep up with the grandchildren.'

'Oh, you have grandchildren?' she asked obediently.

'Yes. I'll spare you the details.' John Kingsley gave her a charming, self-deprecating smile. 'There's nothing more boring than hearing about other people's grandchildren. Especially if you don't have any yourself . . . ?' he added with a lift in his voice, inviting a reply.

'No. I don't. Alexander . . . is gay.' She went on hastily. 'Don't get me wrong. I don't mind. It's the way he is, he's happy, and I'm absolutely fine with it. But there won't be any grandchildren.' She indicated the photo of Alexander and Luke. 'Here he is with his partner. Luke.'

'In my experience, mothers usually cope quite well with gay sons. Sometimes their fathers have a more difficult time.'

Margaret recognized the truth of that. With Alexander, it was as if she had always known – on some level – so that when, as a teen, he'd summoned up the courage to tell his parents, it had taken her a mere split second to assimilate it and reconcile it with her understanding of him as a person. Hal had found it much harder; for months he'd struggled to come to terms with something he'd never even suspected.

'Maybe because mothers usually know their sons better than their fathers do,' she said, half to herself.

'Exactly.' John Kingsley nodded, then took a sip of his wine. 'You're . . . a widow, I believe?' he asked delicately.

'Yes. That is . . .' Her voice trailed off as a stab of pain, almost physical, shot through her, and she gulped at her wine to gain a few seconds. She was, suddenly, filled with an almost irresistible urge to tell this empathetic man the whole distressing story, to pour out the things she'd never dared to tell anyone else. She sensed, somehow, that he would listen and not judge her – not as others would judge her. Not as she judged herself. It would be such a relief to tell him.

Margaret took a deep breath. 'My husband, Hal,' she began, and then the doorbell rang, cutting across her words.

'Oh. That must be Keith,' John Kingsley said.

She sighed. Disappointed? Relieved? 'Yes,' she agreed. 'I'd better get the door, hadn't I?'

Neville rubbed his face with both hands, unconsciously shaking his head.

He was at his desk, alone with the printouts from Sebastian Frost's computer, turning over one page after another.

It didn't get any better. If anything, it got worse.

Neville didn't consider himself particularly shockable; by this stage in his life and career, he'd thought he'd pretty much seen it all. His job brought him, day after day, cheek by jowl with the underbelly of life. He'd seen brutal death, in all its permutations. He'd seen bullying, up close and personal. He'd seen blood flying, heard the crack of flesh against bone. He'd been exposed first hand to the things people were capable of doing to each other, in the name of hate – or in the name of love.

Yet this shocked him, more than he'd thought possible.

The shock he'd felt when he'd first seen the messages – visceral and raw – was reinforced over and over again as he turned the pages. Part of it, he suspected, had to do with the age – fifteen? sixteen? – of the people involved. Kids could be cruel – of course he knew that, from his own childhood. But the language they employed, the filthy words they so deliberately directed at another human being . . .

Had he known words like that at fifteen? Hell, he didn't even know all of them *now*. But he was in no doubt about their intent, if not their exact meaning.

Much of it was homophobic, of course. Neville was amazed at the variety of unpleasant ways that a hatred of homosexuality could be conveyed. Queer and poofter were the mild ones, just the beginning. It went on from there to heights of descriptive vulgarity.

Was Red Dwarf gay? It didn't much matter. They thought he was, and that was all that counted.

Neville had witnessed homophobia before – casual, offhand usually. It wasn't uncommon in the police force, to say the least. His own feelings about it were largely unexamined. Secure in his own sexuality – his strong heterosexual impulses – he had never felt particularly threatened by homosexuality in others. Live and let live, he'd always said, with perhaps a hint of condescension.

But now that he was about to become a father . . .

What if he had a kid who was gay? It could happen.

How would he feel about it? Disappointed? Disgusted?

Or fearful that this kind of thing might be directed at him?

Nothing was being achieved by wallowing in this filth, Neville told himself firmly. He shuffled the pages together and tossed them in his in tray. He was going home.

John Kingsley yawned, covering his mouth. 'Oh, excuse me,' he said.

'I'll make some coffee,' said Margaret. 'Or would you prefer tea?'

He put down his pudding spoon and shook his head. 'I'm really sorry, my dear, but I'm going to have to call it a night. This has been a splendid evening, but I'm afraid it's past my bedtime.'

Margaret escorted him to the door; when she returned, Keith Moody was still at the table. 'I'm not going yet,' he said with a cheeky grin. 'And I'll have some of that coffee you offered.'

'Fine,' she smiled. 'Shall we have it in the drawing room?'

'Sounds good to me.'

Margaret had already laid out a tray with cups and a cafetière in the kitchen, so it was just a matter of boiling the kettle. Switching it on, she removed the third cup from the tray and put it away.

It had been a most successful meal, she reflected, as she waited for the kettle to boil. In spite of her fears about her cooking skills being rusty, all had gone according to plan, and her guests had been enthusiastic about the results.

She had enjoyed herself, as well. John Kingsley was a dear – one of the nicest people she'd ever met, she decided – and the more time she spent with Keith Moody, the better she liked him. Already, with all of the things they'd discovered they had in common, there was such an ease between him that she felt as if she'd known him for years. That, and a little frisson, a niggle, that she wasn't yet ready to examine too closely ...

Keith appeared at the kitchen door just as the kettle boiled. 'Can I carry that tray for you?' he offered.

'Thanks.' Margaret poured the boiling water into the cafetière and replaced its lid.

He took it through into the drawing room.

'It's a shame John had to rush off like that,' Margaret said. 'He really is a lovely man, isn't he?'

'The best,' Keith confirmed with feeling. 'I'd trust him with my life, you know.'

They chatted over their coffee, then Margaret remembered something. 'Oh! I'd meant to offer you a chocolate with your coffee.' She went to the drawer where she'd stashed the large box of chocolates which had been on her desk that morning; she'd put them there mostly to remove them from her sight and minimize the temptation to tuck in.

The appearance of the box of chocolates brought a knowing smile to Keith's face, confirming all of Margaret's suspicions. 'You,' she said. 'You've been leaving the chocolates on my desk, all along. Why?'

'Why not?' he countered. 'Everyone knows that you love chocolate. I wanted to do something nice for you. Because you're special.'

'But you didn't really even know me, when you started doing it.'

He stood up, put his empty cup on the tray, then took the box of chocolates from her and put it down on the coffee table. 'I know you now,' he said. 'And after the last few days, Margaret, I have to tell you something.' Keith paused until she made eye contact. 'I think I've fallen in love with you.'

Margaret stopped breathing for a second. He took a step closer and folded her in his arms; her head nestled into his shoulder naturally, as though it belonged there. She exhaled, then breathed in deeply, savouring the spicy scent of his aftershave, the feel of the tweed against her cheek. Suddenly, inexplicably, she wanted to cry.

But a moment later he kissed her, and crying was the last thing on her mind.

Interlude: from the front page of the Thursday Daily Globe

STABBED BOY WAS A BULLY
By Lilith Noone

Tragic teen Sebastian Frost, who was stabbed on Paddington Green late on Sunday night, was a bully, one of his friends has revealed.

The friend, who has asked not to be named, confirms that another boy at their school (who also cannot be identified, for legal reasons) was the main target of Sebastian's cyber-bullying on a special Facebook page. 'Seb hated his guts,' the friend said. 'We all did, really. I mean, R★★ D★★★★ is just so lame. So f★★★ing g★y.'

He added, 'But it was just a bit of fun, to be honest.'

166

I have to ring Callie, was Mark's first waking thought on Thursday morning. He'd tried to reach her, multiple times, the night before, but her phone had gone straight to voicemail. Either she'd let the battery run down and forgotten to charge it, he surmised, or she'd switched it off while in a setting – a church service, a group session – where a ringing phone would be inappropriate, and not remembered to turn it back on.

Or she didn't want to talk to him.

Either of the first two possibilities he could believe, and he could live with. It wouldn't be the first time.

But what if she didn't want to talk to him?

Why wouldn't she?

His imagination supplied him all too readily with a reason, and a scenario. Adam. Picking up where they'd left off.

Yes, Adam was married now. But there was such a thing as proximity, and opportunity. An old spark, flaring up, overwhelming both of them whether they'd sought it out or not.

He didn't want to think about it. And yet . . .

Mark reached for his phone and pushed the speed dial button.

'The person you are trying to reach is not available,' said the mechanical voice. 'Please leave a message.'

He'd left messages last night. Several of them, and she hadn't rung him back. 'It's me,' he said tersely. 'Ring me when you can.'

Then he went to take his shower, leaving the phone on the edge of the basin so he could hear it if it rang.

It *did* ring, at the worst possible time – just as he was washing his hair under the shower head. He switched off the water, flung open the glass door, and lunged for the phone, a split second before he registered that it wasn't Callie's ringtone.

'Hello?' he barked into the phone.

'Did I catch you at a bad time?' Neville Stewart asked, with patently false sympathy.

Mark's reply was blunt and to the point. 'Yes.' He was starkers, dripping all over the floor – which his flatmate would not appreciate – and shampoo was running into his eyes. And it wasn't the call he'd been waiting for.

'Well, too bad. Things are about to get worse, mate.'

He reached for his towel. 'Tell me.'

'You haven't seen the *Globe* this morning, then?'

It took a second for him to realize what Neville was on about. 'No. Why would I have?'

'Well, then.' Neville paused. 'Brace yourself.'

Getting up on Thursday morning wasn't high on Callie's list of priorities. She'd slept badly, with troubling dreams, so when the bell chimed for Morning Prayer all she wanted to do was pull the duvet over her head and have a lie-in.

She wasn't going to be allowed to do that, she realized, when there was a loud knock on the door.

'Callie? Are you in there?' Tamsin demanded.

She sighed, climbed out of bed and unlocked the door.

'You're not ready for Morning Prayer. Or even breakfast,' Tamsin observed, looking her up and down.

Callie ran her hands through her tousled hair, considered a sarcastic reply, but settled for a neutral one. 'I suppose not.'

'Are you OK?' Tamsin scrutinized her closely. 'We hardly had a word out of you last night. At dinner, and in the bar. Is something the matter?'

'Oh, Tamsin.' Callie plopped back down on the bed. 'It's Adam.'

'*Him* again.' Tamsin snorted in a rather unladylike manner. 'I know he's a pain, but can't you just ignore him, like the rest of us do? I mean, I thought you'd moved on. To your hunky Italian. Remember?'

'He came here yesterday,' Callie blurted out. She hadn't meant to tell Tamsin, but there was no escaping now.

'Adam? To your room?'

She nodded miserably.

'Oh my God. To have his wicked way with you? Just like old times?'

Trust Tamsin. 'No,' Callie said tartly. 'Quite the opposite, in fact. He was very clear about that. God has blessed him with a wife who's great in bed, so he no longer has any interest whatsoever in my body.'

'Then what's the problem?' Tamsin widened her eyes. 'You didn't want to sleep with him, did you?'

'Of course not. Don't be ridiculous.'

168

Tamsin lowered herself into the chair and gave a patient sigh. 'I'm missing something here, clearly. You're going to have to explain it to your thick friend.'

'I just don't understand why I've become so repulsive,' Callie said, round the lump in her throat. 'My fiancé doesn't want to sleep with me. And now my ex makes it very clear that he doesn't, either. What is wrong with me? Am I *that* hideous?'

The inbox on Lilith's computer was full of messages. Ignoring most of them, she opened the one from her editor.

It was brief and to the point. 'Good work, Lilith,' it said. 'More, please.' He'd signed it Rob.

Not Rob Gardiner-Smith. Just Rob.

That was a first. A milestone.

Lilith smiled to herself, triumphant.

The kicker, of course, was the second sentence. She had to produce more. This was just a beginning. She couldn't rest on her laurels now. And where was she going to come up with the next story? In her bones she felt she'd pushed Olly as far as she could. He'd clammed up towards the end, and now that the story was in print, even someone as dim as Olly would realize that he had effectively betrayed his friend into her hands. No, that well was now dry, and surely none of Sebastian's other mates would talk to her either.

Her phone rang; she didn't recognize the number. 'Lilith Noone speaking.'

'This is Detective Inspector Stewart,' said a stiff, barely controlled voice on the other end. 'And I have a question for you, Miss Noone.'

Her day was getting better and better. 'You're not going to insult me by asking for my confidential sources, are you?' she said sweetly.

'Insult you? How is that an insult?'

'It would be an insult to my professional integrity, to imply that I could possibly reveal one of my sources. You know how we journalists operate, Detective Inspector. We're prepared to go to prison if need be, to protect our sources.' She was really enjoying herself now. 'It's one of the cornerstones of our free society. And it's part of my job. I'm afraid you'll have to look elsewhere for someone to help you with *your* job.'

'Bollocks,' he snapped rudely. 'I don't want to hear any of that "you do your job, I'll do mine" crap. My job is catching killers. Yours is selling newspapers. They're not exactly on the same level, are they?'

'Insulting me will get you nowhere, Inspector,' she said. 'And neither will anything else. I'm afraid I can't help you.' With a smile she pushed the button to end the call.

Callie had managed to pull herself together, more or less, with a bit of help from Tamsin. Neither one of them had made it to breakfast, though Tamsin was successful in begging an apple from the cheeky dining hall attendant before he closed the doors. She crunched into it as they made their way to the lecture hall for the morning session.

'Oh, that's better,' she said with feeling. 'I hope there's something good for lunch. I'm starving.'

'Sorry for making you miss your breakfast,' Callie apologized meekly.

'Greater love hath no woman, than she give up her breakfast for her friend,' Tamsin quipped. 'All I can say is, you owe me one, Miss Anson.'

'Big time,' Callie agreed, just as she remembered that she'd left her phone in her room on the charger. She stopped in her tracks. 'You go on ahead,' she said. 'I'll catch you up in a few minutes.'

Tamsin stopped as well and gave her an inquisitive look, her mouth too full of apple to speak.

'Forgot my phone,' she explained over her shoulder as she headed back towards B staircase.

Callie huffed her way quickly up two flights of stairs – not that out of shape, then, she told herself with satisfaction – unlocked her door, grabbed the phone off the charger, and retraced her steps back down the stairs to the courtyard.

Checking her watch quickly for the time – if she was lucky, they might not have started yet – she nearly ran headlong into the principal's secretary. 'Oh, I'm so sorry,' Callie gasped.

Hanna Young seemed equally taken aback. 'My fault. I suppose I wasn't looking where I was going, to be honest.'

'Me, neither,' admitted Callie. She was going to have to start being more careful: this was becoming something of a habit.

Before she could resume her progress, Hanna put out a hand to stop her. 'I suppose I'm a bit upset,' the other woman said. 'I don't really know what to do, to be honest. I could use some advice.'

I don't need this, Callie thought. But she fixed a smile on her face and tried to conceal her impatience to be on her way. 'I'm not sure I'm the best person for that,' she said.

Hanna ignored the demur. 'I've just seen something ... disturbing,' she confided, lowering her voice. 'Dr Moody. You know – Mad Phil, as he's called?'

'Yeees ...' Now Callie was sure she didn't want to hear this. But perhaps it was better for her to be the recipient of whatever scurrilous gossip the woman was now passing out, instead of Nicky or someone else who would disseminate it still further – Jennifer Groves, maybe, or even Tamsin, who wouldn't be able to stop herself from telling Nicky.

'He came into the principal's office. He came up behind her, and touched her on the shoulder.'

'Nothing too scandalous in that, surely?'

'And then he bent over, like he was going to ... like he was about to kiss her! Right there, in her office! But then he caught my eye, and saw that I was watching him, so he stopped.' She drew a ragged breath. 'I had to get out of there, to be honest. I mean, doesn't the man have any shame? He's an absolute menace. A sexual predator.' Hanna said the last words self-consciously, as though it were something she'd heard on the telly, or looked up on the internet.

'But he didn't kiss her,' Callie pointed out. 'All he did was touch her on the shoulder, according to you.'

Hanna widened her eyes. 'And now I've left him alone with her! Who knows what he might be up to, without me there to stop him? I shouldn't have left her!'

'Well, go back, then,' Callie suggested. Was this the advice the woman was looking for? She stifled a sigh of impatience.

'But what should I *do*?' Hanna demanded passionately.

'Nothing. Try to forget about it. Ignore it.'

'Ignore it? But don't you think I need to warn her? The principal? Don't you think I need to tell her what I know about that ... that beastly man?'

For a moment Callie wondered whether Hanna was interested in Mad Phil herself, and this was all just a manifestation of jealousy. Whatever her motive, though, this wasn't healthy. And it could be dangerous: a man's reputation – his very career – was at stake. In a place like this, allegations of sexual impropriety wouldn't be tolerated, especially as the man in question was a priest.

'No,' she said firmly. 'I don't think you should say anything at all to the principal. Promise me you won't.'

Hanna nodded reluctantly, as Callie added, even more firmly, 'Don't say anything to *anyone*.'

'Bloody woman!' Neville shouted, resisting the temptation to hurl the phone across the room.

'Lilith Noone?' Cowley guessed as he came into Neville's office.

'You've got it in one.' Neville scowled at his sergeant. 'I didn't really expect her to co-operate, but she didn't have to be so damned smug and bloody-minded about it.' He slammed the phone down and put his head in his hands. 'Professional integrity, my arse,' he muttered.

'Cheer up, Guv.' Cowley was grinning, which served to enrage Neville even further.

'Why would I want to do that? And by the way,' he added sourly, 'where the hell have you been?'

Cowley whipped his hand from behind his back, like an old-fashioned magician, and flourished a wad of folded-up papers. 'Results!' he announced. 'I've been hassling the kid's service provider, and they've finally come through. In spades!'

'Phone records?' Neville's mood lifted instantly as he stretched out his hand for the papers.

The sergeant held them just out of his reach, evidently enjoying his moment of triumph to the full. 'Text messages,' he announced.

Neville lunged forward and snatched the papers, then smoothed them out on his desk and tried to make sense of the columns of numbers. He'd expected messages, yet saw nothing but digits: dates, times and presumably telephone numbers. There was a pattern here, but it was difficult to tell what it was.

Cowley leaned over his shoulder, pointing. 'Here, Guv. Lots of these texts were to his mates, as you'd expect. Hugo, Olly, Tom. Some to his mum's phone. We know all of those numbers, so we can eliminate them.'

'So what does that leave us?'

'This number here.' Cowley indicated one which appeared on the list with a frequency unmatched by any of the others. 'He texted this number dozens of times, every day.'

'It must be his girlfriend, then. Lexie.' That made sense, Neville reasoned. He would text his girlfriend often, not least to arrange to meet up when the coast was clear. When his parents were working and it was safe for her to come round . . .

'No.'

Neville twisted round to look at him; Cowley was shaking his head. 'That's what I thought at first,' he admitted.

172

'Then who?'

'The bird in charge didn't want to tell me. Customer confidentiality, and all that sort of rubbish.' He grinned again. 'But I ... persuaded her, shall we say.'

Neville wasn't very successful at hiding his impatience. Letting Sid have his little moment of drama was all well and good, but time was passing. After all, at the end of the day, if they wanted to know who the number belonged to, they could always ring it and ask.

'And?' he demanded.

'And the phone is registered to someone called Joshua Bradley. I even managed to get his address off her.' Cowley reached into his pocket and pulled out a slip of paper. 'Using my considerable charm, it must be said.'

'Well, then.' Neville stood up. 'What are we waiting for?'

Margaret had seen the look on her secretary's face as Keith had leaned in to kiss her. She'd seen the expression of absolute horror, the mask of shock, and then an instant later the woman had fled through the door and away.

It was like a faceful of ice water. Like a sucker punch to the stomach.

It was a wake-up call.

'Not now,' she'd said to Keith, pushing him away.

They were already late for the first session, so he seemed to accept the rebuff with equanimity.

Now, as she sat in the back row of the lecture hall, in a seat nowhere near the one Keith had chosen, she didn't hear a word of what John Kingsley was saying.

What, she asked herself, had she done?

Her shame, her mortification must show on her face, she feared. She put her hands to her cheeks and found that they were burning. All she could hope for was that everyone else was focused on the front of the room, and not the back.

What had she done? What had she been thinking?

For a moment – a brief moment, but long enough – she had allowed herself to forget. To forget everything that had happened in her life. To forget Hal. To forget, above all, that she had forfeited the right to enjoy any man's kisses the way she had enjoyed Keith's kisses the night before. To have a man's arms round her – possessive, comforting arms – was something she'd never thought she would experience again.

She had no right to take pleasure in it. Hanna Young, with her scandalized expression, knew that, even if Keith didn't. The look on her secretary's face had told Margaret all she needed to know.

It had brought her back to her senses. Painfully, horribly.

She was a middle-aged woman, with an adult child. A professional woman, a priest in the Church of England. How could she possibly have forgotten herself so thoroughly, and behaved like a hormonal teenager?

And now what?

They'd both said things last night that should never had been said, and done things that should never have been done. Things that couldn't be undone or taken back now.

How could she tell Keith, now, that it was all over, virtually before it had begun? That she'd made a terrible mistake, led him on, when she'd had no right to do so?

At the front of the room, John Kingsley thanked the people who had just engaged in a role-playing exercise, then said something that caught Margaret's attention, in spite of herself.

'We've been exploring all sorts of different areas of ministry over the last few days,' he said. 'We've talked about the nuts-and-bolts things you've all experienced in your first year – the things you've expected and ones that have caught you by surprise, about time management and diary-juggling, about the challenges of sermon-writing, about your relationships with your training incumbents and your parishioners. Now we're going to move on to another area of relationships. We're going to think about the people closest to us – our families and significant others. Spouses, partners, friends – the people we care about the most, and how our call to priesthood affects those relationships. Can you be a good priest, and at the same time be a good husband, wife, parent, friend?'

What a wise man he was, Margaret said to herself. Involuntarily, her eyes sought out Keith Moody.

He was looking at her, and smiling.

Margaret looked away.

Miranda Frost was no longer willing to go on living in limbo, she decided on Thursday morning. What was the point of sitting round, drinking endless cups of coffee and re-living her son's death? Richard might feel differently – he probably did – but she'd had enough. What else could she do at this point? They couldn't make funeral arrangements until the coroner gave the go-ahead; they couldn't even answer the phone themselves in case it was the press.

The family liaison officer was pleasant enough, and reasonably tidy – for a man – but his presence was irksome to her.

She would tell him not to come here tomorrow. And she would go back to work. Why not? Work would be good for her. It would keep her occupied, mind and body. She might even save a life or two. Redress the cosmic balance.

Already she'd arranged for her cleaner, Iris Bolt, to come today. Up till now she'd not been able to face Iris, who had been with them for so many years and had known Sebastian since he was born. Today Miranda was feeling stronger, and noticing the little things in the house that needed doing. There was a film of dust on the surfaces in the sitting room; the kitchen sink could use a good scrub.

She heard Iris's key in the lock, followed by her called greeting – Iris always announced herself. Just in case.

'In here,' Miranda called back from the kitchen, where she was occupying herself by disassembling and cleaning the coffee machine. She braced herself for Iris's inevitable expressions of sympathy and sorrow. Get it over with, she told herself.

Iris dropped her bag on the kitchen table and came to Miranda, folding her in her arms – something no one else would have dared to do, even with a relationship going back nearly twenty years. 'Oh, you poor lamb,' she crooned.

Miranda stood stiffly, enduring the embrace for as long as she could before she disengaged herself. 'Thank you, Iris,' she said.

'To think that someone would kill that dear boy, in cold blood! My own blood runs cold, just thinking about it,' Iris Bolt pronounced. 'I haven't been able to stop thinking about it, not for a minute, since I heard.'

'Thank you,' Miranda repeated.

'And I can just imagine how it must be for you and Dr Frost. I mean, if something like that had ever happened to one of mine . . . oh, it doesn't bear thinking about, and that's God's truth.'

Miranda pressed her lips together.

'I said it to my Ernie this morning. "That poor lamb," I said. "She needs a hug, and that's no mistake."'

'Well, there's plenty to do here, Iris,' Miranda said with forced heartiness. 'You haven't been here since Sunday, and the house has suffered for it.'

175

Iris ignored the hint. 'And I want you to know, Mrs Frost, that I don't believe a word of it. Not a word.'

'A word of what?' Miranda frowned.

'That rubbish about bullying. In the *Daily Globe*. Shocking lies, that's what I call it. Your Sebastian – *our* Sebastian – a bully? I never heard such a pack of lies in all my life!'

Miranda stared at her, astonished.

Halfway through the morning session, there was a break for coffee.

Tamsin narrowed her eyes at Callie over a cup of tepid brew. 'You're awfully quiet,' she stated. 'Please tell me you're not still obsessing over that toerag Adam.'

'No. I'm not.'

Callie had other things to worry about. She wished, in a way, that she hadn't been the recipient of Hanna Young's confidences, but on the other hand, she couldn't help feeling that it was a very good thing indeed that she, and no one else, knew what Hanna had seen.

Was there anything in it? Could there possibly be any truth in Hanna's fevered speculations?

She couldn't help herself, looking first at Mad Phil and then at the principal, then back again.

They were not together. Mad Phil was talking to John Kingsley. It seemed to Callie that the principal was in his line of sight, and he glanced occasionally in her direction. Was he trying to make eye contact with her?

She, though, had her back to him, and was talking – listening, mostly, from what Callie could tell – to Scott Browning. Scott, the bishop-in-waiting, the one in their year, it was commonly agreed, who was most likely to wear a mitre one day. It figured that he would be sucking up to the principal, Callie thought uncharitably. He was probably telling her how useless his training incumbent was, and asking her whether she could find him a better one.

'What's going on?' Tamsin demanded. 'Who are you looking at?'

'Nothing. No one.' Callie frowned. 'I'm not looking at anyone. And there's nothing going on,' she added firmly. 'Absolutely nothing.'

Neville and Cowley didn't have far to go. Joshua Bradley, it transpired, lived in the shadow of the Westway flyover, no more than a ten-minute walk from the police station.

'We'll walk,' Neville decided. It would take less time than faffing about with a car, and trying to find a place to park it when they got there.

Their route took them through the tree-lined walkways of Paddington Green, right past the crime scene. The police tape had been removed, Neville noted, but something else was there: a shrine to the memory of Sebastian Frost, with cellophane-wrapped bunches of flowers heaped up against the iron railings of St Mary's churchyard.

He stopped for a minute to check it out. The flowers were wilting; most of them were dead and beginning to smell a bit rank. No teddy bears, like he'd seen on some of these shrines – from what he knew of Sebastian, he didn't seem like a teddy bear sort of kid – but there were a few *Star Wars* Lego figures. Interesting. Darth Vader . . .

And there were cards and notes, of course. Badly spelled, almost indecipherable in most cases. 'What do they teach these kids in school?' Neville asked sourly. 'I may not be the world's greatest speller, but at least I tried when I was at school. By God, the nuns would have thrashed me within an inch of my life if I'd written anything like this.'

'It's because of all that texting,' Cowley said with maddening patience, as if he were explaining it to some cranky pensioner bemoaning the defunct standards of his long-lost youth. 'They don't learn how to spell properly. And they don't care. My nephew's just the same. He doesn't give a flying monkey's.'

Neville sighed. 'Well, God help us all.' He bent over and plucked one of the notes at random. '"Ul B mist",' he read. 'Give me strength.'

'Do you notice what's *not* here, Guv?'

'Teddy bears?' he hazarded.

'No. Other kids. No one's here.' Cowley gestured round the churchyard.

'True.' Neville straightened up and looked at the empty space. Cowley had a point, he admitted to himself. Where were all of Sebastian's mates now? Had they forgotten about him already?

Someone was loping along the path in their direction, camera bag slung over his shoulder.

Neville vaguely recognized him as a photographer from one of the tabloids: not someone he necessarily wanted to engage with. 'Let's get a move on, Sid,' he suggested, starting off at a brisk walk.

But the man with the camera bag hailed them. 'Yo, Inspector! Hold on a second!'

'What is it?'

'Detective Inspector Stewart, right?'

Neville stopped reluctantly. 'Yes.'

'I'd really like a photo of you, here by the railings. Looking at those flowers, like. Won't take a minute, I promise.'

'No, thanks.'

'But it would be perfect for tomorrow's paper,' the man pleaded.

'I have work to do,' Neville snapped, continuing on his way.

Perfect for tomorrow's paper, indeed. Detective Inspector Stewart, CIO in the Sebastian Frost case, looking at the flowers instead of getting on with catching the killer. 'Dead Flowers for Teen Bully – Police Stop to Smell the Roses', or something along those lines. He could just imagine it.

'This way, Guv.' They got to the end of the green and turned into St Mary's Terrace, a road lined with a mixture of white Georgian terraces, red brick Victorian mansion blocks and ugly post-war blocks of flats. Those German bombs again. You just couldn't get away from it in London, Neville reflected, especially this close to a railway station. It was a double shame: sad that the splendid old buildings had been blown to smithereens, and equally sad that they'd been rebuilt in an age of scarce resources and abysmal architecture.

They turned again, heading towards the flyover, on a road which seemed to have suffered particularly badly from both the bombs and the rebuilding. A stretch of council housing had been thrown up on the right, six-storey blocks of flats in cheap yellow brick, bristling with satellite dishes. On the other side was their destination, the gated entrance to a mews. Low rise, brown brick, still ugly. The gates were there, Neville presumed, mainly to keep unauthorized cars out, as the mews flats were blessed with ground-level garages and private parking bays – a rarity in this part of London.

Of course the gates were locked, and required a key-code to open. Neville pressed the buzzer with the palm of his hand and waited impatiently for the arrival of the attendant, who proved to be surly as well as slow. 'Private property,' he announced. 'No entrance.'

That required production of warrant cards, which they waved at him through the iron bars.

'Which flat do you want then?' the man said reluctantly, pushing a button from within to release the gates.

Neville was in no mood to be forthcoming. 'Bradley.'

The man pointed. 'That one there. But he's not at home,' he added, almost gleefully. 'His car's gone, see? I seen him leave this morning, like always.'

'Thanks.' Neville headed towards the front door of the flat, in an alcove next to the garage door.

'He's not there, I said,' the man called after them.

Neville ignored him and rang the bell. He tapped his foot, suddenly unwilling to wait a moment longer, and pushed the bell again, even as he heard the sound of footsteps descending the steps towards the door.

There was another moment of delay, accompanied by the sound of a bolt being shot and a chain being removed, then the door swung open a little way.

'Yes?'

A boy stood there looking at them. At first Neville took him for a young child, then realized that he was just quite short, and probably several years older than his size would indicate. Fifteen or sixteen, at a guess, given the deepness of his voice and the stubble on his cheeks. Ginger stubble.

Ginger hair.

'Joshua Bradley?' Neville asked.

'That's right. Josh,' he added, widening his eyes.

Neville glanced at Cowley, who nodded. He didn't need to say anything; Neville knew what he was thinking.

They'd just found Red Dwarf.

CHAPTER 15

Mark went to an Italian restaurant in Praed Street, near Paddington Station, for his lunch break. He'd been there before; he knew it wasn't as good as the family restaurant, La Venezia, but he also knew – from experience – that there were far worse, and this one was reliable. And cheap. He could get a plate of pasta, a glass of wine, with a decent shot of espresso after, and not have to take out a bank loan.

He put his phone on the table while he waited for his food. No luck yet in talking to Callie; surely she would ring him soon, or at least turn her phone on so he could reach her.

There was a tumbler of long, crunchy breadsticks on the table. He took one and bit off the end, telling himself not to obsess. She *would* ring. She would. Maybe during her own lunch break. Any time now.

But when the phone rang, it wasn't Callie's ringtone.

Chiara, the caller display revealed. Mark sighed, remembering he'd told his niece she could ring him any time she needed to talk. He just wasn't in the mood for this right now.

'*Ciao, nipotina*,' he said, forcing a cheerful tone of voice.

'Hey, Uncle Marco.'

'What's up?'

'Are you busy tomorrow?' she asked. 'I mean *busy* busy?'

'Well, I'm working. It's Friday. A work day.' He knew he was hedging; Miranda Frost had already told him that he wouldn't be required tomorrow, so in theory he could be a bit flexible, but that wasn't something he was ready to reveal to Chiara.

She sighed. 'And you can't get a day off? For something really, really important?'

'Why don't you just tell me what you need me for.' At least it wasn't his sister, asking him to wait tables at the restaurant. He'd been guilt-tripped into doing that more than once.

'It's a Fun Walk. To raise money for the church. We've all got sponsors and everything. Don't you remember, Uncle Marco? You said you'd give me twenty pounds if I finished.'

He had a vague recollection of saying something like that, but it had been a long time ago. 'That was months ago, wasn't it?'

'Well, I asked you months ago. But the walk is tomorrow.'

'And you need me to come and cheer you on?' he guessed.

'Not exactly. I need you to go with me,' she explained. 'It's a Parent and Child Fun Walk. Kids can't do it on their own – it's part of the rules.'

'But I'm not your parent,' Mark said, just as he realized that he was stepping into the giant chasm that had opened at his feet.

There was a stifled sob on the other end of the phone. 'Dad was supposed to go with me,' Chiara gulped. 'Like you said, it was ages ago. Dad and I. We were going to do it together.'

Madre di Dio. 'Your mother,' he said helplessly. 'She can't . . . ?' Of course she couldn't. She would be working at the restaurant, and that was sacrosanct.

'Mum's working. There's a big party in at lunchtime,' she said, so there's no way she can get away.' Chiara sighed deeply down the phone. 'Please, Uncle Marco? Please? I don't have a dad any longer, but you're my uncle. Isn't there any way you can get off work to go with me? I've been looking forward to it so much. And it's for a good cause. Wouldn't you feel guilty if the church lost all that money, just because my dad died?'

Mark knew when he was beaten. The girl must have taken guilt-trip lessons from her mother and her grandmother; she was world class already, at the age of thirteen. 'I'll see what I can do, *nipotina*,' he conceded. 'I should be able to manage it, without getting sacked.'

Instantly her tone of voice changed. 'Oh, that's brilliant! It's going to be such fun – you'll see. My friend Emilia and her mum are coming, and I hardly ever get to see her because she goes to a different school. She would have been just gutted if I'd had to cancel.'

'What time does it start? And where?'

'Oh, Mum will ring you later about all of that,' she said dismissively. 'The important thing is that you're coming. Love you, Uncle Marco!' she added as she hung up.

'Love you, too.' Mark sighed and dropped the phone back on the table.

Almost immediately it rang again: Callie's tune this time. He snatched it and punched the button. '*Cara mia!*' he said eagerly.

'This is the first chance I've had to ring,' she explained. 'I've been tied up all morning. Marco, it's so good to hear your voice.'

He couldn't help himself. 'But last night . . . ? I left so many messages. Is something wrong?'

'It's good to hear your voice,' Callie repeated.

181

Margaret had no appetite, and even less desire to be sociable, so she slipped away after the morning session and went into the chapel while everyone else trooped to the dining hall for lunch. The chapel was quiet, empty, peaceful. In contrast to the Victorian Gothic style which dominated most of the college, the chapel was decorated simply, with white walls, clear glass windows and movable chairs rather than stationary pews. Margaret always found it a restful haven.

She knelt down at the altar rail and tried to empty her mind of its turmoil, to place herself in God's hands and ask for his forgiveness.

After a few minutes, she was conscious of someone else in the chapel, but she was determined to block out the intrusion and concentrate on her prayers.

It was no good; she couldn't focus. Margaret gave up and rocked back on her heels, tears prickling her eyes.

'I'm so sorry. I hope I didn't disturb you, my dear,' said a soft voice at her side.

She turned to see John Kingsley, crouching down beside her.

'It doesn't matter,' she said dismissively, attempting a smile as she rose to her feet.

'But it does matter. Something is wrong. I can see that.' He put out a hand to stop her before she could flee. 'I've sensed it all morning. Something is troubling you. And it's something that's happened since last evening.'

Not trusting herself to speak, Margaret nodded.

'Would you like to talk about it, my dear?'

She tried to protest. 'You should be having lunch. You're very kind, but you don't have time for all of this, Canon.'

'Please, call me John,' he said. 'And I'm not hungry. You fed me so well last night that I don't think I'll need to eat again for a week.'

In spite of herself, Margaret smiled at the compliment, even as her throat tightened at the man's kindness.

'Come over here,' he urged. 'Let's sit down and talk for a few minutes.'

She had thought she would resist him, but discovered that she didn't really want to. It had been so long since she'd had anyone to talk to, anyone who would listen. Margaret was the one who usually did the listening; the prospect of being on the other side was as comforting as it was terrifying. So much pain . . .

She remembered the fleeting temptation, the night before, to confide in him, and knew now – as she'd known then – that he wouldn't judge her, and that he would truly listen.

'Tell me what's troubling you,' he invited, as they sat side-by-side in adjoining chairs.

'I don't want to burden you,' she protested.

'My dear Margaret, you must know that sharing in others' sorrows, as well as in their joys, is one of the chief privileges of priesthood.'

She *did* know it; she had often felt the same, though she'd rarely heard it so well expressed.

'Tell me,' he repeated.

So she told him.

'I was married,' she began, 'to an exceptional man.' Then she stopped, hardly knowing how to proceed.

'Hal,' he prompted.

Margaret sighed. 'Yes. Hal. I loved him very much. He was clever and kind. And the handsomest man I've ever laid eyes on,' she added. 'I wouldn't mention that, but it does play a part in what happened, I think. His attractiveness, I mean.'

The canon nodded.

'Hal was so supportive of my ministry,' she said. 'When I became an archdeacon, especially. Some men would have been threatened by that. But not Hal. Though he'd been a very successful man in his own right, he was quite happy to take a back seat to my career. He embraced life as a clergy spouse.'

'A rare treasure.'

She smiled. 'Indeed. He'd had a heart attack, you see. Too much job stress. So he gave it all up, sold his business, and became a painter and decorator.'

'Hmm. That could be a dangerous job for an attractive man,' John observed.

He understood! 'Exactly,' she confirmed. 'He was charming, funny, handsome. And doing a job that put him in contact with women, quite a lot of the time.'

'How did you feel about that?'

'I thought it was rather amusing, to tell you the truth,' Margaret admitted. 'He always came home and told me about the women who fell for him – it was sort of a joke between us. Because I trusted him, you see. I knew that he loved me, and I didn't have anything to worry about.'

John said nothing, waiting for her to continue. She swallowed, hard: this was the beginning of the difficult bit. 'But then,' she said at last, 'he did something that neither one of us had ever expected. He fell in love. With a dowdy vicar's wife – not even someone glamorous or beautiful.'

It had been horrible. He hadn't told her; she'd found out about it through a malicious third party. The bottom had dropped out of her secure world. Remembering, she clasped her hands together in her lap so hard that the nails dug into the backs of her hands.

'They didn't have an affair,' she went on, trying to keep the emotion out of her voice. 'They were both too ... good. Too honourable to give in and violate their marriage vows. That's what he told me, and I believed him.'

'But it must have been very painful for you.'

'I just couldn't cope with it,' she confessed. 'He gave her up. Her husband never even knew. Very *Brief Encounter*,' she added with a bitter little smile. 'But I couldn't forget what he'd done to me. The emotional betrayal ... falling in love with someone else. It was worse, in a way, than if he'd slept with her and not loved her, or at least it seemed that way to me at the time. It undermined everything I believed about myself and about our marriage.'

'I can understand that,' he said gravely.

'I tried to carry on. To put it behind us and rebuild our marriage. We both tried. He was determined to make it work. But I just ... couldn't. At the end of the day, I couldn't do it. Every time I looked at him ...' Margaret buried her face in her hands and squeezed her eyes shut.

John waited.

'So I filed for divorce. I didn't see what else I could do in the circumstances. I knew it would damage my career in the Church, but that wasn't my concern. I just ... couldn't bear to look at him. I wanted him out of my life.'

'And?'

'And I got him out of my life, but not in the way I'd planned.' Margaret gulped back a sob. 'He ... died.'

'Oh, my dear.' His voice was compassionate.

'He had another heart attack. A massive one. He died instantly.' She took a deep breath. 'Stress again, the doctor said. And I knew what that meant. Hal didn't want the divorce, but I insisted on it. It meant that it was my fault that he died. I ... I killed him.'

It was the first time she'd ever spoken the words, though she'd thought them, pondered over them, wept over them a thousand and more times. 'I killed him,' she repeated.

184

'Are you treating this boy, this Joshua Bradley, as a suspect?' Detective Superintendent Evans leaned across his desk and stared Neville down with his piggy eyes.

Neville nodded. 'Yes, Sir. That's what I've been trying to tell you.' He ticked the points off on his fingers. 'The dead boy bullied this kid something shocking. He encouraged his friends to do the same. We don't know why he hated him, but he did. That gives Josh Bradley plenty of motive, as far as I'm concerned. And Bradley lives two minutes' walk from Paddington Green, where the murder took place,' he added. 'I think it's very likely that he did it. We certainly don't have anyone else in the picture at the moment. This is the first breakthrough we've had.'

'Then no. Absolutely not. You can't question him.'

'But, Sir. Why not?'

Evans sighed and leaned back in his chair. 'You know the law, Stewart. He's under sixteen. You're not allowed to question him without a parent or "appropriate adult" present. Do I need to quote you chapter and verse of PACE?'

He could do it, too, Neville had no doubt. The Police and Criminal Evidence codes were probably Evans' bedtime reading. 'We've questioned all of Sebastian Frost's mates,' he pointed out. 'Most of them didn't have their parents present.'

'That was different. They weren't suspects, were they?'

'No,' he admitted.

'Surely you can see the difference. They weren't detained or in custody. When you're gathering information, it's one thing. When a kid is in the frame for murder, it's something else entirely.'

Neville knew Evans was right, but it put him in an impossible position. 'What am I supposed to do, then?'

'I suggest that you track down one of the kid's parents, as soon as you can.' Evans bared his teeth in something he would have liked to believe resembled a smile. As far as Neville was concerned, it wasn't even close.

He tried to be patient. 'His mother is dead. His father is a travelling salesman. Travelling. As in on the road. Left home this morning, not expected back until tonight.'

'He leaves his kid alone when he goes on the road?'

'It's the school holidays,' Neville reminded him. 'The kid would usually be in school during the day.'

'Humph.' Evans frowned. 'What sort of a dad would leave a fifteen-year-old on his own all day?'

185

'The sort who has to make a living.' Neville wasn't sure why he was defending the bloke; if it were *his* kid, he probably wouldn't even think of leaving him. It was just that Evans' assumptions annoyed the hell out of him. 'Lots of fifteen-year-olds are capable of looking after themselves for a few hours.'

'Is that the sort who sticks knives in other kids?' Evans enquired sarcastically.

'Point taken,' admitted Neville.

Evans drummed his fingers on his desk. 'Doesn't the bloke have a mobile?'

'He's not answering.'

'Probably in the car, then,' Evans surmised. 'A good, law-abiding bloke who doesn't answer his phone when he's behind the wheel. Even if he does abandon his kid. Keep trying.'

'Yes, Sir.' Neville pressed his lips together. 'I will.'

'I killed Hal,' Margaret said again.

John Kingsley shook his head. 'You mustn't think that.'

'But I do. Because it's true. If I'd been able to forgive him, the way I should have done, he would still be alive today.'

'You don't know that. He had a bad heart, you said—'

She cut across his words. 'And now I can't forgive *myself*. I know that I killed him. And I know, intellectually I suppose, that God forgives me. But that doesn't mean I can forgive myself. It was a horrible thing to do to a man who loved me.'

'You couldn't have known—'

'It doesn't matter,' she stated. 'I failed him. I failed our marriage and I failed my vocation. And because he died before the divorce went through, I actually benefitted by his death. This job here – principal of a fine theological college. It suits me down to the ground, but do you think I'd ever have been offered this job if I'd been divorced? No way.' She gave an emphatic shake of her head. 'Every day, when I wake up in my beautiful lodgings, I feel guilty about that. If Hal hadn't died, I wouldn't be here. I feel such a fraud. People feel sorry for me because my husband died, but they don't have any idea . . .'

For a moment John bowed his head, then he said quietly, 'Why now, Margaret? Why has this suddenly come to the surface, since last night? If you live with this terrible guilt all of the time, and have done so for several years, why now?'

'Because of Keith Moody,' she blurted out. 'He ... cares for me, apparently. And I ... could. Could care for him as well. But I mustn't, because I don't deserve him. I don't deserve any happiness, ever again. Not after what I've done. It would be wrong.'

He shook his head, almost violently. 'Love is never wrong, Margaret. Not when two people are free to care about each other. Love is God's greatest gift to us. He wants his creatures to be happy, not to suffer.'

'But I'm *not* free.'

'Only because you've allowed yourself to be enslaved by guilt and regret. You don't think that God would wish to see you deny yourself happiness, do you, just for the sake of wallowing in your own guilt?'

That was exactly what she *did* think, but hearing him say it like that ...

'You and Keith,' he went on more warmly. 'It's exactly what I would wish for both of you. The two of you have so much to give each other. You're two lovely people. You'd be a great team. You've both suffered, but with God's help, you could heal each other.'

She let out a long, slow sigh. 'If only I could believe that ...'

'You *must* believe it. If you believe in God, as you say you do, you must trust in his absolute forgiveness, then allow him to heal you and grant you another chance of happiness.'

He made it all sound so simple. Could it be true? 'Thank you, John,' she said, feeling dazed. 'I need to think about this. I have to absorb what you've said. Maybe we could talk a bit more ... ?'

The canon nodded. 'I'll be here until Saturday morning, my dear. And you know where to find me.'

Neville was back in his office, trying Josh Bradley's father's mobile yet again, when Sergeant Sally Pratt came in.

'Sorry to disturb you,' she said.

'No problem.' He hung up: still no reply. Not even a voicemail option.

Sally Pratt was the custody officer on duty. Neville had a lot of time for her: she was sensible, kind, intelligent – if decidedly unglamorous. A middle-aged woman with short grey hair, at birth she had been given the unlikely and entirely unsuitable name of Salome; everyone knew her as Sally.

'The lad,' she said. 'Josh. He's asking to see you.'

Neville had left Josh Bradley in Sally's care, even though he was not technically in custody. The boy had come with them voluntarily, not under arrest, and it didn't make sense to book him in until they were able to question him. As soon as Sally booked him into custody, the clock would start running and they would have limited time to conduct interviews.

'Did you tell him that we have to wait until his father gets here?'

'I did.' She put her hands on her ample hips. 'He says he wants to see you anyway. I told him I'd see what I could do.' Sally was the mother of three teenage sons; she'd obviously established a rapport with the boy. Which was why Neville had felt comfortable about leaving him in her care . . .

'I suppose we could have a little chat,' Neville said. 'Off the record. It wouldn't hurt for me to get to know him a bit.'

'It would calm him down, I think. He's awfully jumpy at the moment. And he *is* free to go,' she reminded him. 'I'm afraid he might bolt if he's left alone too long.' She gave him a wink. 'And I won't tell Evans if you won't.'

Evans would probably have a fit. If he knew. But surely there was no harm in an informal chat . . .

'I've found a little room for him,' Sally said as she led him down the corridor. 'I wish there was a place with a telly. Or a computer or something, to keep him occupied. Young lads get bored so easily. My three are always saying they're bored.'

Josh Bradley was sprawled on a hard chair, sipping from a can of Coke. He didn't get up when Neville entered the room.

'Is Sergeant Pratt looking after you all right?' he asked awkwardly.

'Yeah. She's ace,' the boy confirmed. 'She got me a burger for lunch. I was starving.'

'Excellent.' He paused. 'She said you wanted to see me?'

'Yeah.' Josh took a slug of Coke.

'Did the sergeant explain that we need to wait for your father?'

He nodded. 'But I don't see why. I mean, I'm ready to talk.'

'It's the law,' Neville explained. 'You're under age. A juvenile. It's for your protection,' he added. 'Like having a solicitor present. You're allowed to have that, as well, by the way. When the time comes.'

'Can't I have a solicitor instead of my dad?'

'I'm afraid not.'

'Having my dad here won't make any difference,' the boy said defiantly. 'I mean, he'll just try to stop me from telling the truth. Which is that I did it. I killed Seb Frost.'

Callie was feeling a bit uneasy. Something – she wasn't sure what – wasn't quite right.

She'd talked to Marco at last, which was good. But that conversation had been less than satisfactory. He'd been in a restaurant, and when they'd only been talking for a few minutes, his lunch had arrived. Feeling awkward, she'd cut the conversation short.

She missed him. That was part of it: she missed his warm smile, his arms round her, the sheer pleasure of being in his company. Talking to him on the phone was better than nothing, but it was a poor substitute for his physical presence. It had only been four days since she'd seen him; already, when she closed her eyes, she found it difficult to picture his face. She could remember his eyes, his smile, the shape of his ears, the colour of his hair, but those elements failed to assemble themselves into a whole person. That was deeply worrying.

The afternoon session was in full flow; she was trying to pay attention. It was important, she knew: Canon Kingsley was talking about the effect of priesthood on family relationships. She ought to be listening, benefitting from it. Her mother, for instance, had never accepted the validity of her call to the ministry. Disappointed that Callie had given up her secure future in the Civil Service, Laura Anson was virtually in denial about it. And as for Marco, with his Roman Catholic upbringing and very different expectations of the priestly role . . .

She really needed to talk to Marco again. Properly this time. As soon as this session was over, she would ring him.

'It was me. I killed him,' Josh repeated.

That was what Neville wanted to hear, but not now. Not like this, without the proper procedures in place. Josh Bradley hadn't even been cautioned, let alone arrested: this could cause no end of trouble about admissibility. And Evans would have his hide.

'You shouldn't be telling me that,' he said quickly. 'Not without legal advice. And your father present.'

'I don't care. I did it. And I'm not sorry,' the boy blurted out.

Neville sighed and sat down. Too late to pretend he hadn't heard. It couldn't be unsaid now.

Except legally. Once Josh's father told him to deny it, and the solicitor advised him not to say anything to incriminate himself, it would be as though this had never taken place, in the eyes of the law.

'All right,' Neville said, thinking about how he might salvage the situation. 'This is what we'll do. I'll give you some paper, and you can write down what happened. Then when your father gets here, and your solicitor, we can go through it and ask you some questions about your statement at that time.'

'I'll write it down later. But I want to tell you now.' The boy folded his arms across his chest. 'He was a bully, just like it said in the paper. He was horrible. He sent me texts and put up all sorts of stuff on Facebook. All of his mates did it too, but he was the worst. The leader, like. They wouldn't have done it if he hadn't started it. I got sick of it, is all. So I killed him. I texted him and asked him to meet me on Paddington Green, and I stabbed him.'

So that was it: pretty much as Neville had surmised. He clamped his lips together to keep himself from asking any questions. Instead, just to protect himself, he reeled off the words of the caution.

'Joshua Bradley, I'm arresting you for the murder of Sebastian Frost. You do not have to say anything. But it may harm your defence if you do not mention when questioned something which you later rely on in court. Anything you do say may be given in evidence.' It didn't mean a thing, under the circumstances, and would have to be repeated later on, in the presence of the boy's father, but he felt better for having said it.

'Yeah, yeah.' Josh waved his hand dismissively. 'I watch the cop shows on telly. I know all about that stuff. Do you want me to tell you about what happened, or not?'

Neville got out his notebook. His notes wouldn't be admissible, but he could use them to refresh his memory when the formal questioning took place. 'OK,' he said. 'I'm not going to ask you any questions now. I can't, as I explained. You can say whatever you like, though. I'll take notes, if that's all right with you, and we can go through it again later on.'

The boy nodded. 'Like I said, he was a bully. He made fun of me because . . . well, because I'm short. And ginger. He called me Red Dwarf. And the other thing was, he had more money than me. His mum and dad are both doctors, so they have pots of money. My dad, he works hard, but cash is tight.' He took another sip from the Coke. 'He and his mates had all the latest gear, but I can't afford that stuff. He never let me forget it. And that's why I killed him.'

Interesting, thought Neville. Josh hadn't mentioned anything about the homophobia. He wouldn't know that Neville had seen the Facebook postings, with gay-bashing as the dominant theme. Why was he omitting the most important thing about the bullying?

Following the afternoon session, Callie evaded her friends and went back to her room to ring Marco again.

This time she was more fortunate: he was not in the middle of anything important, he assured her, and was free to talk.

'I'm missing you, *cara mia*,' he confessed.

'And I miss you, as well.'

There was a slight pause on his end. 'Do you mean that?' he asked.

'Of course.'

'Because I've been a bit worried. That something's wrong. That you've been having second thoughts about marrying me, after that fiasco on Sunday. And,' he went on, hesitation in his voice, 'I'll be honest. I suppose I've been worried about you being with . . . Adam. That seeing him again, in the place where you were . . . together . . . has . . . oh, I don't know. Rekindled something.'

Ha! She almost laughed out loud. 'Far from it,' she assured him. 'Seeing him again has convinced me more than ever that I had a very lucky escape.' He'd been honest with her, Callie reflected; now she owed it to Marco to be equally honest. 'But it *has* been difficult,' she admitted. 'There are a lot of ghosts here, and I wasn't prepared for how uncomfortable that would be.'

'What do you mean?'

She got up from the chair and crossed to the window, looking out without really seeing. 'I'm in my old room,' she said. 'I think I told you that. It's a nice room, but it's . . . strange. To be back here, I mean. And I found something I'd forgotten about. There's an old fireplace in the room – the chimney's blocked now, but there's a little shelf inside the chimney breast. And I found some letters and things that I'd left there a couple of years ago. It really shook me. You think you've put something behind you, and there it is again, staring you in the face. I sort of . . . freaked out, actually.'

'Adam?' he asked apprehensively.

'Adam. But not *him*, as such,' she assured him. 'It just brought back all of the pain that he put me through.'

'Oh, Callie.' Marco sighed. 'I wish I was there to hold you and support you and make everything better.'

'So do I,' she said softly. 'Marco, so do I.'

'Paul Bradley here,' said the voice on the phone.

At last! Taken aback by his success, Neville was at a momentary loss for words. How, exactly, did one tell a bloke that his son had confessed to murder?

'Mr Bradley, this is Detective Inspector Neville Stewart,' he said, after a fractional pause. 'Metropolitan Police, CID, Paddington Green. We ... um ... have your son Joshua here, and hope that it won't be too inconvenient for you to attend as soon as possible.'

'You have Josh? There? He hasn't done anything, has he?'

Neville swallowed. 'I'm afraid, Mr Bradley, that we're holding him for the murder of Sebastian Frost.'

'But that's absurd! Impossible!'

'I'm afraid not.' He waited for his words to sink in.

'But ... but I should be there! And he needs a solicitor. I'm sure this is just some ridiculous mistake. A joke. My son isn't a murderer.'

'We would appreciate it, as I said, if you could come to the station at your earliest convenience. We need to ask your son some questions, and the law requires that you be present for that.' He added, 'Please do bring your solicitor, or we can make arrangements for you to ring a duty solicitor.'

'Don't worry,' said the voice on the other end. 'I'll be there. With my solicitor. And *you*'d better be prepared to answer some questions yourself, Detective.'

CHAPTER 16

Lilith's phone rang; she could see that the caller was her boss, Rob Gardiner-Smith.

'Hello, Lilith. Are you busy?' he asked.

'Yes,' she fibbed. Her efforts to find a juicy new twist to the story had so far been in vain, but she didn't want to admit that to the boss.

'Well, then, perhaps I'd better look for someone else to deal with this,' he said. 'Something new in the Sebastian Frost murder.'

'No! That is . . .' she back-pedalled. 'I'm sure I can manage.'

'Good woman.' He lowered his voice. 'The thing is, one of my sources tells me that there's been an arrest.'

Lilith's heart started beating faster. 'Paddington Green Station?'

'That's right.'

'Any details?'

'Not yet. That's up to you, Lilith.'

She didn't harbour any great hopes that the police would be more forthcoming than on her last visit, but the police station seemed the most logical place to start. If she played it safe, kept her eyes and ears open . . . 'Thanks, Rob,' she said. 'I'll keep you informed.'

'Just remember the deadline for the morning paper,' he offered as his parting shot.

Callie was determined to enjoy her penultimate evening in Cambridge. She said as much to her friends at dinner, and Tamsin had a suggestion. 'Let's make the most of it,' she said. 'Instead of spending the evening in the college bar, let's go into town. We could go to a pub or two. Maybe catch some live music somewhere, or go to a film. Are you up for it?'

Although Callie's thoughts had run more to a quiet evening in the bar with her friends, she agreed. 'Sounds like fun,' she said gamely.

'I'm definitely up for it,' Nicky concurred.

'I'll see if Jeremy wants to come,' Val suggested.

'The more, the merrier,' Nicky declared. 'Let's see who else we can round up. It will be like old times.'

Tamsin clapped her hands, jubilant. 'Brilliant! Curates on the town.'

'But no clericals,' Nicky warned. 'Dog collars will not be worn. Strictly mufti tonight. We don't want to bring Archbishop Temple House, or the Holy Mother Church for that matter, into disrepute, do we?'

Val frowned. 'Not that we'd do anything to risk that, would we?' she said with a prim set of her mouth.

'I wouldn't be so sure.' Nicky twirled an imaginary moustache and chuckled wickedly. 'We've been working hard all week. It's time to cut loose!'

Adam was walking past the group, returning his tray to the rack. He paused behind Tamsin's chair. 'You're all going out?' he asked. 'Can I come, too?'

There was a moment of sudden preternatural silence, as if the whole dining room was holding its breath; Callie was conscious that everyone's eyes had turned in her direction. Waiting.

She stared straight ahead, willing herself not to make eye contact with anyone. Especially not Adam. She took a deep breath, then let it out.

'Sure,' she said. 'Why not? As Nicky says, the more, the merrier.'

This time Lilith had better luck at the police station. She showed the guard her press pass and engaged in a minute or two of mild flirtation; he waved her through the door with a smile.

This place, she reflected not for the first time, was nothing like *Dixon of Dock Green*, dimly remembered in old repeats from her childhood. No cheery, avuncular desk sergeant, no cosy wood panelling, no venerable oak counter. Just a lot of industrial architecture – stainless steel, Formica – and sour-faced people going about their business.

The person at the reception desk was a woman, and a miserable-looking one at that. No chance of charming that one into revealing anything.

Lilith considered her options: risk asking the miserable cow, or look for someone marginally more sympathetic?

While she was thinking about it, a man strode into the reception area, frowning – a stocky, rather powerfully built chap with an auburn beard. He went straight to the reception desk.

As luck would have it, the miserable cow was at that moment on the phone. She kept her head down and ignored the man, clearly conveying that her conversation was more important than he was.

He pounded on the Formica surface. 'Oy,' he said loudly.

The miserable cow raised her eyes, shook her head and continued talking into the phone.

'Listen here,' he shouted, reaching across the desk and yanking the phone out of her hand. 'I've come to fetch my son. Josh Bradley. Some moron rang to say he'd been arrested for murder. I've never heard such foolishness in all my life. If this isn't someone's idea of a joke, and my son is really here, I want to see him. Now.'

The woman stared him down, unintimidated. 'Mr Bradley,' she said, putting her hand out for the phone. 'We'll have none of that sort of behaviour. Please take a seat. And as soon as I've finished my call, I'll ring Detective Inspector Stewart and tell him you're here.'

The bearded man looked as though he were going to explode, but after locking eyes with her for a moment, he handed the phone over and stalked towards the plastic chairs provided for people on hold.

Lilith, smiling, followed him.

Callie, furious that she'd been backed into a corner and had allowed herself to be intimidated by the fear of what other people would think of her, stomped up the stairs to her room.

It was so unfair! The choice that lay before her now was to go out with her friends, and have a miserable time as she spent the evening avoiding the odious Adam, or to stay behind and be miserable at the thought of what she was missing. Her friends, out having fun without her.

Miserable, either way. Thanks to Adam.

Her gut feeling was that she shouldn't go. She'd ring Tamsin on her mobile, tell her that she'd developed a sudden, blinding migraine. Tamsin wouldn't believe her, of course, and neither would anyone else, but face would be saved.

At the top of the stairs she turned into the corridor and nearly ran head-on into John Kingsley.

'Oh! Excuse me,' she gasped. 'I wasn't paying attention to where I was going.'

He stopped. 'Are you all right, my dear?'

'No. Not really,' she admitted.

'Would you like to tell me about it?'

It was tempting: he was such a good listener, and had given her very sound advice already.

Except that he'd told her to forgive Adam, she recalled suddenly. Not good advice at all. 'You said I needed to forgive Adam,' she said, almost accusingly. 'But he doesn't deserve my forgiveness.'

195

'Oh.' The canon put out a hand to stop her, as she started to squeeze by him and head for her room. 'We definitely need to talk, my dear. Don't run away.'

Reluctantly she stopped. 'I don't think there's much more to say.'

'I think there is.'

Callie allowed him to follow her to her room. She would rather have gone in, locked the door behind her and fumed in private. But she opened the door and gestured him in. 'I'll put the kettle on,' she said automatically.

'A cup of tea would be lovely,' the canon said, and sat on her desk chair as she filled the little kettle from the basin in the corner, plugged it in and reached for the teabags and her mug.

'I only have the one mug,' Callie said. 'One person, one mug.' They were nothing if not efficient here.

'I'll fetch mine.' He disappeared down the corridor for a moment, returning with his own mug just as the kettle boiled.

'It's a shame they can't give us proper milk,' she said, pouring the water into the mugs. 'I hate this UHT stuff.' Along with one mug, they were provided with individual tubs of processed, long-life milk.

'It's not very nice,' he agreed, but when the tea had brewed sufficiently and she'd fished the bags out, he proclaimed the tea to be just to his taste. 'I'm sure you've learned by now,' he said. 'One of the chief indispensable skills of a clergyperson is the making of tea. And the drinking of it. Any time, day or night.'

Callie laughed. 'Too right. I learned that within the first week.'

He resumed sitting on the hard desk chair, leaving her with the comfy armchair. 'Now, my dear,' he said. 'Let's hear about this. What's happened?'

She told him: first about Adam's visit to her room, with his infuriating suggestion that they resume their friendship, and then about tonight's fiasco.

'He is absolutely clueless,' she finished. 'Not only has he not even asked for my forgiveness. He doesn't seem to realize that he needs to. I don't think he's even sorry for what he's done to me! Like I said, he clearly doesn't deserve to be forgiven.'

John Kingsley sipped his tea, regarding her over the top of his mug. 'Think about what you've just said, my dear.'

'I've only said the truth.'

'Do you think that God puts conditions on *his* forgiveness?'

She thought about it for a moment. 'We're supposed to be sorry if we do something wrong. We're supposed to ask him to forgive us.'

'But what if we're not sorry, and we don't ask him? Do you think God forgives us anyway?'

It was something she'd never considered.

'I think he does,' John Kingsley said quietly. 'In my understanding of God – which is as imperfect as anyone else's, I admit – he is supreme love. That's his defining characteristic. Of course he forgives us, even before we ask. That's what I think.'

'But we're told to ask,' she repeated.

'Yes. But the asking ... that's for ourselves, my dear. Not for him. We're the ones who benefit by the asking.'

Callie didn't understand what he was getting at. 'What does that have to do with Adam?'

He regarded her for a moment before answering, and then his reply was oblique. 'Who do you think is suffering because you aren't able to forgive Adam?'

Not Adam, that was for sure. 'If anyone,' she said slowly, 'it's *me*. I'm the one who is all tied up in knots about it.'

'Exactly.'

Again, he waited while she worked through the implications.

'So you're saying that I need to forgive him for *me*, not for him?'

The canon nodded. 'You keep saying that Adam doesn't deserve forgiveness. From God's point of view no one *deserves* forgiveness – it's a free gift, no strings attached.' He smiled at her. 'In the Lord's Prayer, Jesus said "forgive us our trespasses, as we forgive them that trespass against us". He doesn't say "as long as they're sorry about it". Nowhere are we taught that forgiveness has to be conditional. Conditional on repentance, that is. We like to think that it is – if someone comes to you, and says they're really sorry, it would be wrong, as a Christian, not to forgive them. Almost everyone would agree with that. But take it a step further. What if they're *not* sorry, like Adam? Does that remove from you the obligation to forgive?'

She was stunned. 'So you're saying that I could – I *should* – forgive him, whether he's sorry or not?'

'And you're the one who will benefit from it. That's the wonderful thing. If you just let go of your resentment and your anger, hand it all over to God, you'll be so much happier. You can get on with the rest of your life. That,' he added, 'is what I meant when I said yesterday that it's time for you to forgive Adam. Not for his benefit. For *you*. With forgiveness comes freedom.'

Freedom from the pain of the past. She could get on with the rest of her life.

It was a Road to Damascus moment; the scales fell from her eyes.

Callie finished her mug of tea in silence, absorbing the implications of his words.

'Now,' he said, putting down his empty mug, 'I think I'd better be on my way. I believe you're going out with your friends.'

'Yes,' said Callie, smiling. 'That's right. I'm going out with my friends.'

'He's here,' the desk sergeant said when Neville answered his phone. 'Josh Bradley's father. And he's pretty angry,' she added.

Neville wasn't surprised. 'I'll be there in a couple of minutes,' he said.

Before he went down to reception, he rang Cowley on his mobile. Sid had gone to the canteen to get a bite to eat, and had wanted Neville to go with him. Neville, though, had little appetite.

'Heads up, Sid,' he said. 'It's show time.'

'Righto, Guv. I'm nearly finished.'

He didn't wait for Sid to get back, but went straight down to the ground floor.

The first person he saw, to his enormous dismay and displeasure, was Lilith Noone. She was standing close to someone who could only be the elusive Paul Bradley: a stocky, bearded man who was gesticulating and making himself heard throughout the reception area.

'It's absolutely outrageous,' he was saying. 'I had to cut my working day short because of this stupid misunderstanding. They call me and tell me to drop everything and come, then they leave me cooling my heels! I honestly don't know what the police are playing at. But I'm perfectly prepared to sue for defamation of character on my son's behalf, if they don't sort it immediately. To suggest that he is a murderer is beyond a joke.'

If it had been in his power, Neville would have had Lilith Noone arrested on the spot, locked up for the night, preferably sharing a cell with a mean-tempered, drunken hooker. But he couldn't do that. Regrettably.

'I don't suppose it will do any good to ask you not to write a story about this?' he asked her, as civilly as he could manage.

'Not a chance, Detective Inspector.' She smiled sweetly. 'And I don't suppose you would consider making a statement for my readers? About the arrest?'

He told her, in no uncertain terms, and in two words of one syllable, where to go.

'Inspector!' Paul Bradley interposed an outraged face between them. 'Watch your language! There's no need to speak like that to a lady.'

'Oh, she's no lady,' Neville muttered, giving Lilith up as a lost cause and turning to the bearded man. 'I think it's time for us to talk privately,' he said, with a strong emphasis on the last word. He led him towards the stairs.

Bradley hesitated. 'What about my solicitor? He must be on his way. I thought he would be here by now.'

'They'll send him to the right place when he arrives,' Neville assured him.

He took him upstairs to his office. 'While we're waiting for your solicitor,' he said, 'and before Josh gets involved, I think it would be useful for the two of us to have a chat.'

Cowley stuck his head in the door. 'I'm back, Guv.'

'Come in and join us, Sid,' Neville said. 'Mr Bradley, this is my sergeant, DS Cowley.' There was no need to perform an introduction in the other direction.

'Perhaps one or the other of you could explain this outrage to me, then,' Paul Bradley exploded, swivelling his head between them. 'If it's your idea of a joke, it's not funny. And it's gone on long enough. I'll take my son home now, thank you very much.'

'Josh isn't going anywhere for a while,' Neville stated.

'Well, what on earth has put this insane idea in your heads, that my son is a murderer?'

Neville looked at Cowley, who raised his eyebrows. His expression said as clearly as if he'd spoken the words that this one was down to Neville. He was the guv; he was going to have to tell him.

'Well,' said Neville, then cleared his throat. 'Actually, Mr Bradley, your son has confessed. To murder.'

Margaret had done a great deal of thinking, and some praying as well.

John Kingsley was right, she knew now. She'd been beating herself up for a long time, and the only thing it accomplished was to make her feel bad about herself. Her guilt had tainted the memories of the good years she'd had with Hal, paralysed her spiritual life in the present, and poisoned any future she might have had. And all unnecessarily.

God had forgiven her, long ago. Now she could forgive herself.

The realization was like an enormous weight lifting from her soul.

She wanted to tell someone about it, share the wonderful feeling of well-being and wholeness.

After a moment's thought, she rang her son. She couldn't tell him what had happened, of course, but she needed to talk to someone.

'Mum,' Alexander said. 'Great to hear from you. Would you mind if I rang you back? Luke was late getting home from work, and we're just sitting down to supper.'

'Oh, I won't bother you, then. We can talk another time. It wasn't anything important,' she assured him, smiling to herself at the understatement. *Only getting my life back.*

Her doorbell sounded. With a certain sense of inevitability, Margaret went downstairs and opened the door to find Keith Moody standing outside.

'I feel like you've been avoiding me,' he said without preamble.

'Well ... maybe.' She smiled.

He gave an awkward shrug, followed by a nervous laugh. 'May I come in? There's something I'd really like to tell you.'

'Certainly.' She stepped back and let him in.

'Confessed?' Paul Bradley said blankly. 'But that's daft. It's impossible.'

'Irregular,' Neville said, choosing to take his assertion literally, 'but entirely possible. I told him we needed to wait until you got here before he made any statement. But he insisted on telling me that he'd killed Sebastian Frost. The boy who was stabbed on Paddington Green the other night.'

'What?'

Neville decided to be upfront and honest about it. 'I have to tell you, Mr Bradley,' he went on, 'that anything he said to me previously, without you present, is not legally admissible.'

'Then he'll unsay it,' Bradley stated. 'I don't know what's got into the boy, telling porky pies like that. Attention-seeking, I suppose. You hear about things like that – people confessing to crimes just to get attention. And maybe the boy hasn't had enough of that since his mum died.' He shook his head. 'I try my best, of course. But I do have to put food on the table and keep a roof over our heads, Inspector. It's not easy, being a single parent.'

'I'm sure it's not.'

Bradley sighed; the fight seemed to have gone out of him quite suddenly. 'But it's the Lord's will. He needed her more than we did, I suppose. And he – the Lord – sustains us. The church fellowship has been a wonderful support to us. A true blessing.'

A religious nutter, Neville said to himself with disgust. That was all they needed. He risked a quick look at Cowley, who rolled his eyes.

His phone rang. 'Walter Kendrick is in reception,' the desk sergeant told him. 'Mr Bradley's solicitor, apparently.'

Neville thanked her. 'Your solicitor is here,' he told Bradley. 'Mr Kendrick?'

'That's right. Walt Kendrick. A member of our church,' Bradley explained. 'I've never needed to call on his professional services before, of course, being a law-abiding Christian family and all, but I know he's a good man.'

A good man he might be, but Neville had run across Mr Kendrick before, in the course of his job, and had little respect for his professional skills. Not for nothing was he known as 'Wally' to the police.

'Sid,' Neville said, 'could you pop down and fetch Mr Kendrick? And on the way, could you ask Sergeant Pratt to prepare an interview room? And,' he added, 'could you ask her to tell Josh that his father is here?'

'Right, Guv,' Cowley assented.

Margaret led Keith upstairs to her drawing room, then offered him coffee.

'No, thanks,' he demurred. 'I had some after dinner.' He made no attempt to touch her. 'I just ... need to talk to you.'

'I'm glad you've come,' she said, gesturing him into a chair. 'I need to tell *you* something, as well. Something really important.'

He looked apprehensive; she smiled. 'It's something good. I promise.'

Keith relaxed, visibly. 'Then you go first.'

She found it easier than she'd expected. He was a good listener, she discovered, and didn't interrupt at all as she recounted her story.

Margaret told him about Hal, and their marriage. She told him about its tragic conclusion, and the paralysing guilt that had followed. And she told him about her transforming encounter with John Kingsley, who had made her see what she'd done to herself.

'I told you John was a good man,' Keith said, when she'd finished.

'He's ... amazing. That's all I can say.'

'So you're open to ... a new start?' he asked hopefully.

'Yes.' She got up from her chair and stood in front of him.

Keith rose and put his arms round her. 'I'm so glad,' he said.

'So am I.' Once again her head found its natural place, in the curve of his shoulder. For a moment she allowed herself to enjoy the sensation, without a trace of guilt holding her back. Then she remembered, and pulled away slightly, looking up into his face. 'But you wanted to tell me something,' she reminded him.

'It will keep,' he said, his face unreadable.

Neville allowed Paul Bradley to have a few minutes alone with Josh before the formal interview; he was glad he wasn't in the boy's shoes.

But when they emerged from their conference, Josh was smiling and calm. It was his father who was scowling. 'He won't budge,' he said to Neville. 'I don't know what to do with the boy.'

If Josh was determined to incriminate himself, as he seemed to be, there wasn't much his father *could* do, Neville reflected. This was probably not going to be a pleasant interview. But at least there were signs that it could go his way: if Josh didn't retract his confession, and he could get him to repeat it under caution, it should stand as legally valid.

And Josh refused, flat out, to have a private consultation with his father's solicitor before the interview. 'There's no point,' he stated. 'He'll just tell me not to say anything. That would be a waste of everyone's time.'

So they went into the interview room, for the beginning of the formal proceedings.

Neville identified the parties present for the recording, issued the required caution, then tried to clarify some ground rules. 'Mr Bradley,' he said, 'I'll be asking your son a number of questions. This may be difficult for you, but you're not to answer on his behalf. You're here as an observer, and to oversee his interests, as his parent. Your solicitor, Mr Kendrick, may advise Josh on whether he should provide answers to my questions, but Josh is not obliged to take his advice. Do you understand?'

'I understand.'

Taking a seat at the table across from Josh, Neville began by getting straight to the point. 'Josh, did you kill Sebastian Frost?'

'Yeah,' Josh said.

His father jerked forward. 'Isn't that a leading question? Walt, is he allowed to ask him that?'

'Mr Bradley.' Neville kept his voice courteous, but frowned his displeasure; this interview would never end if the man was going to behave like this. 'We're not in a court of law. We're in a police interview room. There's no such thing as a leading question in here.'

'Right.' Bradley subsided back into his chair.

'All right. Josh, would you tell me, in your own words, what happened last Sunday night?'

'You don't have to answer,' Walt Kendrick said.

Josh ignored the solicitor. 'Could I have a Coke?'

Neville sighed. 'Sure. Sergeant Cowley, could you get a Coke for Josh?'

Cowley left the room; Neville announced the change of personnel into the tape machine, and again when he returned with a can.

'Resuming the interview,' he said. 'Josh, what happened on Sunday night?'

The boy popped the seal and took a swig. 'Seb Frost had been on my case all weekend. Guess he didn't have anything better to do, since it was the school holidays. He sent me lots of texts, saying that he hated me and stuff like that. I just got sick of it. I texted him and asked him to meet me on Paddington Green. Then I went to the kitchen and got a knife out of the drawer. I went to Paddington Green, near the church. Seb showed up a little while later. He laughed at me. Said I was a pathetic ginger runt.' The boy ran his finger round the rim of the Coke can. 'So I stabbed him. Then I went home.'

'Did you stay around to see how badly he was hurt?'

'No.' Josh shook his head. 'I didn't care. If he was dead, that was all right by me.'

'It was all right if he was dead?'

He shrugged. 'Yeah. He deserved it.'

Paul Bradley jerked to his feet. 'Josh knows the difference between right and wrong,' he said urgently to Neville. '"Thou shalt not kill" is one of the Ten Commandments. He knows that. He can't be telling the truth about this. His mum and I taught him the Bible from the minute he was born.'

'Sit down, Mr Bradley,' Neville said, more sternly this time, then turned back to Josh. 'What time was this, and where was your father when this happened?'

'It was late. Maybe eleven o'clock, half past. Dad was in bed. Asleep, I guess. He usually goes to bed pretty early.'

'It was Easter Sunday, the day of Our Lord's resurrection from the dead,' Paul Bradley interposed. 'I'd had a busy day, at church. Of course I was in bed at eleven o'clock, even if I didn't have to work the next day.'

He couldn't put him out of the room, but Neville wished it was in his power to gag the boy's father. 'Please,' he said, glaring. 'Josh, did you see anyone else on Paddington Green? Was Sebastian alone, or did he have anyone with him?

There was a tiny hesitation. 'He was alone,' Josh stated.

'And you didn't see anyone else? Dog walkers, or late joggers, or couples . . . courting?'

He shook his head. 'No.'

Neville moved on. 'Josh, what did you do with the knife, after you'd stabbed Sebastian?'

The boy played with the Coke can for a minute, spinning it round on the table. 'I wiped it off in the grass and put it back in my pocket. Then I walked down to the canal, under the flyover, and threw it in.'

That was exactly what Neville would have done, in those circumstances; in the morning he'd have to get them on to dragging the canal. 'And then?'

'Then I went home and went to bed. There weren't any more texts from Seb.' The boy smiled grimly.

His father groaned, but at least he held his tongue.

'Josh, I want to ask you a few questions about these texts you had from Sebastian. And messages on Facebook, I believe?'

The boy shifted in his chair. 'OK.'

'You say he texted you, frequently, and sent you messages on the Facebook social networking website.'

'Yeah.'

'What was the content of these messages?'

Josh cleared his throat. 'Like I said. He called me a ginger runt. Stuff like that.'

'And did he make unkind comments about you not having as much money as he did?'

The boy gave his father a sideways glance. 'Yeah. Because his parents are rich doctors, like.'

Now Neville was getting to the tricky bit. 'Did Sebastian Frost ever make disparaging comments on other aspects of your lifestyle?'

'Lots of stuff,' Josh admitted. 'I mean, he hated me. He said anything that he thought would get on my wick.'

'Why didn't you tell me this, Josh?' his father interposed. 'I had no idea you were being bullied! I would have done something about it!'

He turned to his father. 'Yeah, you would have prayed, I suppose.'

'Yes, I would have!'

Neville wrested back control. 'Please don't speak to your son, Mr Bradley. And Josh,' he commanded, 'look at me.'

Josh raised his eyes. 'Yeah?'

'Did Sebastian Frost ever send you texts or other messages, suggesting that you were . . . homosexual?'

Paul Bradley shot to his feet. 'That is an outrageous question, Inspector, and I will not allow it! Joshua does not even know about such things –

he's a boy who's been brought up in the Lord, brought up to be pure and not polluted by filthy talk like that!'

'Please sit down,' Neville said, as calmly as he could manage. 'Josh, please answer my question. And when you do, I suggest that you remember the things you've been taught by your parents and your Church about lying,' he added, with sudden inspiration.

The boy's father nodded as he sat down. 'False witness,' he said.

'Josh, did Sebastian Frost ever suggest that you were gay?'

Josh looked down at the table. 'He might have done,' he mumbled.

Paul Bradley's fist crashed on to the table. 'That's enough!' he shouted. 'I withdraw my permission for you to question my son. And if you're suggesting, Inspector, that my son is a pervert, a filthy sodomite, then I suggest you think again. You could find yourself looking at a law suit for slander! Isn't that right, Walt?'

Walter – Wally – Kendrick shrugged.

Interlude: from the front page of the Friday Daily Globe

EXCLUSIVE: ARREST IN TEEN BULLY STABBING
By Lilith Noone

This paper can reveal, exclusively, that an arrest has been made in the death of teen bully Sebastian Frost. A juvenile thought to be Joshua Bradley, aged fifteen, from the Paddington area, is being held for questioning at Paddington Green Police Station.

Sebastian Frost was stabbed to death on Paddington Green late on Sunday evening. A friend confirmed that Sebastian was the ringleader of a group who engaged in cyber-bullying, targeting an unpopular schoolmate.

CHAPTER 17

Callie didn't look at the clock when she crawled into bed, but she knew it was well past her usual bedtime. Past midnight, in fact – which meant it was Friday already.

'I'll get up for Morning Prayer,' she said to herself, aware that she'd only made it once during the whole week.

She'd just closed her eyes when the storm hit: a downpour, lashing against her east-facing window, as the wind changed direction and blew rain in from the North Sea.

The unseasonable warm spell was over. *We made it back just in time*, was Callie's last thought before – rain or no rain – she fell into a deep, dreamless sleep.

It had been an entirely knackering day, in all sorts of ways, so Neville had expected to sleep soundly when he finally got to his bed.

But though he dropped off quickly, sometime in the early hours of the morning rain arrived in the form of a windy storm, rattling the windows as it flung moisture against them. Waking, Neville groaned and turned over. He pulled Triona close and buried his face in her cloud of loose hair. 'Mmm,' she murmured as his arm went round her, cupping her bump with his hand.

Unusually, Neville wasn't in the mood for sex. That troubled him for a moment: did it mean he was getting too old, or too domesticated? Did marriage do that to you? He pushed the unwelcome thought away.

'Are you awake?' he whispered.

'I am now,' came her resigned reply.

She'd been in bed already, asleep, when he got home, so he hadn't had the chance to tell her about what had happened.

They hadn't charged Josh Bradley with the murder. It was too late at night; they were all exhausted, and Neville had taken the decision that it could wait until morning. The formalities, the paperwork, the magistrate: there was no rush.

And now ... there was a niggle. Something not quite right. What was it?

Procedurally, they had dotted the i's and crossed the t's – he was sure of it. He'd been more than scrupulous. Why, then, was there this uneasiness? This feeling that something was going to come back and bite them on the bum?

Triona rolled over to face him. 'What is it?' she asked sleepily. 'Is something bothering you?'

'We arrested someone for the murder,' he told her. 'He's confessed.'

'Then you should be happy.'

'I ... am.' Was he? Wide awake now, Neville told her all about the events of the previous day, hoping that in the telling he would realize what was tugging at the back of his mind. 'And you'll never guess who his solicitor is,' he added. 'Wally Kendrick.'

'Oh, Lord! The poor boy!' She sighed. 'Mr Incompetent − a disgrace to my profession. That boy doesn't stand a chance of getting out of there, does he?'

'Not in the short term, I'm afraid. If it wasn't for Sally Pratt, looking out for his interests ...'

'And his father sounds like a real piece of work,' Triona observed. 'With that father, and Wally Kendrick, he's really drawn the short straw.'

'He's afraid of his father,' Neville said, knowing it was true as he said it. 'And because of that, there's something he's holding back. Or lying about. I'm just not sure what it is. I wish I could think ...'

'Sleep on it,' she urged, yawning. 'Maybe your subconscious will work it out by morning.'

But sleep had now eluded him. Neville lay awake as his wife fell asleep beside him. He listened to the rain against the windows; he listened to Triona's even breathing. And he thought about Josh Bradley.

There was no sign of Tamsin at Morning Prayer, and she wasn't in the dining hall either. Callie got her breakfast and slid into the seat across from Nicky, who was picking at a bowl of cereal with a pained expression.

'You look disgustingly cheerful this morning,' he observed. 'You haven't been to Morning Prayer, have you?'

'I have.' She tried not to sound smug. 'But at least you've made it to breakfast, which is more than I can say for Tamsin.'

A few minutes later, though, Tamsin arrived, and went straight for the coffee before she joined them. 'How can you eat?' she demanded. 'How can you even *look* at food?'

Callie popped a bite of sausage into her mouth. 'I obviously didn't have as much to drink as you did last night.'

'That,' said Nicky, 'and the visit to the kebab van in the wee small hours. You were wise to say no to the kebab, Callie. The combination of excess alcohol and kebab grease evidently doesn't agree with our Tamsin.'

Tamsin groaned. 'Why didn't you tell me that last night? You encouraged me, you toerag!'

'You know you wanted to,' he smirked.

'It was a bad idea.' Tamsin gulped at her coffee. 'I really didn't think I was going to make it out of bed this morning,' she confessed.

Adam approached with his breakfast tray. 'That was fun last night,' he said. 'But I had nightmares that someone from my church was in Cambridge and saw me in the pub. And threatened to tell the vicar.'

'Oh, fate worse than death!' Nicky declaimed, clutching his heart. 'A curate in the pub – whatever next?'

Callie patted the chair next to her. 'Come on, Adam,' she said cheerfully. 'Sit down and eat your breakfast. I promise I won't tell your vicar about the pub.'

Tamsin looked up from her coffee and stared across the table at Callie, eyebrows raised almost to her scalp.

The weather had turned overnight, Mark observed as he got up on Friday morning. He looked out of his window to see streets and pavements slick with rain, under grey skies.

What a shame for Chiara's Fun Walk, he thought. It wasn't raining at the moment, but it might start again at any time, and it certainly wouldn't be as warm and pleasant as it was yesterday.

He had resigned himself to going on the walk, and was almost looking forward to it. Mark always enjoyed spending time with Chiara; having a day with her out in the fresh air – never mind the rain – was much more appealing than being cooped up in a house with people who really didn't want him there.

He was owed a day off, he told himself: he'd had to work on Monday, when he should have had a holiday. And Miranda Frost *had* told him not to come.

But when he'd been woken by the rain against his window, in the middle of the night, something had been nagging at him. A loose end, and one that hadn't even occurred to him until he'd talked to Callie yesterday.

That fireplace, in Sebastian's room.

Callie had said there was one in her room at the college, an old one with a hidden shelf inside.

Had anyone thought to check inside Sebastian's chimney breast? The forensics team had been through the room and had found little, they'd said, in the way of personal papers.

Had they missed something that was hiding in plain sight? Had they overlooked the architectural feature dominating the bedroom?

Mark wanted to check it out, just to be sure. Before he did anything else that day.

So he went all the way to the Frosts' house. It was a relief to see that the journalists had departed, a sign, he hoped, that they'd moved on to greener pastures, the next big story. Or maybe they'd just got tired of hanging about with no results.

Miranda frowned when she opened the door to him. 'I told you not to come,' she reminded him. 'I'm going to work later. Do you have some news, or something?'

He hadn't even checked in with Neville to see whether there had been any developments, he thought guiltily. But then surely Neville would have been in touch if anything significant had happened. 'No news,' he said. 'I just need to check something in Sebastian's room. I'll be in and out in five minutes.'

She moved aside reluctantly. 'That room has been checked, top to bottom. I don't know what you think you'll find in there.'

Mark went up the stairs to Sebastian's room, knelt down in front of the fireplace, and extended his arm up into the chimney breast. It was impossible to see anything; his fingers moved over bricks, mortar, then encountered a ledge. He groped a bit higher and felt something soft. Carefully he grasped it and pulled it down and out.

It looked like an old pillowcase, covered in soot and grime – as was his arm, Mark noted regretfully. He was going to have to go home and change his shirt before meeting Chiara; she would be mortified if he turned up looking like a chimney sweep.

He opened the end of the pillowcase and peered inside. There was a stack of magazines, an exercise book, a few loose sheets of paper.

No time to examine anything more closely; he would have to deliver it to Neville and leave it up to him. And he'd have to be quick about it: he'd factored in the time to pay this visit to St Michael's Street, but not the extra time to go to the police station, and then back home for a wardrobe change. He'd promised Chiara that he'd be on time, and he wouldn't disappoint her.

Miranda Frost was standing in the corridor outside Sebastian's door. 'Well?' she demanded.

Mark held up his grimy bundle. 'I found what I was looking for,' he announced with a touch of smugness.

'Can I see it?'

'Not yet,' he said. 'I'll give you a receipt, if you like, but I need to take this to the police station. Right away.'

Margaret had expected to see Keith at Morning Prayer; trying not to be distracted and to focus on the service, she nonetheless was aware of each person who entered the chapel, early birds and latecomers, and felt a stab of disappointment each time when she realized it was someone else.

Perhaps he'd overslept, and gone straight to breakfast.

But when she got to the dining hall, her eyes searched out every table, every corner, in vain. No Keith Moody.

Deciding to skip breakfast herself, she went to her office instead.

Hanna wasn't in yet, which was something of a relief – especially when she found the note on her desk.

Margaret recognized Keith's distinctive handwriting on the envelope and ripped it open eagerly.

'Sorry not to see you this morning,' she read. 'I have to be away from college today. Will ring you later – xxx Keith.'

She sighed. Strange, she thought, that he hadn't mentioned it last night. If he'd known he was going to be away, why hadn't he said? And if not – if it was a spur-of-the-moment thing – it was even more mysterious.

Well, he'd said he would ring. She would have to be satisfied with that, Margaret told herself sternly.

'But the lad's confessed. Tell me what I'm missing.' Evans glowered at Neville through narrowed eyes, beneath lowered caterpillar eyebrows.

Neville sighed. With all that was at stake, how could he possibly make Evans understand his misgivings? 'I just don't want to rush into anything,' he explained. 'If you'll agree to another twelve hours of custody, we'll be able to tie up all the loose ends before we commit ourselves.'

'I repeat. The lad has confessed. What more do you need, before you charge him?' Evans drummed his fingers on his desk.

'He *has* confessed,' Neville agreed. 'But it's just too ... easy. Too pat. He came out with his confession before we'd even had a chance to question him. Before we were *allowed* to question him, technically, with his father not available. It was like he had his story all worked out and just couldn't wait to tell us.'

'Maybe because his story is true,' Evans suggested ironically. 'Did you ever think of that possibility?'

'I want to believe him,' Neville assured him. 'Nothing would make me happier. But I'll say it again. Something's just . . . not right. And I can't, for the life of me, put my finger on it.'

Evans brought his fist down on his desk. 'Can I remind you, Stewart, of what's at stake here? The bloody press have their teeth into it. The *Globe* has even named him, for God's sake! If we let this drag on, it will only get worse. But as soon as he's charged, they're gagged. No more speculation, no more police-bashing.'

That was a valid point, and very tempting. Lilith Noone gagged . . . 'But if we get it wrong, they'll never let it go,' he said, trying to convince himself as much as Evans. 'They'll have an even bigger stick to beat us up with, if we charge him without being one hundred per cent certain.'

'You're the only one who's not one hundred per cent certain,' Evans pointed out. 'As far as I'm concerned, the lad did it. End of story.'

'But I'm the SIO.'

'And I'm beginning to regret it.'

Neville waited. Evans frowned, drummed his fingers, chewed his lip. Then with an abrupt gesture he shooed Neville out of his office. 'All right, Stewart. You can have your twelve hours. Get on with it, and don't waste them.'

Neville went, before Evans could change his mind. He headed back towards his own office; he wanted to have a look at the crime scene photos, the photos of the victim. Perhaps something in them would jog his memory . . .

Going round a corner, he nearly ran headlong into Mark Lombardi.

'Oh!' said Mark. 'Just the man I was looking for, actually. Sid said you'd gone to see Evans.'

Neville stopped, impatient. 'Yes?'

Mark held out what appeared to be a bundle of dirty rags. 'I've found something,' he said. 'In Sebastian Frost's room. It looks like it might be important.'

Brian Stanford enjoyed a fry-up for breakfast, though he didn't very often have one. Such treats were usually reserved for his day off; his customary fare was cereal and toast.

But today Jane had decided to surprise him with eggs, sausage and bacon after Morning Prayer. And that wasn't the only surprise she'd planned: she was going to tell him about the amazing, enthralling, scary thing that was happening to her – to *them*. It was time to share the news that they were going to have a baby.

Her plans received their first setback when she opened the fridge and realized there was no bacon.

Jane looked at the clock. There was time to nip out to the corner shop before Brian got home, if she was quick about it.

Unfortunately it had rained overnight, and was considerably cooler than it had been. Jane grabbed an old cardie, along with her handbag, and headed out for the shop.

While she was paying for the packet of bacon, she glanced at the rack of newspapers. The *Globe* headline jumped out at her: 'ARREST IN TEEN BULLY STABBING.'

On impulse, Jane grabbed a copy of the paper and fished the change out of her purse. She took it home and read the article at the kitchen table while the kettle boiled and the frying pan heated up; Brian should be home any minute now, and he liked his breakfast on the table as soon as he came in.

But Brian didn't come home – not then, and not for another half an hour. By then the tea was stewed, the eggs were cold, and the bacon and sausage congealed in their own fat.

Jane was not amused.

'Oh, Janey!' Brian said at the sight of his ruined breakfast. 'A fry-up! What a nice surprise.'

She relented. 'I'll start over, shall I?'

'No, don't bother. I don't mind.' He sat down at the table and tucked into the disgusting mess. 'Sorry I was delayed,' he said, between mouthfuls. 'Liz Gresham came to the service. I hadn't had a chance for a word with her before now, so I took the opportunity to catch her afterwards.'

'Oh!' Jane dumped the stewed tea in the sink and switched the kettle on. 'What did she say?'

'She's very worried about Tom. She said he's a nervous wreck, but won't talk to her. And you know that the police have questioned him. Twice.'

'But they've made an arrest!' Jane grabbed the paper and flourished it at him. 'Liz can stop worrying. They've caught the boy who did it. Someone called Joshua Bradley. So Tom's in the clear.'

'Sorry I'm late.' Hanna propped her umbrella by the door. 'My car wouldn't start, so I had to take the bus.' Averting her face from Margaret, she went past her towards her own office at the back.

'No problem.' Margaret, at her desk, was trying to clear her post before the first session, so she didn't pay that much attention to her secretary's whereabouts.

After a few minutes, though, it struck her as strange that she hadn't had a full account of Hanna's trials and tribulations in getting to work. That would have been the usual thing; clearly something was wrong. 'Hanna?' she called.

There was no reply.

Margaret got up from her desk and went to the little secretarial office. Hanna was standing by a pulled-out file drawer with her back to Margaret, holding a file. It was, Margaret saw, a personnel file, meant to be confidential.

'What are you doing?' she asked, more sharply than she'd intended.

Hanna jumped, then turned with a frown. 'I was ... checking something, to be honest,' she said, not meeting Margaret's eyes.

'Checking what?' She plucked the file from her secretary's hands. It was Keith Moody's file.

'Mad Phil ... Dr Moody's file,' Hanna admitted, still not looking at her. 'It says he's ... single.'

'Yes, he's single. What of it?'

Her secretary looked down at the floor. 'It's just that ...' Hanna's voice trailed off.

'What?'

'Well, to be honest, I promised I wouldn't say anything to you.'

'Say anything to *me*?' Margaret's voice sounded to her own ears as though it were coming from a long way off. From another room. From another universe, even. 'Whatever it is, Hanna, tell me,' she demanded. 'Now.'

Neville emptied the pillowcase on to his desk. 'What the hell?' he said aloud, to himself; Mark, having explained his find, had already gone.

There was a bound exercise book, the sort used for schoolwork. There was a bundle of magazines, and some folded-up bits of paper.

He pulled out one of the magazines. Porn, he suspected – just the sort of thing a teenage boy would hide in his secret cache from his parents' prying eyes, and from the conscientious cleaning lady.

It *was* porn.

213

Gay porn.

Neville's jaw dropped. 'Bloody hell,' he breathed.

He'd seen plenty of porn in his day – of course he had; he was a red-blooded man and unashamed of that – but he'd never seen anything like this. Graphic, both visually and verbally. So much male flesh on show, doing things to each other that in his wildest imagination he couldn't have thought of – and wouldn't want to, quite frankly. 'Jesus, Mary and Joseph,' he said as he flipped the pages, not really wanting to look but unable to stop himself.

He reached for his phone and rang Cowley. 'Sid, where are you?' he asked.

'I'm with Sally Pratt. We're trying to sort something out for Josh,' he said, resentment in his voice. 'Guv, do you know how many problems you've caused by delaying the inevitable? Josh's father is screaming, and Sally's having a fit.'

'Never mind that,' Neville said. 'Come to my office. Now.'

By the time Cowley got there, Neville had reached saturation point with the porn and had moved on to the exercise book.

'What's this all about?' Cowley demanded.

Neville looked up. 'He was gay.'

'Well, we know that. Although he denies it, of course. Not surprising, with his father ranting and raving about perverts and poofters and sodomites. He couldn't very well admit it, could he?'

'Not Josh. He is, obviously, but I'm talking about Sebastian Frost.'

That stopped Cowley in his tracks. 'What? What are you talking about?'

Neville pushed a magazine across the desk with one finger, as though it were coated in a toxic substance. 'Take a look at this, Sid. And I hope you have a strong stomach.'

Cowley picked up the magazine and flipped through it. His eyes widened; he whistled. 'Cor, Guv. This is disgusting. Hard core. Where did you get it?'

'From Sebastian's bedroom. Where it was well hidden, I can assure you.'

'Maybe he was keeping it . . . for a friend, or something.'

Neville shook his head and waved the exercise book. 'It's all in here. Sort of a journal, where he wrote down all of his feelings.'

'Gay feelings, you mean?'

He dropped the book back on his desk and nodded. 'To make a long story short, he was in love with Tom. One of his best mates. He knew

214

that was unacceptable, so he used this like an escape valve. He wrote stuff down because he couldn't act on his feelings. He says as much in here.'

'Tom is straight, I take it?'

'Very, apparently.' Neville smiled wryly. 'Sebastian writes about Tom's girlfriend Becca, and how it made him feel when Tom talked about shagging her. And these,' he added, indicating the folded papers. 'These are letters he wrote to Tom – love letters – but of course he knew he couldn't ever send them. So he kept them hidden with his magazines and his journal.'

Cowley leaned against the wall. 'Wait a minute, Guv,' he said slowly. 'Are we talking about the same Sebastian Frost who was shagging Sexy Lexie every chance he got? Who posted such poisonous gay-bashing stuff about Josh Bradley on Facebook? Who sent him text messages calling him every gay slur in the book? And you're saying he was a poofter himself? It just doesn't make sense.'

'It doesn't,' Neville admitted. 'Though in a funny way it does. I'm no psychiatrist, Sid. But they would probably tell you that it has something to do with denial. It was the way he could prove to his mates that he was as straight as they were – by leading the attack on some other poor gay kid. They always do say that the most virulent homophobes are people who are afraid of it in themselves.'

'And he got himself killed for it.'

'*If* Josh killed him,' Neville said thoughtfully.

'He's confessed, Guv,' Cowley reminded him. 'All of this doesn't change that fact. And whether Seb Frost was a closet poofter or not, Josh had plenty of motive.'

'But it sure does raise a few interesting questions.' Neville leaned back in his chair and closed his eyes. 'One of which is Lexie. And how she fits into all of this. Did she, for instance, know that her boyfriend was gay?'

'I'll ask her, Guv,' Cowley volunteered promptly.

'Tell me,' Margaret repeated with all the authority of her position.

Her secretary still wouldn't meet her eyes. 'Dr Moody,' she said. 'I saw him, just now. In his car. I was on the bus, and I saw him.'

She was worried that Keith was skiving off when he was supposed to be in college? Margaret exhaled a small sigh of relief. 'Oh, that's all right,' she said. 'He ... notified me that he would be away today.'

'He wasn't alone,' Hanna said in a low voice.

'Not alone?' Whatever did she mean?

'It was the girl. He stopped his car in front of a block of student housing – undergraduate flats. She came out and got in his car.'

'Girl?' Margaret said blankly. Her brain wasn't working – she wasn't following. 'What girl?'

'The same girl. Oh, I did promise I wouldn't tell you!' Hanna crossed her arms and turned her back on Margaret.

Margaret fought back a strong urge to take her by the shoulders and shake her. 'I don't know what you're talking about, but you had better explain yourself.'

'To be honest, I thought I should tell you, all along,' Hanna said. 'I mean, you're the principal. You ought to know what goes on in your college.'

'Then *tell* me.'

Hanna turned back to face her and braced her shoulders. 'Everyone in the college is talking about it, to be honest. You're probably the only one who doesn't know. Mad Phil ... Dr Moody. He has a girlfriend. A very young girl, probably an undergraduate.'

'That,' said Margaret numbly, 'is a ridiculous lie.' Again her words sounded to her as though they were coming from a long way off.

'But it's not. I saw them myself, a few days ago. They were hugging. And kissing. Very close, they were. Intimate, to be honest. I could tell.'

Margaret's words were automatic. 'You must have been mistaken. It must have been someone who looked like Dr Moody. Or ...'

'They were coming out of his house. It couldn't have been anyone else, to be honest.'

'I don't believe it.'

Hanna gave an anguished little sob. 'It's not my fault! And I tried to tell you the next day, to be honest. But he came into your office and interrupted me. And then something else happened,' she added. 'Everyone was talking about it. One of the women in his tutor group found some stuff in his bathroom. Stuff that belonged to the girl. I thought I ought to tell you. Especially when I saw him trying to make a pass at *you*.'

Oh, God. Margaret's head was pounding, with the onset of the sort of migraine she hadn't had for years. Zigzags of flashing lights danced in front of her eyes, obscuring her secretary's face.

'But you promised him that you wouldn't tell me?'

'No, not him,' Hanna admitted. 'One of the deacons, to be honest. She said it wouldn't do any good to tell you.'

216

So everyone *did* know. And it was true, obviously – Hanna was incapable of inventing anything that vile, and why would she?

And people were trying to protect her. Somehow that made it even worse.

'I have a headache,' she said with as much dignity as she could muster. 'I'm going upstairs now. Please tell anyone who asks that I'm unavailable for the rest of the day.'

When Mark got home to change his shirt, he looked in the mirror and saw that the soot had transferred itself from his hands to his face. That meant a quick shower and scrub, which put him even farther behind. And Mark didn't like being late.

He was to meet Chiara at the Italian church; the walkers were gathering there and would depart after preliminary refreshments and a briefing.

Fortunately the church wasn't too far from his flat; as he sped there on foot, he rang Chiara's mobile to let her know he was on the way.

'I was worried, Uncle Marco,' she said. 'I thought maybe you weren't coming.'

'I'll be there in five minutes, *nipotina*,' he assured her.

Her smile, when he arrived, was one of relief mingled with anticipation.

'Too bad about the weather,' he said, giving her a quick hug.

'Never mind. We're going to have a brilliant time.' She indicated the refreshment table. 'Do you want some coffee before we all start off?'

'Good idea.'

'And you have to meet my friend and her mum. We're going to walk together,' Chiara informed him.

They were near the refreshment table, so as soon as he'd grabbed a cup of coffee she dragged Mark towards them. 'This is Emilia,' Chiara said. 'And her mum. This is my Uncle Marco.'

A pretty little girl, shorter than Chiara, with big brown eyes and dark hair. And her mother, who was much the same: small and trim, with dark hair and eyes, and a nice smile.

Mark stared at her for a split second. 'Do I know you?' he said, afraid as he said it that it sounded rude. But she was so very familiar . . .

'Giulia Bonner,' she said, putting out her hand. 'I used to be Giulia Trezzi. We were in the church youth group together, a long time ago. I remember you – Marco Lombardi.'

217

'Of course!' He took her hand. 'Giulia – I do remember you. It's been a long time.'

Half a lifetime ago, in fact. When he'd been fifteen or sixteen, he'd thought she was the prettiest girl in the world. It all came back to him now, in a heady rush: long-buried memories of his first – and unrequited – love. A face like a flower, a name like poetry. Giulia.

CHAPTER 18

One more session to go. Tomorrow she'd be back home.

Callie finished her lunch and went out to get a bit of fresh air in the courtyard. The rain had cleared, and the sun was struggling to come out from behind the lingering clouds, but the damage had been done. The cherry blossom was one visible casualty: the grass was covered with damp pink petals, leaving the trees with only their small, tender leaves. Daffodils had been beaten down and crocuses shredded by the force of the storm.

Glad she'd put on a warm jumper, Callie wrapped her arms round herself as she sat on her favourite bench for a few minutes, lifting her face to the weak sun. She closed her eyes, thinking about Marco, longing to see him. This week had been good in so many ways, but she was ready to go home. Ready to have Marco's arms round her instead of her own . . .

'Callie?'

She sighed, and took a moment to open her eyes. 'Hello, Adam.'

'I'm leaving for home as soon as the last session is over,' he said. 'So this might be our last chance to talk.'

Fine with her. 'OK.'

Adam hesitated a minute. 'Do you mind if I sit down? I'd like to ask you something.'

'Help yourself.' She scooted over to give him a bit more room – and to put some distance between them.

'It's just that . . . I don't quite understand the way you've been treating me,' he said.

'Treating you?'

'This week. I mean, at first you ignored me like I wasn't even there, and wouldn't talk to me. I tried to be friendly. I came to your room the other day to sort things out, hoping we could be friends again, and you chucked me out!' He shook his head in bafflement. 'No explanation or anything. And then all of a sudden you're being nice. Last night, at the pub. We actually had a normal conversation! And this morning at breakfast. What's going on, Callie?'

Was he really that oblivious? She decided to cut to the heart of things. 'What's going on,' she said, 'is that I've decided to forgive you. We'll never be friends again, Adam. You can forget that little plan – I'm not that much of a masochist. But I can be civil to you, like I would be to anyone else whose company I don't particularly enjoy.'

'But ...' he sputtered, staring at her. 'I don't understand!'

'No, you don't,' she agreed pleasantly. 'You never have. And as far as I'm concerned, that doesn't matter. I'm not going to try to explain it to you, Adam. If you want someone to tell you about the way women's hearts work, maybe you should ask your wife to explain it.' Preferably in words of one syllable, she added to herself as she got to her feet; he was obviously as dim as Pippa. Why had she never realized that? 'I'm going up to my room now. And if I don't see you to talk to before you leave, travel safely.' Callie paused. 'And have a nice life.'

Neville had hoped to interview Josh as soon as the boy had had his lunch, but that proved to be impossible.

'His father's not here,' Sally Pratt told him. 'He got fed up with waiting round all morning, and went off to do a few things.'

'Bugger,' said Neville.

'He said to remind you that he's a working man, it's a working day for him, and he has better things to do than sitting round a police station. He'll be back later, he said. Paul Bradley is an angry man,' she added unnecessarily.

'But that's not good enough! He knows full well that we can't interview Josh without him. And we only have ...' Neville looked at his watch, 'nine hours, tops.'

She merely raised her eyebrows; Neville interpreted that to mean she was exercising extreme forbearance in not reminding him that it was his own fault. If he'd done the interview first thing this morning it wouldn't have been a problem. Hell, she was probably still fuming that they hadn't charged Josh yet. From what Cowley had told him, the arrangements she'd had to make to keep the boy in custody had taxed even her considerable powers.

'So will you let me know when Paul Bradley deigns to show up?'

Sally Pratt nodded. 'I'll give you a ring, shall I? And I assume you'd like me to arrange an interview room?'

'Yes, please. To both.' Neville forced a smile, knowing how important it was to keep Sally Pratt on side. 'Ring me on my mobile.'

He'd better make use of this enforced hiatus to follow other lines of enquiry, he decided. The revelation of Sebastian Frost's unsuspected sexual orientation raised quite a few questions, and made it necessary to rethink things Neville had taken for granted.

Had Seb's parents even suspected? What about his mates?

Was *anyone* actually telling the truth?

They were going to have to talk to Tom again, and observe his reaction to the revelation that one of his best mates had been in love with him. Eventually they would need to talk to Hugo and Olly as well. And Miranda and Richard Frost . . .

For now, though, he would get Cowley out of harm's way by sending him to supervise the dragging of the canal for the murder weapon. And while Cowley was occupied with that, Neville would tackle Lexie.

From the Italian church the walkers headed due south to the river. During that initial part of the walk they were travelling through the heart of the City of London, on pavements thronged with workers and tourists, so they more or less needed to go single file in an unsociable formation.

But when they reached the river and the Victoria Embankment, they were able to spread out a bit. Their route took them the entire length of the embankment, all the way to Westminster, where they would turn by the Houses of Parliament and enter St James's Park, along Birdcage Walk, and thence to Green Park and Hyde Park.

Unsurprisingly, Chiara and her friend Emilia skipped ahead along the embankment, chattering to each other and in high spirits. That meant that Mark found himself walking with Giulia Bonner.

If she felt any awkwardness, she didn't display it. 'The girls so enjoy each other's company,' she said as they went by Somerset House. 'Their friendship has been good for them, since they've both lost their fathers.'

'Oh,' said Mark, caught out. 'Your husband . . . ?'

'My husband was killed in Afghanistan, just about a year ago.'

'Oh, I'm so sorry.'

She shrugged. 'It was pretty horrible. But it happens. You get on with things.'

Over the course of the next hour or so, in an ongoing conversation that was neither forced nor maudlin, he learned the story of Giulia Bonner's life.

When he'd known her, all those years ago, one of the reasons that she'd been so inaccessible, so far beyond his reach, was that she already had a serious boyfriend: Colin Bonner. She'd married him as soon as she left school, and at that point had vanished from the Italian church youth group, and from Mark Lombardi's life.

Colin had joined the army; they'd embarked upon a peripatetic military existence, moving from one base to another. Emilia had come along quite quickly, and a few years later there was another child, Enrico.

'The marriage wasn't particularly happy,' she said candidly. 'I was frustrated. Pretty quickly I regretted the fact that I'd married so young, and hadn't gone to university. I couldn't get a decent job without a degree, especially the way we moved round the country. And Colin didn't think it was important. He was happy for me to stay at home with the children, and occasionally get a part-time job stocking shelves at the NAAFI or waiting tables at a local café.'

'What would you like to have done?' Mark asked.

'Graphic design,' she said without hesitation. 'I was always good at drawing, at school. It's my dream, to be a proper graphic designer.'

'It's not too late, you know.'

'I know.' She was, it transpired, working on it: she was doing an Open University degree course, while working as a teaching assistant at Emilia's school. 'The job allows me to have the same hours as the children, so I can be at home when they are, and have the holidays with them as well.'

'Where is Enrico today, then?'

'Ah.' She gave a rueful smile, then explained. Since they'd always lived in army accommodation, when her husband was killed she'd had nowhere to go. Her own parents were dead, so she'd ended up bringing her children to the London suburbs to live with Colin's mother, with whom she had a difficult relationship.

'She adores the children, of course. And she's always happy to look after them – she'll drop everything to do it if I need her help. But she's so . . . controlling. Things have to be just so. Her house is neat as a pin, and the children know they have to keep it that way. It's not . . . natural. They're not allowed to be themselves.'

'And you don't get on with her?'

'I try my best. After all, I'm living under her roof. But I was never good enough for her. She didn't want Colin to marry me, and she still thinks he made a dreadful mistake, marrying a *foreigner*.' Giulia gave the word ironic emphasis. 'And a Roman Catholic, at that. She hates it that I bring the children to the Italian church. I mean, she's churchwarden at her parish church, and thinks that's where we all belong. As a family, you know. But St Peter's is what keeps me sane. It keeps me connected to my roots.'

'Yes, I can understand that.' Mark *did* understand, though as far as he was concerned it was a mixed blessing.

'She tries to pretend that the children are English,' she said, with a passionate hand gesture which took Mark back with a jolt to his adolescent self: her expressive hands were one of the things he'd once found so enchanting about Giulia Trezzi. 'She calls them Emily and Henry, for God's sake! And insists that I do the same! She's trying to erase their heritage!' With a grimace she added, 'She calls me Julie. I can't bear it.'

'If I were you, I'd try to find my own place, as soon as possible.'

'Believe me, I dream of the day I can do that. When I've finished my degree, when I can get a proper job and don't have to rely on the charity of a woman like Colin's mother . . .' Giulia sighed. 'Sometimes I think I should have listened to my own mother – *che Dio l'abbia in gloria*. She said it was a mistake to marry someone from a different culture. "*Mogli e buoi dei paesi tuoi.*" Have you ever heard that?'

Mark had, more than once, from his own mother. It meant that spouses and cows should come from your own country, and was a sentiment with which he heartily disagreed – though he didn't feel it would be very diplomatic to say so at this point.

'Yes,' he admitted. 'My mother says that as well.'

They were in front of Buckingham Palace, about to cross the Mall into Green Park. Keeping an eye on the girls to make sure they were OK, he offered his arm to Giulia and escorted her across the road.

'How very gallant,' she laughed when they'd reached the other side. Then she favoured him with a smile – as dazzling as the ones he used to dream of receiving from her. 'I've been talking a lot about myself, Marco,' she said. 'Now it's your turn. What about *you*?'

The same young girl opened the door to Neville at the flat off the Edgware Road. 'Mum's not at home,' she said, with a suspicious squint of her eyes.

'How about your sister? Lexie?'

The girl nodded. 'But she can't be disturbed right now.'

Neville wracked his brains for the girl's name. Something boyish, he recalled. Charlie? No, that wasn't it. Not Bobbie, either.

Georgie. That's what Lexie had called her.

'Georgie?' he said tentatively.

She nodded again. 'You've been here before, haven't you?'

'Yes. I'm a policeman, Georgie. And it's important that I talk to your sister. Can I come in?'

'I s'pose so.' She stood aside to let him through the door. 'I was watching Jeremy Kyle. Wanta watch?'

'All right.'

Neville had never seen *The Jeremy Kyle Show*, and the first few minutes were a revelation. Pasty-faced people with tattooed arms, appalling teeth, bizarre hair styles and multiple facial piercings shouted at each other from chairs on opposite sides of a stage. 'You're a slapper!' 'Bleep you, bleephead.' The man in the middle egged them on. 'Why are you calling her a slapper, mate? You were happy enough to sleep with her, even when you knew full well she was your father's girlfriend.' The audience catcalled their agreement.

Did Georgie's mother know that her child was watching this? Lexie obviously didn't care – but then Lexie was the one who was in the habit of going out and leaving the child on her own ...

'I'm waiting for the DNA results,' Georgie said conversationally. 'They're going to find out whether her baby's father is him, or his father. If it's his, Jeremy will tell him that he has to step up to the mark and be a real dad.'

Good God. 'You watch this a lot, then?' Neville couldn't help sounding horrified as he rapidly adjusted his preconceptions about the innocence of childhood.

'It's my favourite,' she confirmed. 'But I only get to watch it during school holidays.'

Jeremy Kyle looked into the camera with an earnest expression. 'We're waiting for those all-important DNA results. Is Den the father of Tracy's baby, or are he and baby Tiger actually brothers? We'll find out, after the break.'

An advert for online bingo replaced Jeremy's smirking visage; Neville took the opportunity to ask Georgie a question. 'Why can't Lexie be disturbed? And when do you think I'll be able to talk to her?'

'She's in her room. The "Do not disturb' sign is hanging on the doorknob. That means she'll kill me if I disturb her. Or you,' she added. 'And she'll come out when she feels like it.'

Had Lexie been a fifteen-year-old boy rather than a fifteen-year-old girl, Neville would have understood immediately: it would have indicated the kind of forbidden behaviour which Father Flynn had insisted would make you go blind.

Surely girls didn't do that sort of thing?

'Do you know why she doesn't want to be disturbed?' he couldn't help asking.

Georgie shrugged. 'None of my business.'

Which meant, Neville suspected, that she knew very well, but chose not to say.

'You could send her a text,' Georgie suggested helpfully. 'Sometimes that works.'

Neville fished his phone out of his pocket and handed it to the girl. 'You do it for me.'

She looked at his phone with disapproval. 'This phone is really old,' she said. But she pressed a few buttons, then her thumbs worked rapidly over the keys. 'Done,' she pronounced.

'Does your mother know that Lexie shuts herself in her room like this?' Neville asked, to satisfy his own curiosity.

'No. She doesn't do it when Mum's at home,' admitted Georgie.

'Just like your mum doesn't know that she used to leave you here alone to . . . visit her boyfriend?'

Georgie looked at him blankly. 'She's never left me alone. Mum really would kill her if she did that.'

'What?' Neville was baffled. Lexie had admitted it to him. Maybe, he reasoned, she had managed to sneak out somehow so that her sister didn't know she was gone. 'Are you sure, Georgie?'

'Course I'm sure. Her mates come here sometimes and hang out while Mum's at work, but Lexie doesn't go out. Not that I'd care if she *did* leave,' Georgie added. 'I can look after myself. But she wouldn't. She'd be afraid that I'd tell Mum. Then she'd be grounded for like the rest of her life.'

'What's going on? Who wants to see me?' Lexie appeared in the doorway. 'Oh, it's *you*,' she said flatly, glaring at Neville. 'This had better be important.'

'And now,' said Jeremy Kyle, on the screen, 'for those all-important DNA results.'

Neville sighed; he supposed he would never know now whether Tiger was Den's son, or his brother.

'What about *you*? What have you been doing with your life?' Giulia asked him.

Mark hardly knew where to begin. It had been so many years since he'd seen her, and how interested was she, really, in what those years had held for him? Not very, he suspected.

'I'm a police officer,' he said – the easiest option. 'I'm with the Met.'

'Oh, I wouldn't have guessed that. Was it what you always wanted to do?' She was smiling encouragingly.

'Actually, it was,' he confirmed.

'My mother-in-law thinks it's regrettable, but I love watching police dramas on the telly,' Giulia confided. 'Tell me about your job. Are you a beat cop, or something else?'

'Something more interesting, you mean?'

'I suppose that *is* what I meant,' she admitted.

Chiara and Emilia, who had been walking in front of them, suddenly turned and waited for them to catch up. 'Ice cream,' said Chiara to her uncle, pointing at a van by the side of the path. 'There's an ice cream van, Uncle Marco. Please, can we have an ice cream?'

'Please, Mum?' Emilia entreated Giulia.

Mark reached for his wallet. 'Sounds like a good plan. What would you like, ladies?'

They placed their orders; he paid the vendor, collected the ice creams, and handed them round with a little bow to each, which delighted the girls and seemed to embarrass Giulia. 'You didn't have to pay for ours,' she said, shaking her head.

'My pleasure.'

'Then thank you.'

They resumed walking. Giulia ate her cornetto daintily, nibbling round the edge of the cone. Mark wished he'd made a more sensible choice as he peeled the paper from his Magnum bar and bit into it, shattering the chocolate covering. Bits of chocolate went everywhere, most of it on to the pavement.

'I should have had a cornetto,' he said ruefully.

'You were telling me about your job,' Giulia reminded him.

Giving up on the Magnum bar before the rest of it melted all over him, Mark took one last bite out of it and dropped the remainder in the nearest bin they passed, then scrubbed at his hands with the flimsy serviette he'd been given.

'I'm a family liaison officer,' he said, licking a blob of chocolate off his finger. 'Abbreviated to FLO. That means I deal, mostly, with bereaved families.'

'How fascinating. I've seen FLOs on some of the police dramas. I'd love to hear more.'

Mark found her interest flattering, and was persuaded to tell her about some of his previous cases. Before he knew it, they were circumnavigating Hyde Park, heading for Kensington Gardens.

'I'm sure I've bored you enough,' he said at last, with a self-deprecating laugh.

Giulia gave a vigorous shake of her head. 'Not at all. It's better than watching telly.'

'I'm glad you think so.'

'But what about your personal life, Marco?' she turned her face to look at him. 'Wife? *Bambini*?'

'No. None of the above.'

'The police on telly always seem to have such complicated personal lives,' she said before he could elaborate. 'Have you never married, then?'

'Not yet,' he said. He thought about Callie, and knew he was smiling. The next words slipped out before he could stop them. 'But I'm engaged. I hope to be married quite soon. Maybe sometime this summer.'

Giulia's eyes widened. 'Oh! I didn't ... Serena didn't ...' She rushed on, seeming flustered. 'But who? Who is the lucky woman, then?'

'*I'm* the lucky one – she's the most wonderful woman in the world. She's called Callie Anson.' Just saying her name made him ridiculously happy. And she was coming home tomorrow! The week without her had seemed interminable; he couldn't wait to see her.

Lexie led Neville to her bedroom again. This time, conscious as he'd become of the strict rules governing the interviewing of juveniles, he wondered about the wisdom of this. What if she were to accuse him of something improper? Legally, he wouldn't have a leg to stand on.

'So what's this about, then?' she demanded, taking a seat on the bed and folding her hands primly in her lap. 'I told you everything I could about Seb. And I saw on the internet that you've arrested Josh Bradley. What more do you need from me?'

'Just tying up loose ends,' Neville said, as reassuringly as he could manage.

'All right, then.'

He decided not to beat about the bush; there wasn't time for that. 'It seems that you haven't been entirely honest with me, Lexie.'

With one hand she flicked the fringe out of her eyes, momentarily obscuring her face, but her voice maintained her attitude of bravado. 'What do you mean?'

'Why didn't you tell me that your so-called boyfriend was gay? You must have known.'

Her eyes widened. She pressed her lips together.

'I've read his journal,' Neville added. 'He wasn't interested in girls. At all. He might have fooled his parents, and his mates, but I don't see how he could have fooled *you*.'

Lexie's expression changed as a variety of emotions played themselves out on her face, in the space of a heartbeat. Then her shoulders slumped and she turned her face away. 'Yes, all right,' she said softly. 'I knew. Of course I did.'

'Do you want to tell me about it?'

She shrugged. 'Seb's dead. I suppose it doesn't matter now. But I promised, see. I promised him I'd never tell a soul.'

'If you tell me what you know, it might help me to understand what happened to him,' Neville pointed out.

Now she looked confused. 'But you've arrested Josh!'

For what that was worth. 'There are still a lot of questions to be answered. Like for instance, what *was* your relationship with Sebastian? He wasn't really your boyfriend, was he?'

'No,' Lexie admitted. 'We were friends, though. Mates. I liked Seb.'

'Why did you tell me you'd shagged him?' Neville pressed her.

She gave him a faint, ironic smile. 'I didn't tell you that. Think about it, Inspector. You're the one that said it, and I went along with it.'

Neville cast his mind back to their earlier interview: she was right. It was Hugo who had told him that Seb was shagging Lexie, not Lexie herself.

'But I went along with it because I'd promised him,' she added. She opened her hands out in a gesture of appeal. 'You have to understand about me and Seb,' she said. 'He was like a brother to me. He talked to me, told me things he couldn't tell his other mates.'

'Like the fact that he was gay.'

'Yeah.' Lexie smiled again. 'And there was another reason I hung out with Seb, to be honest. You know he was in love with Tom?'

Neville nodded. 'His journal made that pretty clear.'

'Well, me too. That is, I fancy Tom something rotten. So we had that in common, I guess. It was, like, a bond between us, I s'pose you'd say.'

And by spending time with Sebastian, Neville reasoned, she'd have a better chance of seeing the object of their mutual lust.

'There's something else I'd like to ask you about,' he said. More to satisfy his own curiosity than anything else, he admitted to himself. 'You didn't go out and meet Sebastian at night, then. When his parents were working.'

'No. Never. We talked a lot at night, though – on our mobiles, some, but mostly on the webcam.' She indicated the laptop computer on her desk, its lid shut.

'There's a camera on that thing?'

'Sure.' She gave him a pitying look.

'Your sister says that when you put the "Do not disturb" sign on your door, it's more than her life is worth to interrupt you. What's that about, then?'

Lexie frowned and evaded his eyes. 'I don't have to tell you.'

'No, you don't,' he agreed. 'Not if it isn't relevant to Sebastian's death. But is that what you did when you were talking to him? Put the sign on your door?'

'Sort of.' She played with the ends of her hair, still not looking at Neville.

'I won't tell your mum, if that's what you're worried about. I'd just like to know.'

Lexie got up and opened the lid of her laptop. 'My mum doesn't have much money,' she said defensively. 'The pay at Tesco is crap. And like I said before, my dad pays our school fees out of guilt for dumping Mum. And buys me stuff like this computer. But I need cash for clothes and stuff. I can't get a job, 'cause I have to stay at home with Georgie while Mum's working. So I have to do something to earn a bit of spending money.'

She was using her computer to earn money? What an enterprising girl, Neville said to himself.

'There's a lot of randy old blokes out there,' she went on. 'All you have to do is find them. Sad, but there it is. And I've got the equipment, so why not?'

What on earth was she talking about? 'I don't understand,' he admitted.

She gave him another pitying, condescending look. 'Simple,' she said. 'I put the webcam on. Then I take my clothes off. Not all my clothes – just my shirt, usually. Then I dance round a bit. And they pay me – straight into my PayPal account. It's like, free dosh. It doesn't hurt anyone. In fact, it's kind of a public service. But,' she added, 'if my mum found out, she'd kill me.'

The Fun Walk had ended – quite successfully – at Marble Arch. There the walkers had dispersed. Giulia Bonner and her daughter had boarded a bus to take them back to her mother-in-law's suburban home, and a few minutes later Mark and Chiara caught the Number 55 towards Clerkenwell.

Mark flourished his Oyster card, but Chiara had left hers at home, which meant that Mark had to come up with enough change to pay her fare. They found a pair of empty seats; Chiara took the window seat and sighed happily.

Still thinking about Callie, Mark pulled his phone out and rang her, though he didn't really expect her to pick up the call.

She answered after the first ring. 'Marco!'

'*Cara mia!*' He smiled. 'I'm glad I caught you.'

'We've just finished the afternoon session,' she said. 'The final session, in fact. Now I'm on my way to have tea.'

Again, he was overwhelmed with the need to see her. 'If it was the final session, can't you leave now?' he suggested. 'You could be home by early evening.'

'I wish,' she said with an audible sigh. 'But there's a dinner tonight. A posh, dress-up dinner to finish off the week in style.'

'Too bad.' He could imagine her, wearing a filmy frock. Sitting next to Adam.

As if reading his mind, she said, 'I have to tell you something, Marco. About Adam.'

Mark's heart gave an unpleasant lurch.

'I'm free of him,' she stated. 'I've come to terms with it all, and I'm ready – really ready – to move on. With you. And I've told him, basically, that I don't want to have anything more to do with him. Ever.'

'Oh! That's wonderful.' The best news in a long time.

'And I'll see you tomorrow,' Callie added. 'I should be home by lunch time, if you're—' She broke off, then said, 'Sorry, Marco. I've got to go now. Love you.'

'Love you, *cara mia.*' He caressed the phone, unthinkingly, before stowing it back in his pocket.

He would have preferred to spend the rest of the bus journey in silence, savouring the prospect of seeing Callie in less than twenty-four hours, but with Chiara sitting beside him, it wasn't going to happen. 'Wasn't that fun, Uncle Marco?' she said as soon as he'd put his phone away.

'Super,' he agreed. 'We were lucky that it didn't rain.'

'Isn't Emilia nice?'

He hadn't had much meaningful interaction with Emilia, but he nodded agreement. 'Very nice.'

'And her mum.'

'Yes, very nice.'

'Mum really likes her,' Chiara stated.

'Oh, your mother knows her?' he asked, then realized that of course she would; Serena would make it her business to know her daughter's friends, and their families.

And then he remembered something that had passed him by while he daydreamed about Callie – Giulia Bonner's evident surprise when he'd told her of his engagement. 'Serena didn't . . .' she'd said.

Serena hadn't told her that he was engaged.

There was a good reason for that, of course. Serena didn't know.

And then he saw it all, in a flash.

How naïve he'd been.

Serena had planned this – had planned for him to meet Giulia Bonner. A suitable match for him: Italian, a respectable widow, the right age. She'd probably told Giulia all about him – her handsome brother, who needed a nice Italian wife. Not about Callie, of course. Not that he was already attached, because that wasn't part of her plans for him. Callie was irrelevant as far as Serena was concerned, no more than a slight inconvenience in her master plan to marry him off to an acceptable woman.

Did Serena know that he and Giulia had been acquainted a long time ago? She couldn't possibly have known about his adolescent longings and dreams of the beautiful Giulia, because he hadn't told a soul – then or ever.

But that didn't matter. She'd seen a way to get him away from Callie and into the arms of a woman of her own choosing. She probably envisioned it as a double benefit, delivering Giulia from her evil mother-in-law at the same time as she rescued her brother from his unsuitable attachment.

Serena, the master string-puller.

Mark's anger flared, hot and immediate. His Italian temper didn't surface very often, but when it did, it was something to be reckoned with. He tried to bring it under control as he addressed Chiara.

'Was it your mother's idea to ask me to go with you on the walk today?'

She nodded innocently. 'Nonno said he'd take me. But Mum said I should ring *you*. She said to remind you that my father was dead, so you wouldn't be able to say no.'

Lexie had closed her bedroom door in Neville's face, leaving him to find his own way out.

On impulse, he stopped by the lounge, where Georgie was still watching the telly. Jeremy Kyle was over, evidently; she was now watching an ancient episode of *Star Trek*.

Star Trek. Star Wars.

'Georgie,' he said, 'could I ask you something?'

She turned. 'Sure.'

'Lexie's mates. You said they hang out here sometimes.'

'Yeah.' Georgie nodded. 'When Mum's at work. They watch telly, or just sit round talking and stuff.'

'Do you ever listen to what they talk about?' he suggested delicately.

She shrugged her thin shoulders. 'They never pay much attention to me. I'm just Lexie's little sister. Part of the furniture.'

Neville took that as a 'yes'; he didn't imagine that Georgie missed much that went on in that flat. 'Have you ever heard them talk about . . . bullying? Cyber-bullying?' he added self-consciously.

'All the time.' Her voice was matter-of-fact, almost bored. 'There's this kid they hate. Josh, he's called. They sit round and send him nasty texts, and talk about what they're going to put up on Facebook about him.'

'Lexie, too?'

'Of course.' She rolled her eyes; clearly she had no illusions about her sister.

Cautiously, Neville probed a bit further. 'I think they all use different names. On Facebook. Is that right?'

She nodded. 'Mostly *Star Wars* names. I think it was Seb who started that. He was Darth Vader.'

'And the others? Do you know their names?'

'Lexie is Princess Leia. That figures, doesn't it?' she grinned. 'Hugo – he's Luke Skywalker.'

Neville suppressed a smile: he'd been right about that, then.

'Tom is Han Solo. Olly's Chewbacca. I wouldn't want to be Chewbacca,' she added. 'But Olly thinks it's cool. And Becca – she's Tom's girlfriend – she's Padmé. She wanted to be Princess Leia, but Lexie got there first.'

'What about you?' he couldn't help asking. 'Do you have a name?'

Georgie made a face. 'They call me Yoda, sometimes,' she admitted. 'That was Tom's idea.'

Yoda, Neville seemed to recall, was wise – sort of an oracle. 'I'd take that as a compliment.'

'I don't,' she said flatly. 'They don't mean for it to be one.'

232

'Just one more question,' he said before he took his leave. 'Tiger – son or brother?'

'Son,' said Georgie. 'Poor little sod.'

Callie was on the phone with Marco when she saw Adam striding across the courtyard towards the porters' lodge, his duffel bag slung over his shoulder. Good riddance, she said to herself.

A minute later she spotted John Kingsley on his way to the common room for tea. This would be a good opportunity to catch him, she thought, just in case he didn't attend the dinner and there was no further chance to speak to him before the week ended. So she said a quick goodbye to Marco, pocketed her phone, and caught up with the canon just as he joined the queue.

She slotted into the queue behind him. 'Oh, hello, my dear,' he said, smiling. 'Glad it's all over?'

'It will be good to get home,' she acknowledged.

'I hope it hasn't been too painful.'

'Not at all.' Well, maybe it had been, she acknowledged to herself. But the end result was well worth it. 'It's been a wonderful week,' she added. 'And I wanted to thank you for all you've done to ensure that. So much hard work . . .'

'You, and your fellow deacons, have done all of the work,' he demurred. 'It's been a privilege for me to be on this journey with you.'

Callie looked round to make sure that none of her friends were within earshot, then she lowered her voice. 'And as far as my . . . personal . . . issues are concerned, everything is sorted. I've even talked to Adam and told him that there's no place for him in my life.'

'Well done!' John Kingsley gave her an approving smile.

'So I owe you so much. And I wanted you to know how much I appreciate everything.'

He put his hand up like a stop sign. 'You don't have to thank me. I just . . . facilitated, that's all. You would have worked it all out for yourself, eventually.'

'Eventually is right!' Maybe she would have got there in the end, but how long, she wondered, would it have taken her, without his help?

Hanna Young came up behind Callie in the slowly moving tea queue, and Canon Kingsley turned to speak to her. 'I must thank *you*, Miss Young, for your help with all of the photocopying, and everything else you've done this week.'

'It's my job, to be honest,' Hanna said, but she looked pleased.

233

The canon looked round. 'I don't see the principal,' he observed. 'Come to think of it, I haven't seen her since breakfast. Is she all right, do you know?' He'd got to the front of the queue, and reached for a cup of tea.

'I'm not really sure, to be honest,' admitted Hanna. 'She said she had a headache this morning. And she said to tell anyone who asked that she wasn't available. That's all I know – I thought she would have got over it and put in an appearance before now.' She frowned thoughtfully, then directed an apologetic shrug in Callie's direction. 'I know I promised you that I wouldn't tell her about Dr Moody, but she made me tell her. To be honest, she did seem quite upset.'

'What's all this about?' John Kingsley wanted to know. He was frowning as well – the first time Callie had seen him do so.

Callie took her tea and quickly snatched a biscuit from the plate, then moved out of the way to allow Hanna access to the serving table.

Hanna's face settled into a self-righteous expression. 'I told her about Dr Moody's girlfriend. She must have been the only person in college who didn't know about it, to be honest. And like I said, she made me tell her.'

'Girlfriend?' The canon's frown deepened. 'What on earth are you talking about?'

'To be honest, I thought she deserved to know,' she said to Callie, then addressed the canon. 'Don't tell me *you* don't know about it. I thought everyone did. And you can't say I'm making it up, because I saw it with my own eyes. I saw him kissing and hugging a young girl. That's not right, no matter what you say.'

John Kingsley was staring at her with an appalled expression. 'Let me get this straight,' he said quietly. 'You told the principal that you saw Keith Moody kissing—'

'She was *very* young,' Hanna stated. 'It was positively indecent. I mean, he's practically an old man, to be honest. No offence, Canon Kingsley,' she added.

He seemed to be making a great effort to keep from spilling his tea, and after steadying the cup with his hand, he placed it carefully on the nearest table. 'Excuse me,' he said. 'But you had no right. And I need to talk to her. Now.'

CHAPTER 19

Neville still hadn't heard from Sergeant Pratt when he returned to the station, so he stopped by to see her.

She shook her head before he could speak. 'No,' she said. 'Paul Bradley isn't here yet.'

'But . . .' Neville looked at his watch. 'What is he playing at? Is he just hoping to run the clock out, so we'll have to let his son go?'

'Probably.'

He brought his fist down, hard, on her desk in a gesture of frustration, and instantly regretted it. 'Isn't there anything we can do?'

Sally Pratt grimaced in sympathy as he shook his throbbing hand. 'I've been checking the codes,' she said. 'If he doesn't show, and we can't reach him, I think it would be permissible to get a social worker to sit in on the interview. *In loco parentis.*'

'Well, then. Do it.'

She nodded. 'Right, Guv.'

Neville headed for his office. There was something he'd been planning to do, hours ago, before he'd been sidetracked by the bombshell about Sebastian. He wanted to have another look at the crime scene photos, and read through the post-mortem report thoroughly. That nagging feeling that he'd missed something hadn't gone away; it had only intensified.

Something not quite right.

He rummaged through his in tray and found the envelope of photos, buried under all sorts of things he didn't recognize and didn't want to think about. With a sweep of his hand he shoved aside all of the papers which had collected on the surface of his desk, pushing them into an untidy pile, to make room for the task at hand.

Neville sat down and spread the photos out across his desk, then tried to empty his mind of preconceptions as he studied them. What if he knew nothing about this case, and was looking at these photos for the first time? What would he notice?

The photos, taken from all angles, showed a tall, lean youth with curly dark hair, sprawled on the ground. The fatal stab wound, in his throat, was clearly visible.

It was in his throat. Not in his chest, as was often the case. According to the pathologist, it had severed the jugular, and death had been almost instantaneous.

His throat.

Presumably he had been standing when the fatal wound had been administered. Not lying on the ground like this.

He was a tall boy. The post-mortem report would give his actual height, but Neville guessed it to be close to six feet.

How tall was Josh Bradley? No more than five foot three or four, and possibly less. Red Dwarf: they'd called him that for a reason.

Neville found the post-mortem report in his in tray and scanned it until he found the relevant bit: the description of the knife wound which had killed Sebastian Frost. Did the angle of the wound indicate that it was an upward stab, struck from below?

No. Dr Tompkins, in his usual precise way, was very clear about it. The force indicated by the depth of the wound, and its angle, meant that the knife had been virtually level when it entered the boy's throat.

So if Sebastian Frost had been standing – not kneeling, not sitting, not lying down – there was no way that Josh Bradley, slashing out with a kitchen knife, could have stabbed him – fatally – in the throat. Arm, maybe, or chest, but not throat.

Neville groaned, vindicated but at the same time robbed of his only viable suspect.

'Josh probably couldn't have done it,' he said aloud, then reached for his phone to ring Sid Cowley.

Hours ago, Margaret had taken a sedative. She still had a few left in the bottle in the bathroom cabinet, issued to her in those dreadful days after Hal's death. She didn't like to take them; nothing but the severity of her migraine would have induced her to do so. But with the flashing lights and the stabbing pain pushing on her skull from the inside out, she decided that if she could only sleep through the migraine, perhaps she would have a chance of surviving it.

The sedative was a strong one, and it worked. Margaret slept through the afternoon, dragged back to consciousness only by the persistent ringing of her doorbell.

'Whazzat?' she said aloud as the noise penetrated her deep sleep. She prised her eyes open, squinting in the dim light of her bedroom.

The migraine was still there, pounding away, and her stomach churned with nausea.

Keith. She remembered, and squeezed her eyes shut again, pulling the covers over her head, trying to keep still. If she didn't move, maybe it wouldn't hurt as much.

But the doorbell didn't stop.

Who could it be? What could possibly be so urgent? Was the college burning down? Had a nuclear holocaust been unleashed?

Eventually, when it became clear that it wasn't going to stop, Margaret pulled the covers back and swung her legs over the side of the bed. The top of her head felt as if it were going to come off, but after a moment her feet found her slippers and she reached for her dressing gown.

'This had better be important,' she said as she crossed the seemingly endless expanse of carpet, one step at a time, then clung to the bannister and went down the stairs to the door.

She'd bolted the door, so she drew back the bolt and pulled on the handle.

The expression on John Kingsley's face told her that she looked every bit as bad as she felt – probably worse, even. 'What is it?' she said, trying not to sound too rude.

'Oh, Margaret. I'm so sorry.' His own face was paler than usual, creased with concern. 'Sorry to disturb you.'

'Headache,' she said. 'Migraine.' She didn't think she was capable of any more detailed explanation of her state.

'I need to talk to you.' He put a hand on her arm, as if he feared she was about to close the door in his face. 'It's very important. I wouldn't bother you if it wasn't.'

She wanted to tell him to go away. If it had been anyone else, she would have. But John Kingsley had given her back her life. Margaret squeezed her eyes shut; now it felt as though someone were pushing on her eyeballs from behind. By force of will she opened her eyes and managed a thin smile.

'Come in, then,' she said.

'You don't have to come all the way home with me, Uncle Marco,' Chiara said as the Number 55 bus trundled along High Holborn, close to Mark's flat. 'I can get home myself from here, if you want to get off.'

'No, that's all right. I want to have a word with your mother.'

That was an understatement: Mark had a good many words he wanted to share with Serena. And she wasn't going to like any of them.

They got off the bus in Clerkenwell Road and walked the short distance to the di Stefano house, to find Angelina sprawled on the sofa in front of the telly in the lounge.

'Did you have a good walk?' she asked.

Chiara's smile was dazzling. 'It was brilliant. Emilia and I had the best time. And we did the whole course, so everyone has to give us lots of sponsorship money.'

Mark wasn't in the mood for small talk. 'Is your mother at home?' he asked tersely.

'Yes, she's back from the lunch shift,' Angelina confirmed. 'She's in the kitchen, I think. Putting together some supper for us before she has to go back for the dinner shift.'

'I'll tell her about the walk,' Chiara stated, heading for the kitchen.

Mark caught up with her and put a hand on her shoulder. '*Nipotina*, would you do me a big favour?'

'Sure.' She turned, smiling.

'Would you mind going to your room for – say, ten minutes? I need to talk to your mother in private.'

Chiara looked puzzled, but nodded agreement. 'OK.'

He pushed open the door of the kitchen and went in. 'Serena,' he said. 'We're back.'

She was stirring something on the cooker and didn't turn round. 'Oh, *ciao*, Marco. Did Chiara have anything to eat this afternoon? She was so excited before she went that she wouldn't sit down and eat something properly.'

'She had an ice cream,' he said, briefly sidetracked.

'Then I'd better make sure to leave her a proper supper. Some protein. You should have got her a sandwich or something, not just an ice cream,' Serena added disapprovingly.

Her bossy tone of voice was enough to bring his focus back. 'Don't you tell me what to do.' He spoke in a soft but emphatic voice.

'Marco?' She turned round and looked at him, eyebrows raised.

'How dare you?' His volume went up a notch. 'How dare you try to interfere in my life?'

'What are you talking about?'

'You know damn well what I'm talking about! That woman. Giulia Bonner. You . . . you set it up! Don't try to deny it.'

Serena crossed her arms across her chest. 'OK, I set it up. For your own good, Marco. She's perfect for you. I just thought—'

Mark cut across her words. 'You *thought*? For my own good?' He shook his head. 'Has it escaped your notice, Serena, that I already have a girlfriend? One I've managed to find for myself, without any help from you?'

'But Giulia's perfect for you,' she repeated.

'And Callie's not? Just because you didn't pick her out?' His hands were clenched into fists. 'That's the problem, isn't it? You want to control my life, and Callie is outside of your control.'

'You must admit she's not ideal,' Serena stated. 'I mean, she doesn't really fit into the family, does she? She's a nice enough girl, and she tries, but—'

'Stop it!' Consciously he unclenched his fists. 'Do you have any idea how hurtful that is? How disrespectful? It's disrespectful to Callie, and it's disrespectful to me. It's downright insulting, in fact. Don't you think I'm capable of making my own choices?'

'I just don't want you to make a big mistake,' she said, with a placatory gesture.

'A mistake? Finding Callie is the best thing that's ever happened to me.' Mark swallowed, then narrowed his eyes at his sister. 'I love her. In fact, I'm going to marry her. I've asked her, and she's said yes. We'll be married as soon as we can. Whether you like it or not, Serena. Whether *la famiglia* approves or not. I'm going to marry her. And if you can't accept that – and accept that I'm not going to change my mind, no matter how many nice Italian women you dangle in front of me – then I don't need *you* in my life any longer. I've made my choice.' He turned and headed for the door, adding over his shoulder, 'I choose Callie.'

Mark slammed the door behind him.

'I'll put the kettle on, shall I?' suggested John Kingsley.

Margaret didn't have the strength or the will to refuse. 'All right.'

She sat at the kitchen table, head in her hands, while the canon switched on the kettle and found what he needed by trial and error. At last he set a mug in front of her.

'Sweet tea,' he said. 'Plenty of sugar.'

Margaret hated sweet tea. But she knew that it was supposed to be good for shock, so she drank it obediently, grimacing at its taste.

'Now,' he said. 'We need to talk.'

She shook her head, and instantly regretted it; she hadn't thought the pain in her head could possibly get any worse, but she'd been wrong. 'There's nothing to say.'

'There's a great deal to say. I understand that your secretary has been telling you some rather . . . ill-advised . . . gossip. About Keith.'

'It's not gossip. She saw it herself. And obviously everyone in college knew about it. Everyone but me.'

'No,' said John Kingsley firmly. 'I didn't know. If I had done, I would have said something. To her, and to anyone who was passing on such nonsense. Because it's not true.'

'She saw it,' Margaret repeated. 'She saw them kissing. And I feel . . . such a fool.' That, she acknowledged to herself, was the bitterest pill of all to swallow. The fact that she had invested so much hope, so much emotion, in this new relationship, to see it all turn to dust and ashes, was bad enough. But the fact that everyone knew about it, that people were talking about her, laughing at her behind her back . . .

John reached across the table, took her hand and gave it a squeeze. 'It's not what it seems to be,' he stated. 'You have to trust me on that, Margaret.'

'If you know so much about it, then explain it to me. In words of one syllable, since I'm evidently so thick that I can't see the obvious.'

'Do you remember yesterday, when we talked? And I said that I thought you and Keith would be good for each other, because you'd both suffered and could help each other to heal?'

She sighed. 'Of course I remember.'

He poured himself a mug of tea. 'I assumed that Keith had told you about his own . . . troubles, and that you knew what I was talking about. It seems I was wrong.'

'He hasn't told me anything.' Suddenly Margaret recalled that Keith had tried to tell her something last night, and she'd forestalled him with her confessions about Hal. But . . . what? What could it be, that would explain the sort of behaviour he'd demonstrated?

'You mustn't think badly of him for that,' John Kingsley said, sipping his tea. 'It would have been very difficult for him to share it.'

'Well, tell me, then!' she demanded. 'If you know what's going on, then you'd better tell me now.'

He shook his head. 'I can't. I'm very sorry, my dear, but it isn't my story to tell. Keith will have to tell you himself. Until then, you'll just have to trust me. Keith hasn't done anything . . . dishonourable. I promise you that.' He paused, then went on, 'He loves you. I'm sure of that. Trust me – and trust *him*.'

Margaret closed her eyes.

Neville was still looking at the crime scene photos when Cowley arrived, in response to his urgent summons.

'What's up, Guv?' Cowley asked. 'No luck so far with finding the knife, I'm afraid. It's a big canal, you know. It might take days to find it.'

'Never mind that.' If Neville's hunch was right, and Josh hadn't stabbed Sebastian, then the knife could be anywhere, and dragging the canal would turn out to be a total waste of police resources. 'Give them a call. Tell them to suspend the search,' he decided.

Cowley obeyed, with a quizzical look. 'What's up?' he repeated when he'd finished.

Neville explained, indicating the photos. 'I just don't think that Josh could have done it. He's too short. See how tall Sebastian was? I mean, Sid, this one's a no-brainer. We saw the body. We should have realized.'

'Red Dwarf.' Cowley might not be the most sensitive officer on the force, but at least he was reasonably sharp, Neville recognized with gratitude.

'Exactly.'

'There's something else,' Cowley offered. 'When we interviewed Josh. Did he ever mention the second stab wound?'

Neville shook his head. 'No.'

'He said he went home after he stabbed him in the neck, didn't he?'

'After he got rid of the knife.' There was something else he hadn't mentioned, Neville realized: the smashed phone. He hadn't mentioned Sebastian's phone at all. 'And then there's the phone,' he said; Sid's grimace told him that no further explanation was necessary.

Cowley sagged back against the wall. 'I hate to say it, Guv, but it sounds like we're on to a loser.'

'Oh, Sid.' Neville groaned, then rubbed his face between his hands. 'We're going to have to let him go.'

'Which leaves us with . . . nothing,' Cowley pointed out glumly.

'Bloody hell, Sid.' Neville shuffled the photos back into a pile as the implications of it all began to sink in. 'How on earth am I going to tell Evans that after nearly five days of this damned investigation, we're back to square one?'

Trying not to let her imagination run wild about what was going on with Mad Phil and the principal, Callie went back to her room to pack her case. If she packed most of her stuff now, she reasoned, she could get an early start in the morning.

First, though, she pulled out the dress she'd packed in the event that there would be an occasion for a posh frock – she would wear it for the dinner tonight – and put it on a hanger. It was tried-and-true: a pretty flowered dress which fell below the knee, suitable for dinner parties and even for parish events. Not exciting, but safe.

As she hung it in the wardrobe, she discovered, to her dismay, that it had a conspicuous stain down the front of the skirt. Tea or coffee, it looked like. And then she remembered: the last time she'd worn it, to a concert in church a few weeks ago, someone had jogged her elbow while she was drinking her interval coffee. She'd intended to wash it out as soon as she got home, or take it to the dry cleaners if necessary, but something had distracted her and she'd put it back in her wardrobe untreated.

And now it was too late.

'Oh, no . . .' Callie said aloud.

No use trying to borrow something from Tamsin. Even if Tamsin had a spare frock with her, she was entirely the wrong shape.

Val, then? Val had fewer curves than Callie, and was a bit taller, but she might have something that would do. And since she lived in college, her entire wardrobe was in close proximity.

Callie rang Val and explained her dilemma. 'Do you think you might have anything that would fit me?' she concluded.

'Well, I might. But what's the matter with the dress you bought the other day?' Val asked. 'Why don't you wear *that*?'

The dress she'd bought the other day. Callie hadn't even thought about it.

She'd bought it under duress – Tamsin, Nicky and Val had insisted upon it. It wasn't at all the sort of dress she would normally even look at, but it had been displayed in the window of a shop in Rose Crescent and Tamsin had gone into raptures about it.

'I couldn't wear it in a million years,' Tamsin had said, 'but it would look great on *you*, Callie.'

Against her better judgement she'd tried it on, admitted that it fitted perfectly and looked good, and had been persuaded to buy it.

A little black dress – she'd never owned one before. Elegant, understated and more than just a little bit sexy. 'I'll never wear it,' she'd protested.

'You *will*,' Tamsin had stated.

And it looked as if Tamsin might have been right, sooner than she could have imagined.

Did she dare wear it tonight? Callie retrieved it from the bottom of the shopping bag, where it was carefully wrapped in tissue paper, shook it out and held it up against her.

It was way shorter than anything Callie had ever worn – well above the knees. But she *did* have decent legs, she admitted to herself, even if they were usually covered up.

Nicky had whistled admiringly when she'd tried it on and modelled it, reluctantly, for her friends. 'You look stunning, darling,' he'd declared. 'Almost enough to turn me.'

She didn't want to be responsible for *that*, she told herself, smiling, unless Tamsin were the eventual beneficiary.

Why not wear it? Callie decided. It wasn't as if she had many other choices. And since Adam wouldn't be there to see her, and possibly suspect her of ulterior motives, she wouldn't need to worry about that source of embarrassment.

She would have to wear the new underthings, of course – the dress wouldn't look or feel right with her plain vanilla Marks & Spencer's bra and knickers, so scorned by Tamsin.

But why not?

The deed had been done: Josh Bradley was released without charge, free to go home. Though that, Neville reflected, was something of a mixed blessing for the boy, with that father in residence.

It was, by now, late enough that Neville could have gone home himself, and had a fresh start in the morning. But he was loath to do that. He needed to think through the state of play, and try to approach the situation from a different direction.

'Shall we go for a drink?' he suggested to Cowley. 'Or do you have other plans for the evening?'

Cowley hesitated for just a second. 'I do, as a matter of fact. But I could manage a quick one, Guv.'

They went to the nearest pub, which was less than salubrious, but had the advantage of an awning over the smokers' terrace at the rear. Rain was threatening again; dark clouds massed overhead as they took their pints outside to the tables provided for those for whom drinking and smoking were inextricably linked.

Cowley lit up as Neville took his first sip of Guinness.

'OK,' said Neville, wiping the froth from his upper lip. 'Josh Bradley didn't do it. But he wanted us to believe that he did. Why? Why would he insist on confessing?'

'He was protecting someone,' Cowley replied promptly.

'And why would he do that?'

'Because he's afraid of them?' Cowley closed his eyes, concentrating on getting that first lungful of smoke.

'Or in love with them, maybe.'

The sergeant nodded; he exhaled slowly. 'Could be, Guv. Who, then?'

Neville tapped his fingers on the table. 'I can't help feeling that this all has something to do with the bullying. There was a whole gang of them at it. And we know who most of them were, thanks to Lexie's little sister. Apart from Sebastian, there was Hugo, Lexie, Olly, Tom. And Tom's girlfriend, apparently.'

'So you think one of them killed him, and Josh was protecting them, for whatever reason?'

Neville took another sip, then shook his head. 'I don't know. All I can say is, since Josh and Sebastian were both gay, it was unlikely to involve a fight over a girl.' He gave an unamused snort.

There was a crack of thunder overhead, startling and unexpected. A few seconds later the rain started, pounding on the awning above them – no gentle shower, but a sudden fierce downpour.

Cowley raised his voice a notch to compensate for the racket over-head. 'Maybe we ought to look at it another way, Guv.'

'What do you mean?'

'Maybe we ought to ask ourselves, which of those kids is tall enough?'

Tall enough to have done it. Neville stared at his sergeant.

It was so simple, when you looked at it that way.

'Hugo.' Cowley answered his own question. 'And Tom.'

Neville grinned, then reached for his pint. The sooner he finished it, the sooner they could go and talk to Hugo and Tom again – in spite of the rain, in spite of Cowley's plans for the evening.

'Sid, I could kiss you,' he declared.

The look on Cowley's face was priceless. 'No, thanks, Guv,' he said quickly. 'I appreciate the sentiment, but I'm not a flamin' poofter!'

Determined that tonight she would share the big news with Brian, Jane made his favourite steak and kidney pie for supper. But halfway through the meal – which he seemed to be enjoying hugely – Brian had a phone call from one of his churchwardens. As he explained to Jane, Philip Page had been in the church – changing some light bulbs – when the heavy rains started, and water was pouring through the roof in various places.

'I need to get over there straight away,' Brian said ruefully, eyeing the remains of his steak and kidney pie.

'But what can *you* do?' Jane frowned. 'He's the churchwarden. He should sort it.'

'He needs help. He can't get the bowls and buckets emptied fast enough by himself.'

Crossly, Jane scraped the contents of Brian's plate into the bin and did the washing-up. She'd nearly finished when the phone went again. '*Now* what?' she muttered.

It was Liz Gresham, asking for the vicar. 'I'm afraid that Brian's not here,' Jane told her. 'I don't know when he'll be back. And tomorrow's his day off, you know. Can it wait until Sunday?'

'I don't think so,' the other woman said, her voice shaky with evident distress. 'Can *you* come over, Jane? I'd really appreciate it.'

Jane looked at the window: the rain was coming straight down in torrents. The last thing she wanted to do was venture out into that deluge.

'It's my son. Tom ... I'm so worried about him,' Liz added. 'I just don't know where else to turn. My husband is away on business, in New York, so there's no one else here.'

It was part of being a vicar's wife, Jane told herself with stoicism. She wasn't sure what she could do in a practical way, but if her moral support was really required ...

'All right,' she said, feeling virtuous. 'I'll be there as soon as I can.'

Mark paced up and down the lounge of his flat, the noise of the storm outside a fitting background to the tumultuous emotions which gripped him.

He was angrier than he'd ever been in his life. Serena – whom he'd trusted, given the benefit of the doubt, even made excuses for – had betrayed him. He meant what he said: given a choice between his sister and Callie, he was prepared to cut Serena out of his life. Whatever the consequences, however poignant and heart-rending Mamma's tears. He would continue to see the girls, somehow, but at this moment he didn't care whether he ever laid eyes on Serena again.

And he owed Callie an apology. She'd known all along that Serena didn't like her, hadn't even begun to accept her, but Mark had refused to acknowledge it. At all costs, he'd wanted to make his family happy, to preserve the unity of *la famiglia Lombardi*. He'd subsumed his own happiness to that impossible ideal. In fact, somehow he'd accepted the

245

unstated assumption that he didn't actually deserve anything for himself. He'd been conditioned, all of his life, into the belief that *la famiglia* must always come first.

Gradually Mark turned his anger on himself. He didn't *deserve* Callie, he told himself furiously. He'd been weak – more of a mouse than a man. It was a wonder that she hadn't walked away from him months ago. He wouldn't have blamed her if she had.

He needed to tell her how sorry he was, to promise her that from now on he would put her first. To make himself worthy of her – and her love.

Tomorrow, he thought, and then his flatmate came through the door.

Geoff Brownlow was dripping wet. 'It's pitching down out there,' he said conversationally. 'Forgot my brolly this morning. Bad move.' He stripped off his sodden jacket and draped it over a chair. 'So that means a change of plan for tonight. I was going to meet some mates after work, and go down the pub to watch the football on the big screen. But now I don't fancy going back out again, so I think I'll just stay in and watch the match here. I hope there's some beer in the fridge,' he added. 'One or two of my mates will probably drop by. Feel free to join us if you like.'

That did it. Not tomorrow. Tonight. 'I'm going out,' Mark announced abruptly.

'Don't forget your brolly!'

But Mark didn't care about little things like getting wet. He was going to Cambridge. Now.

Liz Gresham, her face creased with worry, let Jane in and took her dripping raincoat.

'I'll put my brolly here,' Jane said, propping it by the door. No danger she'd forget it, if the rain continued like this.

She followed Liz into the sitting room, just to the left of the front door, still unsure what she was expected to do. Liz gestured her into a chair.

'Would you like something to drink?' Liz offered. 'Coffee? Tea? Or a glass of wine, perhaps?'

As if this were a social call, Jane thought. 'Only if you're having something.'

Liz produced a bottle of red wine and uncorked it with trembling hands, sloshing it into two glasses. 'From my husband's wine cellar,' she

246

said as she brought one of the glasses to Jane. 'He's into fine wines in a big way, and this is one of his favourites.'

Jane remembered suddenly that she shouldn't be drinking wine, but it was too late to turn it down now without arousing suspicion. She accepted the glass and took a sip. She was certainly no judge of fine wines, having had scarce opportunity to sample such things in her life, but this one tasted very good indeed to her untutored palate, and the label on the bottle was impressively ornate, with a large house on it.

'It's very kind of you to come,' Liz said, sitting down across from Jane. 'As I said, I just didn't know where to turn.'

'Do you want to . . . talk about it?' Jane invited obediently.

Liz gulped down about half a glass of her wine. 'It's Tom,' she said. 'My son. Our youngest. He's been so . . . depressed . . . lately. Distracted. Upset. Withdrawn. He broke up with his girlfriend recently,' she explained. 'Becca. Such a sweet girl. I'm not sure what happened between them. But he's taken it so badly. And then his good friend Sebastian was killed. Murdered,' she added, frowning. 'Since then he's been even worse. He won't talk to me or his father. He just says it's none of our business, and he's dealing with it.'

'How old is Tom?'

'He's sixteen. Just – as of last week.' With her head she indicated the birthday cards on the mantelpiece.

'Young teenagers can be very moody,' Jane said reassuringly, remembering it very well. 'My boys were the same. Simon, especially. He's a very sensitive boy, and something like losing a girlfriend can seem like the end of the world.' Now he was barely nineteen, and coping with the prospect of fatherhood before he hit twenty. Jane pushed the thought away from her; she couldn't afford to be distracted by that worry just now. 'I'm sure he'll come through it eventually. Just give him time.'

'That's what we thought, at first.' Liz finished off her glass of wine and moved to refill it. 'Even though our older two were just fine – no problems with them at all. But with Tom it just gets worse and worse. And tonight – he won't even come out of his room. I called him for supper, and he told me to go away.'

'He'll come out when he gets hungry enough,' Jane predicted. And it probably wouldn't take long. Her boys were bottomless pits when it came to food consumption; she couldn't imagine them passing up a meal for any reason. If their legs were broken, she was certain that they would crawl to the table.

'I'm not so sure.' Liz shook her head, a worried frown line between her drawn brows.

'Maybe you should take his supper up to him,' Jane suggested.

Liz knocked down another half a glass of wine. 'I tried,' she said. 'I tried his door. It's locked. From the inside. And now he won't even answer me.'

Jane felt a faint twitch of real unease. Was she out of her depth here? This sounded like more – much more – than a teenage strop.

The doorbell rang; Liz started. 'Who could be out on a filthy night like this?' she wondered, heading for the door.

The voices carried into the sitting room. 'Mrs Gresham, we're really sorry to bother you again, but it's very important that we talk to Tom.'

'Now?' she said, her voice rising. 'But you've talked to him already. Twice. And now's not a good time,' she added. 'Can't you come back tomorrow?'

'I'm afraid not,' said a determined Irish voice – a man. 'We need to talk to him *now*.'

'But he won't come out of his room. Not for me, and certainly not for *you*.'

'Then we'll go to him.'

'We'll leave our brollies here,' said another male voice – Cockney this time.

Jane had a brief glimpse of the two men as they went past the sitting room door towards the stairs. Liz, following them, paused at the door for a second to catch Jane's eye and mouth the word 'police'.

Without even thinking about it, Jane went after them.

At the top of the stairs, the two men looked at Liz for guidance. She indicated a closed door with one trembling finger.

'Tom?' said the Irish one, putting his face close to the door. 'This is Detective Inspector Stewart. We need to talk to you, mate.'

There was no reply.

'It's important,' he said, a bit louder.

Still no reply.

He tried the doorknob. It didn't budge. 'Do you have a key, then?' he asked Liz.

She shook her head, her eyes huge with shock. 'It's on the inside.'

Turning to his companion, he raised his eyebrows in silent communication, then addressed Liz again with an apologetic shrug. 'Sorry about this, Mrs Gresham.' He stepped aside; the Cockney policeman put his shoulder to the door and slammed it, hard.

After the fourth slam, the door frame began to give way; two slams later, with a splintering of wood, the lock was ripped from the frame and the door flew open.

The Irish policeman was through in an instant, while his Cockney companion rubbed his shoulder in the corridor, grimacing in pain.

After that, everything happened so fast. 'Tom!' the Irish policeman shouted, then, 'Oh, dear God!'

Liz pushed past the Cockney policeman, who put out his arm to stop her.

'He's taken something,' called the Irish policeman in an urgent voice. 'He's unconscious. For the love of God, Sid, call an ambulance! *Now!*'

Callie came out of the dining hall before the general exodus. The wine was still flowing freely, and many people were still partaking of it, but she felt a bit tired after the late night before and wanted to finish her packing before she went to bed. And if it wasn't too late, she would ring Marco one more time.

Fortunately, it wasn't raining. But her heart gave a little lurch when she saw someone standing, quite still, under one of the arches in the courtyard. A man who looked as though he'd been rained upon rather thoroughly.

And then he spoke, almost tentatively. '*Cara mia?*'

Marco. Her heart lurched again as she moved towards him as quickly as her high heels would take her. 'Marco? What on earth are you doing here?'

He spoke at the same time. '*Cara mia!* You look amazing! I hardly recognized you!'

Callie stopped short, suddenly self-conscious. The dress. The underwear, for heaven's sake. She went hot all over: what would he think? He'd never seen her dressed like this.

But his expression, as he examined her from top to toe, was far from disapproving.

'What are you doing here?' she demanded again, to cover her embarrassment. 'I'm going home tomorrow, you know.'

'I had to see you,' Marco said. 'I just couldn't wait till tomorrow.'

'But . . . why?'

Concisely, he told her. 'I had a row with Serena. I told her that if she's not prepared to accept you as part of my life – as my *wife* – then I don't need her. And I mean it, *cara mia*. I've been so . . . blind. I've let

249

my family boss me about, and I've put them first, instead of trusting my own instincts and looking after my own needs. Instead of cherishing *you*.'

He stopped for breath. She stared at him wonderingly.

'But you're the best thing that's ever happened to me,' he went on. 'And if you'll forgive me for being so ... so stupid, then I'll spend the rest of my life making it up to you. Making you happy, my darling, darling Callie,' he said as he crossed the few steps between them and wrapped his arms round her.

He was as wet as he looked. Callie remembered, inconsequentially, how Bella had knocked him over in the middle of his proposal of marriage. It had rather spoiled the solemnity of the moment. This was a bit like that, but she didn't mind.

'You're all wet,' she said, against his sodden shoulder.

Marco laughed joyously. 'I came out without my brolly. I couldn't wait to see you.'

'But you've been waiting ... ?'

'It's seemed like hours,' he said. 'The porter wasn't amused at being called out, and he took a great deal of persuasion to let me in. Even when I told him I was your fiancé. I don't think he believed me.'

'Then he's not going to want to find a room for you, at this hour of the night.' She twisted her head to smile at him.

He spoke quietly, but without hesitation. 'In that case, I suppose I'll have to share your room.'

'There's only one bed.' Callie swallowed hard, feeling suddenly breathless. 'And it's not very big.'

Marco's hands slid from her back to her waist, then moved farther south. 'I think we'll manage,' he said.

CHAPTER 20

It wasn't that Neville didn't get to bed at all on Friday night – it only felt that way. Especially when his phone rang, very early, on Saturday morning.

The night had seemed endless: the rush to the hospital, then sitting there for hours with Tom Gresham's mother and the vicar's wife, waiting for the news that he was going to pull through after his drug overdose.

That news had come in the wee hours of the morning, along with the doctor's verdict that the police wouldn't be allowed to see Tom until the next day. After that Neville had gone home, only to find that Triona wasn't there. According to the note she'd left for him, she'd got tired of waiting for his return, and had gone to visit her friend Frances, where she would probably stay the night.

Put out at the time, Neville was now grateful that she wasn't there as he groped for his phone on the bedside table. Triona didn't deserve to be woken up at six-something on a Saturday morning.

Neither did he. Not after the day he'd had yesterday. Not after a night at the hospital.

Probably Evans, he thought with a mixture of resignation and trepidation as his hand connected with the phone and he brought it close enough to his face to see the display.

It wasn't Evans. It wasn't even Cowley – Sid, who had left the hospital hours before he did, to keep his Friday night assignation.

It wasn't a number he recognized at all.

Squinting, he punched the little green button. 'Hello?'

'Mr Policeman?' whispered a small voice.

'Yes . . . ?'

'It's me. Georgie.'

Lexie's little sister. Neville sighed. 'What can I do for you, Georgie?'

'You gave me your number,' she reminded him. 'You said I should ring you if I thought of anything. And I did.'

Something that wouldn't wait until daybreak? 'I'm listening,' he said, deliberately patient.

'I'm ringing early, before Lexie and Mum get up,' she explained. 'I even set my alarm. It's something I thought you'd want to know about. And Lexie wouldn't like it if she knew I was telling you.'

That sounded promising; Neville tried not to get his hopes up. 'OK,' he said. 'Tell me.'

'Did you know that Lexie fancies Tom?' she whispered.

In spite of himself, he felt a twinge of disappointment. 'Yes, I knew that.'

'Oh. Well.' She sounded a bit deflated. 'Did you know that Tom broke up with his girlfriend, Becca?'

He hadn't known it until the night before when, sitting in the hospital, he'd had to listen to Mrs Gresham going over and over the reasons for Tom's apparent suicide attempt. Was it significant?

But, Neville realized, Georgie hadn't known it the day before; when he'd talked to her, she'd spoken of Tom's girlfriend in the present tense. 'How did you find out?' he asked.

She gave a soft chuckle. 'Lexie would kill me. She sleeps really soundly, you know? Sometimes I sneak into her room in the night and pinch her laptop. I log into her Facebook account. Just so I can see what she's been up to, and her mates as well.'

Neville was scandalized by her behaviour and her forthright admission, though in his reaction there was also a sneaking admiration for her resourcefulness: Georgie would make a bloody good detective.

'You know her password and everything?'

'Course,' she said scornfully. 'Anyway, there was loads of stuff on Tom's Facebook page. About breaking up with Becca and stuff like that. And then there was a really weird post, last night. He said how sorry he was for everything, and there was no other way out.'

A suicide note, via Facebook.

Neville tried to get his head round it. Why not? This was the Facebook generation; they lived their lives on the internet. They did their bullying on the internet, for God's sake. Why not post their suicide notes as well? It was efficient, notifying all of their friends at once, and forestalling the possibility that a note would be overlooked or not found.

And this pretty much proved that Tom's overdose on his mother's prescription medication *was* a suicide attempt, and not just an accident.

'Thanks, Georgie,' he said. 'That's really helpful. Thank you for ringing.'

'Don't you want to know what I remembered?' she put in quickly. 'The reason I rang you?'

'That wasn't it?'

'No. I was just telling you *why* I remembered.'

'Then carry on,' he said, bemused.

Her voice dropped back to a barely audible whisper. 'It was Sunday night. Late. I was in bed in my room, playing with my Nintendo DS. Dad got it for me for my birthday. I usually would be asleep by then, but there was no school the next day.'

'And?'

'I heard some voices in another room, near the front door I thought, and some other noises. I looked out of my window, and saw someone coming out of the flats.'

'Who was it?'

'I was pretty sure it was Tom,' she said. 'Course it was dark, but I thought it was him. 'Cause he's tall. I wondered whether he and Lexie were ... well, you know. I thought maybe he was cheating on Becca, and since Lexie fancies him something rotten ...'

Sunday night.

Neville forced himself to keep his mouth shut, not to press her to get to the point.

'Anyway,' she went on, 'the next morning I spilled some juice on the tablecloth. Mum was furious, and said I'd have to put it in the washing machine myself.'

Where on earth, he wondered, could this be leading?

'So I did. But there was already something in there, wet. Ready to be put in the tumble dryer. So I put it in the dryer. And you know what? When I went to treat the juice stain before I washed the tablecloth, the Vanish stain remover was completely empty. Not a drop left.'

'The stain remover?' he repeated, baffled.

'All gone.'

Neville could contain himself no longer. 'So what was it? The thing that was in the washing machine?'

'Didn't I say?' Georgie paused, clucking at her oversight. 'It was Tom's grey hoody. His Superdry one.'

For a second Neville forgot to breathe. 'Tom's? You're sure it was his?'

'Course,' Georgie asserted. 'I've seen him wearing it like a million times. Trust me. It was his. Do you think it's important?'

After a second dose of her sedatives, Margaret slept through the night. She woke early, feeling much better than she'd expected – headache-free and rested.

She still couldn't make sense of the events of yesterday. What was she to make of Hanna's allegations about Keith? If John Kingsley were to be believed, there was no truth in them, and she should feel ashamed of herself for giving any credence to her secretary's tales rather than having faith in the man she was beginning to fall in love with.

Hanna had seemed so sure, as if there were no shadow of a doubt. But why would John Kingsley tell her anything other than the truth? And he was in a position to know. He had been Keith's training incumbent; they'd been friends for many years.

Margaret put on her cassock and went downstairs to her office. There would be things to catch up with, after she had been away from her desk all day yesterday, and as it was Saturday, Hanna wouldn't be coming in. It would be good to get an early start; she wanted to be available to say goodbye to the deacons as they left, and especially to speak to Canon Kingsley before he went.

Efficient Hanna had opened her post and left it stacked on her desk. Margaret sat down and began to go through it systematically, forcing herself to concentrate on the business at hand.

But it was with a certain sense of inevitability that she heard a soft knock on her office door. Before the door opened, she knew who was on the other side of it.

'Come in,' she called, keeping her voice as calm as she could, though her heart had begun to pound more quickly. 'It's open.' She didn't stand up. Suddenly she wasn't at all sure that her legs would support her.

Keith wasn't smiling. He walked over to her desk, facing Margaret, put his hands on the desk, and leaned over to look into her eyes. 'This isn't the first time I've said this,' he stated. 'I seem to have been sidetracked. But there's something I want to tell you.'

Brian Stanford's weekly day off, on a Saturday, was sacrosanct: no meetings, no services, no calls or visits from troublesome parishioners. Any attempt at the latter would be headed off at the pass by Jane, who protected Brian's days off with relentless ferocity. So she was looking forward to the luxury of a lie-in, especially after the lateness of her return home the night before.

But she'd reckoned without Brian's curiosity. He'd been asleep by the time she got home, and this morning he wanted to know what had kept her out so late.

'Janey?' he whispered, close to her ear. 'Are you awake?'

'I am now.' She rolled over and squinted at him. 'What time is it?'

'The church bells have just rung eight.'

She'd hoped for at least another hour of sleep. Never mind.

'Where *were* you last night, Janey? I got home about nine and you weren't here. Just a brief note, saying you'd gone to the Greshams'.'

'I didn't think I'd be away so long,' she admitted.

'I waited up till nearly midnight! Couldn't you have rung?'

Ringing Brian had been the last thing on her mind, with everything that had happened. But she couldn't very well tell him that it hadn't even occurred to her to absent herself from the unfolding drama to ring her husband, so she just shook her head.

'I was worried,' Brian admitted.

Not too worried to go to bed without her, or too worried to wake up when she crept into bed well after midnight, she thought with uncharacteristic disloyalty. Not that she'd have been capable of much discussion at the time – she'd been relieved, in fact, that she could go straight to sleep without being quizzed on her whereabouts.

'Liz was desperate for someone to talk to, and you weren't here,' she said. Then she explained: Liz's admission of her worries about Tom, the unexpected arrival of the police. The discovery of Tom, unconscious from a suspected drug overdose. The frantic trip to hospital with Liz, following the ambulance. The hours in A & E, sitting with Liz and the policeman. 'When the doctor came out and told Liz he was going to pull through, that's when I decided it was time for me to leave. I tried to persuade Liz to go home as well, and get some sleep, but I don't think she paid any attention to me.'

'Drugs!' Brian said in a shocked voice. 'I must say, that does surprise me. I don't think Liz had any idea that he was a drug user. Not from what she said to me the other day.'

Jane shook her head. 'Not a user, probably – they think it was a suicide attempt. He'd taken some of Liz's prescription painkillers – they're not sure how much he took, but they found the bottle in his room. Empty.'

'Good Lord.'

'I know. It's so sad to think of a young man with all of his life ahead of him – he's younger than the twins, you know – feeling that things were that desperate. That there was no other way out. And just because his girlfriend broke up with him? I can't imagine it.'

'We must pray for him, and for his parents,' said Brian.

Margaret took a deep breath, then let it out slowly. 'I'm listening,' she said levelly.

'This isn't easy for me,' Keith admitted. 'I know I should have told you sooner, and I did try. But I'm not the sort of person who talks easily about myself, and it isn't a very pretty story in any case.'

She wasn't sure what she was expecting, but it certainly wasn't the tale that emerged, in fits and starts, over the next quarter of an hour, from the man on the other side of her desk.

'In the first place,' he began, 'I usually describe myself as a bachelor.'

'And you're not?'

'Oh, I am – in the sense that I'm not currently married,' Keith explained. 'But most people take that to mean that I've never been married. And I have been.'

Margaret found that she wasn't all that surprised. 'I see.'

'It was a while ago, and it turned out to be a big mistake on my part. But at the time, no one could have talked me out of it. And a few people tried,' he added with a wry smile. 'John Kingsley among them, though I don't suppose he'd admit to it now. In the gentlest possible way, he tried to make me see that it wouldn't work.'

Gemma had, he went on to relate, been one of his parishioners. Not a churchgoer, but a troubled young woman who had come to him for help and advice. He'd fallen head over heels for her. 'I was in my thirties, but quite naïve,' he admitted candidly. 'I hadn't had all that much experience with women. She wasn't yet twenty, and the most beautiful creature I'd ever seen. Gemma – my gem of a girl. No fool like an old fool, they say, and it's true.'

He married her in spite of all advice to the contrary, and they moved to another parish, away from the controlling parents who had been the cause of her initial contact with him. Within the year they'd been blessed with a baby girl.

'Flora,' he said, smiling. 'The apple of my eye.'

Margaret still didn't see where all this was leading.

'As far as I was concerned, we were a happy family. I had a lovely wife whom I worshipped, a beautiful and enchanting child whom I adored. Gemma never really took to being a vicar's wife, but it's not a role for everyone, and she was very young – I didn't hold it against her,' he added. 'I suppose I convinced myself that everything was perfect, because I needed to believe it. I had to prove them all wrong – all those people who said I shouldn't marry her.'

Keith grimaced. 'And then, quite suddenly, it all fell apart. About ten years ago, when Flora was eight.'

'What happened?' she couldn't help asking.

'A man turned up. Out of the blue. An old boyfriend of my wife's, as it turned out.'

Now, instead of maintaining eye contact with Margaret, Keith inspected his fingernails as he told her the next part. The man's relationship with Gemma, when they were both quite young, had been a main cause of her problems with her protective parents, and had been carried out furtively. The habit of secrecy well established, Gemma had continued seeing him for a while, even after she and Keith had married, until they moved away. She loved him then; she continued to love him.

She had never loved her husband. He, poor besotted fool, was merely an expedient way for her to escape from her parents. The other man had been in no position to marry her, so she'd taken the first alternative who had come along – Keith, the smitten vicar.

And then the real shocker: the man claimed that he was Flora's biological father. A blood test had proved it.

'I don't know whether you can imagine what I went through,' Keith said softly, still not looking at her. 'My darling daughter . . . wasn't mine. And when Gemma announced that she was divorcing me and going off with him, there was nothing I could do to stop her.'

'And Flora?' Margaret's heart ached for him.

'I had no legal rights to her at all. Even though my name was on the birth certificate, it had been proven that I wasn't her father. They took her away. They changed her surname to his. And they wouldn't let me see her – they didn't even let me know where she was.' He swallowed. 'I left my parish, of course. There was no way I could stay. That's when I applied to come here, as a tutor in theology. And I put "single" on my application form. Because I was.'

She was beginning to have a glimmer of the truth. 'Flora?' she prompted again.

'Last autumn she came to Cambridge, as an undergraduate. I had no idea, of course, and she had no way of knowing that I was here. We hadn't been allowed any contact for nearly ten years.' Keith smiled now, a smile that lit his face and made it almost handsome. 'We ran into each other, just by chance. Literally. In the fog, on the bridge over the river at Garret Hostel Lane. I was cycling one way, late for a tutorial, and she was cycling the other way, late for a lecture. Her cycle clipped mine, or the other way round. We both went down. And then . . . It was . . . a magical moment. When we recognized each other.'

Margaret was able to imagine it, vividly.

So the girl he'd been kissing was his daughter. Or not his daughter, but someone whom he had regarded as such since the moment of her birth.

'She's beautiful,' he said proudly. 'My Flora. And clever, as well, of course. Having her back in my life has been the most wonderful gift. We just picked up where we left off – father and daughter, in every way that matters.'

'Her mother. Gemma . . .'

'She doesn't know. Flora feels guilty, keeping it from her. But it's the only way we can continue to see each other. And that's something neither one of us is willing to give up.' He shook his head, bemused. 'The other day – the day your secretary must have seen us together – I rang Flora up in a panic, because you were coming to tea. I needed her help. She bakes the most wonderful chocolate cakes, and I had to have one. For you.'

He looked at her at last. Margaret's throat closed up; her eyes welled with tears.

'It was too soon, then, to tell her why I needed the cake. But things have . . . happened this week. Marvellous things. So yesterday I took her out for the day, to a pub in the country, to tell her about you. She was so pleased that I'd found someone, after all these years.' Keith smiled. 'She wants to meet you, Margaret. I hope . . .'

Margaret blinked back the tears. 'I'd love to meet her,' she said huskily. 'She sounds wonderful.'

Afterwards she wasn't sure which of them had made the first move, reaching across the desk. But their hands met halfway, clasped and held on tight.

Neville had a short list of two people whom he wished to interview as a matter of urgency. A call to the hospital ascertained that Tom Gresham was definitely out of the woods, which was the good news. The bad news was that he would not be well enough to be questioned by the police until later in the day – sometime in the afternoon.

'I'll ring you when he's ready,' the doctor promised.

The other person on Neville's list was Josh Bradley. There was no point going to the Bradleys' flat too early, Neville reflected; as it was Saturday, he was taking a chance in going at all. He just had to hope that Paul Bradley would be out – doing something at his church, or catching up with lost work.

Josh was no longer a suspect in Sebastian Frost's murder, which meant that he could be questioned without his obstructive father present. That, too, was good news. Still, Neville couldn't help feeling that the boy held the key to what had happened that night, and he had a list of questions for him that needed answers.

Once again he walked through Paddington Green, past the site of the murder. If anything the shrine was even more dilapidated than it had been – the flowers deader, the notes and cards sodden from the heavy rains, their messages obliterated. No one there to mourn a dead friend. An unpleasant pong of decay wafted from the pile of flowers. Neville wrinkled his nose.

He reached the gates of the mews and pressed the buzzer, warrant card at the ready this time. The unpleasant gatekeeper glowered, nodded and swung the gates open.

'Is Mr Bradley at home this morning, do you know?' Neville asked.

'Nah,' the man stated smugly, little realizing that it was an answer to gladden Neville's heart. 'I seen him go, not thirty minutes ago. You missed him again.'

'Thanks, mate,' Neville said cheerily. He went to the flat and rang the bell.

'I said he's gone!' the man called after him. Neville ignored him and pushed the bell again.

Déjà vu, all over again. Footsteps on the stairs, the bolt drawn back, the chain released. The door opening a crack, revealing Josh's scared face.

'Hi, Josh,' said Neville.

The boy didn't reply. He wouldn't even make eye contact.

'I think it's time we had a little talk, don't you?'

Josh stood back and opened the door, just enough for Neville to squeeze through.

After the rains of the night before, the sun was shining as Callie and Marco stepped out into the courtyard on their way to breakfast. The sky seemed newly washed to Callie, pale blue and cloudless, and the spring flowers looked to her like brave, battered warriors, their scents intensified by the moisture. A glorious morning; she couldn't remember ever being happier.

Walking hand in hand through the courtyard, they hadn't quite arrived at the dining hall when they were overtaken by a breathless Tamsin.

'Oh. My. God,' she gasped. 'You're Marco!'

'I believe so,' he smiled. 'And you're . . .'

Callie performed an extravagant flourish with her arm. 'Marco, may I present my dear friend Tamsin? And Tamsin, as you've surmised, this is Marco. My fiancé,' she added proudly, and was rewarded with a warm smile and a squeeze of her hand.

'Tamsin, it's a great pleasure to meet you,' Marco said, with a courtly little bow. 'Callie's told me so much about you.'

'And she's told me so much about *you*.' Tamsin seemed about to say something else; Callie shot her a warning look.

'We're going to have some breakfast,' Marco said. 'Would you care to join us?'

'I'd love to.' Tamsin fell into step beside Callie as they resumed their progress towards the dining hall. 'Mission accomplished?' she whispered.

Callie turned her head and caught Tamsin's eye. 'Mission accomplished,' she mouthed, with a wide grin. She didn't even blush.

It wasn't that the Bradleys' flat was dirty – it wasn't. But there was something about it, Neville realized immediately, that indicated the lack of a female presence: a certain staleness in the air, a general feeling that corners had been cut, or more likely just overlooked.

To Neville's surprise, Josh took him not to the lounge, but to the kitchen. There the boy sprawled on a hard wooden chair, leaning his elbows on the table. The table was covered with a faded floral oilcloth, easy – Neville suspected – to wipe clean after meals. On one end of the table, a plastic tray held a pair of salt-and-pepper shakers in the shape of dogs, one black and one white, as well as a bottle of tomato ketchup and another of brown sauce.

To his further surprise, Neville found himself feeling sorry for the boy. What kind of a life was it for a young lad, being brought up by a religious nutter? 'Your father isn't here?' he asked unnecessarily.

'He's gone to church,' said Josh. 'Weekends, he spends most of his time there. Saturdays he helps to get things set up for Sunday.'

'Your mother,' Neville said. 'How long has she been ... gone?'

Josh swallowed, his Adam's apple visibly bobbing up and down. 'Nearly a year. It'll be a year in June since cancer killed Mum.'

'You must miss her.'

The boy nodded. 'This was her favourite room. She used to be in here all the time, cooking, ironing, pottering about. I'd come home from school and sit here to do my homework and talk to her.'

That explained why he'd chosen this room for the interview, then – it was his comfort zone. On impulse, Neville asked him, 'Did your mum know that you're gay?'

Josh nodded again. 'I could talk to her about it, no problem. She said she'd always known, ever since I was little. It didn't bother her. She said it was just part of me, who I am.'

'But your father doesn't feel the same.'

'No way.' Josh snorted. 'You've heard him. He thinks gay people are the devil's spawn. He'd kill me if I told him.'

Or at least subject him to some horrible exorcism, or enrol him in a programme to straighten him out, Neville reckoned.

'Not that I've actually . . . you know. *Done* anything,' Josh said, averting his eyes and blushing. 'With anyone else, I mean. But as far as my dad's concerned, you don't have to. Just being gay makes you evil and sinful. That's why I couldn't answer your questions at the police station, when he was there.'

'Well, he's not here now.' Neville leaned back in his chair. 'So I can ask you some things, and you'll give me proper answers, right?'

'I'll try.'

No point beating about the bush. 'OK, Josh. The first thing I'd like to know is this: why did you confess? Why did you tell me that you'd killed Sebastian, when you didn't do it?'

This evidently wasn't the question Josh had been expecting. He frowned, hesitated, and said, 'I'm afraid I can't tell you that.'

'You're protecting someone, aren't you?'

'How did you—' The boy bit off the end of his startled exclamation; to cover his confusion he got up and went to the fridge, turning his back on Neville as he pulled out a can of Coke. 'Do you want one?' he offered.

'No, thanks. But I'd like you to answer my question, Josh. Because I know that you're protecting someone. And I think I know who it is.'

'You couldn't know.' As soon as he'd said the words, Josh looked as if he wished he could call them back.

'Right. Now we know where we stand.' Neville waited while Josh sat back down, popped the tab on the can, and gulped down some Coke.

Josh avoided his eyes. 'You couldn't know,' he repeated stubbornly.

'It's Tom Gresham, isn't it?'

The boy raised his eyes and stared at him.

Neville fired off another shot in the dark. 'And you're protecting him because you're in love with him, aren't you?'

Josh pressed his lips together, lowering his head.

'All right, Josh,' Neville said in a reasonable voice. 'I can understand protecting someone you love. I might even do the same. But what I

261

can't understand is how you can be in love with someone who bullies you. Someone who calls you filthy names and posts horrible things on Facebook about you.'

Once again Josh spoke without thinking. 'He doesn't!'

'Oh, but he does. He and Sebastian were friends – you know that. He's one of that little gang who've turned picking on you into an art form.'

Josh must have realized that he'd already gone too far to deny it all now. 'He told me that he didn't,' he muttered. 'He said it was Seb and Hugo. Darth Vader and Luke Skywalker. And some of their other friends.'

'Tom is Han Solo,' Neville said, watching as Josh went pale and silent, working out the implications. He allowed him just enough time to let it sink in before firing his next question. 'What really happened that night, Josh?' He added, a bit more gently, 'I think you know that you have to tell me. It's no good trying to protect Tom. He doesn't deserve it, and it's too late. We're on to him.'

The boy's shoulders sagged in defeat; he squeezed his eyes shut. 'I was there that night,' he whispered, almost inaudibly. 'Paddington Green.'

'So you saw what happened?'

'No.' Josh gave an emphatic shake of his head. 'I don't know what happened. That's the thing.'

Neville took a deep breath; for the first time since he'd stood over Sebastian's body on Paddington Green, he felt that he might actually be getting close to the truth. 'Tell me what you *do* know,' he said gently.

'I was there,' Josh repeated. 'Earlier than I said. My dad went to bed early. And like I told you, I got the kitchen knife out of the drawer.' His eyes tracked to the other side of the kitchen, to one of the drawers.

'So you were intending to . . . hurt someone?'

'Myself.' He spat the word out as if it were poison. 'I didn't text Seb. I texted Tom. I told him to meet me on Paddington Green. I said I needed to talk to him.'

'And did he come?'

Josh nodded. 'I knew all along, deep down, that Tom would never love me. I mean, he's straight. You can tell that. He has a girlfriend. And I'm a freak – a red dwarf,' he added bitterly. 'Even if he was gay, he wouldn't want me. But I was desperate. And so unhappy, because I love him so much. And I wanted him to know it.'

'So what happened?'

'I told him that I loved him. He laughed at me.' Josh gulped back a sob. 'I showed him the knife. I told him that I was going to kill myself, and it was all because of him. And I meant it, too.'

This wasn't what Neville was expecting. He waited, afraid to say anything.

'He laughed again. He said I was a silly little wanker, and not to be so bloody stupid. But I didn't care what he said, because . . . well, you know. Then he . . . he took the knife off me. Just grabbed it out of my hand. He laughed, and told me to go home.'

'And did you?'

'Yeah.' Josh sighed. 'I came back home. But the next day . . . well, when I heard that Seb was dead, and had been stabbed with a knife . . .' He shook his head. 'I knew that Tom had something to do with it – he had the knife, didn't he? And he was on Paddington Green, right where it happened. So when you found me, and took me to the police station to answer some questions, I did the only thing I could think of to protect him. I told you I'd killed Seb.'

Neville processed that for a few seconds. It might not have been what he expected, but it did make a weird kind of sense. 'I have just one more question for you, Josh,' he said. 'What was Tom wearing that night? Can you remember?'

Once again, it clearly wasn't the question he was anticipating. Josh frowned, but answered immediately. 'His grey Superdry hoody. It's his favourite.'

'You're sure?'

'Oh, yeah,' said Josh, nodding. 'I'm sure.'

CHAPTER 21

Repeated calls to Liz's home number, made by Jane through the morning, resulted in nothing but a series of messages left on the call minder. 'She must be at the hospital,' Jane reported to Brian. 'If he's out of danger, I suppose they would let her stay in his room and sit with him.'

'Do you think I ought to go to the hospital to support her?' Brian asked doubtfully.

'It's your day off. She wouldn't expect it. And there's nothing you could do, really,' Jane stated, supplying the answer she knew he wanted.

'I'm sure you're right.'

But Brian seemed restless, unsure what to do with his day off. Once he'd had his breakfast and a bath, rather than his customary shower, he said to her, with uncharacteristic impulsiveness, 'Let's do something today, Janey. Something different. Let's get out of the parish.'

Usually, if they went somewhere on Brian's day off, Jane was the one who planned it, in advance, and it had always – until a few months ago – been planned with the boys in mind. Trips to the London Transport Museum or the Museum of Natural History, picnics in Hyde Park, or the odd train journey to the seaside, on the rare occasion that the weather was suitable. Brian had always been happy to go along, but he'd never suggested anything himself.

'What did you have in mind?' Jane asked blankly.

'Oh, I don't know. We could take a train to Oxford and surprise Charlie. Or we could go to the cinema. Or ...it's such a beautiful day – we could even go to Kew Gardens.'

'Kew Gardens sounds wonderful,' said Jane. They'd been, once, a long time ago, but the twins had been bored and fractious and as she recalled it, the weather had been less than ideal.

'That's what we'll do, then. We'll have a lovely day out, looking at the gardens, and then a cream tea in the Orangery. How soon can you be ready, Janey?'

The doctor rang Neville on his mobile, as promised, early in the afternoon. Tom Gresham was – he said – conscious, stable, and well enough to be questioned.

Neville went straight to the hospital, switching off his phone as he entered. He figured out where he needed to go, then headed for the lift. Someone else was waiting for it as well. He realized with a shock that it was Miranda Frost.

He knew she worked at the hospital, of course, and he knew – from talking with Mark Lombardi – that she had gone back to work a day or two ago, so it shouldn't have been such a surprise. But his previous encounters with her had been in other places, and he'd never seen her in scrubs.

They got in the lift together. 'Hello, Mrs Frost,' he said, feeling awkward.

She nodded in acknowledgement as they punched their respective buttons. 'Good afternoon, Detective Inspector.'

'You're ... back at work.'

'As you see.' Her tone was cool, verging on tart. 'There are lives to be saved. And nothing to be gained by sitting at home, waiting for you and your colleagues to catch my son's murderer.'

Stung to defensiveness, Neville said, 'We're getting close, Mrs Frost.'

The lift slowed at her floor; the doors opened. 'I'm pleased to hear it,' she said. 'You will let me know, won't you?'

Why did she have such a knack for making him feel guilty? He might have been more diligent in keeping the Frosts up to date with the police enquiries, he acknowledged to himself. But that was what they had family liaison officers for. Nonetheless, he forced a smile and nodded as she stepped off.

'I will,' he stated. 'I promise.'

The lift went up another floor. Neville got off and followed the signs down the corridor to the ward where he'd been told he would find Tom Gresham.

He stopped at the nurses' station and asked for the boy's location. 'He's not on the general ward,' the sister on duty informed him. 'He's in a private room. Just there.' She pointed across the corridor to a half-open door.

His parents would be paying privately for that, Neville assumed. He pushed on the door and went into a small room with drawn curtains, his eyes adjusting slowly to the dimness after being in the brightly lit corridor.

Mrs Gresham was sitting by the bed, holding her son's hand. She looked up at him and smiled. 'Thank you for coming. It's very kind.

My husband . . . he's on his way back from New York, but he won't be here until late tonight.'

'This isn't a social call, Mrs Gresham,' Neville informed her. 'The doctor said it would be all right for me to talk to Tom. To ask him a few questions.'

She nodded, but showed no signs of moving.

'In private,' he added, thanking his lucky stars for that providential sixteenth birthday.

'We *are* private. Close the door, if you like.'

He was going to have to be more direct. 'I'm afraid you'll need to leave us alone, Mrs Gresham. For a few minutes. Wouldn't you like to go and get a coffee, or something to eat?'

Tom's mother frowned and looked as if she were about to protest, but then she shrugged, rising from her chair. 'All right, then. But don't tire him out. He's still very weak. And possibly confused,' she added.

Neville waited until she was gone, then closed the door behind her and sat down in the chair she'd vacated. 'Hello, Tom,' he said. 'I think it's time for us to have a little chat. Just the two of us. Don't you?'

Frustratingly, the train from Cambridge back to King's Cross was delayed, stopping between stations, for reasons which remained unexplained to the passengers.

While they were waiting for the train to start again, Callie got out her phone. 'I'll ring Peter,' she said. 'I'll let him know that we're on the way. And I want to make sure he's not planning on hanging about, once we get there.'

Mark laughed at her determined expression. He pulled out his own phone, which he'd switched off before he arrived in Cambridge, feeling a bit guilty that he hadn't checked in with Neville for over twenty-four hours. Had Josh Bradley been charged with the murder? Mark could only assume so, given the state of play the last time he'd talked to Neville. He'd scanned the front-page headlines of the tabloids at the station, but remained unenlightened. The *Globe* had moved on to other things, and none of the other papers featured the story either. He really ought to find out what was going on, and make the time to pay a visit to Miranda and Richard Frost.

But when he tried Neville's number, it went straight to voicemail. Mark left a brief message, shrugged, and pocketed the phone.

* * *

'Tom?'

For the first time the boy rolled his head on his pillow to face Neville. 'Yeah?'

'I said, we need to have a little chat.'

'If you say so.'

Now that the moment was finally upon him, Neville felt weary. All those days of looking for answers; now he was about to get some. He had no appetite for playing games, so he went straight to the point.

'What happened that night, Tom?'

'I took some pills,' the boy said, wilfully misunderstanding him. 'Quite a few, as a matter of fact.'

'I didn't say last night. I said *that* night, and I meant Sunday. As you very well know.'

Tom closed his eyes with a weary sigh. 'I don't know what you mean.'

'Don't try that with me, Sunshine,' Neville snapped. 'You know exactly what I mean.' Cards on the table time, then. 'You stabbed Sebastian Frost. You killed one of your best mates. I know it, you know it. So there's no point wasting my time by pretending otherwise.'

The boy's eyes flew open; he paused for a moment to assimilate the situation. 'Did that little freak rat on me, then?' he sneered. 'I knew he would, as soon as I heard he'd been arrested.'

Neville felt absurdly protective of Josh. After all, Josh had been willing to take the rap for a murder he hadn't committed, out of love for this spoiled brat. He resisted the temptation to tell Tom exactly that.

'So that's why you swallowed the pills, I suppose. You thought you were going to get caught, so you went for the easy way out. Or tried to.'

Tom turned his head away.

'It didn't have anything to do with all that crap your mum believes – that you were depressed because your girlfriend dumped you,' Neville went on. 'You tried to kill yourself because of what happened on Sunday night. But you failed, son. You're still alive. You're still here. So am I. And I'm not going anywhere until you start answering some questions.'

'Like . . . what?'

There was one thing, in puzzling out the events of that night and the circumstances leading up to it, that Neville didn't understand: that was where he would begin, and work up to the rest of it.

267

'Josh Bradley,' he said. 'Red Dwarf. You despised him, like all of your mates did. You bullied and persecuted him, along with the rest of them. And yet you led him on. You made him think that you weren't involved in the bullying. You must have been at least a bit nice to him, or he wouldn't have been so besotted with you. And when he texted you that night, and asked you to meet him on Paddington Green, you went. Why?'

That brought a smirk to Tom's face. 'He was ... useful.'

'Useful? In what way?' Apart, that is, from the buzz Tom must have got from knowing that the kid was in love with him. As he must have known that Lexie fancied him.

'He ... did things for me.'

Things. Not sexual, surely. What, then? 'What sort of things?'

'My parents ... expect a lot of me,' Tom said obliquely, looking towards the window, its drawn curtains allowing in just a thin shaft of sunlight where they didn't quite meet. 'At school and stuff. They expect good marks, good exam results. And I'm not as clever as Seb. Not as clever as Josh, come to that. So Josh ... helps me, sometimes.'

It was beginning to make sense. 'He helps you cheat, you mean? To get better marks?'

Tom shrugged in acknowledgement. 'If that's what you want to call it. Sometimes he does my homework for me. And once he stole an exam paper from the office, with the answers and everything. He'd do anything for me,' he added, with a touch of smugness that made Neville want to give him a good smack.

Instead he balled his fists and pressed on. 'So on Sunday night, Josh called you and asked you to meet him on Paddington Green. You went. He threatened to kill himself. You took the knife off him and sent him home. What happened after that?'

Tom looked at him for a moment, as if trying to decide what to say. Neville waited.

'OK,' said Tom, sighing. 'I'll tell you.'

Suddenly Neville found the darkness of the room oppressive. In a gesture that he knew to be symbolic as well as practical, he crossed to the window and pushed the curtains to either side, flooding the room with afternoon sunlight.

Tom winced at the glare. 'Did you have to do that?'

'Yes.' He crossed his arms and stood by the bed. Waiting.

'I texted Seb,' Tom said quietly, after a moment of silence. 'I told him to come to Paddington Green.'

'Why?'

'I wanted to tell him about what had happened with Red Dwarf. I thought it was a real laugh, you know? I mean, we'd been putting stuff on the Facebook page, telling him to kill himself and stuff, because he's such a waste of space, and then the little wanker says he's going to off himself with a kitchen knife. Because he loves me! How funny is that?'

Not very, in Neville's opinion. 'And?' he said.

'Seb came. His parents were working, he said, and he was bored. So we just hung out for a while. I told him about Red Dwarf, then we planned some more things to put on Facebook.'

Neville tried to picture the scene: the two boys, lounging on the grass, possibly even sitting on the bench in the churchyard where he'd sat with Cowley later that night. 'Where was the knife all this time?' he wanted to know.

'I had it. I was playing with it, like. Just messing about.'

'Then what happened?'

Tom turned his head to look out of the window, taking a moment to answer. 'I said something like, if I was going to turn into a bloody poofter, I'd do it with someone better than Red Dwarf. Someone more like Seb. I was just joking, see? Messing about.'

Oh, no, thought Neville. Here it comes.

'Seb stood up. I thought he was going to go home, but he said there was something he had to tell me.' Then the words came out in a rush. 'He said he loved me. He said he would never have said anything, he'd been holding it in for ages, but now maybe there was a chance so he had to take it. And since I'd broken up with Becca, he thought that meant something, that he had a chance with me. I was like, gobsmacked. I had no idea.'

'And then what?'

'I stood up, and he ... he grabbed me.' Tom gave a little shudder. 'He put his arms round me. Without any warning. And he kissed me. Stuck his tongue down my throat. It was ... so gross. Horrid. Disgusting.' He closed his eyes for a second. 'The knife was still in my hand. He had my arm pinned up against him, like, but my hand was by his neck, and I just ...' He stopped.

Neville held his breath.

'I stabbed him,' Tom said, with a little sob. 'I didn't mean to. I was just trying to get him off me. I didn't mean to kill him.'

'Well?' said Rob Gardiner-Smith, sitting behind his vast desk. He raised his eyebrows, looked at Lilith, and waited.

'The trail's gone cold,' Lilith admitted. 'They released that boy Josh. And as far as I can tell, they haven't arrested anyone else.'

'My source would let me know if they had done,' he pointed out.

'Well, then.' She shrugged. 'What else can I do? Apart from having a go at the police for dropping the ball, leaving a major murder unsolved after nearly a week.'

Rob Gardiner-Smith tented his fingers in front of him. 'You could start there. Lay on the outrage, and hit the "parents' anguish" angle again. Any chance of talking to the parents again?'

Lilith shook her head with regret. 'I don't think so.'

'How about the boy? The one they arrested? Josh, is it? You could interview him, and do a "My night of hell in the slammer" sort of story. Police bungling, arresting the wrong person – a poor, innocent lad who was minding his own business.'

She liked that idea, and could see the possibilities there. The father: a religious headcase, from what she'd seen of him. He was bound to be indignant about the treatment his son had received at the police's hands, and he didn't seem to be shy about sharing his feelings.

'Leave it with me,' said Lilith confidently. 'I'll come up with something. I promise.'

'He was my mate. I didn't mean to kill him,' Tom repeated. 'You have to believe me.'

He *didn't* have to believe him, but Neville did. It sounded right; it explained everything. Or almost everything. 'Tell me what happened after that,' he said.

'I realized . . . he was dead. Straight away. He didn't, like, bleed to death slowly or anything. He didn't scream or yell. He just . . . died. I couldn't believe what had happened, what I'd done. One minute he was sticking his tongue down my throat, and the next minute he was dead.' Tom rubbed his eyes with his hand. 'I suppose I freaked out at that point.'

That sounded about right, too.

'Because of what he did to me, I like freaked out and . . . did something weird. He was laying on the ground, and I cut his tongue.'

That box was ticked, then. And Neville hadn't even had to ask.

'And then I thought about how I'd sent him a text. Anyone who found his phone would, like, know that he was meeting me there. So I took his phone out of his pocket, and smashed it.'

Everything accounted for, then. Except . . .

270

Tom closed his eyes. 'Then I threw the knife in the canal.'

So Josh's fictional account of disposing of the knife had been right on the mark, Neville thought with a certain grim satisfaction.

'And I realized that there was blood on my hoody. Seb's blood.' He shuddered. 'I thought about chucking it in the canal as well. I might not be that good at science, but I figured it might float.' His mouth twisted in a half-smile. 'Then I thought about Lexie. Seb's girlfriend. I've always known she fancies me. And she doesn't live too far away. So I texted her and asked her if she'd do me a favour.'

'You wanted her to wash your hoody,' Neville stated.

'Yeah. I took it round. I told her if she got the stain out, she could keep it. She always said she liked that hoody.'

That raised another question in Neville's mind. 'How did you explain the blood?'

Tom shrugged. 'I told her it was chilli sauce. From a kebab.'

Had Lexie believed such a flagrant lie? She wasn't a stupid girl, by any means. How much, then, had she guessed or surmised, when Sebastian turned up dead? Questions for another day, thought Neville wearily.

The door opened and Mrs Gresham came into the room, crossing to her son's bed. She bent over him protectively and put a hand on his forehead.

'Tom, you look pale. All done in. I hope you haven't upset him, Detective Inspector,' she addressed Neville with a frown. 'Maybe you'd better go now.'

'I will,' he said. 'But first I'd like a word with you, Mrs Gresham. In the corridor.'

Jane had always liked watching families. She enjoyed speculating about their relationships, and observing the variations and repetitions in their genetic codes: the curve of a nose, repeated through generations, or the peculiar whorl of an ear, handed down from father to son.

There were plenty of families for her to observe at Kew Gardens on that beautiful Saturday afternoon. Parents with young children in prams and pushchairs, extended families with reluctant teenagers lagging behind, grandparents and offspring in all sorts of combinations.

After walking quite a bit, and taking the little train round vast tracts of gardens, Brian declared it was time to have their cream tea at the Orangery. They chose a table outside where they could enjoy the sunshine.

'This *is* lovely,' Jane said contentedly, lifting her face to the sun while they waited for their tea to arrive.

A large family group arrived nearby, moving tables together to create more room. There was an older couple and two younger couples, as well as assorted children. Jane watched their efforts with interest.

'How do you think they're related?' Brian asked. 'Do you think those two women are sisters?'

She scrutinized them covertly, not wanting to be caught staring. 'No,' she said at last. 'They don't look anything alike. I think the two men are brothers. Look – they both have the same pattern baldness. The one just took his baseball cap off to scratch his head, and his hair is just like the other one, even though it's cut shorter. And the older man,' she added. 'He's obviously their dad. He hardly has any hair at all.'

Brian, who was rather sensitive about his own receding hairline, smoothed back the strands on his forehead. 'Poor chaps,' he said.

The older woman plucked a fat baby out of its pushchair and dandled it on her knee, crooning wordlessly, while the older man leaned over her shoulder and pulled faces at the baby.

Jane smiled.

'Look at that,' said Brian, smiling as well. 'Just think, Janey. One day we'll be like that. Granny and Granddad.'

One day.

Jane took a deep breath. Perhaps there would never be a better opening. 'Actually,' she said, 'it's not that far off.'

Her husband gave her a quizzical look. 'What do you mean?'

'Simon,' she said quickly, before she lost her nerve. 'He and Ellie . . . are having a baby. They're going to get married,' she added.

Brian's jaw dropped. 'But they're too young! And we're far too young to be grandparents.'

'I agree, but it's going to happen anyway.' Now that she was on the other side of the fence, arguing for it rather than against, she found herself echoing Simon's words. 'They'll make it work. You'll see, Brian. They've thought it all through. And they love each other.'

'How long have you known about this?'

'A few days,' she confessed. 'Simon left it to me to break the news to you.'

He sighed and shook his head. 'It's not the way we did it in our day.'

'I know.'

'In our day there was none of this living together nonsense,' he pronounced gloomily. 'You got married, then after a decent interval you had your babies.'

Jane couldn't help laughing: he sounded like a grumpy old man, sixty-something instead of forty-something. 'But you know how much things have changed,' she pointed out to him. 'How many of the couples who come to you to marry them are living together?'

'All of them, or nearly all,' he admitted. 'That's just taken for granted now.'

The server arrived with their cream teas, which seemed to improve Brian's frame of mind considerably. 'Splendid,' he said, rubbing his hands together. He split a scone and slathered it with clotted cream and jam.

Jane poured the tea. 'I know it's a shock,' she said. 'About Simon and Ellie, I mean.'

'Oh, well.' He gave a philosophic shrug. 'Ellie's a lovely girl. And Simon's mad about her. I'm sure they'll make a go of it. And,' he added, 'I suppose it will be lovely to have a grandchild. It will keep us young, Janey.'

It was now or never, she told herself. And never wasn't an option. 'Actually,' she said quietly, feeling herself blushing, 'we won't have to rely on our grandchild to do that. I . . . we . . . are going to have a baby. As well.' She stared down at her scone, afraid to look at him.

'But . . . but . . .'

Jane looked up and watched as Brian's expression of slack-jawed incomprehension slowly transformed itself into a delighted grin.

'I don't believe it!' he said. 'You're sure?'

'I'm sure.'

'Janey, you *are* a clever thing,' he announced, abandoning his scone and reaching for her hand.

Neville sagged wearily against the wall of the hospital corridor for a moment, closing his eyes to shut out the glare of the fluorescent lights.

Parenthood: it was a mug's game, he reflected.

If people knew, or even gave half a thought, to what having a kid was going to do to them, they'd probably never go down that path. They would stay out of the bedroom altogether, or at the very least make damned sure that there was no chance that anything would come of it. Not just contraception, but sterilization.

273

It was too late for him. Way too late for the Greshams. And for the Frosts.

The trouble was, kids didn't come with any guarantees. You could be the best parent in the world – knock yourself out for your kids, lavish everything that money could buy on them – and it could still end in tears. A dead son. Or a son who was capable of sticking a knife into one of his best mates.

Heartache. That's what kids brought you.

He'd already had to see it inflicted it on one woman today, when he told Mrs Gresham what her cherished boy had done, and explained what was likely to come out of it. Even if Tom Gresham managed to avoid the worst of the possible legal consequences, by reason of his age or the unpremeditated nature of his crime, he would have to live with what he'd done for the rest of his life. A young life shattered; a family in ruins.

And the Frosts? They'd lost their only son, their link to the future of the planet. Their lives would certainly never be the same, even if they managed to pull together as a couple and survive the anger and acrimony that Sebastian's death had caused – or uncovered? – in their marriage.

Now it was time for him to tell another woman that her son had been killed – needlessly, senselessly – by his close friend. He didn't want to do it. But he'd promised.

It was only after he'd accomplished that that he would be able to return to the police station, to set in train the endless, hateful quantities of paperwork necessary to bring this case to its conclusion.

And after he'd done that, he could return home to his pregnant wife. To pretend to her that all was now right with the world. To try to convince himself that he wasn't actually terrified about being a father, and that, contrary to everything his head was telling him, their kid would turn out just fine.

Neville sighed, squared his shoulders, and went in search of Miranda Frost.

When Detective Inspector Stewart had gone, Miranda Frost continued to sit in the little cubicle which served as her office, staring at the blank wall for a very long time.

Sebastian's killer had been found. Had confessed, and this time the confession was accepted by the police as the truth.

He was here in the hospital now, the boy who had stabbed her son.

Tom. His friend.

Not a random maniac. Not even a bitter and twisted outsider, jealous of Sebastian's gifts. His friend.

She couldn't believe it. Couldn't get her head round it.

And all because Sebastian . . . was *gay*?

How could that be? And how could she not have known?

Miranda picked up the framed photo of Sebastian from her desk and examined it, with an intense scrutiny she'd never before subjected it to.

Sebastian, smiling. Just as in life. Nothing to indicate that he was anything other than the gifted, sunny boy she had always believed him to be.

But behind that smiling face, there had been inner torment. DI Stewart had told her of his secret journals, full of suppressed passion and misery. She hadn't known, hadn't even suspected.

Had she ever really known her son at all? That was the question with which Miranda now tortured herself.

First there had been the bullying. She'd been so sure that it couldn't be true, until the hard proof had established it beyond any doubt. Her lovely son had demonstrated a deliberate cruelty towards another human being of which she would never have believed him capable.

And now this. Gay.

How could she not have known?

It didn't really bother her that he'd been gay. What bothered her was that she'd had not the slightest inkling of it.

Why hadn't he told her, confided in her, shared his distress? And why had she not seen the signs? Had he been so adept at hiding them, or did she really, on a deep level, not want to know?

She had, she was beginning to realize now, constructed an image of Sebastian as she wanted him to be: clever, popular, sporty, gifted in so many ways. Perhaps he wasn't any of those things. Had he known that she couldn't cope with the real Sebastian, and thus been complicit in projecting to her the qualities she wanted to see?

How could you live with someone for more than fifteen years – the entire span of that person's life – and not know him?

Sebastian had been an easy child, fitting in with her punishing schedule and not making unreasonable demands of her. He knew – he'd been told often enough – that both of his parents were busy people, performing essential work, committed to saving lives.

Yes, she was busy. She had a demanding career. That had always been her excuse. But it was no excuse, really.

There *was* no excuse. Nothing should have been more important to her than her child.

And in that she had failed him. She'd never made an effort to go beneath the image of the ideal Sebastian, to get to know the real one. As long as he seemed to be everything she wanted him to be, she was happy.

Was that why she'd been so angry, in those days after his death?

Her anger had been directed chiefly at Richard – an easy target, and someone else whom it was convenient to take at face value. Their marriage had largely been lived out on the surface. She'd never had the commitment or the inclination to find out what really made her husband tick.

What was all that anger really about? Not about Richard at all.

Was she angry at Sebastian, for disrupting her carefully constructed life? Or angry at herself?

Had she felt, on some level, that she bore a share of the responsibility for her son's death? Yes, someone else had struck the fatal blow. But she had failed him. If she'd taken the time and made the effort to know her son better, he might have been a happier, better adjusted person. He might never have become a bully. He might have been comfortable with his own sexuality, rather than torturing himself in private. He might never have gone to Paddington Green that night . . .

Miranda realized that she was crying, silent tears streaming down her face. Tears for Sebastian – the one she'd thought she knew, and the real one she'd never known. Tears for her marriage: was it too late to save it?

Tears for herself.

Callie climbed the steps to her flat above the church hall with mixed emotions. Part of her was still with Marco, from whom she'd parted at King's Cross as he went to his flat to shower and change his clothes. He would join her here later, probably with food to cook for their supper. And possibly with an overnight bag as well . . .

Her main emotion, though, was the sheer joy of homecoming, tinged with apprehension. Would Peter have trashed the place? Would he break his promise to leave, and be ensconced for another prolonged stay?

She needn't have worried, she realized as she pushed the door open. Yes, there were a few telltale signs of his occupancy, but by and large he seemed to have made an effort to tidy up. And his bag, stuffed full and zipped up, was by the door.

Callie sighed with relief as a black and white bundle of fur cannoned into her legs, ecstatic at her return. She went down on her knees to hug Bella and receive her welcoming kisses.

Peter appeared from the kitchen. 'I've just made myself a coffee. Would you like one?' He'd given her the fancy capsule-based coffee machine the last time he'd been to stay, and he was the only one who used it. Callie usually preferred tea, and Marco made his coffee the old-fashioned Italian way, on the hob.

'No, thanks.'

'Well, I'll just drink this, then I'll be off.'

Overwhelmed with gratitude that he was really leaving, she said, 'Thanks so much for looking after everything. Bella's been OK?'

'She's been a darling. As usual. Though of course she's missed you.'

'And I've missed *you*,' she addressed her dog, kissing the top of her head and scratching behind her floppy ears. Bella rolled over on her back, legs in the air.

'Shameless, isn't she?' Peter said cheerfully.

'Takes one to know one.'

'Ooooh!' he went, in his best Kenneth Williams voice. 'Get you!' He put his coffee cup down and grabbed the strap of his bag, slinging it over his shoulder.

'Do you have somewhere to go, then?' Callie didn't want to ask, but in all good conscience she couldn't put him out on the street without making sure.

'I told you, Sis. I had a flat lined up. I signed the papers yesterday, and moved most of my stuff in this morning. So I'm sorted. But thanks for asking,' he added with a grin. 'Very noble, I'm sure. Though I'm not going to ask what you would have done if I'd said no.'

What *would* she have done? Fortunately, she wasn't being put to the test.

Callie got up from the floor. 'Maybe we can have lunch one day next week, and catch up.' She put her hand on his arm and gave him a kiss on the cheek.

'Sis!' He grabbed her hand. 'What is *this*?'

'I believe it's commonly known as an engagement ring,' she said smugly.

'That's fantastic! Good old Mark popped the question, did he?'

'He did.' She wasn't about to tell him anything more than that, so she just smiled.

'We'll definitely have lunch,' Peter promised. 'I want to hear all about it.'

With a wave he was gone. Callie closed the door behind him and leaned her back against it.

The only sound was Bella's tail, thumping on the floor.

Callie opened her arms wide, symbolically embracing her flat. 'There's no place like home,' she said aloud.